BOYOS

A NOVEL

BY RICHARD MARINICK

KATE'S MYSTERY BOOKS

JUSTIN, CHARLES & CO. PUBLISHERS

BOSTON

Library of Congress Cataloging-in-Publication Data
Marinick, Richard, 1951–
    Boyos : a novel / Richard Marinick.
        p.cm.
    ISBN 1-932112-32-4 (cl.)
    ISBN 1-932112-42-1 (pa.)
    1. South Boston (Boston, Mass.) — Fiction. 2. Criminals — Fiction. I. Title.
    PS3613.A748B69 2004
    813'.6—dc22   2004054843

Published in the United States by Kate's Mystery Books,
an imprint of Justin, Charles & Co., Publishers,
www.justincharlesbooks.com
Distributed by National Book Network, Lanham, Maryland
www.nbnbooks.com

10 9 8 7 6 5 4 3 2 1

Printed in the United States of America

Book design by Boskydell Studio

PRAISE FOR BOYOS

"This gritty tale of South Boston street gangs comes from the voice of experience. This first-time author ran with the Southie gangs as a youth and learned to write in prison. Not for the faint of heart, *Boyos* is the story of the brutish Curran brothers. Their cold-blooded plottings and run-ins with rival gangs are slightly tempered by their occasional doubts about street life. *Boyos* has the feel of a cult classic."
— *USA Today*

"Although *Boyos* is a work of fiction, the characters who spring from the pages and haunt the reader are a compilation of the real-life characters Marinick met in Southie barrooms, boxing rings, and dim street corners during the darkest times of his life." — *Boston Metro*

"A Southie sizzler. Richard Marinick brings real-life experience — as a member of an Irish gang during the Whitey Bulger era — to this gritty thriller."
— *Boston Herald*

"*Boyos* triggers the kind of buzz that makes Hollywood agents and literary magazines fawn . . . Rick Marinick, an ex-con one strike away from a life sentence, is a wanted man again. Crime gave him stories to tell, fiction a way to tell them."
— *Baltimore Sun*

"A hardboiled debut as fresh and authentic as it is uncompromisingly ugly. Pusher, cold-blooded killer, amoralist, and antihero, Jack has almost no redeeming qualities, but you won't easily forget him."
— *Starred Kirkus Reviews*

"Set in the dense working-class neighborhoods where *boyo* is slang for an Irish street hood . . . Marinick gives us Jack "Wacko" Curran, an existential street samurai with his hand in coke, armed robbery, and loan-sharking. Marinick has a true insider's knowledge of the dead-end world of the streets."
— *Penthouse Magazine*

Where before I took chances, now they are given to me. My thanks to Mum, my wife Elaine for her love and patient listening, my brothers Bob, Ron, and Scot who always believed in me. The Boston University Prison Program and its wonderful and capable professors, the late Lou Stein, Paula Verdet, and Michael Koran among them. Jean Fain for her support. Sisters Kathleen and Ruth of Bethany House. Former Harvard University Professor Munroe Engel. Walter Collins for his loyalty. John Rapinchuk for his insight. Kate Mattes for reading and recommending the original manuscript, and Steve Hull for believing in, and publishing it. And finally my thanks to Frank Oreto who made a tough time easier and, in his own way, helped me to write this book.

TO THE READER

My name is Richard Marinick and I live in South Boston. I've been a short-order cook, junior civil engineer, automobile painter, nightclub bouncer, administrative assistant to the Norfolk County District Attorney, and a Massachusetts state trooper. During my mid-twenties, I became loosely connected with a group of young "up and comers" in the South Boston underworld. We all trained at the same boxing gym, "the Munie," attached to the South Boston District Court building. From there our friendship expanded.

My wife at the time had expensive tastes that I could not begin to satisfy. I watched my underworld friends get rich, and eventually had had enough of the slow-lane, no-money life of a citizen. My wife and I split and I became an active full-time member of Southie's criminal clique. Over the course of the next eight years I was involved in an array of criminal activities before my friends and I stepped up to the big time of armored car heists.

I was on a roll for years, reveling in the money, using way too much cocaine. In 1984, following a violent armored car shootout, I watched my best friend die in the back seat of a speeding, bullet-riddled getaway car. Shortly after that I decided to change my life, and put myself into a drug and alcohol rehab program. I came out sober and tried to go straight. I got a non-union construction job, but only made pennies and could barely afford to live. I returned to robbing banks and armored cars.

In 1986 I was the head of a crew involved in an armored car hold up. It was a beautiful score and we planned to take the entire truck, but bad luck plagued us that day, and after a fifteen-mile chase through the mountains of western Massachusetts, we were apprehended at a police roadblock.

I received an eighteen-to-twenty year sentence, and spent more than ten years in state prison. I had just turned 35 when I went in. I was 46 when I came out. My prison time was a period of great reflection and I vowed during the earliest months of my incarceration that, because I knew I had better in me, I was going to change my life.

I spent my time in prison wisely. I went through seven years of weekly psychological counseling, attended NA/AA meetings, and Mass once a week. I immersed myself in the Boston University Prison Education Program, and in the space of six years earned a bachelor's degree (magna cum laude) and a master's degree (summa cum laude).

While behind the walls I took many creative writing courses, and even had a short story published in a British literary magazine. When I was released in 1996, I was reluctant to write about crime. I tried to distance myself from it in every way. I was afraid that if I relived my past, even through writing, it might pull me back, like a terrible drug, into a life that would eventually destroy me. But my writing professors encouraged me to write about the street life I knew so well.

I first came up with a title, **BOYOS**, then wrote the story around it. In the *Oxford English Dictionary* "boyo" is defined as an English/ Irish slang word for boy or lad. Italian organized crime figures are called "wiseguys." Their Irish mob counterparts in South Boston and New York are sometimes referred to as "boyos." In Southie a "boyo" has money and respect. He lives by a set of rules, but not the rules of a citizen, a taxpaying nine-to-fiver, which I've now become.

I worked on the novel for three years, taking it to work everyday as a member of Local 88/The Tunnel Workers Union, working on Boston's Big Dig. As the "top man's" helper I sat on a perch overlooking the 230 foot shaft, exposed to the elements year round, writing whenever I could. When they shifted me to the yard crew, I wrote behind storage tanks in the snow, or inside leaky electrical sheds out of the rain. I wrote at lunch. I wrote.

And I finished. And I learned the computer and put it all in and I rewrote, rewrote, rewrote the material I had already rewritten in longhand five or six times. I got good feedback and then, through a fortunate series of events, (which I attribute to God) I was directed to Kate Mattes, owner of Kate's Mystery Books in Cambridge, Massachusetts. She read the first third of the manuscript, told me it should be published, and asked for the rest. I gave her the remainder of the book. She loved it and sent it to a publisher, Justin, Charles & Co. in Boston. A few months later I signed a publishing contract.

I am now pretty far along into my next book, a private eye mystery. I lie in bed at night thinking about dialogue and blocks of narrative, then get up and make notes in the dark so as not to awaken my sweet wife, Elaine. It's maddening at times. My plan is to someday help other guys, by example and through my writing, to stay out of prison. I am convinced that the penal system is *designed* so that men will recidivate.

Gotta throw them a curveball.

Richard Marinick
South Boston, 2004

EVERYTHING YOU CAN IMAGINE IS REAL.

— PABLO PICASSO

BOYOS

1

IT WAS LATE MAY, following an unusually warm winter, and Jack "Wacko" Curran turned the wheel of his favorite car, his midnight blue Mercury Marquis, right off Dorchester Street onto East Seventh Street. As he followed a familiar route through the maze of streets and courtyards of South Boston's Old Colony housing projects, sets of dark, unfamiliar eyes followed him closely. As he pulled to the left and double-parked in front of 19 Pilsudski Way, he felt like he just passed through a colon.

He got out of the car and checked both ends of the street before he opened the rear door and removed an overflowing bag of groceries from the seat. Securing the bag under his left arm, Wacko pushed through the maroon exterior door of the brown brick, three-story building. His right hand was strategically placed near his hip as he climbed the green cement stairway to the second-floor landing, where he paused, his ears pricked for following sounds. Hearing none, he continued to climb until the third floor, turning left at the top of the stairs and stopping in front of a battered steel, olive-colored door on his right, with the number 14 painted above the busted out peephole.

As he glanced sideways towards the stairs, he simultaneously pulled back on his nylon windbreaker, his right hand exposing the hard rubber grip of the two-inch Smith & Wesson .38 revolver on his hip. He shoved the gun deeper into his belt before he softly knocked three times. He stepped back from the door as he waited, eyeing the stairwell every few seconds, as though he were expecting someone. With no response from within, he pulled a lone key, attached to a silver ring, from his pocket and stuck it into the lock.

The door swung easily open, and Wacko Curran leaned in. "Ma? Kevin, anyone home?" he said, before stepping into the front room of the neat but sparsely furnished apartment. He crossed the room towards two partially opened windows in the wall on his left and placed the groceries on a couch, its fabric sprayed like buckshot with small embroidered roses. A slight breeze from two-inch openings at the bottoms of the storm windows rustled the curtains. Wacko lifted the half-drawn shade with one finger and checked the street below, saw nothing unusual, then removed a half gallon of milk from the bag along with some butter and cottage cheese. He carried the groceries into the kitchen and put everything in the refrigerator, then grabbed a Flintstones glass from the cabinet and filled it with water from the tap. As he drank he noticed a note beneath a saltshaker on the table. Wacko picked it up. It read:

> Boys,
>   If you stopped by, thank you. Went to lunch with Rita Moynihan, down the hall (who's been bugging me to go for weeks, tired of ducking her). If you get a sec, help your old Ma, and pull down my screens, can't get the storm windows up. Bugs getting in. Call me, your fingers aren't broken.
>   Love you both. Mum xxoo (one each).

Wacko put the empty glass in the sink just as a yellow cab pulled up in front of the building. The back door blew open, and a wiry young man burst from the car, hitting the sidewalk running. In a heartbeat the driver was outside and rounding the bumper. The cabbie screamed, "Stop, you son-of-a-bitch!" He halfheartedly ran to the maroon door his passenger had seconds before entered, then jerked to a stop and threw up his hands like he was attached to a chain. In the hallway outside the door, Wacko heard the familiar cackling laughter of his brother, and the peculiar thundering echo of footsteps ascending housing project stairs. He opened the door in time to see Kevin rounding the landing, then bolting the final few feet to the door.

"I beat the bum, Jackie," Kevin said as he slipped past his brother, stroking his stylishly cut brown hair into place with his fingers. Kevin kneeled on the couch and looked out the window. "Look at him, pussy's scared to come into the building, afraid he'd catch a beatin'." Wacko walked into the kitchen, pinched the side of the curtain and peeked down. Kevin came up behind him. "Where's Mum?" he said.

"Out to lunch, like you. That cabbie's still down there lookin' around," Wacko said.

"Fuck him, let him look. Ma got any Kool-Aid?" Kevin said, rummaging through the cabinets over the sink. "It's gettin' hot outside, she oughta stock up."

"What the fuck's wrong with you?" Wacko said, releasing the curtain. "You need money, tell me, you'd take a pinch in Ma's house over a lousy cab fare?"

"Relax, Jack, no one's gettin' pinched. Here it is," Kevin said, pulling a pack of Kool-Aid from the back of a drawer next to the stove. The torn top was folded, secured by a paper clip. Kevin sniffed the package and jerked his head back. "Damn, smells like Ma's slippers." He burst out laughing and wrapped his arm around Wacko's shoulders. Wacko picked the note off the table and handed it to his brother.

"We got work to do, Ma's got bugs in the house," Wacko said. Kevin opened the Kool-Aid and stuck his tongue inside. As he read the note he made a face like he had just sucked a bad egg. "Damn . . . I don't see no bugs," Kevin said, smacking his lips, looking around the room.

"Check the bathroom . . . the mirror," Wacko said.

"You're a funny man, Jack, a real funny prick," Kevin said, throwing the Kool-Aid into the trash. He turned on the kitchen tap and stuck his tongue under the water just as the cell phone on Wacko's hip rang.

"Ya," Wacko said, looking at Kevin. He nodded. "You want the same as last time? I told you it was a good read. Same place, okay?" Wacko closed the phone. "Leppy Mullins needs to re-up," he said. Kevin wiped his mouth with a paper towel.

"Already? He's movin', pissed through that shit pretty quick," Kevin said.

"He got four ounces of blow last week, give him five today," Wacko said.

"Cash?"

"Cash for four, he'll cuff the fifth," Wacko said.

"He know he's cuffing?" Kevin said.

"When you meet him in an hour in front of Albany Radiator he will," Wacko said.

Kevin made a face. "We're low, Jack, we got maybe six ounces left at Story Street, we gotta see Marty soon," Kevin said.

Wacko's cell phone rang again and he jerked it to his ear. "Ya, what? Christ, are you whacked? I told you, same place, listen the fuck up," he said and snapped the phone shut. "I hope Leppy's not usin' his own shit again; he does, he's through."

Wacko kneeled on the couch, opened the inside window all the way, slid the storm up behind it, and lowered the screen. He glanced over his shoulder. "You gonna watch me do all the fucking work? Start in the bedrooms, and take this," Wacko said, tossing Kevin the cell phone. "If Leppy calls again I'm in no mood to chat."

As he lowered the screen in the kitchen window, Wacko noticed the cab was gone. Somewhere in the apartment he heard his cell phone ring, and Kevin appeared in the entrance to the kitchen. "Jack, you better take this one," he said, raising his eyebrows twice. Wacko took the phone.

"Ya?" Wacko said.

"Got somethin' for you, Jack," said a voice on the other end that Wacko recognized as belonging to a smash and grab artist by the name of Sean Brancaccio.

"Ya, what?"

"Ice, a bucketful," Sean said.

"How much we talkin'?"

"Retail, over a million, a cakewalk, believe me."

"Hold on," Wacko said, looking out the window. He walked into the living room, kneeled on the couch, and moved the curtain aside with the phone. Across the street on the sidewalk, two old ladies with small bundles in their arms stood and chatted. A short distance past them a black Ford Crown Victoria, with black-walled tires and small silver hubcaps, had pulled up and sat double-parked and idling. The driver turned his head and stared directly at Wacko's window. Wacko pushed himself away from the couch and stood up. "Sean, meet me in a half hour in front of the IA," he said, something sharp edged and dark passed in front of his eyes. "Be there, don't fuck up." Wacko closed the phone. Somewhere in the apartment a window screen lowered and clicked into place, then Kevin came bounding into the living room.

"I think we got somethin', diamonds, gotta hook up with Sean Brancaccio," Wacko said.

Kevin gleefully rubbed his hands together. "I'm goin' with you," he said.

"No, you're not, you're stayin' and doin' the windows for Ma. Besides, the cops are out front, probably because of that cab. This shit's gotta stop, Kevin, you're creatin' problems," Wacko said.

"Only problem I got, I'm hungry. How 'bout I go with you, get somethin' to eat, come back?" Kevin said.

"Forget about it. You're hungry, there's food in the fridge," Wacko said, pulling his keys out of his pocket.

"Nothin' but cheese and some old bread," Kevin said.

"Then make yourself a grilled cheese. I'll be back in an hour, finish the windows," Wacko said.

"They're done," Kevin said.

"Then wash 'em, eat some grilled cheese, and stay the fuck inside," Wacko Curran said.

2

DANNY KING ROLLED OVER, checked the clock, and farted what was left of last night's beer through his Yogi Bear sheets. His stomach grumbled, and he wondered how he'd eat today. The night before he'd blown all he had, every dime of his last five hundred dollars, at the Pen Tavern, and the thought of hitting someone up for a loan made his stomach twitch. It was always the same, make a score, then blow it on beer, cocaine, and keno. He was tired of loan sharks, but he'd be fucked if he'd go back to budging cans of tuna off the shelves of Flanagan's market. Sticking them inside his belt and praying they wouldn't fall out before he left the place. He had a rep, he was a consummate thief, proficient stickup man; Danny King even stole his own cars. He was a man just now coming into his own, and here he was broke again and the pressure was on.

Danny convinced himself that he liked the pressure. He prided himself on the fact that he always left for a score with a single dollar bill in his pocket, the last one. There'd be no turning back, he'd be either dead, or in jail, or that dollar bill would soon have a bunch of companions. That Danny had balls was a fact not lost on others in the South Boston underworld. Hadn't Wacko Curran, or at least his brother, Kevin, invited him in on an armored car score? They called it a piggy bank on wheels, and he wouldn't let them down.

At thirty-one Danny King remained an athlete, and he still had the moves. When you were out there working the streets, pulling scores, it paid to be in shape. After he pissed, washed his face, and swilled a cup of instant Maxwell House, he sat on his bed and knotted the laces of a pair of New Balance running shoes. They were good shoes but not his best; the other pair, the ASICS, he only wore on scores. They had never seen the streets, only the polished tiles of lending institutions.

Danny closed the door to his M Street apartment, took a left at the bottom of the stairs, and trotted easterly towards Day Boulevard. He crossed the busy thoroughfare and followed the sidewalk towards Castle Island; on his right Boston Harbor sparkled in the early morning sun. Occasionally cars passed and tooted their horns and Danny waved even when he failed to recognize the drivers.

At Kelly's Landing, Danny King spit over the green iron railing into the water, then took a right at the site of the old Head House, into the area of the Lagoon known as the Sugar Bowl. He followed the narrow access road that shot straight into the harbor for a quarter mile before arcing left, eventually connecting with Castle Island, the site of a huge granite fort, a half mile across the Lagoon. As he ran his lungs filled with the sixty-degree air, and he reminisced about a much colder run seven years before.

It was winter, the night before a heist down the Cape in Falmouth, and he was unable to sleep. A midnight run to Castle Island was better than Valium, so he dressed and headed out under a canopy of crisp, white stars. He followed the empty boulevard to the Sugar Bowl and the access road, into the harbor, which was bordered on either side by green chain-link fence.

As he approached the halfway point, he saw something on the fence that electrified the hairs on the back of his neck. It was a visitor from Spectacle Island, a giant arctic snowy owl. He slowed to a walk as he drew up on the bird, which seemed large enough to carry him away, and he fought the urge to turn and run. In an instant it unfurled its wings and rose, like smoke from a Boston Edison stack, spiraling upwards until it blended with the stars. He finished his run that night fearing the bird's return and wondered if he'd see it again.

■　■　■

Wacko Curran traveled north on Day Boulevard in the blue Marquis. As he passed the Ocean Kai restaurant on the left, he angrily poked the seek button on the radio with his right index finger. "You like this shit? You really do? Listen on your own time," Wacko said. Kevin laughed and slapped the dashboard like a conga drum.

"Oh, Jack, man, get with it. Hip-hop's happenin', baby! A little OutKast, DMX, Biggie Smalls can't hurt ya. Lighten up," Kevin said.

"How 'bout I lighten the fucking car up?" Wacko said, tightening his grip on the wheel. "Speakin' of which, speakin' of which, you get Ma anything for her birthday yet?"

Kevin stopped drumming, looked at him like he was crazy. "Ma's birthday's two months away."

"Two months, five weeks, so what, you eat there, what, three nights a week?" Wacko said. He slapped Kevin on the back of the head. Kevin's Vuarnet wrap-a-round sunglasses tumbled off his face into his lap.

"Hey, that's only because you can't cook," Kevin said. He poked his brother in the ribs, and Wacko swerved into the oncoming lane.

"Cut the shit, you'll kill us," Wacko said.

"Ain't worried about no traffic accident," Kevin said, checking himself in the sun visor mirror. He pushed the hair down behind his ears and readjusted the Vuarnets as Wacko stamped his foot and tapped the brakes.

"There's our man now," Wacko said. He turned left near M Street and backed twenty feet up the one-way street, then stopped. Danny King was nearing the end of his run a hundred yards northeast of the L Street Bathhouse, a building dating back to the early part of the twentieth century, when he heard the horn. He glanced to his right, and wiped the sweat from his eyes, and looked over his shoulder. The car horn sounded again. Danny stopped and waved in Wacko's direction, signaling a car on the boulevard to continue before he stepped off the curb.

"What's up, Jack?" he said, jogging up to the Marquis driver's side window. "Hi, Kev." Kevin didn't reply but waved, as if he were flicking spit off a finger, and stared straight ahead.

"You guys don't seem too . . ."

"You still in, Danny? I've called, been to your house twice this week, no answer, no note, nothing. You too busy?" Wacko said.

Danny stepped away from the car. "Jack, of course still I'm in." He thumped his heart with an open palm. "I've been runnin' around with this broad." He spun, staggered, and almost collapsed onto the street before he caught himself. "This broad, Jack, never seen anything like it, fucking me to death," Danny said.

Wacko smirked. "That's a healthy way to die," he said. "I know worse." Danny's eyes pleaded, and he shrugged before Wacko continued. "Look, Danny, if you're supposed to be home when we come, be fucking home. I'm no messenger boy; I don't knock on empty doors. If you ain't goin' to be there, call. I've got this crazy imagination that takes me to dark places when I think I'm gettin' stiffed."

"I wouldn't stiff you, Jack," Danny said.

"You not being where you're supposed to stiffs me, Danny. I don't search for my guys, got it?" Wacko said.

"I got it, Jack, sorry," Danny said, reaching into the car and grabbing Wacko playfully behind the neck.

"Hey, get outta here, ya bum, you're all sweaty," Wacko said, starting the car. "Someday soon I'll call you, early morning, before you run. We'll meet and check the play on that armored car score we got," Wacko said.

Danny King stepped away from the car, grabbed and pulled his balls. "I'm ready when you are, boss," he said.

Wacko hit the up button on the window and nosed the Ford into the boulevard, then pulled into the right lane, slowed, and locked his eyes on the rearview mirror. "That prick's still standing there watchin' us. Something about him, Kevin, something's missin'," Wacko said.

"What do you think?" Kevin said. He hit the down button for the window and spit over the top of the glass. "Balls? He's got balls, Jack, seen him in action myself."

"Seen what, him boltin' some jewelry store, hittin' some seventy-year-old drop in the South End?" Wacko said.

"He does banks, Jack."

"With a gun or note?"

"He uses a piece."

"That's a start, but we ain't talkin' banks, we're talkin' armored cars, different as weasels and wolverines. I just don't know if Danny boy is up to it," Wacko said, punching the steering wheel. "If Mitch Cochran hadn't taken that stupid pinch over that douche bag he calls a girlfriend, he'd be out here with us, and we wouldn't be dealin' with the likes of Danny King," Wacko said.

"Mitch is doin' a skid bit, Jack, eighteen months, maybe we should wait," Kevin said.

Wacko shook his head. "I ain't waitin' eighteen months to make a move. I don't trust Marty Fallon no more. The more money we make the more he wants, then he's nervous because we're makin' moves and money. Marty gets nervous, people get hurt, fact," Wacko said.

"What do we do?" Kevin said.

"The armored car. We whack that, we don't need no one," Wacko said.

At the traffic lights at I Street, Wacko turned right. A half a block up he nodded at the ice cream shop on the left. "Want something at Frosty Village?"

"Pass, I'm watchin' my weight. Which reminds me, I'm feeling a little heavier than usual around my balls," Kevin said. He reached down into his pants and fumbled around his crotch. "Ah, here's the culprit," Kevin said. He pulled out a small plastic bag with a knotted top. "Want some?" he said, biting off the knot.

At the East Eighth Street intersection, Wacko slowed and opened his right hand. Kevin poured a tiny pile of white powder and yellow-tinged pebbles into it. Wacko tossed the contents into his mouth like he was eating peanuts. He licked his palm.

"Man, how you do that?" Kevin said, sticking a rolled-up dollar bill directly into the bag, then up one nostril. He gently inhaled and coughed.

"So I won't do that," Wacko said. At East Seventh Street he turned a lazy right and followed the road until L Street, where he turned left. A few blocks up on the right he pulled over and stopped in front of the L Street Diner. "That cook in there pay you for the cuff last week?" Wacko said.

"Not yet, Jack, but Billy Rilke's cool, he gets paid today, I'll get it," Kevin said.

Wacko pulled back into traffic. "I think you're too easy on these bums. Let's go see Marty," he said, turning left at East Fourth Street. They cruised past the Stop & Shop supermarket on the right then stopped in front of the fire station. Across from them, on the corner of K Street and Emerson, was the Dudley Tavern. A dark blue Chevy Impala sat double-parked out front. "He's in there," Wacko said, making a U-turn. They cut through the Stop & Shop lot to Broadway, then looped back, traveling down one-way Emerson Street to the Dudley Tavern. They pulled behind the Impala and stopped. Wacko hit the horn twice, and a face appeared in the tiny rectangle of glass of the tavern door. The door opened a crack, and a hand waved them in.

"Seems Marty's holdin' court," Kevin said, wiping his nose. "How I look?" He turned towards Wacko and jutted out his chin.

Wacko pointed at his nose. "A stalactite in the corner; another reason I don't do that," he said.

Kevin turned the rearview mirror in his direction and hastily wiped his nose. "Ah, perfect, all I need is a fucking tie," he said, exiting the car.

"And a fucking brain," Wacko said, throwing his sunglasses onto the dashboard.

3

MIKE JANOWSKI HAD A LOT to be thankful for since his release from MCI Cedar Junction six months earlier. As a favor, he'd been hired to tend bar at the Teamsters Pub. The Teamsters, on the corner of D and West Second Streets, was a rough-and-tumble joint frequented by blue-collar types, ex-cons, and union men. The bar was owned by Marty Fallon.

Marty Fallon was to South Boston what a canker sore was to a mouth, everything had to get by it before it got to a place where it would do any good. He was one of those guys, that rare breed, that when people mentioned his name they'd automatically lower their voices and mentally make the sign of the cross. Little moved through South Boston without Marty tearing off a piece. A "Fallon Tax" he called it.

In order to avoid being hijacked or, at the very least, having their tires slashed at traffic lights, city and suburban truck firms delivering beer, wine, and hard liquor to South Boston bars and package stores paid the Fallon Tax. Every bar owner in Southie made bimonthly payments to Fallon's hulking enforcer, Andre Athanas, in order to avoid the stink bombs or tear gas canisters heaved through the doors of those establishments hesitant to pay. Owners of variety stores, clothing stores, even toy shops paid the Fallon Tax for the privilege of operating with all their teeth.

When Mike Janowski hit the streets, he respectfully called in a favor, the result of a chance encounter with Marty Fallon six years before. It was late Monday night, and Mike Janowski was in his second-floor apartment on Bantry Way when a pounding at the door interrupted what had been a very enjoyable task. Earlier that day he and a friend, Webby Downs, had robbed the Merchants Bank on Tyler Street in Chinatown of its weekend receipts.

Before the bank had opened, and after the manager and two blue-haired tellers went in, they pounded their way through the double, glass front doors with ten-pound sledge-hammers. After tossing the terrified manager and tellers to the floor, they scooped the night deposit bags out of the laundry cart they'd been collected in, filling a huge, double-ply trash bag, before making their escape.

Mike's end was $114,000, and he was in the process of re-counting it when came the fateful knock at the door. He thought it was the cops and froze, until he heard the voice.

Marty Fallon, with whom he'd dealt briefly in the past, stepped through the door that night, the collar of his green army jacket pulled up, the lid of his baseball cap down, and the stench of gasoline emanating from his clothes. Marty eyeballed the cash, laid in rows on the floor, as he explained how he'd just torched a Lincoln Continental down the street, and how his driver, Eddie O'Brien, had panicked and left Marty behind when the car failed to ignite the first time. Marty wasn't known as a quitter and completed the task. Mike allowed him to stay until the night absorbed the sounds of fire trucks and scurrying emergency vehicles.

It wasn't until the following morning, long after Marty Fallon had gone, that Mike discovered the one small element he had neglected to mention. Inside the Lincoln was the body of a man, badly charred like the rest of the car, but still enough of him left to bring the cops swarming through the neighborhood, questioning anything that moved for the next eight hours.

Mike Janowski knew something was up when Eddie O'Brien, Marty's driver, had gone missing in the days that followed. Eddie was old, had retired to Florida they said, or maybe Marty had dug a hole. You didn't leave someone like Marty Fallon high and dry next to a corpse and expect a high five, but Marty wasn't saying much. Marty wasn't saying period.

4

THE CURRANS ENTERED the Dudley Tavern. While Wacko found seats at the bar, Kevin remained at the door and talked with the spotter. As he spoke, Kevin was inches from the spotter's face. "I'm telling you, Dinny, the blow's excellent, you won't regret it," Kevin said. He reached into his back pocket, pulled out a small brown notepad and flipped it open. "Here, to make things straight, because I like ya, I'll knock two hundred dollars off the last batch you bought, how's that?" The spotter smiled and both men shook hands. Kevin sat down at the bar next to his brother.

"Straightened out?" Wacko said, eyeing the spotter. "You shouldn't have cut him any slack, Kev. This is business not charity, let the buyer beware."

"I couldn't do that to him, Jack; he's a slob, a workin' stiff who's always up-front with his cash, unlike a lot of the bums we deal with. I don't blame him being pissed, they whacked his coke with aspirin," Kevin said.

Wacko grabbed Kevin's forearm. "Not so loud, you fucking nut, 'they' is us, remember that," Wacko said.

Kevin pulled his arm away. "But aspirin, they were hardly ground up; ever hear of a fucking Derring? Couldn't Marty at least pretend he's human, cut his coke with anesitol?"

Wacko looked away from his brother, then quickly turned back. "Listen, Marty Fallon got a bad batch, what's he supposed to do, eat it? We wholesale and move his product, that's what we do. Whatever he gives us we move to guys like Dinny Moynihan over there, and he moves it to his customers. It ain't going to be good all the time, what is?" Wacko said.

"It ain't right," Kevin said.

"Again, what is, relax," Wacko said.

Wacko handed a long-necked Bud Light to his brother and one to a wiry little man, wearing sneakers, dungarees, and a white Polo shirt with the collar up, to his right. The little man poured his beer into an overused glass, then removed his frayed gray scally cap and pulled a piece of paper from inside the brim. He waved it at Kevin.

"Who you got, Molly?" Kevin said.

Molly winked. "I got the Red Sox to win against Atlanta for three sixty, Kev. The line's one eighty to one hundred. I'll make the deuce, the Sox are hot."

"Maybe I'll take a little," Kevin said.

"You'll take nothin'," Wacko said. "Molly, leave him the hell out of your business."

Molly hurriedly pulled on his cap.

"S-sorry, Jack, didn't mean nothin," he said.

"It ain't you, Molly, it's him," Wacko said, sipping his beer.

"C'mon, Jack, a couple of bucks," Kevin said.

Wacko put down his beer. "Look, I promised Ma you'd be doin' no gamblin' when you're with me," Wacko said.

Kevin leaned into his brother. "You're right, Jack, I promised her too," he said.

"Have some fucking discipline, Kevin. Instead of being my partner, people are lookin' at you like you're some kind of mascot. It ain't good," Wacko said.

"All right, no gamblin', but I think I got some discipline left over down here. Want some?" Kevin said patting his crotch.

"Hold off on the coke, I don't want you jekylled up in front of Marty," Wacko said.

Kevin looked past his brother and nodded towards the rear of the bar. He exaggerated the shakes. "Oh-oh, monsters in the house," he said.

In the tavern's back wall a mahogany door near the men's room opened, the frame immediately filled by an enormous figure. Andre Athanas stepped into the room. Kevin slid off the barstool and patted his crotch again. "I'll go do my business in the men's room. Don't worry, Jack, I'll be cool," he said. As they crossed paths, Andre and Kevin eyeballed each other, like each had been informed they were married to the same woman.

"Marty'll see you in a minute, Jack," Andre said, staring at the men's room door. He looked over his shoulder up the stairway leading to the second floor. "While I'm down here, boss, you want a Coke or somethin'?" Andre said. Wacko heard a voice at the top of the stairs say something about onion and garlic chips. "I gotta go across the street to Joseph's for them, boss, Frankie don't have 'em," Andre said. He scowled at the bartender, who blushed and furiously scrubbed a glass. "You can go up, Wacko . . . er, Jackie," Andre said. Wacko hopped off the barstool and eyed the giant hard, while the big man pursed his lips and stared at the ceiling like he was counting clouds.

"Outta my way," Wacko said, passing in front of Andre who followed close behind him up the stairs.

Wacko hated the nickname he'd reluctantly carried since he was nineteen years old. At the time, Kevin, who was six years younger, had gone to a Bruins game at the Garden with a few friends on a Sunday afternoon and returned looking like something from a horror movie. He and his friends had been set upon by a group of older men, the same age as Wacko. The ringleader, the son of a North End Mafioso, believing himself to be immune from retaliation, had delivered the most damaging blows. Wacko had grabbed a hockey stick and, by himself, taken a cab to the corner of Atlantic Ave and Hanover Street, where the men were said to hang out. Wacko found the ringleader and three of his friends and beat them all senseless, actually using the splintered remains of the broken stick to nearly fatally stab two of them. There was heat, but in the end the wiseguys backed off, deciding the beating was justified, there'd be no retaliation. The word was out; not only did the kid from South Boston have enormous cojones but he was crazy, out of his mind, wacko. The name stuck, though no one called him that to his face.

In a room across the linoleum-covered hallway at the top of the stairs, Marty Fallon sat behind a cheap wooden desk. A heavyset man in a swivel chair sat to his left, with his back to the door. The other man spun around in the chair as Wacko walked into the office. Wacko recognized him as Jerry Callahan, one of Marty's main Dorchester bookmakers. Jerry looked bloated, and his skin had a shine to it like someone was operating a bicycle pump up his ass. Wacko stopped in front of the desk and nodded.

"Andre, close the door and leave us alone. Have a seat," Marty said, indicating a metal fold-out chair beneath a television mounted on the wall. The TV was on, a little too loud, and Bob Barker was explaining the rules of some game to one of his contestants. He made it sound easy. Wacko thought it was a lot like Marty Fallon, everything was easy as long as someone else was doing it. Wacko sat down in the chair.

The other two men spoke in whispers a few more minutes, then Jerry Callahan stood up and tugged at the crease in his pants. "So, Jack, how's tricks? Kevin leavin' the sports book alone?" he said. Like he was getting up, Wacko put his hands on his knees, then relaxed and leaned back into the chair.

"What's your problem, Jerry? He paid what he owed you, so whatever else he's up to's his fucking business," Wacko said. Jerry glanced at Marty, who smiled, put his hands behind his head, and leaned back into the heavily padded leather chair.

"Don't get me wrong, Wacko, I'm happy, really, he's not gamblin' no more, only makes it hard on himself," Jerry said. Wacko leaped to his feet, and Jerry half-stepped quickly to the side and glanced towards the door.

"Hey you, sit the fuck down," Marty said to Wacko. "And you, watch your mouth, you know he don't like —"

"Wacko?" Jerry said, bolting to the door. He pulled it open, jumped outside, then stuck his head back in. "You're lucky, Jack, it's colorful, accurate. Wish I had a nickname."

"You got one, Callahan, and one day I'll whisper it into your ear," Wacko said. Jerry slammed the door.

Marty Fallon stood up. "You two, since you were kids, fightin' like cats and dogs; I don't get it," he said. He took a few steps to the right and stopped in front of a small white refrigerator with a lock on it. He opened the door, took out a bottle of San Pellegrino spring water, and cracked the top. To the right of the refrigerator stretched a red leather couch. Wacko could smell the new leather and figured the couch was probably tribute from one of the hijacking crews that operated in the area.

He remembered back to the days when he was a kid, boosting from the backs of tractor trailers stopped at the lights in front of the projects, at the intersection of Dorchester Street and Old Colony Avenue. With the driver unaware, they'd use a bolt cutter on the lock, pop the back door, and toss cases of whatever was inside — Polo shirts, Nike sneakers, sirloin steaks — out to chase cars that followed directly behind the slow-moving trucks as they rolled, after the lights had changed, through the heavy traffic. Wacko also remembered afterwards heading back to the Dudley Tavern to give Marty Fallon an end, since he was the man, the one everyone wanted to be. Marty got his piece then, and he always would.

"So, what's goin' on?" Marty said, drinking deep from the bottle.

Wacko waited until the air bubbles stopped percolating to the bottom before he spoke. "Not much, Marty. Gotta re-up, same amount . . . maybe a little more than last week, I'm working on a couple of new venues." Wacko said.

"Where?"

"In Quincy. I figure, since I got that condo in Squantum, I may as well support the community," Wacko said.

Marty screwed the cap back on the bottle and tossed the empty into the bucket. "Squantum's a small place, think it's smart?" he said.

"I don't shit in my backyard; I'm not talkin' about movin' coke in Squantum. I'm talking a couple of taverns in Hough's Neck. I'm workin' on two bars down there, dumps, but they do an all right business, and another joint, a nicer place up in North Quincy, a place where they got no problem payin' for a good product," Wacko said.

"Anyone movin' in those joints now?" Marty said.

"There's a local smuck, Peter Viro . . . Vino something, Italian, he's movin' a little coke, thinks he's a hit man. Flippy Condon's gonna talk to him," Wacko said.

"Flippy's a nut," Marty said. He sat down in his chair and played with an unopened pack of Marlboros.

"Ya, but he's our nut and he'll talk to the guy. I've clocked this Vino character. I know where he lives, what he drives, where he hangs. We'll find the right spot and have a good talk with him," Wacko said.

Marty motioned Wacko closer. "Think he'll listen?" he said, motioning Wacko even closer before picking up the remote device and pointing it at the television. Wacko nodded. The volume increased. Bob Barker ranted on about the final showcase. "If he don't listen, what you gonna do?" Marty said, directly into Wacko's ear. Wacko could smell Old Spice deodorant and fennel seeds on his breath.

"That's on him, Marty. I'm only gonna ask him once. He says no, that's okay." Wacko said, then shrugged.

Marty leaned back in the chair and put his cowboy boots up on the desk. "Nice boots," Wacko said, thinking they made Marty look like a faggot. "Thinkin' about getting a pair myself."

"So you get Quincy, Jack, those bars on line, how much more weight we talkin' you movin'?" Marty said.

Wacko closed his eyes and stroked his chin with his right hand. "We're talkin' maybe another half pound," he said.

Marty winced. "A small return, seems like a lot of work," he said.

Wacko clapped his hands together. "You're talkin'minimum, an extra kilo a month, right? C'mon, Marty, a little sauce, a bit of cheese, what ya got? A big fucking pizza."

"Ya, but you need heat to cook that pizza, and heat I don't need," Marty said. Andre knocked and opened the door. He tossed a bag of onion-garlic chips to Wacko and put two on Marty's desk near his feet.

"Don't like 'em," Wacko said, tossing the bag sideways into Andre's chest.

"Eat them," Marty said, crunching some in his mouth. "Onion and garlic are good for you." Andre handed Wacko back the bag. Wacko opened it, smiled, and put a chip in his mouth.

"Not bad," Wacko said. Andre smirked.

"Jack, Mary Rose O'Connell seen your car. She's parked down on K waitin' for ya. What I tell her, boss?" Andre said.

"Me and Jack here are almost done. Tell her to sit and wait, he'll be out in a minute. How's she doin', Jack?" Marty said.

"Consistent, two, sometimes three ounces a week, pays up-front, no complaints."

Marty pointed at the television. "Jackie, check this guy out, Bob Barker, close to a hundred and look at them teeth," he said. He turned off the television. "I hear Mary Rose is a hustler, but she's a broad, Jack, be careful. She ain't doin' any time for you, not fifteen minutes."

"She knows the rules, Marty, she's a project kid. Her older brother Stevie, they're close, he's up The Hill doin' a dime, he schooled her good," Wacko said.

"She better have a college degree for your sake," Marty said, his eyes piercing and dark.

Wacko shifted uneasily; the eyes were something he never got used to. When he was a kid he'd read about a place called La Brea, somewhere in California, with tar pits that trapped huge, powerful animals and pulled them down. Marty's eyes were everything like that, black pools from which nothing, even light, escaped.

Wacko broke the spell and stood up. "So, ah, I meet Andre at the regular spot for the pickup?"

Marty Fallon got up and moved to the window in the wall behind the chair. He shifted the blinds, looked out. "Ya, the same place. You said you wanted extra. You're movin' twenty ounces a week, I'll give you thirty."

Wacko opened his mouth to speak but Marty cut him off. "Cash on the first twenty, like always, the others you cuff," he said.

Wacko shook his head. "Naw, think I'll pass, Marty. It's gonna take time to get those Quincy joints up and runnin'. I don't want —"

"Naw, you take 'em," Marty said. He let the blind drop with a bang on the glass, then came around the desk and faced Wacko. "Jack, you're like a son, you're my top mover, my main guy, you can do this, just get rid of them." Marty winked and put his hand on Wacko's shoulder, escorting the younger man out the door. "Do this for me," he said, closing the door.

As he headed downstairs, Wacko knew he'd been had. He'd end up eating the coke if the Quincy bars didn't come on line fast enough, paying cash, ten grand, to Marty Fallon for something he didn't want. It was almost as if Marty hoped that if he loaded Wacko up enough, he'd do something stupid, move it too quickly, get busted and go under.

Wacko opened the door at the bottom of the stairs but didn't have to look far for Kevin. At the end of the bar, his younger brother shadowboxed in front of the giant Andre, who stood and stared at him like a Cape buffalo measuring a jackal just beyond the reach of its horns. Kevin snorted through his nose and windmilled his arms. "I won't show you the secret combination I use to take out goons like you, Andre, too complicated and you'd lose track," Kevin said.

"Knock it off, Kevin," Wacko said.

"One of these days it's gonna be just you and me," Andre said, taking a step towards Kevin.

Wacko stuck two fingers through Andre's belt and tugged him back. "But not today, Andre," he said.

"Mary Rose is waitin' outside, Jack," Andre said, his eyes burning a hole through Kevin.

Wacko grabbed his brother by the arm and dragged him laughing out the door. "You gotta stop messin' with the goon," he said.

"He's a joke, Jack, a big fucking joke," Kevin said.

"He may be a joke, but he's a dangerous joke, don't forget it," Wacko said, pointing down K Street. "Look, ain't that Mary Rose?"

A half block down K Street, Mary Rose O'Connell sat inside a red Ford Thunderbird and fixed her makeup in the rearview mirror. She smiled at herself as the Currans walked out of the Dudley Tavern.

5

MARY ROSE O'CONNELL hated her name. The Mary part belonged to her mother, whom she couldn't stand, and the Rose to a grandmother she never knew and who was rumored to have been a drunk. She stood, with her mouth open, in front of the bedroom mirror as she dabbed at her eyes with mascara.

"Gonna catch flies, Mary Rose," her eight-year-old brother, Logan, said, peeking around the door. Mary Rose's mouth snapped shut, and she glared at the mirror.

"Get outta here, ya brat," she said, knowing, even as the head disappeared, it had a return date booked. What the hell, she thought, not much longer, she'd almost had enough.

It had taken her, what, ten weeks to save first, last, and security deposit for a nice little place over the bridge in Quincy. If she'd only begun moving the coke earlier, but she'd been afraid, people had warned her. Jealous people? Stupid people? Hell, it was easier than she had imagined. Soon she'd be able to quit her waitressing job at Amrhein's. No more standing in front of the mirror she shared with two other sisters. No more eating welfare cheese and hearing the next-door neighbors argue so close you could almost smell the Budweiser on their breath. No more a lot of things.

Mary closed the bathroom door and put her back against it. She withdrew a dark blue plastic makeup pouch from her pocketbook, unzipped it, and poured out the contents. She counted thirty-five small plastic bags, each secured at the top by a tiny knot. "Twenty forties and fifteen eighties," she whispered to herself. She'd unload most of the forties at work and the larger bags, after work, at places like Triple-O's and Kelly's. People were always well on their way by then, always looking to score after twelve, after they'd been drinking and doing lines all night. They didn't care about the cost, only if you had it, and have it she did these days, all the time. The mutts would be lined up at the door waiting for her. Cash only, though some would beg for a cuff. The same bums who begged for credit now never acknowledged her in the old days. Now everyone wanted to be her brother or sister, whatever, but all Mary wanted was the green. No cuff, don't ask, take a fucking hike.

Yes, Mary Rose was almost through with Amrhein's and the Old Harbor housing projects. Someday, when she had enough, she'd be through moving the coke too. She'd have a nice place and a decent job. Hell, maybe even a man. First things first, but there was nothing wrong with having plans. She did not call them dreams anymore. The marching powder would help march her out of South Boston, over the bridge into a better life. All she had to do was keep moving, and she would. She had the rhythm now.

6

MARY ROSE O'CONNELL CHECKED her face in the rearview mirror of the red Ford Thunderbird, then with both hands gave her hair one last flip before she popped the door, narrowly avoiding a battered gold Plymouth Duster speeding south on K Street. The driver leaned on the horn and swerved at the last second, missing both the door and the crazy blond who leaped from the car. In the middle of the street Mary Rose jumped in the air and gave the guy the finger, then both fingers, before she daintily spun and headed towards the Curran brothers, who stood in front of the Dudley Tavern and watched in amazement.

Wacko looked at his brother. "Great ass, see it flex when she jumped? I'd wear that thing like a catcher's mask," Wacko said.

"Ya, great ass. I'm hungry, want anything at Joseph's?" Kevin said.

"You're hungry? How can you eat all jekylled up on that shit?"

"Easy. Us mascots can do things real people can't," Kevin said, crossing the street. He high-fived Mary Rose, halfway through the intersection, as they passed.

Mary Rose O'Connell gave Wacko Curran a kiss on the cheek and a hug. She had known him for years, genuinely liked the man, and wasn't at all intimidated by his fearsome reputation. How could she be scared of a guy she remembered as a kid running around the projects in Flintstone's pajamas? Still, Mary Rose knew her place, what to say, how to say it, and especially how to carry herself around a guy like him. Never show him fear or nervousness, always be on time, and of course it didn't hurt to smell good and look pretty when meeting the boss. It was certainly true Mary Rose was her own boss, she moved her product where she wanted and when, but Wacko was her connection, her source, and without him, in this part of town, she'd be moving nothing, and for this she was grateful.

Wacko accepted the kiss from Mary Rose and inhaled her scent. Jesus, she smelled as good as she looked, he thought. "How're you doin', pal, how's the family?" he said, checking out the curve of her eyelashes.

"Things are great, gettin' better," Mary Rose said. "My sister Meghan got into Boston Latin; at least one of us got brains, and Sheila's graduatin' from Mt. St. Joseph's next year. Big brother Stevie's up for parole next month, and the younger two, well, they're kids and act it. Pain in the ass, but I love them, what can you do?"

"You're a good girl, Mary Rose, and your brother Stevie's a good man, you tell him I was asking for him. As a matter of fact. . . ." Wacko pulled a thick roll of bills, bound by an elastic band, out of his pocket and peeled off three twenties. "Put this in his canteen account when you see him next, okay?"

"I'm headin' up there Saturday. It's a tough day for visits, it's wall-to-wall maggots and the guards are pricks, but it's the only day I can make it. I'll tell him you asked for him. He'll be grateful, fact," Mary Rose said.

"How's everything on the other end?" Wacko said.

"Moving right along. I was thinkin' about grabbing a little more this week, maybe an extra ounce or so. I'm pickin' up new customers. There's so much crap out there, and people are tired of getting stiffed. I ain't beatin' my coke to death, everyone loves it. As a matter of fact, just make that an extra ounce even, don't want to owe too much," Mary Rose said.

"I ain't worried, Mary, your credit's good, you want more you got it."

"I appreciate it, Jack, but an extra ounce is enough."

"It's your operation, no problem," Wacko said.

Kevin came out of Joseph's carrying a foot-long sandwich and whistled at Mary Rose.

"Hi, Kev," she said, turning to wave. Wacko checked out her ass again.

"Kevin, go back into Joseph's and come out again," Wacko said. Kevin looked confused. Wacko stretched out his arm, pointed at the sidewalk, and made little circles with his index finger. "I want to see her turn." Mary Rose giggled and slapped Wacko's shoulder.

"You guys are all the same," she said, purposefully flexing her butt cheeks as she turned towards Kevin. Kevin wolf-whistled.

"Kevin, you cute thing, get over here and give me a bite of your spucky," Mary Rose said.

Kevin took a bite of the sandwich and crossed the street. He stopped in front of the pretty blond and crazily chewed. "I'll do you one better, Mary Rose, how about doin' a blast?" he said.

"Do you believe this guy eats when he's wired?" Wacko said.

"Well, I ain't eatin', and a blast sounds good, you carryin'?" Mary Rose said.

"I'll meet you at your car in a minute," Kevin said.

Wacko gave the back of her blouse a little tug. "Kevin will meet you tonight at six in front of the Beer Garden to take care of business," he said.

With both of hers Mary Rose grasped one of Wacko's hands. "Make it seven, hon. I gotta watch my brothers until Ma gets home from work."

"Seven it is," Wacko said.

Mary Rose grinned. "Ooo, you guys are so good to me. See you at the car, Kev." She pinched Wacko's cheek and turned away. As she headed down K Street, both men were mesmerized by the way the cheeks of her butt threw themselves into each other with such abandon.

"When you meet her tonight, give her four ounces," Wacko said, his eyes locked on the receding figure of Mary Rose O'Connell.

"Four? She usually gets two," Kevin said.

"She asked for three, give her four. Look, I'm tryin' to help her here. She'll just cuff what she don't have the cash for."

7

SNOOPY COSTA WAS PISSED. He'd been crouched on this flat roof above the night-deposit box of the Mariner's Bank for almost two hours, and its surface gravel felt irrevocably embedded into his knees. In the parking lot, twelve feet below, his friend and partner, Alby Litiff, sat in his green Trans Am, a hundred yards out and he hoped awake.

Snoopy and Alby had been partners since their release from the Suffolk County House of Correction two years before. Both men were petty crooks, small-timers doing nickel-dime scores, but like most of their kind they always had one eye turned for the big one . . . and the big one was just around the corner.

Thursday nights for the past three weeks Snoopy Costa had perched on this very same roof, kneeling in the darkness, miserable but optimistic as he waited for Manny Goldstein. Manny was the big one.

Most Thursday nights — but not always because he was cute — Manny Goldstein would arrive at the Mariner's Bank on Northern Avenue, sometime after seven, to deposit the considerable take from the four economy gas stations he owned in South Boston and Dorchester. Other guys, too, knew about Manny and in the past had tried to rob him. One attempt, two years earlier, had ended with the assailant being fatally shot. Manny Goldstein was too cheap to hire security and prided himself on the fact he had a permit to carry, as well as on his proficiency as a marksman. Manny believed in the axiom kill one, scare a thousand, and in his mind the thousand had been scared.

Sometime after seven o'clock, Manny Goldstein pulled into the Mariner's bank parking lot and, as usual, carefully surveyed the scene before he got out. When he did, he held the model 1911 Colt .45 automatic tightly in his right hand. The heavy money bag was firmly in his left.

As he crouched on the roof above, Snoopy Costa heard Manny's car door open with the engine still running. He stared across the darkness of the parking lot. All Alby had to do was signal with his headlamps when the time came for Snoopy to stand and get the drop on Manny Goldstein.

Alby's headlights flashed, and Snoopy slowly rose, the gravel falling from his knees onto the roof so loud Snoopy wondered if Manny could hear it too. Manny Goldstein was twenty feet from the night-deposit box when he heard it. It sounded like falling gravel. He raised his line of vision. There on the edge of the flat roof above him stood a figure in black, wearing a ski mask, pointing a pump shotgun directly at his head. The barrel looked like the opening to a manhole as the gunman chambered a round. "Drop that gun or you're fucking dead," Snoopy Costa said.

"What the?" Manny heard himself say. The next sound he heard was that of his own gun hitting the pavement. A car pulled up behind him, and the door opened.

"Hit the ground, fuckface," Alby Litiff said, sprinting out.

Manny dropped to his knees, then flattened out. "Don't kill me, I got family," he said.

"Ya, and tonight I'm takin' your *family* with me," Alby said, picking up the money bag. A kick sent the .45 clattering away.

"From the roof I never expected," Manny said into the pavement.

"A beautiful thing, huh?" Alby said, backing towards the car.

Manny heard the bank's copper rain gutter creak as Snoopy swung himself down. The shotgun walked by Manny's head, the car doors slammed, and the vehicle drove away. The figure on the ground hammered his fist into the pavement. "Motherfucker," Manny Goldstein said.

8

SNOOPY COSTA SAT in his kitchen, in the back of his apartment at 50 O Street, and lazily chopped up a thick line of Colombian coke with someone else's credit card. He'd been up for two and a half days straight and was finally coming down. Two nights earlier, Snoopy and his partner Alby Litiff had grabbed $38,000. from the old Jew, Manny Goldstein, and Snoopy's end was enough to keep him zipping along on the Colombian marching powder for the next eight weeks.

Convinced it was morning, he shifted the shade on the window next to him to peek outside. He was shocked to see the blue-white arc of streetlamps lining East Third Street to the right of the empty, trash-strewn lot behind his apartment. The cat clock on the kitchen wall said eight o'clock, and here he sat telling himself it was morning; he had totally lost track of the time. The message that dripped through the gauze in his skull said it was time to come down off the shit.

Sure, what people said about him being paranoid was true, but these days, it seemed, everyone *was* out to get him. He'd spent the past two days on window duty, high on coke, peeking through cracks in the shades, listening to the walls, and looking out the front door mail slot for people looking for him. He had a gun or a knife in every room of his first-floor apartment and a hand grenade, with a straightened pin, was duct-taped to the knob of the cellar door in the kitchen. The pin was attached to the doorframe by a wire and a sheet metal screw. If someone came at him from below, he'd find a hellava surprise at the top of the stairs.

No matter how much Snoopy told himself it was only his head playing tricks, hadn't he still lain on his bed for hours pointing a gun at whatever, whoever was crawling on the other side of the drop ceiling? He had held the gun up until the muscles in his arms and back spasmed and the pain became too great and he had to run from the room. He carried a heavy revolver, buried deep in his budge, everywhere he went. The gun bruised his hip but would remain there until he came down off the coke.

Snoopy was out of beer; he checked his watch and found there was still time to grab a thirty-pack from the package store two blocks away. He'd do a line just to get up there, come back, relax, and crash for the night.

Snoopy dragged himself into the bathroom but avoided the mirror. The water was cold, brutal to the touch, but he forced himself to wash his face. The task complete, he dirty-toweled away the residue, brushed the shit taste out of his mouth, and ran his fingers through his greasy hair. He sniffed his shirt as he pulled it over his head, wrinkled his nose, threw it into the shower, and cranked on the water.

Snoopy entered the living room and pulled on a T-shirt that had a red anchor beneath the words THE FARGO CLUB in white across the chest. He went to the window and tugged at the side of the shade, looking out onto O Street. Seeing nothing suspicious, he turned to admire the brand-new, thirty-six-inch Sony TV he'd bought hot following the score. Across from it he sat in a chair, picked up the remote device, and pointed it at the screen. Nothing happened. He hadn't plugged it in yet, but there'd be time for watching TV. He didn't grab nineteen large every day. After the celebration was over he'd lay off the coke. He'd eat better, put the weight back on, shower, shave, and shit, none of which he'd done in the past two days.

He tossed the remote onto the cushion of a dirty brown couch to his right and vaguely remembered that his girlfriend, Janey, had called a few times, worried. She left messages until he disconnected the phone. The bitch knew better than to bother him, like he couldn't take care of himself. She made him feel guilty, Janey. His mother was another pissa. Obviously, both of them suffered from short attention spans. Did Janey forget the diamond tennis bracelet he bought her last Easter and Ma the washer-dryer combo he had delivered to her door around the same time? He had even put some thought into what he would buy them from this score, but when he tried to remember he couldn't. No big deal, all he needed was a few more beers and some sleep.

He had to sleep. He really didn't feel strong enough to make the walk to the packy, but the thought of chugging down a bottle of NyQuil to knock him out made him gag. He'd buy a thirty-pack of Bud Light, come home and watch his new TV, maybe throw on a boxing video before he went to sleep. Ya, there'd be plenty of time for sleep after the celebration was over.

Snoopy took a deep breath, readjusted the gun, then covered it with his sweatshirt before he opened the door. Outside he checked both ends of the street before he descended the steps. Near the bottom he hooked his toe on the last step, pitched forward. He looked around, embarrassed, and was thankful the package store was close.

Halfway up the next block, Snoopy spotted a dark blue Chevy Impala on his side of the street parked facing the wrong way. The engine was running. As he got close, the passenger window went down and an arm came out the window. Andre Athanas playfully made a grab for him. "My main man, Snoop. Been lookin' for you, pal," Andre said.

Snoopy stopped short and felt the small amount of life remaining in his legs drain out and puddle on the sidewalk. "Andre, Marty, what's up? I'm . . . I'm on my way to the packy; catch yous on the way back," he said, forcing his legs to move. Marty Fallon leaned across Andre's chest.

"Hold on, Snoopy, we got beer in the car, why don't we head to your place for a drink, talk about a few things?" he said.

"I don't know, Marty," Snoopy said, desperately wishing he wasn't so fucked up.

"Or you could get in the car," Marty said, indicating the backseat with his thumb. The power door locks popped up, and before Snoopy could move, Andre was outside the car. "Let's head to your place, Snoop, you don't look so good," Andre said. The giant wrapped one huge arm around Snoopy's shoulder and looked everywhere but at Snoopy.

Marty got out, came around the front of the car, and grabbed Snoopy by the elbow. His feet barely touched the ground as both men dragged him back towards the apartment. "Andre was right, Snoop, you don't look so good." Marty said, looking over his shoulder.

Snoopy was relieved he hadn't locked the front door when they pushed him face-first into it. He stumbled into the hallway, and his gun fell out and hit the floor. Andre lunged, kicked it away, then grabbed Snoopy by the back of the shirt, lifted him, and tossed him like a doll sideways into the living room. Marty followed him close behind, heading to the windows and pulling both shades tight to the sills. Andre came into the room carrying a small wooden chair from the kitchen and placed it a few feet in front of the Sony.

"Sit," Marty said. Snoopy sat down. "Expecting anyone else?" Snoopy shook his head.

"Marty, please I. . . . ," Snoopy said.

"Shut up." Marty motioned for Andre to check the place.

The giant returned seconds later. "Joint's empty, boss," he said. Marty smiled, then slowly turned, twisted his hips, and viciously drove his right fist into Snoopy's face. The force of the blow almost tipped the chair over before Andre grabbed it and forced the legs back down. Like a boxer, Marty Fallon crouched, tilted his upper body to the side, and fired a left uppercut into Snoopy Costa's solar plexus.

He never saw it coming. Snoopy had been eyeing the hallway when the first blow landed. He was faintly aware of a thud and then saw stars in front of his eyes. He had opened his mouth to scream just as the chair was being righted when the second punch dug deep into his chest, sucking the air from his lungs. Snoopy choked, then vomited slightly before tilting to the left and falling off the seat.

He was faintly aware of a voice somewhere above asking him, "Is it? Is it?" He didn't understand. He felt the enormous weight of Andre's knee on his chest.

"Where is it, you fucking punk? I'll kill you, you cocksucker, I'll cut your heart out," Marty said, bending over him. Snoopy heard a distinct metallic click above his head, then something sharp and twisting like a snake entered the outside of his knee. He heard the sound of gristle being snapped and sheared as his kneecap was almost pried off, and then he heard the scream. It was high-pitched, inhuman, almost catlike, but brief as another meaty fist slammed into his mouth. Snoopy gurgled and choked as he inhaled his own blood into his throat. He feebly struggled with the giant and tried to push against the floor with his feet, but strangely, only one of them worked; the other was folded, useless, under his ass, and he was only too aware of the pain in his knee that spread towards his groin like a trail of lit gasoline.

Marty grabbed him by the windpipe and squeezed. "Where is it, you fuck, you dirty little fuck?" he said while Andre wrapped his forearm under Snoopy's chin and lifted him from the floor.

"Marty, he's bitin' my jacket," Andre said.

"I'll buy you a new one — with his money," Marty said, grabbing Snoopy's balls and squeezing. Snoopy was aware of the pressure, but oddly, he felt no pain. "Where is the money, we just want the money. Tell me and we'll end this thing, drop you at a medical center, I promise," Marty said.

Marty nodded at Andre, who dropped his victim to the floor. Andre wiped the spittle from his sleeve and examined the puncture marks. "You little prick," he said, raising his foot over Snoopy's head.

Marty shoved him back. "Leave the kid alone, he's had enough. Haven't you, Snoop?" Marty said. With his one good eye, Snoopy stared at the ceiling. Something sharp was in the back of his throat, then it shifted to his airway and he coughed. A broken molar skittered across the floor.

"I've . . . had enough, please, Marty, you got it," Snoopy said.

"Where is it?" Marty said.

"In the cellar, all of it except what's wrapped in tinfoil in the freezer. Take it all," Snoopy said, covering his blood-smeared face with his hands.

Marty nodded at Andre, who left the room.

Snoopy spoke between his hands. "I'm bleedin' bad, Marty, get me a doctor please. You got the dough, there ain't a problem, you got the dough, help me, a doctor," he said.

Andre came back into the room. "There's a fucking hand grenade on the cellar door," he said.

Marty looked at Snoopy and smiled. "Then stick it up your ass, Andre, eat it, I don't care. Get down that fucking cellar."

His one good eye closing fast, Snoopy thought, If I get out of this I'm through, no more scores. I'll work do anything. Take care of Mum. Marry Janey, she's good, good for me. God, what have I done?

Andre reentered the living room carrying three foil-wrapped packages. "I did the kitchen first, boss." He tore the cover off one, crumpled it, and dropped the shiny ball on Snoopy's chest. "It's here, boss, looks like two grand in this one, all of them probably."

Snoopy's knee felt like a blowtorch was being held behind it. He was faintly aware of footsteps descending the cellar stairs, then Andre reentered the room holding more foil-wrapped packages in his arms. "It's all there, boss. There's an empty chamber in the top of the water heater where the money is. It's a good chunk of change, this little prick's sharp," he said.

Snoopy groaned. "Doctor, Marty, you promised," Snoopy said.

Marty folded his knife. "Ya, we'll take care of you," he said, motioning Andre to pick him up. Andre did and dropped Snoopy in the chair and pulled back hard enough on his shoulders that his legs kicked out in front. Andre pulled off his belt. "Call the doctor," Marty said. In one fluid motion, Andre wrapped the belt around Snoopy's throat, twisted it, and yanked back towards his massive chest.

Snoopy Costa failed to recognize the terrified, openmouthed countenance reflected back from the darkened screen of the thirty-six inch Sony in front of him. Then his legs began to kick again.

9

"SO, HOW'S IT LOOK?" Wacko Curran said. He picked a flattened can of Bud Light off the sidewalk and flipped it like a Frisbee over the green iron railing bordering Castle Island, which constituted the easternmost tip of the South Boston peninsula, into Boston Harbor twenty feet below. Wacko loved Castle Island, with its Civil War era fort and wide open spaces that offered few hiding places for police surveillance.

Sean Brancaccio threw up his arms and stretched like a cat. "It's a beautiful thing, Jack, a real pretty score, almost as pretty as this place in the morning. Nothing beats Castle Island, huh, but the trick is to get here before the morons arrive. The working-stiff citizens with their coffee cups trying to shake the stink of the wife and kids out their clothes, grab one last lungful of fresh air before they head downtown to their fucking cubicles," Sean said.

"Sorry sons-of-bitches," Kevin said, shaking his head.

"So, Sean, you've seen the play, actually seen it yourself?" Wacko said.

The other man nodded.

"Tell me exactly what you saw," Wacko said. He draped his arm around Sean's shoulder and continued to walk him north towards the Clipper Ship monument.

"See, this flashy bastard jeweler lives out in Westwood with the rest of the rich assholes. Every day he arrives at his store in Abington same time, six forty-five, except on the third Wednesday of the month. That's the day he meets his connection, this Hasidic Jew who comes down from New York City, the Diamond District. They hook up at the Sonesta in Cambridge to do their business. On that day the jeweler, the guy's name is Armand Capizzo, closes the store, but he reopens the following morning."

"So you're saying when this guy shows up at his store out in Abington he's carrying everything with him?" Wacko said.

"Exactly. My source, this girl who worked for him for five years, tells me he walks in with everything he's bought the day before. He's got this safe in the back room of the store. It's a small place, Jack. He's an importer, all he does is diamonds. People make appointments, come in and buy them. He don't need much, a little room is all, better for you."

"Tell me about the layout of the area," Wacko said.

"He's in a small strip mall, ten, twelve shops. To the right of his store is a vacuum repair shop, doesn't open until nine. On the left a tax joint only open about four months a year," Sean said.

"Inside, what's it look like?" Wacko said.

"Go through the front door you're in the main room, it's maybe eighteen by twenty. Near the wall in back there's a desk where he does all his business. Behind the desk to the left is a door. It's a folding door, has vents in it like a shutter. It leads to a little room where all there is is a watercooler, file cabinet, and a safe."

"Could we take the safe with us if we had to?" Wacko said.

"Naw, too big and it's secured to the floor with Hilte bolts, eight inch jobs, you'd need a tow truck to rip it out," Sean Brancaccio said.

"So, this broad your source, how long she work for this guy and why is she giving him up?" Wacko said.

"She worked for him for five years. He's a Valentino type, a real smoothie, been tapping her since she was eighteen, knocked her up a few years back, made her get rid of the kid. He's a nice married man, his wife wouldn't understand," Sean said.

"A feminist," Kevin said.

"Maybe," Sean said. "But whose wife would?"

"After a while, like most, he gets tired of the broad, dumps her for a younger model. The new broad works in the area, comes in every day, and Valentino's rubbing the old girlfriend's nose in it, which drives her crazy and she quits. This guy ain't so smart."

"Where'd you meet her?" Wacko said.

"I'm gettin' there. I'm sitting at the bar at the Old Colony House down on Morrissey Boulevard one night, and she's next to me. She's cute, in a chubby kinda way, and we start talking. After a few drinks, a few more drinks, and a couple of lines out in the parking lot, she starts to tell me about her former boss. Bing, the bell goes off, a jeweler? Now I'm a sympathetic listener. No man should treat a woman this way, I tell her. He needs to be taught a lesson, I tell her, and she agrees. A few more lines of coke and she's telling me everything about the guy—how much he makes, what he sells, where, to who, where the hide is, everything. I didn't know Santa Claus had tits."

"So, where you figure the best place to take him, outside the shop?" Wacko said.

Sean grimaced. "Outside the shop is dead, too busy. Like I said, it's a strip mall, but not too far from a MBTA station. There are too many cheap pricks who park in the strip mall lot in the morning to avoid paying the rate at the T lot."

Wacko sat down on a bench directly across from a cement pier that extended thirty feet out from the seawall, from which a handful of old men hung fishing poles over the railing into the harbor. "What you think they catch out there?" Kevin said, sitting down and throwing his arms over the back of the bench.

"Every once and a while stripers, but mostly colds," Sean said. "They're out there year-round."

"So why haven't you taken this guy yourself, banged him out at the Sonesta, you never tried?" Wacko said.

"We tried, Jack. This Armand Capizzo character parks in the garage underneath the hotel, but he's sharp and he packs, he's always packing. Another thing, like every guinea I know, he thinks he's connected, Mafia bullshit, and he's got this real aggressive attitude. I'm not into guns, I'm allergic to bullets, break out in holes when I come in contact with 'em, but we took a shot," Sean said.

"What happened?" Wacko said.

"We're down there a few months ago Thursday morning, me and one of the Sullys, you know them the nuts from Gold Street? We got nine irons to tee off on this jeweler's head with, but we can't get close. Fifty yards out from his car, the guy makes us. Sully pretends, in the middle of the fucking garage, he's on a puttin' green, hittin' an invisible ball, but the guy pulls his piece and points it at his head. Sully drops the club and runs. I just walked away; almost shit myself waiting for a bullet in the back. I told myself, Never again, I'm leavin' it to the pros."

"You gotta be good to use those nine irons," Kevin said. "You land 'em wrong and the shaft bends like a fucking hula hoop. I say if you can get that close, stab 'em, never broke a blade."

Sean waved his hands in front of his chest. "Whoa, I'm not into killing no one," he said.

Wacko glared at his brother. "What's the matter with you? What are you scarin' Sean for? No one's gettin' hurt here, Sean, relax. We'll take this guy down, and Don Corleone and Al Pacino together won't be able to stop it," Wacko said.

"How much were you thinking about gettin' your end?" he asked.

Sean scratched his head. "I'm not greedy, Jack. I'm thinkin' the usual twenty percent's good enough."

"Not greedy and smart, a good combination. Give me a minute alone to discuss this with my business associate here," Wacko said.

"I'll stretch my legs," Sean said, getting up and walking away.

"What you think?" Kevin said.

"I like this kid, and his information has been good in the past. Anyways, we'll watch for ourselves this week won't we, and if our jeweler friend is closed next Wednesday, Thursday we tear his head off," Wacko said.

"How much are we talking here?" Kevin said.

"Sean's talkin' over a million retail, quality stuff."

"We piecemeal it, we'll get more money than if we sold it in one lot," Kevin said.

"Naw, we'll unload it all at once up Hanover Street. Them North End guineas got the dough, especially Alby Canatta. He's fair, should give us a little over a fifth of the retail; that's a good day's pay, why be greedy?" Wacko said.

"What about Marty, Jack? He'll want an end of this. We cut him out of the truckload of cigarettes last month. You said he wouldn't find out, he did," Kevin said.

"He still ain't sure who did that," Wacko said.

"Well, I'm thinkin' he knows, and he's waitin' for us to kick something in, fact."

"Let him wait. I'm through payin' him, Kevin, we're through. Why should Marty Fallon get an end of everything we make sittin' on his ass up the Dudley?"

"Because he always has?"

"Always ain't forever. I'm sick of the small shit we deal in, all of it, the shylocking, the drugs, nickels and dimes, too much exposure, it's a house of cards gonna collapse on us and I don't want to go back to the can. Kevin, you've never been in, got no idea. You don't know the boredom, how all the time you're angry because some screw or maggot inmate fucked with ya. Every night watchin' the evening news, seein' rush-hour traffic, people in their cars standin' bumper to bumper, miserable, and me wishin', with all my heart, I was sittin' be-hind a wheel in it somewhere. We're into everything and it ain't work-ing fast enough. We deal drugs, we deal Marty Fallon's drugs. We got money on the street, we use his bank, his connections." Wacko said.

"We're doin' all right," Kevin said.

"What the fuck's wrong with you? You just want to 'do all right', be under his thumb for the rest of your life? I'd rather be dead," Wacko said.

"So, what we gonna to do? He ain't going to let us operate on our own." Kevin jumped to his feet, thrust his hands into his pockets, took a few steps, then turned around. "Ya know, if you're thinkin' about makin' a move, it better be right, cause we won't get more than one chance."

"I realize that, and if we're going to break from Marty Fallon, we'll need a serious cash flow," Wacko said "After we hit that ar-mored truck, we won't need no one. We need muscle we'll buy it, there's an army out there that'll follow the cash. I don't care what it takes, Kevin, we gotta do this, we gotta break away. Workin' for Marty Fallon's like chewing off your body parts one at a time, even-tually there's nothing left."

Almost imperceptibly, Wacko shook his head as he stared at the sidewalk. "Heads up, Kevin, here comes Brancaccio. Let's finish put-ting this thing together."

Wacko got up and shook Sean's hand while Kevin patted him on the back. "Sean, my man, Kevin and I are onboard," Wacko said.

"How you want to do this?" Sean Brancaccio said.

"You and me are gonna drive out to Abington this week to check out the play, see what his routine is. If I like what I see next week, the third week of the month, we'll hit this bag of shit then," Wacko said.

He checked the time on his wrist. "I'm leavin', got someplace to go. What about you guys?"

"I'm going to stop by the house and see my kid," Sean said. "I hear the ex-old lady's been whacked on blow the past few days, just want to make sure the kid's all right." He drove his fist into his open palm. "Ya know, when we were together all she did was complain how I was getting high all the time. Pot. Big deal, a little coke now and then. I get sick of listening to her, hit the bricks, and bang, she's on the coke twenty-four-seven like something from a monster movie, and who suffers? The kid. I'd like to crack her head."

The three men followed the sidewalk around Fort Independence towards the parking lot. "Sean, I haven't heard anything good about your ex-wife lately, but sure as shit she's heard nothin' good about me," Kevin said. He burst out laughing and took off his ball cap.

"Be cool with that shit, Kevin, there's people around," Wacko said, as Kevin pulled a small plastic bag from inside the hat.

"What, those people?" Kevin said, tilting his head towards a small group on a hill at the base of one of the walls of the fort who were practicing Tai Chi "I start worrying about nuts like them I stop eatin' donuts."

He bit the knot off the bag as he walked and poured a pile of cocaine out on the top of his hand. He sucked half of it up, then coughed. He passed the bag to Sean, who inserted a rolled dollar bill into it and daintily sucked around the inner edges. Kevin licked the back of his hand. "You know, Jack, eatin' coke you might have something here." He inhaled sharply and swallowed. "Wow, nice drip."

Kevin looked around again. "When I was a kid they weren't out here, not in droves like now," he said.

"Who's they?" Wacko said.

"Nuts. Look at them, every-fucking-where you look you got nuts. Nuts joggin', over there, see. Nuts stretchin'. Nuts doing crazy Chinaman dances on the fucking hill . . . in Southie. I see outsiders, people all the time these days I've never seen before, we're being invaded. It was never like that, Jack, Sean, am I right, huh? The newcomers, half 'em are nuts, fucking nutcappas. Here we go, look at this." Kevin pointed and stared at a middle-aged woman approaching from the opposite direction walking a Dalmatian. The woman spotted Kevin glaring at her and, fearful, jerked her dog closer as she made a wide berth around him.

"We seein' the same thing here, am I crazy? Did you see the lips on that broad? They were like this big." He held his hands apart about a foot. "They couldn't have been real. Fucking yuppie must have had them lip injections rich people get. I seen it on TV. They end up with their lips looking like fucking inner tubes," Kevin said.

"Halogen," Sean said.

"What?"

"It's what they shoot their lips with, halogen."

"Don't matter, they're fucking nuts. Nuts that end up at Castle

Island first thing in the morning with crazy fake faces scarin' people. Even her dog looked scared," Kevin said.

Wacko shoved his brother. "I ain't listenin' to this shit, you're the fucking nut; I'm dropping you at Jolly's. I'm going to Elaine's." he said. "And both of you wipe that shit off your face."

Both men wiped their noses and Kevin tucked the nearly empty bag of coke into his cheek.

Wacko looked at him incredulously.

"What?" Kevin said.

Sean stopped at the edge of the parking lot, unrolled his dollar bill, bent his knee, then pulled the bill back and forth across it like he was polishing a shoe. He stopped and plucked something minuscule from the fabric, placed it on the tip of his tongue, and smiled. "You guys always get the best product. When this thing goes down, I want a part of my end in rock," he said.

Wacko pulled out his car keys. "Sean, this thing's what you say it is, rock gets rock."

10

WACKO CURRAN SCRAPED the right front tire of the Marquis as he pulled to the curb in front of 595 East Fifth Street; he softly swore and shut off the engine. He scrutinized the two windows of the first-floor apartment. The shades were up, but the windows were closed. There was no indication that Elaine Ramsey was home.

Elaine was special, one of an extremely small number of people who Wacko would listen to or even defer to at times. Elaine had a boyfriend, David, she said she was in love with, and that was fine, Wacko had no time for relationships, but there was something between them he could not put a finger on.

Elaine Ramsey, and her large extended family, was as much a part of the fabric of South Boston as he was. To Wacko, Southie was like a great oak tree, its many parts extending in complete opposite directions. South Boston families were often like that; immediate family members became politicians or police, gangsters or priests. There wasn't any doubt what Wacko was, and there were days he felt like a leaf on that tree nearing the end of its cycle, the greenness diminishing, turning orange, and Wacko sensed a cold wind coming that eventually would twist him until he fell. His life was insane. There was nothing normal about associating with killers, selling drugs, or sticking a gun in someone's face taking what was theirs. But what was he supposed to do, be a sucker, get a job?

With both hands resting on the wheel, Wacko sat in his car and stared at Elaine's windows. Maybe she wasn't up yet or was already at work. He almost hated to bother her she was so different, so gentle. She with the tumbling red curls, her home like a fortune-teller's teahouse filled with incense angels and flowers. She was as beautiful as a fairy. Something you might find in the old country, if you looked hard enough, staring up from beneath a bough. Something caught by surprise but never angry.

Wacko got out of the car, locked the door, and felt a nudge at his leg. Heidi, the next-door neighbor's black and white Labrador mix, her eyes shining expectantly, stared up at her friend. "Hey, you old mooch, how you doin'?" Wacko said, scratching the dog's head. He bent down and examined the dog's paws. Each of her toenails was painted a different color. "Poor bastard, your owners still messin' with your head?"

Wacko unlocked his car and grabbed a small bag of corn chips off the front seat. He poured them out in a pile on the sidewalk. "Dogs like corn chips? Guess they do," he said, climbing Elaine's front steps.

Once inside, he walked down a small corridor to the left of a stairway leading up and stopped in front of a brown wooden door. He balled his fist and held it for a second in front of the door before he knocked. On the other side soft footsteps approached, and the door swung open. "Why, Jackie Curran, to what do I owe the honor?" Elaine said. The scent of espresso was in the air, and Vivaldi played softly in the background. "Come in," she said, bending and sweeping her right arm low in a mock curtsy.

Wacko stepped through the door and was instantly, sensuously enveloped by her arms. She sighed and nestled her head on his shoulder. Like he was a blanket, she nuzzled deeper and pulled him closer to her neck.

"I was in the neighborhood," he said into her curls, which held the faint scent of lilacs. "Was out the island and thought of you, time to stop by, ya know?"

Elaine released him and rested her palms on his chest as she looked over his shoulder into the hallway. "And where's your shadow?"

"Kevin? I dropped him down Jolly's. The kid's got crazy eatin' habits, loves them donuts."

Elaine wrinkled her nose and poked him playfully in the stomach. "*Both* of you have horrible eating habits. Now go to the kitchen, sit at the table. I'll make you some toast and honey no butter; I think I'm out of butter. And some tea?"

"Sounds great," Wacko said. He walked into the kitchen and sat at a small, red table next to a pair of half-opened windows. A slight, warm breeze rustled the curtains. "I thought about maybe you and me next week for lunch?" Elaine checked the yellow teapot on the stove almost ready to boil.

"You said the same things six weeks ago, Jack, haven't seen you since." Elaine placed a small white plate bordered by blue Chinese dragons in front of him.

Wacko closed his eyes and covered his ears. "Sorry, Elaine, so how's David?" he said, looking out the window at the house directly behind Elaine's. Someone was in the third floor window watching. "Hey, Elaine, behind you the third-floor, you got nosy neighbors?"

Elaine closed the refrigerator door and placed a small pitcher of milk on the table and some toast on the dish followed by two steaming cups of tea. "David's fine and you just relax. That's Mrs. Moore in her wheelchair. Sits there eight hours a day watching the birds, everything really. She doesn't miss a trick."

"She's starin' down here like she knows me," Wacko said, picking up his toast. He took a bite and sipped his tea.

"Jackie, dear," Elaine said from behind into his ear. "There's no one here to harm you. Mrs. Moore doesn't know you, and I don't talk about my friends. Now eat your toast, your tea's getting cold."

Elaine sat down opposite him and stared into his eyes. The sunlight played tag in her hair as she spoke. "Thanks for asking about David. He's back to work after that horrible accident and has got full use of his hand again, thank God." She took a bite of his toast. Her lips were smeared with just a hint of honey and looked like tiny pillows. She distracted him.

"Anything I can do for you, pal, anything I can help you with?" Wacko said, taking another bite of toast.

Elaine shook her head. "God's good, Jack, he could be good to you too if you'd let him."

"I've prayed at times, doesn't work much," Wacko said.

"That's good you've prayed, but there's more. You're a good man, Jack, you could do good things." Elaine looked out the window and waved to Mrs. Moore, who quickly disappeared behind a twist of curtain. Elaine giggled.

"I've got tickets to a play at the Colonial two weeks from tomorrow, interested?" Elaine said. Her eyes were kind and loving.

He was uneasy and felt transparent in front of her. He got up and looked out the window. "I don't like people starin', Lainey. That old broad's a nosey bitch." Wacko gave her the finger. Mrs. Moore disappeared again in a flash of curtains.

Elaine shook her finger disapprovingly at Wacko. "Hey there, she's my neighbor," she said.

"She was my neighbor she wouldn't be for long," Wacko said grimly. He reached into his pocket and pulled out a roll of bills, removed the elastic band, and began peeling twenties. "Hey, I'm sorry, it's not my house. Elaine . . ."

Elaine came around the table and put both her hands around his hand and the bills.

"Jackie, I don't want your money, thank you. What I do want is to see you now and again, and for you to be healthy and safe, especially safe."

"I gotta go," Wacko said.

Elaine followed him to the door and he turned. Wacko traced the back of his finger along the line of her jaw and stopped beneath her chin. He tenderly raised it, and she closed her eyes, her lips slightly parted. Wacko pressed his cheek to hers, lingered for a second, then kissed her there.

"I'll let you know soon about the play," he said, opening the door. Tiny wind chimes sounded from somewhere in the kitchen. "Thanks for the chow, Elaine, you're a friend."

"Ya, I'm a pal," Elaine said, guiding him out the door. "Your hand's not broken, call me sometime."

Wacko frowned. "I don't know, Elaine, you know about me and

phones. The feds are up my ass. I don't want people thinking there's a link between you and me."

"But there is, Jack, we're friends. It's illegal to be your friend?"

"Elaine . . ."

"Jack, I know, just come by again soon, be safe. Don't forget about the Colonial, okay?"

"I'm looking forward to it, lady."

"God bless," Elaine said.

"Even me?"

"Even you, Jack," Elaine said, then blew him a kiss and closed the door.

11

KEVIN CURRAN STEPPED OFF the curb at the corner of Old Colony Avenue and Dorchester Street, opened the door to Wacko's car, got in. "So, how's Elaine?" he said, unraveling the top of a white waxed paper bag. "Got your favorites, chocolate glazed and coconut chocolate."

Wacko reached into the bag and pulled out a donut. He looked at it for a second, then dropped it back in like it had suddenly grown hot in his hand. "Elaine's good but she says donuts will kill you, don't want any," Wacko said, turning right onto Dorchester Street, heading towards Broadway.

Kevin looked at him stunned. "But you like —"

"Used to like, Kevin, things change," Wacko said.

"Well, I hope you still like this," Kevin said, reaching into the bag and pulling out two thick stacks of bills secured by thin rubber bands. "Saw Dizzo before I went into Jolly's. He had our money on him, said he'd been lookin' for us since yesterday."

"Lookin' for us, huh? Dizzo doesn't have my number, but Leppy Mullins does. He sees Leppy all the time, knows Leppy's with us, he should've told him," Wacko said.

"Anyways, Dizzo told me he wants four ounces tomorrow, the

kid's always on time with the payments, Jack, I wish we had a dozen more like him," Kevin said. "After I saw Dizzo, I'm sitting at the counter in Jolly's, Lena, the waitress is waitin' on me, what a set of tits. Anyways, I'm on my third donut and who walks in — that piece of shit Denny Myers. I act like I don't see him, but he sees me. He gets to the counter, then pretends like he left something in his car. He walks out the door, but I'm right behind him. Outside in the parkin' lot, I come up behind and say, Where's our fucking money? He turns, gives me this little song and dance about why he don't have it, the guy's good. He hasn't been duckin' us, he says, he's been out of town trying to hook up some action down in Providence, Rhode Island, he says."

"Sure it ain't Provincetown?" Wacko said.

"Ya, could be he's a strange duck. But I got him on a roll so I ask him how you going to fund this action of yours when you're owin' us money, and he tells me how he's got a little money put aside at his house for emergencies."

"That's our fucking money!" Wacko said, punching the center of the steering column.

"Correct," said Kevin. "So I say let's forget about Providence, Rhode Island, and remember Jackie Curran, who hasn't forgotten you. In fact he's got a hammer with your name on it he's dyin' to introduce you to."

"So, what happened?" Wacko said

"I got it, all of it," Kevin said, reaching back into the bag and tossing a rubber-banded wad of money into the air. He also produced two small ceramic figures with flakes of sugar glaze and coconut falling from them. "When we went to his house for the dough he went into the kitchen, I grabbed these Hummels off the mantel kinda like a fine," Kevin said.

"Court's in session," Wacko said before cutting the wheel to the left and skirting a long row of double-parked cars in front of O'Brien's Funeral Home on Dorchester Street. "Because of their lazy fucking ways, Denny Myers and guys like him are forcing us to hurt them. And what pisses me off is if we did bang him out, break a few bones, he'd run straight to the cops or his wife would."

"Then we'd cave her head in too," Kevin said.

"And that brings heat, which means Marty Fallon will be callin' us in on the carpet to explain what happened, then he'll explain how it's gonna take a grand or two to 'smooth' things with the cops down District Six. It's a lose, lose situation, Kevin, and I don't like losin'. The kid wants coke, it's cash up-front from now on," Wacko said.

"Then we'll lose Denny as a customer, Jack, because he never has the cake up-front," Kevin said.

"Lose him then. Customers like that we'd end up diggin' a hole for, like that fuck from Charlestown last year who got cute thinkin' he didn't have to pay us," Wacko said.

"That was bad news."

"But the good news it put pressure on our regular customers to pay up on time. Everyone's happy."

"Except for Jimbo Culnahane, but he wasn't very happy before we clipped him either," Kevin said, throwing the money back into the bag.

Wacko grabbed his brother's shoulder and slammed him hard enough into the door that Kevin banged his head on the glass. "I told you before, don't ever mention his name."

"Hey, Jack, relax, you're fucking crazy," Kevin said, rubbing the side of his head.

"Relax nothin', kid. I told you forget the names of people we've had problems with and taken care of. You forget them. You don't, one day you get stupid and mention this guy or that guy's name to someone who has it in for us, they go to the cops, now the cops got evidence, maybe enough to hang us. It doesn't take much a guy stands before a grand jury and says, 'Ya, Kevin Curran told me himself, said, Ya we clipped so-and-so.' Maybe you're high. Maybe you're tired and got sloppy, don't matter, you throw out names they'll come back to haunt you. Forget the names, understand, forget them," Wacko said.

"You're right," Kevin said.

"I know I'm right."

"Sorry."

At West Broadway, Wacko turned the wheel of the big Mercury and a few blocks down passed a group of older teenagers hanging on the corner of F Street. Two of them coolly waved. Wacko dead-eyed the crew and gave them the nod as he passed. Kevin slapped his knee. "God, see the look on little Jimmy Kline's face, that wannabe son-of-a-bitch. You, Jackie Curran acknowledgin' him made his fucking day. You'd think the Queen knighted him. They all want to be us, Jack, every fucking one of them."

"And we wanted to be Marty Fallon, go figure," Wacko said. "Hey, speakin' about queens, every queen's got a joker right? Looks like the joker's over there."

Near the corner of E Street and West Broadway, a thin man wearing a green leather jacket, dusty black jeans, and a pair of Converse high-tops stood in front of the Lithuanian Club. He waved them over. Kevin rolled down the window. "Hey, Skinny, what's up, donut, you don't look so good."

Skinny waved the bag off. "Naw, no donuts, Kevin, thanks. Thanks, Jack," Skinny said. He shifted from one foot to the other and nervously looked up and down the street.

"You got a vibrator in your pants, Skinny, what's up?" Wacko said.

"That kid you was lookin' for . . ." Skinny said.

"Which one, Alby Litiff?" Wacko said.

"Naw, haven't seen him for a week, the other one."

"Frankie Popeo?" Wacko said.

Skinny wiped sweat from around his mouth with the back of his hand. Kevin handed him a napkin from the donut bag. "Thanks, Kevin, thanks, Jack, ya Popeo, you got it, Frankie Pop. He's down Mul's; at least he was ten minutes ago," Skinny said.

"By himself?" Kevin said.

"Ya, eatin' eggs," Skinny said.

"You sure it was Frankie Pop and not his brother, Johnny, eatin' eggs?" Wacko said.

"Frankie with the scar on his head looks like he parts his hair wrong, Frankie," Skinny said.

Wacko rubbed his hands together. "Okay, Skinny, that's good, that's real good. "Kevin . . ." Wacko nodded at his brother, who reached down his underwear and pulled out a bundle of small plastic bags. "An eighty," Wacko said. Kevin removed one of the larger bags, an eighty, then pulled out a coconut donut, stuck it in the hole, and passed it to Skinny.

"Thanks for the donut, guys," Skinny said out loud, backing away from the car.

"Watch out, Skinny, those things will kill ya," Kevin said, rolling up the window.

Just after the lights at D Street, Wacko pulled to the curb and stopped in front of Whitey McGrail's old bar on West Broadway. He

not. "There's Dinty Clanahan over there with the wife and little piglets, I hear he just made lieutenant. Hi, Dint," Kevin said, nodding and waving. Dinty waved back. "When that prick waves," Kevin said, smiling, "you better make sure both his hands are empty. Shake your hand with the right and stab you with the left."

"Just like us," Wacko said, accepting the cold beer but refusing the glass.

"Ya, at least we don't hide behind a fucking badge," Kevin said, clinking bottles with his brother.

Mary Rose returned to the table carrying rolls and butter. "So, what are you guys up to or should I ask?" she said.

Wacko leaned back in the chair. "We're out and about, gonna hit the Bayside for Timmy McCarthy's time later tonight," he said.

Mary Rose looked pained. "The poor kid, I bought a ticket too, I'm goin' after work. The drugs got him finally, suicide, can you imagine?"

"Horrible thing," Kevin said, thinking how Timmy McCarthy died owing him $250.

"And what about poor Snoopy Costa, ya hear? They found him today in his apartment," Mary Rose said.

"Another suicide," Wacko said. "The kid had a bad coke problem."

"Oh, I don't think it was suicide," Mary Rose said. "I've been hearin' things."

"Talk's cheap," Wacko said, picking up the menu.

"Ya, you're right, Jack, it is," Mary Rose said, taking the cue. "I'll be back in a minute to take your order."

"Funny about Snoopy, huh? I heard on the street he was one of the guys who knocked over Manny Goldstein," Wacko said. "I half-expected to hear from him. Figured he'd pay up what he owes us and try to score some more blow."

"Jack, did you really think those two coke bombs would be beatin' down our door when they owe us twenty-five hundred? If they banged out Manny Goldstein, then they had enough to pay us for the coke they bought and buy half a ton more, but a junkie don't think like that. He only thinks how much more he can buy if he don't pay what he owes," Kevin said.

"So, I hear instead of doin' the right thing by us, Snoopy sends his brother Mark the mailman directly to Andre with five grand for coke," Wacko said. "I figure Mark's all jekylled up, yappin' away telling his 'friend' Andre how his little brother and Alby made this big move."

"You think Andre got ideas?" Kevin said.

Wacko smirked. "Andre never had an original idea in his life. Snoopy and Alby were losers to the end. To beat us out of a lousy twenty-five hundred, which we would've gotten from them eventually, they went to Marty Fallon's dog for the coke. Now both of 'em are dead and we're out twenty-five hundred. Do you believe it?"

"You think they got Alby too?" Kevin said.

"I guarantee they got Alby."

Mary Rose returned holding her order pad out. "So?" she said. "What's it gonna be?"

"I'll have the prime rib, mashed, and string beans," Wacko said.

"I'll have the same but chicken parm," Kevin said, winking at his brother.

Mary Rose shook her head. "I gotta get out of this business," she said.

"You're in the right business, don't worry," Wacko said. "How're things?"

Mary Rose leaned closer to the table, stared at her pad when she spoke. "Everyone loves your product, Jack, ecstatic, no complaints, and you were right, I moved the extra you gave me, so I got all the money I owe ya. Business is almost too good."

"Bring what you owe us to the Bayside tonight after work, okay? We'll be there until closing. How're you holdin'?" Wacko said.

"I got enough left to last the weekend. If I'm runnin' low I'll give ya's a call, believe me."

■　　■　　■

The Bayside Club, on the corner of East Eighth and Covington Streets, nestled on the side of a hill overlooking Day Boulevard and Carson Beach, was a popular venue for times. The upper portion of the two-story building was a function hall, and downstairs was a rollicky nightclub. Sometime after eleven the Currans pulled up to the front door of the Bayside, on East Eighth Street; the place had been rocking for hours.

Two large men, both in their early twenties with flattened noses, worked the door, ensuring that everyone who entered had bought a ticket to Timmy McCarthy's time. Wacko got out and left Kevin to park the car.

"Hey, Jack, how're you doin'?" one of the doormen said. Wacko smiled and nodded. He reached into his pocket for the ticket. The doorman waved his hands. "No problem, Jack, you're good, come right in." The other bouncer said nothing but turned and ordered a group gathered near the inside door to move out of the way. One young reveler with a buzz on started to give the bouncer lip, then spotted Wacko Curran and discreetly stepped aside.

"How . . . you doin', Jack?" he said.

Wacko grinned. "Fine, boys, how are you tonight, havin' a good time?" he said, moving past them.

Wacko stood at the edge of the crowd and surveyed the dimly lit room. Its only light source seemed to be the mirrored, rotating ball suspended from the center of the dropped ceiling. One by one Wacko picked out the various crews in the room. A raucous clique of Old Colony boys who smirked and laughed and shoved one another, hung in front of the bar on the right; D Streeters, looking dark and dangerous, clustered in a semicircle around the rear of the dance floor. The Point Crew, middle-class college boys most of them, were on the right against the wall. The Point Crew was composed mostly of small drug dealers, but to their lace-curtain Irish peers they were men of respect. Wacko referred to them as "panty gangsters" but figured as long as they bought their coke from him he could tolerate their posturing. A couple of them noticed Wacko and a visible ripple went through the crew. Two of them waved, then broadly grinned when Wacko returned it.

One of the doormen approached Wacko from behind and tapped him on the shoulder. The doorman indicated an area in the back of the room with his head. "Jack, your guys are over there in the corner," he said. In the far left corner of the room, near a window, Marty Fallon and Andre Athanas were exactly where Wacko thought they'd be. A cue ball straight shot from the corner to the door allowed Marty the knowledge of everyone who entered or left the time for Timmy McCarthy. Wacko turned and slipped a folded twenty into the doorman's hand.

"Do me a favor, my friend, when my brother Kevin comes in, send him to that corner table, okay?" Wacko said.

K.C. and the Sunshine Band's "I'm Your Boogie Man" blared

from the eight speakers strategically placed throughout the room. Wacko had to shout into Marty's ear. "Not a bad turnout, huh?"

Marty remained seated, his arm around Wacko's lower back. He motioned to someone, and a waitress miraculously appeared. "A Bud Light for my friend here," Marty said.

"Two, Kevin's on the way," Wacko said.

"Two," Marty said to the waitress. "And this is on — that young guy over there with the black leather trench coat and the white shirt." Marty signaled to the man across the floor who was standing with a beer in his hand with six other men dressed basically the same. All of them discreetly but intently were eyeballing Marty's table. The man Marty indicated held up his bottle in a toast and, obviously pleased by the recognition, smiled.

"I try to give each of the different crews here tonight a chance to pay for our booze," Marty said. "It makes them feel as though they're in the loop; ya know, part of the machine. We drink all night, and they pay as they should." Wacko eyed the group and nodded. Three of them raised their glasses and nodded back.

"All of them, everyone thinks they're the up-and-comers. They really don't realize what it takes, Jack, the patience, the sense of timing," Marty said. He sipped his soda water and lime. "Timin's so important. The willingness to risk it all and then, when the shit hits the fan, to take it like a fucking man. They don't know that, but then most of them won't have to because they don't fucking have what it takes."

Kevin joined them at the table. "Where'd you go, China?" Wacko said.

"Pretty close, it's crowded around out there, had to park all the way down by the Ocean Kai," Kevin said. Wacko handed him a beer.

Kevin took a sip and leaned closer. "I just seen Mark Costa, Snoopy's brother, down the street. He was headin' up here, all fucked up. He's tellin' me that his brother's death wasn't suicide. He blames himself, Jack, for tellin' the guys next to you about the Goldstein score, what really went down. He thinks, he said he knows our friends here whacked his brother and took the money. He's really fucked up over this and talkin' some shit."

"What's he sayin'?" Wacko said, waving to a heavyset woman wiggling on the dance floor. He touched Marty's arm and pointed. "That's Mary Rose O'Connell's mum."

"Looks like Mary Rose got her looks from her father," Marty said.

Kevin continued. "Jack, Mark Costa was high as a kite, coked to the gills, but I understand — his brother, you know? This guy's got a good job at the post office, he's some kind of supervisor, and now he's out there runnin' around gunnin' for these madmen? Brother or no, he crazy?"

"Get to the point. What's he sayin'?" Wacko said.

"He's sayin' Marty killed his brother, straight out, and that this ain't over; Marty's in for a big surprise," Kevin said.

"He say that, a big surprise?" Wacko said.

"His exact words, Jack, this ain't over. I got nervous and stuck him in a cab and sent him home with a package."

Wacko patted his brother's hand. "Smart move, Kev, don't say a word about this to anyone ya hear? I gotta think this over."

"You going to tell Marty?"

"What, you don't understand American? I gotta think about this, I'll handle it, all right?" Wacko said.

He put his arm around Marty's shoulder and pulled him close. "Marty, I think that little blond over there is giving you the eye. Maybe I should flag her over?"

"Naw, not tonight, Jack, I already had some of that this morning." Marty winked. "The one I had was fifteen and sweet, couldn't get enough of me. That one over there's giving you the eye, she's homin' in, let's see what you can do with it."

A pretty young blond wearing a blue leather halter top and skintight black pants with expensive pumps boldly approached the table. Andre stood up, ready to shoo her away, but an unseen signal from Marty stopped him.

"Thanks, Marty, you're a sweetie," she said. "Naughty boy," she said to Andre, shaking her finger at him. The girl put her hand on Wacko's shoulder. "Hi, Jackie, you know my sister Maureen — Maureen Daley? I'm Diva."

"Rhymes with beaver," Marty said. Diva and Wacko ignored him.

"Oh, how is your sister?" Wacko said, not having a fucking clue who Maureen Daley was.

"She's fine; I'll tell her you were askin' for her, handsome," Diva Daley said.

"On the outside she's eighteen," Marty said into Wacko's ear.

Wacko felt his cheeks flush red, and he turned to find Diva impishly staring into his eyes.

"Wanna dance with me, handsome?" Her breath smelled like cherries. She took his hand and led him to the dance floor.

"So, Kevin, what you been hearin'?" Marty said. Both men watched as Wacko awkwardly maneuvered the dance floor while Diva twirled like Tinkerbell around him.

"Not much, Marty, the usual. Been keeping a low profile, getting things done. Jack's all low profile these days," Kevin said.

"Except down in front of Mul's," Marty said.

Kevin looked at him, smiled, and shook his head. "Hey, what can I say, Marty, the guy owes us and he's gotta pay and that's the good news. Good news travels fast, huh?"

Marty laughed and patted Kevin's back. "Of course he's gotta pay. I'm with you guys, Kevin, we're together, he owes you he owes me. In fact I see that son-of-a-bitch I'll tell him he better pay up or I may tell him he owes us nothin' now, nothin' at all, and that will be on him."

"I don't think he'll want to hear that," Kevin said.

"He better know how to pray I say that," Marty said.

▪ ▪ ▪

In a slippery darkness, like he was inside an engine, Wacko stumbled over something that felt like a body. He regained his balance, held his arms out in front, and took baby steps, searching for a wall, a door, anything. Suddenly, from behind, there was a sound like something feverishly skidding across an icy pond, and then it was upon him, pulling him down. He drove his head back, twisted at the hips, and threw an elbow at his attacker. The elbow dug deep into the shoulder of Diva Daley, and she yowled like someone had pitchforked her eye.

"Hey, what the fuck!" Wacko yelled, sitting up and almost falling out of bed. Diva Daley stood naked next to the bed, rubbing her shoulder.

"What's the matter with you, you crazy, you hurt me," she said. She pulled the pillow off the bed and hugged it as she slowly rocked side to side. "I was tryin' to get close, I put my hands on your shoulders, and you hurt me." Her eyes welled up with tears, even angry and half awake she was beautiful; it almost hurt Wacko's eyes to look at her.

"I'm sorry, baby, bad dream. I dreamt it was last night and we were still at the Bayside dancin', havin' a good time, and this tough redhead tried to cut in and dance with me. You wouldn't let her; she insulted you and tried to push me aside to get to you. I elbowed her good in the head."

Diva threw the pillow on the bed and pressed her open hands against her cheeks.

"Ooh, Jack, you poor thing, I'm so sorry," Diva said. She climbed onto the bed and crawled towards him like a lioness. "My hero. You defended my honor, and for that you get a nice reward."

13

INSIDE THE L STREET DINER, Wacko Curran sat opposite his brother in a red vinyl booth. "So, where'd you bang into Mike Janowski?" he said.

"I'll get to that, check this out first," Kevin said, producing a thick white envelope from inside his nylon windbreaker. "I got Leppy Mullins's dough here. I counted forty-eight hundred, sound right? Leppy, that nut, marched right up to me on Broadway, in front of Brigham's, and handed it to me there."

A tired looking, middle-aged waitress approached the table. "Something to drink?" she said. Wacko looked at her.

"Take a hike," he said. The waitress spun around and headed in the opposite direction. "There should be over five grand there, Kevin. Leppy's still not square with what he owes from last month, two hundred and fifty bucks. Lep's a good mover, but you can't let him slide. I try to give these guys some play, but no one's fucking me. Frankie Popeo got himself in a jam not because he owes us, hell, half of Southie owes us either for shylock or dope. We accept that because in the business we're in sometimes we gotta wait for our money; you can't get blood out of a stone. But when you got guys like Frankie Popeo tellin' people who in turn tell me that he ain't payin', I can go fuck myself, what am I supposed to do, take it?"

"He must have been whacked out when he said it," Kevin said.

Wacko leaned close to his brother. "He's lucky he didn't get whacked." The veins bulged in his neck. "You can't get blood out of a stone? I should have used one on his head."

"Come on, Jack, relax, it's over. I guarantee Frankie Pop is collecting what he owes as we speak," Kevin said.

Wacko opened the clear-plastic-covered menu. "I'll tell you what we're gonna to do. We'll give Leppy a break cause he's a good man and a good mover. Tell him for the next two weeks he owes us an extra hundred. Tack that onto his regular coke bill and we're even. He's getting his break, okay? Pay that on time, plus what he normally does for the product, and we'll call it even. It's only a lousy fifty bucks but it's the principle, get it? If I didn't like the little prick I'd hammer him with a hundred-dollar-a-week vig on the two fifty he owes us."

Wacko dropped the menu on the table and rubbed his eyes. "I don't know, maybe I'm just gettin' tired of all the bullshit, Kevin. Tired of chasin' these assholes, they got no morals. I'm thinkin' if I only had enough to get the fuck out, would I?"

"And do what, sell cars?" Kevin said.

Wacko picked up the menu again. "Tuna fish, I'm sick of fucking tuna fish. Tell me about you and Mike Janowski."

Kevin partially closed his menu and leaned closer. "Last night, after the Bayside — that was a good time, huh? Of course you and Diva had a better time, you know I think she's got a better ass than Mary Rose, and I thought, you know, that was impossible, until I saw you and her on the dance floor. Barry White's singin', 'Baby, sweet baby, what am I gonna do?' I'm lookin' at Diva's ass thinking, Don't have to tell me twice."

Wacko put the menu down. "Fuck the Bayside. Fuck Diva." he said.

"You did?" Kevin said, dropping his menu on the table.

"I did," Wacko said.

Kevin grabbed his own hair with both hands. "Oh, Christ, Jack, what she look like without clothes?"

"One more time, Kevin, Janowski, where'd you see him?" Wacko said.

Kevin lowered his chin to his chest. "Okay, okay, I'm trying to get that image out of my mind, Christ, it's hard — Buzzy's."

"What?"

"Ya, after you took off with the hoodsie, me, Skippy Aucoin, Stick, and Stevie Dells went to Buzzy's Roast Beef. Haven't been there in years, nothin's changed. It's two in the morning and we're standin' in line checkin' out the freaks and drunks and saw a fight, two broads, ugly broads, teeing off on each other," Kevin said.

"Get to the point," Wacko said.

The waitress returned to the table. Wacko glared at her. "I said take a hike. I want you I'll use my dog whistle, now blow." She gasped and scurried away.

Kevin looked at him. "You don't have a dog whistle. Used to though, remember when we were kids? Threw it away, couldn't tell if the fucking thing worked."

Wacko slowly closed his eyes, then snapped them open.

"Okay, be cool, I'm gettin' there, Jack. So, we're standin' in line waitin' to order, and I look over to the next line, you know how they got three windows, well now they got five, and there's Janowski," Kevin said.

"How'd he look?"

Kevin pinched his cheek. "He looked good, Jack. No drugs, booze, not high, nothin', well hungry, he was hungry. So, after we both got our food, we're standin' there on the sidewalk at the rotary eatin' and he asks me if there was anything going on, if we could use some help doin' anything, you know. He's a good soldier, Jack, and I'm thinkin' right off about our pal Danny King and his lack of en- thusiasm for real work. I'm thinkin' maybe we could put this Mike in the batter's box case Danny takes a hit from the pitcher. I told Mike to meet us here today around one. Figured it was okay." Kevin stared past Wacko towards the door and raised his eyebrows. "Speakin' of fucking Satan, here's my man now."

Mike Janowski entered the L Street Diner, removed his sun- glasses, and looked around. He noticed Wacko and Kevin right off but still got a take on every face in the room. Before he moved towards them he focused on a middle-aged woman seated at a win- dow table eating a sandwich while reading a newspaper laying flat be- fore her.

"Hi, Mike, how's things?" Kevin said, sliding over. Mike shook both their hands and sat down.

"See someone you know?" Wacko said, tilting his head to the side.

"She's a something, a clerk maybe, at the federal courthouse, Jack," Mike said.

"Oh, ya?" Wacko said, his eyebrows rising. "She do your trial?"

"Naw, must have seen her around is all," Mike said.

Wacko looked at the woman. "You think she may be a clerk, what about a cop, maybe a marshal?"

Mike shook his head. "She's no cop, but you're right to be suspicious, can't be too careful."

Wacko waved his menu in the air. At the end of the counter the waitress pointed to herself, Wacko nodded, she tentatively crossed the room.

"Tuna fish," Wacko said. He looked at Kevin and Mike. "Make it three, white bread, lettuce." The waitress nodded and left. Wacko folded the menu and stuck it next to the napkin dispenser.

"Mikey, let's get to the point, I may have something comin' up. One of — how should I say this — one of the parts of my machine might be breaking down. I'll have to replace it. I do, you interested, can I count on you?"

"You can. What would I be doin'?" Mike said.

"Drivin'," Wacko said.

"And my end of this would be?"

"At least a hundred grand. You got a driver's license?" Mike nodded. "Good, then think about it, get back to me."

"I don't have to think about it, I'm in," Mike said.

"Good," Wacko said. "One more thing, you mention our conversation to no one. Things have a way of gettin' back to me, and if they do concerning this, we have a problem on our hands."

Kevin tapped Mike's wrist. "*You've* got the problem," he said.

"And we take care of our problems," Wacko said. He focused on Mike's face like he was picking just one star out of a winter's night sky. Mike didn't blink; Wacko liked that.

"I understand, Jack, I ain't a fuckup, you know my pedigree."

"I do, and that's why you're here," Wacko said. The waitress brought over the sandwiches and left.

Wacko shifted his attention to his brother. "Now, Kevin, about that Frankie Pop thing, I want you to . . ." Wacko eyeballed Mike. "Mike, could you give us a minute?" Mike nodded like he'd just been hit by a large drop of water on the forehead.

"No problem, Jack," he said, getting up. Wacko clapped his hands, laughed, and pointed at Mike. "Sit down, relax. I almost had him, Kevin. You stay, Mike, you're one of us now," Wacko said, motioning the waitress back over. "Now, what are we gettin' to drink?"

14

THERE WAS NOTHING UNUSUAL about the Mason's Mall in Weymouth. There were eleven stores, half of them barely surviving and none except a Dunkin' Donuts opened before ten. It was midmorning and a gold Ford Explorer was parked to the left of the center of the half-empty lot.

Kevin Curran sat in the front seat behind the wheel and lazily played with a Burger King action figure as he stared through the windshield across the parking lot to Middle Street, where traffic passed by intermittently.

"So, tell me again what we doing here?" Kevin said.

Wacko sighed. "For chrissakes, what's the matter, I told you, listen up. We're here because we met two girls at the Roxy last night, okay, two local girls."

"And we don't know their names, right?" Kevin said.

"Look, we have to let me do the talkin'," Wacko said. "Cops don't like two people talkin' at once. Come to think of it, I don't either, and when you're high it's like three people." Wacko gave his brother a little shove. "Listen, it's easy. We met them last night and agreed to meet them for coffee this morning at ten thirty in front of the Dunkin' Donuts over there. See, it don't matter what the excuse is as long as we got one for being here and we're on the same page with that excuse, get it? No cop is going to ask who the girls are or what they look like. Cops are men, most of 'em, and men understand that other men will go way the fuck out of the way when it comes to scorin' pussy, especially nightclub, dance floor pussy."

Kevin rubbed his hands together. "Hate to say it, bro, but you had to dance well to score pussy, you'd be jackin' off in a phone booth somewhere."

Wacko glared at him.

"You may be right about this alibi stuff, Jack, but it still seems crazy. Hell, this is a free country, right? Why should the cops bug us, the car's legal, nice of Leppy to loan us his, we're not doin' nothin'," Kevin said.

"What are you, a moron? We're not locals, we're Southie guys, sittin' here in the Masons Mall in Weymouth, Massachusetts, at ten in the morning. Minutes from now a Massca Armored truck will pull up to make a delivery at the World Bank and Trust over there. Cops are nosy by nature, and to some we may look suspicious. Now if they pull alongside and start askin' questions, what we going say? We're sittin' here watchin' that armored truck or we're waitin' for some nightclub snatch from last night? What's the right answer here?" Wacko said.

"Okay, I understand already, Jesus," Kevin said. He looked out the side window then out the back.

"Relax, there's no heat around here," Wacko said. "I've been here a few times already and only seen one cruiser, once, make a pass through the lot. These local cops are on coffee break until noon."

"Not looking for cops, lookin' for chicks," Kevin said. "Imagine we were actually meetin' some from last night? Instead of sittin' here workin'? Wow!" Kevin looked around again.

"Things go right, we tip this truck, you'll have enough pussy to turn you queer," Wacko said. "I can't believe how much this thing holds. Every week's the same, it takes two guys almost twenty minutes to load it from the bank, it's incredible."

"Too bad we can't hit them here," Kevin said.

"Can't, too much traffic, it's wide open and we need time. If we hit them here we grab twenty bags, gotta be two million, but it's too risky. Can't spend a dime in Ten Block," Wacko said. "I have a better place to nail it. Less money, but the switch is classic."

"You going to have the other guy look at this, give us his take on it?" Kevin said.

"No, you deaf, I told you, no more bringin' Marty Fallon in on anything. He's already taught us everything he knows, but the students have passed the teacher. Marty's never made a score this big. His score days are over, been over for years. He's strictly a gangster, good luck to him, but us, we're workin' men. Someday we'll be like him, we'll be out of this racket, but that takes money; this could be the one," Wacko said.

"Not invited, no piece of the action, Marty's going to be pissed," Kevin said.

"You're right, he will be pissed, but at who? I ain't tellin' him, are you? He'd hate to see us pull this down. No one likes to see anyone else do good. You're down and out, everybody loves ya. Do well, they hate ya, can't wait to rat you out or take what's yours. We hit this, there will be lots of jealous people, Kevin; we'll have to be on our toes for months."

"I can handle it," Kevin said. He dug into his pocket and popped a large vitamin capsule into his mouth. Wacko looked at him suspiciously. Kevin poked Wacko in the ribs. "Don't get the wrong idea, Jack, it ain't vitamins. It's coke. I buy these huge vitamin C capsules, dump out the poison, fill 'em with real vitamin C. Can't be sittin' here doing lines, can I?" Kevin said.

Wacko shut his eyes. "You should shrink wrap your head. You can't operate without that shit," Wacko said. "You're sick."

"I don't need no shrink; I like to get high, what's the big deal?"

"I'm not talkin' no shrink, I'm saying wrap your banana-head in plastic, kill yourself, you're doin' it anyways. I'm sick of you always — Hey, hey, heads up, here they come," Wacko said, motioning with his head.

Both men locked their eyes on a Massca Armored truck as it lazily turned right off of Middle Street into the mall parking lot. The World Bank and Trust Company sat squarely in the center. Wacko pulled the brim of his baseball cap down and took a half-filled, cold cup of coffee out of a holder on the dashboard. He held it to his lips but didn't drink.

Eighty yards away from the Explorer, the truck circled the bank once, then put on its emergency flashers and slowly backed up to a door at the rear of the building and stopped. A guard, in a gray uniform, his right hand on his gun, got out of the passenger side, scanned the parking lot, then walked over and knocked twice on the back door of the building. The door opened, and a man wearing a dark suit, white shirt, and tie came out.

The guard signaled the side mirror of the truck, and inside the driver pushed a button near the sun visor that released the rear door lock. The guard at the rear responded to the pop, click of the lock and pulled open the door. Suddenly a third man appeared, dressed the same as the first, from inside the bank carrying a canvas bag in each hand, which he handed to the guard.

The money brigade continued back and forth for twenty minutes, the men carrying bags out of the bank, the guard stacking them in rows inside the truck. Finally, the job complete, the guard locked the back door of the truck and climbed in next to the driver. The emergency flashers blinked off, and the truck pulled away from the bank.

Thirty seconds after the Massca truck left the parking lot heading east on Middle Street, the gold Ford Explorer followed it and paced the truck five hundred feet behind. "Not too close," Wacko said. "I don't want them to make us."

"Not like them other guys, eh, Jack?" Kevin said, checking the rearview mirror. "Tommy Sullivan told me the story too about when the cops pulled him over for tailin' that truck in Somerville. Cop came up and asked him direct, Why you tailing that armored truck? But he played Mickey the Dunce."

"He's a natural," Wacko said. "What he say?"

"He said, 'What truck?'" Kevin said.

"The cop says, 'What truck? The one you were so close we thought they were towing you.'"

"They didn't go for it cause Tommy looks about as innocent as Charles Manson," Wacko said.

"Who?" Kevin said.

"Someone who looks like Tommy," Wacko said. "I remember they pinched him after they ran him through NCIC, found he had a ticket out on him out of the BMC for bad checks. It was one big headache and all because he followed too close. Hey, he's takin' a right at the lights onto Washington Street. That's it, nice and slow. His next stop's a bank about a mile down the road."

After passing a seafood joint on the right, the Massca truck's turn signal on the same side flared and it pulled into the parking lot of the Union Bank. The front door of the bunkerlike bank was sixty feet from the road, the drive-through window located on the right side. The truck stopped in front of the building and was sitting there idling when Wacko and Kevin entered the lot. They kept to the right and drove around back.

"I'll show you the rear door, we'll park on the other side," Wacko said. "We'll watch the play from there. We don't need a teller in the drive-through window, some biddy, eyeballin' us as we eyeball the truck."

On the other side Kevin pulled the Explorer into a space parallel to but facing away from the front door and parked. He adjusted the rearview mirror. "Don't turn around, use the mirror. These guards are creatures of habit; follow the same routine every week." Wacko pulled down the sun visor and slid a small door in it to the right exposing a mirror.

"How many times you seen the play?" Kevin said.

"Seen it four times myself. Dangerous both of us being here. A guy sittin' in a car alone isn't suspicious, but two guys might raise the hair on their backs. I like to plan these things alone, Kev. I don't throw off the crazy aura you do; you're whacked out half the time and people sense it, fact. Here we go," Wacko said, nodding at the mirror.

The passenger door of the truck swung open and the guard got out. As he checked the parking lot, he spoke to the driver, then laughed about something, turned, and waved his finger at him before closing the door.

Curbside he stuck a key attached to a long chain from his waist into the side door of the truck and pulled the door open. He climbed into the truck, then, seconds later, reemerged and lowered an aluminum dolly to the pavement. He jumped out and casually looked around once more but gave no indication he noticed the gold Ford Explorer before he turned and began loading canvas bags from the truck, piling them neatly in a stack onto the dolly.

At nine bags the guard stopped loading, said something to someone inside, then closed the door. Kevin leaned closer to the mirror and adjusted it slightly towards the windshield. "Who's he talkin' to? You think there might be another guard in back? Sometimes, ya know, there's three," Kevin said.

Wacko leaned back into the seat, his eyes glued to the mirror. "Naw, two, I've never seen three in this truck, not that they might not slip one in. This guy's just talkin' to the driver; like people everywhere, they're bored, and that's the way we like it." He sat up. "Here we go, he's rollin' again, watch," Wacko said. He smiled. "That's a good boy, both hands on the dolly, pull it to the door of the bank.

Now once he gets past the outside doors, he's got one more set to go through before he's into the bank.

"The layout's like this inside, to the right are the tellers' cages, the bank officers' cubicles are on the left. It's a straight shot from one end of the building. He's gotta walk the entire length to reach the door he wants at the end of the tellers' cages. That door's about six feet away from the back door of the bank that we'll be coming through; the guy who designed this place ought to get some kind of plaque for being a moron. We'll time it right, get the drop on him, he's dead meat," Wacko said.

Wacko closed the mirror and raised the visor. "We're finished here today. We don't have to watch him come out. Let's go home."

Kevin fired up the engine, backed up, and pulled onto Washington Street heading north towards Quincy.

"So, what's Danny's job?" Kevin said. "Peek man?"

"Ya, he's the peek man. I don't want to be in the parking lot, even around back, when that truck arrives in case it circles the place before it stops at the front door. We'll let the truck pull in first, then we'll pull in after it and wait around back. Danny King, Mike Janowski, whoever, will be sittin' across the street in that furniture store parking lot. He'll be parked way over to the left, at an angle to the front door of the bank. That way he'll have a clear view of the guard when he gets out. Naturally, Danny will have a police scanner, a walkie-talkie. He hears or sees anything crazy, he gives us a heads up, we pass. If everything's cool, that guy gets out of the truck, and as soon as Danny sees him drag that dolly through the first set of doors, he'll give us the signal and leave the lot. Exactly twelve seconds from the time we get that signal, we march through the back doors. That guard should be close enough by that time, to get the drop on him and take him down," Wacko said.

"Okay, we got the guard, then what?"

"We take his gun, throw a tie wrap around his ankles quick. You take the dolly. I'll hold the door for you and cover the floor. Outside we got the van with a sliding door, which we'll leave open; we throw the dolly and money in together. You jump in back and I drive.

"They'll be hittin' the alarm as soon as we go through the door, fact, the cops will be comin' quick." Kevin said.

"Fuck 'em, you'll be back there with the Spaz. They come on us, break the back window and open up with that cannon, a few rounds of double-o buckshot and magnum deer slugs will stop 'em. We're caught, it's life for me. I ain't going back to the can, Kevin, rather die in the street and take them with me. There are a lot of cops in hell," Wacko said.

"Play the tune, brother, I'm dancin'. How're we gettin' out of there?" Kevin said.

"Let's get a coffee first," Wacko said.

At the bottom of the steep hill leading into Weymouth Landing, Wacko pulled to the curb in front of a Catholic church. "Stay here," he said. He got out of the car, crossed the street, and entered a coffee shop on the corner, then came out with a cup in either hand and got back into the car. He handed one to Kevin.

"I don't know, this shit gets me wired," Kevin said, staring at the cup.

Wacko ignored him. "You notice, Kev, how the parking lot of the bank is bordered on both sides by that brown wooden fence?"

"Ya, what's your point?"

"My point's this. In back there's no fence, it's bordered by hedges."

"So?"

"So, behind those hedges is a house. Either side of that house a straight shot to the street," Wacko said.

"We drive through the bushes?" Kevin said, resting his cup on the dash.

"Why not? The cops will never suspect it. We tunnel the bushes, then drive another half mile to a strip mall where Danny King will be waitin'. He'll be parked on the side in back of a Dumpster. Can't be seen from the street. We make the switch there.

"From the bank to the first switch we're talking two minutes tops. We leave that lot, drive one point six miles further, there's a Kmart on the left. We make the second switch there," Wacko said.

"They got security cameras in the Kmart lot, we'll be on film," Kevin said.

"They also got a blind spot in an area at the back edge of the lot where they allow tractor trailer trucks to park overnight. There's usually two or three trailers just sitting there, no trucks attached, no nosy drivers. We switch behind them and we're home free," Wacko said.

"Sounds like a plan," Kevin said.

"Gotta have one, there are no dry runs on these things. The cops will block off both ends of Washington Street, but we'll be on Route 3 before they realize they've been had," Wacko said.

Kevin started the car and headed towards Quincy Avenue.

"One more thing, like always we get there early and check the area, have to make sure it's clean before we step," Wacko said. "We can't forget what happened to Billy McGee and his brothers up in Lexington."

"The cops were layin' for them," Kevin said.

"And why? Because one of his crew shot his mouth off in a bar. The next thing you know, the cops are on to them and sittin' there waitin' come score day. I hear there was fifty of them, and when Billy, Jimmy, and the other guy got out of the car, all hell broke loose. Those fifty cops fired over eight hundred rounds, got them all. When cops yell 'freeze' it's only in the movies, for real they shoot first cause they're scared to death. Killed Jimmy outright, still had his gun in his pocket, wounded Billy bad. The other guy —"

"Weasel Williams?"

"Ya, Weasel jumped back into the car and took off. The cops put at least thirty slugs into that thing, bullets flying everywhere, but not a scratch on Weasel. He bailed out of the car, but they caught him later taking a cab over in Waltham," Wacko said.

"They got them, all right, they're still in," Kevin said.

"But they ain't gettin' us, fact," Wacko said, crushing his cup. He threw it at Kevin.

"Fact," Kevin said.

"We'll do our homework and then do it again. Weymouth's a good score, but there are other scores. The North End deal I told you about ain't bad either, more money but more exposure. I've watched the play on that thing twice, a month and a half apart, it stayed the same. We'll check it again. That one we tell no one about. Far as Danny King goes, Weymouth's the score. We'll see if he's with us, find out just how much of a work ethic this guy's really got."

15

IT WAS LATE AFTERNOON, and two men sat in a new black Ford LTD in front of Linda Mae's restaurant off Morrissey Boulevard. The larger of the two rolled the window down and poured the remainder of his coffee on the ground. He tossed the empty container over his shoulder into the backseat. "So, how you know?" the fat man said. His beefy right hand went to the knot in his tie and twisted it slightly side to side before he opened the top button.

"My information been good in the past?" the other man said. He was about the same age and height as the fat man but thinner and more muscular. "Mind if I smoke?"

"Ya, I do, I thought you quit," the fat man said. "Your information's been good in the past, but being good has been good for you."

"Hey, you gotta give to get. Are you interested? I don't like wastin' time, yours or mine," the other man said.

"Relax already, I'm interested. Go on," the fat man said.

"What I'm sayin' is on. Two cokeheads, Leppy Mullins and his cousin Mickey Flatly, killed those other two cokeheads, Snoopy Costa and Alby Litiff, fact," the other man said.

"For thirty-eight grand?" the fat man said. He pulled at the bottom of his red tie. "Can someone tell me why field agents have to wear these fucking things? I mean, who wears ties these days? Come home at night, take this noose off, and my neck looks like I've been the guest of honor at a lynching."

"Maybe you dropped a few pounds," the other man said. "I've got a friend owns a health club down the waterfront. You want you're in, free, you use it."

The fat man jerked the end of his tie, then threw it over his left shoulder. "But kill them?" he said. "These guys, this Lep fella, no record of violence, a couple of drunk beefs, a credit card thing, and a slew of Chapter Ninety violations, but being a lousy driver doesn't make you a killer."

"People kill for fifty cents," the other man said. "My source tells me that Leppy Mullins and his cousin Flatly were on a coke bender for two days, all jekylled up. Leppy moves the shit and also uses his own product. I hear Lep and Quirk found out about Snoopy and rode in on him and his stash, made short work of him. They must have gotten the information from Alby Litiff, another cokehead and Snoopy's partner on the Goldstein score, cause he's among the missing. Word is that Leppy owed big bucks to his cocaine connection, a couple of guys who, I can't really say for certain at this point, but they're real bad dudes."

"And you don't know those people you're not sure of?" the fat man said.

"Let's just say I've got an idea who they are but I'd like to be sure of my information one hundred percent. Don't like to bum beef people, that's not my style," the other man said.

"So, when you get your facts straight, we'll talk some more?" the fat man said.

The other man nodded as he wrote on a small pad of paper. He tore off the top piece and handed it to the fat man. "The two guys' names. I don't know Leppy's real name, but I'm sure your guys can find out."

"The bureau doesn't have jurisdiction on this. I'll forward what you're giving me to Boston homicide. If it pans out, I owe ya," the fat man said. With his right index finger he flicked at a heavy gold chain around the other man's neck. "This new?"

"Ya, I almost forgot, funny story," the other man said. He put a cigarette in his mouth but didn't light it. "Went to a bachelor party down the D two weekends ago."

"You, hanging in the housing projects?" the fat man said.

"Ya, well my girl's brother's gettin' married. Had the bachelor party in the North End, Terra Mia, great place, incredible manicotti," the other man said.

"Been there, good," the fat man said.

"Then we all went to the Foxy Lady down in Brockton. Nice, tight little operation they got there. After closin' we head to the best man's place on Orton Marotta Way in the projects," the other man said. Now we're in the apartment, the music's blastin', there're girls, little fucking knockouts from some other party, the place is rockin', and I'm tryin' to relax, which, for me, ain't easy."

"How were you, buzzed?" the fat man said.

"Naw, you know me, I don't. Two glasses of Pinot Grigio the entire night. So, I'm sittin' there on the couch, it's after four for chrissakes, and then it happens, whoomp, the building shakes. I say to myself, what the — and look around. The music's blasting, Barry Manilow's singing "Copacabana," and there's this seminude conga line making its way through the living room. No one else seemed to notice, so I'm thinkin' maybe some fresh prick put something in my wine and I'm getting steamed," the other man said. He took the cigarette out of his mouth and put it back into the pack. then pushed the cigarette lighter in.

"Then I hear it again, whoomp, and the floor vibrates, but this time they're playing something softer and some of the other guys hear it too. I run outside, and next to the buildin' there's this kid, Mark Boocasian, bending over this Mosler safe that's partially embedded in the fucking asphalt. I say, What's up? And he looks at me. Now in Southie this kid's a legend, known for his strength. Up the Munie he literally tears the heavy bags out of the ceiling, done it twenty times. They hate to see him comin', but no one says much," the other man said.

"Big guy?" the fat man said.

"Not real big, six two, two hundred and ten, two fifteen, but animal strong. He bends over and picks up this fucking safe must have weighed three hundred pounds and awkward, man," the other man said.

"What's he doing?" the fat man said.

"He walks by me with this thing in a bear hug. Says excuse me as he passes and heads into the building and climbs three flights to the roof. 'Heads up,' he yells and throws the thing over the edge. Whoomp-boom, it hits, and I hear him runnin' down the stairs. He passes me again, by now the party's moved outside, there's probably fifty people watching this, and he says, 'Is it cracked yet?' I walk over, and surer than shit it is in the corner. 'Good', he says, and picks it up again and runs inside. A few seconds later 'Heads up,' and the thing's on its way down."

"What's everyone else doing?" the fat man said.

"You gotta remember we're in the project, it's a cuckoo's nest. Someone's put the stereo speakers in the window, and now the music's blastin' outside. Two couples are slow-dancin' about three feet apart under a streetlight to that movie *The Bodyguard* song, Whitney

Houston. This other kid's out there between them doing lines of coke off his hand. There's this other asshole just past them doing that mime crap, putting his face in a box with his hands raisin' his eyebrows until some other kid with no shoes on walks up and slaps him good. The rest of the crowd is into Boocasian's show, all laughin', screamin', eggin' him on. It's like I'm watchin' *The Outer Limits*, ya know?" the other man said.

"Anyways, Boocasian throws the safe off the roof one last time, and it cracks like Humpty Dumpty. The crowd goes wild. He runs downstairs, puts his hand inside, and pulls up a fistful of velvet pouches with gold chains danglin' from them. He passes three or four of the chains out, gives me a couple, and scoops the rest. Told me later how he had hid in the Jewelers Building downtown on Washington Street earlier that night. I guess they were renovating this office in there somewhere and it was empty. Said he went through the Sheetrock wall into the shop next door and whipped the safe, threw the fucking thing out the window into the alley."

"Incredible," the fat man said.

"That reminds me, I got a souvenir for you," the other man said, reaching into the pocket of his green Polo jacket. He handed the fat man a thick gold chain. "They call it flat gold, see, but it's eighteen carat and pretty thick for flat. Like it?"

The fat man smiled and said nothing. He put the gold chain in his pocket.

"So, what's this kid's name?" he said, taking out a pad and pen.

"Mark, Mark Boocasian," the other man said.

"Locals will want to talk with him. Anything else?" the fat man said.

"On that other thing, what happened to poor Snoopy Costa, like I said I got no videotape but I stand by my source. These mutts make us all look bad." The other man opened the door and got out. "If anything more comes up, I'll let you know."

"You do that," the fat man said. "And thanks for the souvenir."

16

WHEN WACKO CURRAN pulled the late-model, gold Toyota Camry up in front of the Bayshore Apartments on Quincy Shore Drive, Kevin Curran was waiting on the sidewalk. "How was the show at the Colonial last night with Elaine?" Kevin said, getting into the passenger side of the car. Wacko pulled away from the curb and immediately moved across the road into the left lane to make a U-turn at the lights.

"Whose wheels?"

Wacko said, "It's Philadelphia Phil's, he lends it to me whenever I tell him to, and ya the Colonial was crowded last night. Saw the play *Chorus Line,* it was really somethin', Kevin, helluva show, and beautiful girls? It was all tits and ass-kickin', struttin', sweating."

Kevin laughed.

"I was in a play once," Kevin said. Wacko looked at him suspiciously. "Ya, at the Condon School I played this farmer who saw the moon in a puddle and had to save it, ya know, the reflection, and I'm, ya know, the farmer is out there with a pitchfork, a hammer, and finally a crowbar trying to free the moon before it drowns. It was weird. But I was real serious about it, and Ma loved it. I had a wig on made of steel wool or some kind of shit; my neck broke out in a brutal fucking rash after the moon drowned. I tell you, to this day whenever I see the moon I itch."

"Still thinkin' about savin' the moon?" Wacko said, banging the U-turn and heading back towards the Neponset Bridge.

"Ya, but I'm smarter now. I'd use a tow truck," Kevin said.

They crossed the bridge, passed under the expressway, and headed west on Gallivan Boulevard. "Elaine, she like the play too?" Kevin said.

"Loved it. She was beautiful, Kevin, knew all these people. She just kind of floats around the place and smiles, they come to her. Remember when we were kids we'd rub a balloon against our pants and it got this energy that made everything stick to it. She's got that kind of energy. She smiles at me, something inside me shifts. Makes me uncomfortable, but I love bein' around her," Wacko said.

"Then do something about it," Kevin said.

"No time for that shit, Kevin, we got things to do," Wacko said. They took the ramp off Granite Avenue onto the expressway heading south.

"What time Sean Brancaccio say this clown shows up?" Kevin said.

"About ten o'clock," Wacko said. "You got our story straight in case we get pulled over? What are you going to say to the cops, huh?"

"I'll say we met two floozies at the Roxy last night and when we get to Abington we'll pick out some spot where we're supposed to meet them, right?" Kevin said.

"You're learning," Wacko said.

At the Braintree split, Wacko followed Route 3 east towards the Cape. The traffic was light; at nine in the morning everyone else was heading north to their jobs in the city. Wacko turned on the radio and punched in a classic rock station. Eric Clapton sang "Layla."

"What else you hear from Snoopy Costa's brother? Mark still talkin' the same shit?" Wacko said.

"Haven't heard but wouldn't doubt it. That happened to my brother, the thought of whackin' Marty Fallon would be first up my hit parade every mornin' I woke. Mark's a nutcappa, Jack, six short of a full deck, fact. I don't care he's a citizen, he's dangerous," Kevin said.

Wacko nodded; his mouth was a grim line. "Some people think because he's a workin' stiff, the post office gig, he's some kinda pushover, big mistake. He's one of those guys could have gone either way. For the most part Snoopy Costa was an easy going slob, could be nasty but it took a lot; Mark's an ex-marine, a hard rock for real; could have been badder than his brother if he chose that life. People should be happy he's sortin' letters," Wacko said.

"Remember seven, eight years ago when that half a fag T.C. was dating Eileen Costa and how he beat her to a pulp one night and she came cryin' to Snoopy? Well, everyone knows Snoopy was capable but cozy capable, he wasn't into doing anything without puttin' a lot of thought into it, but Mark was a different story. He was what, maybe seventeen. Mark clocks T.C. for about a week, gets his routine down good, sees how he spends time down the E and Fifth Variety puttin' the moves on that cute little broad, Zoe, the owner's daughter who works the counter there. One night Mark grabs a piece, puts on a Bill Clinton mask, comes up on T.C. as that piece of shit's walkin' out the E and Fifth Variety downin' a Coke. He puts one right through T.C.'s neck. T.C. almost bled to death on the spot," Kevin said.

"I see Mark two weeks later and, ya know, we're talkin' and he tells me how the night he straightened out T.C. he's wearin' a hooded sweatshirt. How he sees the guy come out the store and he's on him. As he gets close he pulls the hood tighter and the mask shifts, he can't see for shit. He's got his gun out, there's no turning back, so he tilts his head back, he's lookin' out of Clinton's nose as he lets T.C. have it in the head; only the head turns out to be the neck. Close but no potato," Kevin said.

"T.C.'s lucky, he had it comin'," Wacko said. "Me, I had a problem with Mark Costa, I'd definitely take care of it."

"I'm kind of amazed Marty hasn't," Kevin said.

"That's if Marty knows about Mark and if he had something to do with Snoopy's death in the first place, remember that," Wacko said.

Kevin rolled his eyes. "C'mon, Jack," he said.

Wacko's face contorted. "What? You know for sure? Don't go pointin' fingers; you might get 'em hacked off."

"Then how would I pick my nose?" Kevin said.

"With your coke straw, you fucking bug," Wacko said, taking the Route 18 Abington exit. Wacko accelerated hard into the back curve of the ramp.

"Maybe we should try one of these Camrys out in a score someday, four doors, handles great, got balls," Wacko said, tugging the wheel.

Kevin made a face. "Pass, not heavy enough, Jack, we gotta ram, the cops, anyone, we need somethin' in the ass to back us up. Me, I like steel around me in a score, lots of good American steel. We're Americans, Jack, steal American."

The two men followed Route 18 through Weymouth into Abington. A half mile past Abington High School, they turned right at the lights at the top of the hill and followed the road another fifth of a mile before turning right again into a strip mall. They stopped just inside the parking lot and looked around.

BNT Diamond Importers was located to the right at the end of the small block of stores, next to Empire Vacuum Repair and Sales. "Ain't a lot of cars in this parkin' lot. Hope this guy don't make us," Kevin said, snapping his gum. He pointed to a girl in what appeared to be a waitress uniform getting out of a small foreign job a few hundred yards away to the left. She entered the Honeydew Donut Shop. "Check out the donut babe. Going to work in her cute little pink apron. Who said donuts were bad for you?"

"She's cute like a million like her. Forget her and worry about the jeweler. According to Sean this guy's punctual, always here between ten and ten fifteen. I like punctual," Wacko said.

"Ya? Punctual makes me hungry. I'm gettin' donuts, what you want?" Kevin said, getting out of the car.

"Chocolate glazed, and don't waste time waltzin' with that donut chick, if you ate her your cholesterol would skyrocket," Wacko said.

Kevin thumped the roof and laughed. "Calories in pussy, never heard," he said. "Jack, you're a serious fucking degenerate . . . but that's why I love ya." He slammed the door and extended his arms around an invisible partner, then waltzed across the parking lot towards the donut shop.

Ten minutes later Wacko had just taken bite number two from his chocolate glazed donut when Armand Capizzo pulled up in his pearl white Lincoln Town Car. The morning sun reflected off every polished surface; even the tires had an extraordinary sheen to them. Before he got out, the men watched as Capizzo combed his hair in the mirror, tilted his head, then made a few more passes with the comb before popping the trunk from the inside. He got out, walked around back, and retrieved a leather attaché case and a suit on a hanger covered in clear plastic. He closed the trunk, checked his watch, and briskly walked to the door of BNT Diamond Importers, where he keyed in numbers on a small alarm pad to the left of the door. "Look at him, this is beautiful, not a care in the world," Wacko said.

Suddenly, three doors down, the donut shop door flew open. Capizzo looked to the left. The donut babe ran towards him, her breasts bouncing magnificently in the cool morning air; she held a tray in both hands. All smiles, she handed him the tray with coffee and donuts on it, then touched his arm. "What have we here?" Kevin said, leaning forward. He shoved the remainder of his donut into his mouth. "That mutt fucking with my fiancée?" He looked at his brother and stopped chewing.

Wacko's face involuntarily twitched. He pulled on the steering wheel until his knuckles turned white. "Look . . . look at this guinea prick standin' there with his little hoodsie and his fucking pinkie ring. You gonna fuck with me, huh, you fucking king of the strip mall? I'll hit you now, walk up and stick my fucking Glock through your eye. Give me my diamonds, you son-of-a-bitch, you son-of-a-bitch." Wacko punched the dashboard twice.

Kevin knew better than to try to restrain him. It was a part of his brother he never understood but also never questioned. For Kevin scores were only part of doing business, but for Wacko it was different. At times he'd develop a seething hatred for his targets. It was the only time Kevin thought his brother might actually lose control. Wacko never told his brother that part of it was ritual, something he used to pump himself up, though there were times when he actually believed his twisted feelings. Come "game day," as he called it, he was ready, really ready, and his victims never were. After Capizzo and the girl went into the store, Wacko started the car.

"This guy is ours," he said, calming down. He pulled a tissue from his pocket and wiped his eyes.

"Just a punk, Jack, a rich punk," Kevin said.

"Ya, he's cute, confident, a ladies' man, Kevin. Watch, next week we'll put his confidence through a wood chipper."

17

MARY ROSE O'CONNELL SAT on the barstool nearest the front door of the Playwright Pub on East Broadway. She pushed her half-empty glass away and her ass off the stool. "Gotta powder my nose," she said into the ear of Megan Sullivan, who mirrored her actions and dutifully followed behind.

"Tryin' to lose me?" Megan said.

"I could no more lose you than a dog its fucking tail," Mary Rose said.

Two men at the other end of the bar followed their approach with interest. One of them grabbed Mary Rose, gently but firmly, by the arm as she passed. "Mary Rose, how are things, glad to see ya," the man said. He raised his eyebrows twice at her, then smiled at his friend.

Mary Rose ripped her arm away. "I seen you, Kiernan, that's why we're down the other end. You owe me one hundred and sixty bucks, you promised," she said, trying to remain calm.

"Honey, you'll get it tomorrow. My brother owes me four hundred dollars, he's an ironworker, Local Seven, makes good dough, doesn't spend it. He gets paid today; I didn't have a chance to stop by and pick it up is all. Throw me another eighty, that'll make it an even two forty, hey, I'll throw in an extra ten for your trouble, okay, two fifty even, come on," Kiernan said.

"I can't," Mary Rose said. "Too many people owe me already. Hell, I started this business no cuff, next thing you know my regulars are beggin' me, now I'm chasin' them, ain't right." She wiped her nose with her sleeve. "I'm hittin' the ladies' room, nature calls. I'll talk to you later."

Mary Rose entered the bathroom stall and sat down on the toilet. She closed the rust-and-graffiti-stained door, then tried, without success, to make the busted latch work. She got up, her back against the door, and ignored the insistent knocking of Megan as she counted the small bags in the ziplock she took from her purse. She had begun the night with thirty, now only eleven remained.

She recounted her cash but could account for only eight of the bags. She remembered putting two on the cuff for little Jeanne Cotter. Jeanne used to pay on time; now it was installments, and the payments fewer and longer in between. Well, that would be the end, she had had enough of little Jeanne and all the rest, they were out of the fucking car. Cash or nothing from now on and then she'd catch up. She and Megan had done at least four of the bags that night, or was it six? Megan, a recent best friend, was fast becoming a pain in the ass.

The knocking continued. "Mary Rose, it's me, Megan, open up," she said. Mary Rose slammed the busted latch down for emphasis. What was happening to her? She had missed her last payment, for the first time, to Kevin Curran. She was glad she dealt with Kevin; Jack was nice but too unpredictable. She'd make up the difference to the boyos this week if only the people who owed her paid. Either way she'd be fine, she had plenty in the bank. No big deal, she'd take some out and get straight with Wacko, then go after the deadbeats who owed her. Maybe she'd ask Wacko to put out the word for her, a little muscle never hurt collections.

Mary Rose bit open one of the larger bags and poured a pile of the white powder on top of the toilet paper dispenser. It did not have the same sparkling texture her earlier stuff had. Maybe Wacko was selling her an inferior product, taking advantage of her loyalty and prompt payments. Maybe the stuff she was using to cut it wasn't what they said it was, or maybe was she using too much? No matter, the stiffs she dealt with wouldn't know the difference. She snorted up the coke and wiped her nose, then ran her finger across the dispenser before putting it in her mouth.

Megan knocked again. "I gotta talk with you Mary Rose, it's important."

Mary Rose frowned and tore open another forty bag, and poured out half the contents on the toilet paper dispenser. She opened the stall door.

"Do that, Megan, and leave me alone, okay? I gotta figure out what I owe here. Must have dropped some. I'm going to check the floor outside. I couldn't have . . . we couldn't have done all this, could we?"

Megan shook her head and quickly passed by Mary Rose, and sunk the rolled-up dollar bill she held into the tiny pile. "Naw, no way," Megan said, inhaling then coughing. "You hadda have dropped it. Relax, we'll find it, I'll help you."

18

IN A PARKING LOT near the corner of Athens and Dorchester Streets, behind a row of stores and a bank, Wacko Curran strolled, like a customer at a used car lot, around a white Mercedes. He spit on the ground. "What's the matter with this kid, he needs printed directions? He grabs us a diesel, a diesel? You order a burner, explain to this moron exactly what you need, and he brings you this? My fish, my fucking fish runs faster than a diesel. I pay three hundred bucks for a hotbox, I better get what I ordered," Wacko said.

"I told him a Camry, get us a Camry," Kevin said.

Wacko beamed. "A Camry, really, Kevin? You're the balls," Wacko said.

"But he got us this, I don't get it," Kevin said. "Don't worry, Kano's grabbin' us the switch car, he's gettin' us a Conty, boosting it out of this Mercury dealership in Watertown, deliverin' it sometime this mornin'. That kid's got his shit together, goes to the dealership in a mechanic's uniform, walks around lookin' like he belongs. When he sees something he likes with the keys in it he grabs it, the kid's good. Sometimes he'll go into the dealership in a suit and tie wearing glasses lookin' like Clark fucking Kent. He'll carry a briefcase with dealer plates in it. When he finds what he's lookin' for, he slaps the plate on, and bing, he's gone," Kevin said.

"Kano's a good thief, always made a buck movin' cigarettes, he still into that?" Wacko said.

Kevin nodded. "He does that on the side, Jack. Bangs the cigarette trucks out of that warehouse in Randolph. He follows them, knows all their routes. They're Volvo trucks, and he's got the master key. The truck stops to make a delivery, and he jumps in, bye-bye. The kid makes a bundle on the butts, makes you wonder why he's stealin' cars," Kevin said, scratching his head. "Roots, must be his roots. His father stole cars, all his brothers too, some guys don't want to let go," Kevin said, answering his own question. "He should, though, before it's too late. They stick it up your ass these days for stealin' cars. Hate to see him go to the can; he's a good, solid kid."

"Ya, he is unlike his former partner, Arnie Davis, that rat piece of shit. Because of Arnie Davis four good men are scattered throughout the feds doing phone numbers," Wacko said.

"What happened? I was too young then," Kevin said.

Wacko made a face like Kevin had just cut some serious cheese. "Arnie, Kano, and the rest of the crew were stealing cars for the score boys. He personally grabbed all the burners for Jamo McDermott's crew outta Charlestown, and in them days those guys were busy: banks, jewelry outlets, supermarkets, even whacked protected book-makers; if you had money they'd hit you. One day they whacked an armored car over in Revere, turned into a fiasco; they shot the guard, burned the getaway cars afterwards, only one car didn't burn so good.

Inside the trunk the cops found evidence, charred food stamps and canceled bank checks."

"That same night Arnie Davis is watchin' the news. Now here's a guy who usually only watched cartoons, but this night he catches the news, and what's he see? One of the cars he sold Jamo McDermott involved in an armored car hit, a dead guard, and even Arnie was bright enough to know he's looking at accessory before and after the fact. He shit his pants and ran straight to the cops. Next thing you know, Arnie's in the Witness Protection Program lining Jamo and his crew up like ducks in a row smokin' them for the feds," Wacko said.

"I know stuff like that happens, but I dunno, there's something about stealin' cars I hate," Kevin said. "Don't mind suitin' up, stickin' a Mossberg in someone's face, but stealin' cars . . ."

"People think it's easy," Wacko said. "A few years back it's night-time, I'm in the Somerville Mall with Timmy Fitz shoppin' for burners. I find this Ford station wagon I like and go after it. Now, I'm inside the car, got this dent puller in the ignition, bam, I'm pulling, bam, the ignition's comin' out and I look in the mirror. Right behind me's one of them rent-a-cops, sittin' watching me in a fucking Hyundai with a revolving yellow light on the roof."

"Now Timmy Fitz, who drove me there, is supposed to be keepin' the peek, but he ain't. He's just sittin' there in his Plymouth Duster lookin' straight ahead like there's no one else in the world 'cept him and his cigarette. The cop sees me, I see the cop but he don't move, so I leave the dent puller in the Ford ignition, bobbing like a hard-on, and exit the car real cool. I get into Timmy's car and we drive away. The rent-a-dick stays put, don't even bother to chase us, but still it shook me plenty."

"Pain in the ass or not, for the armored car we're stealin' our own," Wacko went on. "I'm not goin' into a score, have something go wrong, maybe someone gets killed, then have to worry about the guy who stole our cars out on the street smokin' and jokin', doin' lines with his buddies saying, 'Ya, I'm with those guys, got the wheels for them.' Word gets back to the cops, and it will, they grab this car thief, pressure him, next thing ya know he's testifyin' against us. Naw, for that we steal our own cars."

"I'm with you," Kevin said. "So today we pass on the Mercedes. What we tell the guy who stole it?"

"Tell him nothin', leave the car here and let him sell it to someone else."

Both men got back into the blue Marquis, and Wacko's cell phone rang. "Ya . . ." He looked at Kevin. "You tell Moses Halleran we needed a car? Talk to him." He handed Kevin the phone.

"Moses . . . who you think it is, you fucking moron? You got it, good," Kevin said. He covered the mouthpiece with his hand. "He got a Camry." He uncovered the phone. "Ya, two hundred, where are you? Okay, stay put, we're down the street, be there in a minute." Kevin closed the phone. "Head to Bell's," he said, as Wacko pulled out of the parking lot onto Dorchester Street.

At the lights at Eighth Street, Wacko took a left, parked, and got out. He came around the corner and stopped in front of Sullivan's Tavern. "Looney, looking for Moses, seen him?" Wacko said to an old-timer standing near the doorway.

Looney nodded down the street to the next corner. "Outside Bell's about ten minutes ago. Wacko pressed a five-dollar bill into Looney's hand.

"How's the missus?" Wacko said.

"Alive last I seen," Looney said, heading into the bar.

A silver Toyota Camry sat parked in front of Bell's Market. A kid about twelve leaned against the fender, sucked on a cigarette, his interest riveted on a scratch ticket he furiously stroked with a nickel.

Kevin came up on him. "Another lucky loser," Kevin said. "Get the fuck off my car, Meany." The kid's cigarette bucked and the ash flew up and hit his cheek.

"Uh, Kevin, Wack — Jackie, sorry," Meany said, flicking at his cheek. He shifted his ass off the fender, and the toe of his sneaker caught the edge of the curb; he stumbled and dropped the ticket. Kevin kicked the ten-dollar Mountain O' Gold scratch ticket into the gutter.

"Meany, you're too young for scratch tickets. Go to fucking school," Kevin said.

"Okay, Kev, okay," the kid said, inhaling deeply on the cigarette. He expertly flicked it twenty feet into the street with his middle finger as he walked away. "You guys have a good day, huh?" Meany said over his shoulder.

Moses Halleran exited Bell's Market with half a sandwich in his left hand and a hunk of corned beef hanging from the corner of his mouth. He wiped his mouth with the back of his hand; the meat clung to it for a moment before falling to the ground. "Hey, guys, what's up?" Moses said before stuffing the remainder of the sandwich into his mouth. He reached into the pocket of his windbreaker, pulled out a bottle of Diet Pepsi, unscrewed the cap, took a hit from the bottle, replaced the cap. "Got it this mornin' at the Braintree T station, like it?" Moses said, pointing at the Camry with the bottle. He returned the bottle to his pocket and wiped his mouth again.

Wacko nodded to Kevin, who pulled a roll secured by a rubber band from his pocket. He peeled off some bills and handed them to Moses as Wacko looked through the passenger window of the Camry at the rag draped across the middle of the steering column. "You peeled the column?" Wacko said.

"Gotta do what ya gotta do. Want it or no?" Moses said. Wacko first looked at Kevin, then Moses. "How bout I peel your face?" he said, straightening up. Moses took a step back and glanced over his shoulder towards the doorway to the market. "Maybe you got another sandwich comin'?" Wacko said.

"Hey, Jack, hey, please, I had to peel the column, can't get keys for every car I grab," Moses said.

"I ain't askin' every car, only the ones we take; like I'm supposed to take a pinch because some cop looks inside, sees the busted out column, knows the car's stolen. In the future you got shit like this, don't bother callin'," Wacko said, signaling Kevin to get into the Camry. "I'll get the car. Park that piece of shit that's got 'I'm stolen' written all over it in the garage, I'll meet you there," Wacko said.

▪ ▪ ▪

Kevin walked out of the commercial garage on the corner of D and Baxter Streets hitting the automatic close button on the inside wall as he did. The huge rolling steel door had just clanked shut on the concrete behind him when Wacko pulled up in the blue Marquis. "Good timing," Kevin said, getting into the car.

"You say we're all set for tomorrow getting all the cars up there to Abington?" Wacko said.

Kevin grinned and turned on the radio. A barely audible Coolio sang "Gangsta's Paradise" on a jammin' hip-hop station. "Ya, Jack, we're all set. I called Stouie last night, he's meetin' me down Mul's to-morrow morning at six. He's psyched, a fast two hundred's a big deal to him."

"You told him nothin', right? I don't care he's our cousin, a good kid, but he don't know our business," Wacko said.

"He knows nothin"cept we're bringin' cars out to Abington. The kid ain't stupid, Jack, he knows what's up, he just don't know, you know, no reason to," Kevin said.

"I figure first we'll leave the Conty outside the gym at Abington High School. An hour later there'll be a hundred more cars in the lot, no one will notice. We'll leave my Camaro at the train station on Route 18, near the old Welcome Farms ice cream joint, and take the seven o'clock train back into South Station. You pick us up there in the Camry, drop Stouie off in Southie, then you and me head out to Abington to meet Mr. Capizzo. After we score his diamonds, I figure it will take us all of twelve minutes to make the switch to the Conty, then the second switch to my car in the MBTA lot. If there's a lot of heat, we can even take the train back to town," Kevin said.

"Stouie's a good kid; if he's interested we'll make room for him with us when he's old enough. Who knows, Kev, the kid's smart, maybe he'll be a college boy," Wacko said.

"Brings back memories," Kevin said.

"Ya, you went to fucking Harvard."

"I wasn't college material? How soon they forget. Remember I used to rob Service Merchandise, their gold. Come in dressed like a square, carrying books and a three-ring binder? Sucked them in good. Papers called me 'The College Boy Robber' — close to college I'll ever get," Kevin said.

"Ya, I remember, you were the professor, but I'm the fucking dean," Wacko said, high-fiving his brother. "We'll take someone else to school tomorrow when we introduce ourselves to Mr. Armand Capizzo. I hope he says to me, 'Do you know who I am?' cause the answer ain't gonna be multiple choice."

19

AS HE STOOD IN THE BATHROOM, Armand Capizzo looked in the mirror and liked what he saw. It wasn't hard. He was financially well off, the owner of his own diamond wholesale-retail business, and looked at least ten years younger than his thirty-eight years. With his right hand he stroked his still jet-black hair straight back with an Italian tortoiseshell comb and with his left removed a dollop of shaving cream from his ear. Before heading downstairs, he splashed Chanel Égoïste on his face and actually waved good-bye to the mirror.

Capizzo entered the kitchen and kissed his wife on the cheek as she hovered over a large flat pan full of silver-dollar pancakes. She served him at the table with real maple syrup, and he listened as he ate while his twin seven-year-old daughters described, in detail, their latest school art project. Capizzo feigned interest and watched their tiny hands draw giraffes and lions in the air, but he had bigger things on his mind.

He finished eating, wiped his mouth, and graciously accepted a kiss from each girl when the school bus sounded its horn at the end of his two-hundred-foot driveway that curved to the left behind a veil of trees.

Capizzo went down into the basement and got onto his knees next to a gleaming mahogany pool table with hand-stitched leather pockets the dealer told him was at least one hundred years old. With a house key he pried up the edge of an aquamarine ceramic tile that he lifted out. He reached down and spun the dial of the small Mosler safe beneath the floor, and a warm flush spread through his cheeks as he extracted a black leather fanny pack from it.

He unzipped the bag, examined its sparkling contents, smiled, and secured the belt around his waist, comfortable in the knowledge that the profit on the sale of these stones would increase his personal worth by at least $100,000.

He reached back into the safe and withdrew a seven-ounce, two inch, .38 Smith & Wesson five-shot revolver. A woman's gun they called it, but it would kill you like a man's. He shoved the gun into the custom-made gray suede holster on his right hip.

Before he left the house he kissed his wife on the cheek. She tiredly accepted it and patted him twice on the back before closing the door behind him. Soon he was out of the town of Westwood, his cruise control set at sixty-seven, heading south on route 128 towards Braintree.

At the Braintree split he pointed the Lincoln Town Car east on Route 3, punched the preselect button on his radio and hit number two. WODS, the classic rock station, came on, and the Platters sang "Only You." The music reminded him that he was born at the wrong time, but he figured if he couldn't have everything he had just about everything else.

Later today two dealers from large South Shore Plaza jewelry stores and another guy, a sharpie like himself who moved a lot of stones up the North Shore and Burlington way were scheduled to take half the stones in his fanny pack. If things went right, he'd make for himself over fifty dimes, a huge score. He planned to move the rest of the stones over the next month to smaller dealers and "friends" and make the same money, maybe a little more.

As he passed the South Braintree exit, Capizzo stroked his hair and checked himself in the mirror for the fourth time that morning, and then it hit him. If only that little fuck Harvey Ketchman had come up with the dough he owed him. Harvey was a middleman who had a lot of contacts in the Jewelers Building on Washington Street in Boston. Harvey promised, if Armand would front him some stones, a quick turnover from a dealer in the building, a relative who was a real hustler. Capizzo had learned a hard lesson; never cuff your product to a degenerate gambler, and now it appeared that it was Capizzo who was hustled. Ketchman was into him for twenty-five large, money that should have been the down payment for the second store Capizzo wanted up in Saugus. Capizzo had saved the money, two thousand a month, by not insuring his diamonds. Why pay for insurance? He had it, courtesy of Smith & Wesson. He had other insurance too.

He'd been supplying beautiful stones, at cut rate, to some of the "boys" from the North End for years. Only last week Sal "the Butcher boy" Montillio had bought a six-carat tennis bracelet for his little cupcake, Lola. Was anyone really named Lola these days? Three days later he buys a pair of two-carat diamond earring studs for his wife. Guilt, but who cared? Guilt made Armand Capizzo a wealthy man. Soon some of the boys, his insurance "adjusters," would be talking to Harvey Ketchman and anyone else who fucked with him because all it took was a phone call.

At the Route 18A exit off Route 3 he punched the seek button twice, passing on a Bach concerto and some hip-hop crap, before settling on Barry Manilow singing "Mandy." At a red light in Weymouth, a Blockbuster Video on his left, Capizzo still sang the words. He looked to his right and saw a pretty blond in a yellow Mustang convertible give him the eye and smile. "Oh, Mandy, you kissed me and stopped me from shaking," he sang to her through the glass. She laughed, twiddled her fingers at him, and accelerated on the green.

At the lights on the top of the hill past Abington High School, Capizzo turned right and wondered if Mora from the donut shop next to his store was working today. Great cup of coffee, beautiful legs, incredible fuck. He smiled thinking about her and how much weight those half-carat studs he gave her carried. He met her once a week after work at her little place at the Elmwood Arms, down the street on Route 18. He'd leave there dizzy. Life was good.

Capizzo pulled into the strip mall parking lot, parked his Town Car directly in front of BNT Diamond Importers, and killed the engine. He ran his comb through his hair as he looked towards the donut shop for signs of Mora, then popped a breath mint in his mouth.

He opened the glove box and with his right index finger hit the trunk release button. He heard the click of the trunk behind him and involuntarily put his hand on his gun. Enjoying the feel of the rubber grip, he withdrew it a half inch before pushing it gently back down into the gray suede holster.

Outside he headed to the rear of the car and opened the trunk. He retrieved his briefcase and closed it; still no sign of Mora.

Capizzo climbed two steps, turned right, and stopped at the entrance to his store. He punched 42974 into the keypad to the right of the door, and the red alarm light blinked to green. He entered the office, hit the light switch on his left, and lay his briefcase down on the only desk in the room.

Behind him the electric door chime sounded. Without turning he said, "Hey, baby doll, what's up for the weekend?"

"Anything you're up for, big boy," said the voice. Capizzo's sphincter tightened, and he turned to his left, pulling back on his jacket.

"Whoa, one more inch, you guinea fuck, I'll spray your brains on the wall. Hands up, into the back room, move," the voice ordered. Capizzo obeyed; raising his arms, he looked over his left shoulder. Twelve feet behind him two men stood facing him side by side, one slightly taller than the other. Both men wore dark, red-framed safety glasses; both had mustaches and huge, bushy eyebrows. Both men wore dark blue running suits, the Nike swoop prominent over the heart of the larger of the two. Both men pointed large-caliber automatics, held low at their hips, at him.

"Expectin' anyone else, any appointments?" the Nike man said.

"What?" Capizzo said.

"Anyone else due here this morning?"

"Ya, er, later I —"

"Shut the fuck up, move," the Nike man said. "Watch for the girl."

"Make my donut chocolate glazed," the other man said. Capizzo's stomach jumped as he passed around the left side of his desk and headed into the back room. Cold steel pressed into the base of his skull.

"Blink and you're dead. Where's the gun?"

"Right side, my right hip," Capizzo said. A hand fumbled at his side. The gun was so light he barely noticed the difference with it gone.

"This thing real?" the Nike man said.

"Ya, it's —"

"Shut up," the Nike man said, pushing him into the wall.

"I want you to lay facedown on the floor, hands clasped behind your neck, got it? Don't make me kill you. We only want the stones, where are they?"

Capizzo responded to the command, but as he lay on his stomach had to turn his head to the side to interlock his fingers. A foot away from his head he could see a pair of double-tied black Converse basketball sneakers. The blue nylon running pants had a thin red stripe down the side. Capizzo dared not look any higher.

"Any more guns, on your legs maybe?" the Nike man said, patting Capizzo's legs.

"No, no guns."

"Better not be lying. Now where are the stones?" the Nike man said.

"Around my waist, fanny pack," Capizzo said. Oddly, he couldn't clear from his mind the image of his wife serving silver-dollar pancakes to him an hour before.

"How's it lookin' out there?" the Nike man said.

"All clear. Almost done?" the other man said.

A pair of legs straddled his hips, and Capizzo heard a knife click open. His testicles rose in his sac as he was relieved of the diamonds.

"The safe, open it," the Nike man said.

"You got enough, get the fuck out," Capizzo said, fighting to control his voice.

"Got enough? Let me check," the Nike man said, raising his gun. Capizzo saw stars, bright comets, planets trailing fire, then he felt the pain. A knee dug deep into his back, and blood tickled behind an ear as his head was yanked back by the hair. Hands grabbed his shoulders and flipped him onto his back.

The Nike man pointed a gun directly between his eyes "The safe, open the fucking safe," he said.

Capizzo was crying now. "I'm connected, you cocksucker, I'll —"

"Ya, connected to your dick." The Nike man brought the butt of the gun down so hard on Capizzo's nose his safety glasses almost fell off. Again Capizzo saw stars and gagged as he inhaled his own blood.

"Okay, okay," he said. He raised himself up on his right elbow and with his left hand spun the dial of the safe against the wall. The tumblers clicked into place, and he pulled back on the door, then covered his nose with his hand. "Oh, God, I think you broke it," he said.

"If I didn't I'm losin' my touch," the Nike man said. He put his right foot on Capizzo's shoulder and shoved him out of the way.

"Is this all of it?" the Nike man said, bending down in front of the safe and pulling out a black box filled with small cellophane envelopes.

"That's it, that's all, take it, please, leave," Capizzo said.

"Any alarms to the cops?" the Nike man said, looking under a table and up the walls.

"No, none," Capizzo said.

"Back on your stomach. How is it out there?" the Nike man said.

"Cool, no problem, let's go," the voice in the other room said.

"Hands behind your back, feet together. I'm going to tie-wrap you. Move you're dead, got it?"

The tie wrap cinched around Capizzo's wrists. "It's too tight, please," he said.

"You bitch," the Nike man said, snugging the tie wrap around his ankles.

The door chime sounded again seconds after the Nike man left the room.

The man on the floor cried softly. "Mora," Armand Capizzo said.

20

"WE GOT TO DO SOMETHING about this shit," the fat man said, popping a clam into his mouth.

"I thought that's what we were doin'," the other man said. "What I hear I think is on the money. My guys are out there watching. I'm just waitin' for someone to show up at my door sellin' ice, lots of ice."

"I'm not talking about that shit, this." The fat man pointed a greasy finger at the windshield. "This beach, Wollaston, when I was a kid you could swim in Wollaston Beach. Tide came in, went out, nothing but water came in, went out with it. Now what you got? Shit, lots of shit. Had a friend a few years back, sidestroking, as was his habit, out there one morning, and clomph, he hits a jellyfish. That in itself is no big deal, jellyfish everywhere on this beach. He finishes his swim, comes out of the water, and part of this "jellyfish" is still clinging to his beard, only it ain't a jellyfish it's shit, still had peanuts in it. He freaked. Some days out there you got beach whistles washing up enough to start your own fucking band."

"They're doin' it, though, they're cleanin' it up," the other man said, throwing a pack of Marlboros into the air and catching it. He tossed it to the other hand and repeated the process. "Big project, Boston Harbor Project they call it; they're out there on Deer Island building a new shit plant as we speak. Them sandhogs, Local Eighty-eight, are digging this huge fucking tunnel, my cousin Mark's one of 'em there. Nine miles out this tunnel goes, gonna flush all this new processed shit into the sea. Everyone's happy, the harbor gets buffed, the politicians look good, even the fucking whales gotta be smiling — they got clean shit in their yard where before they had the stuff with peanuts in it."

"Save the whales," the fat man said, biting into a huge onion ring. "Hungry? Got these at Tony's Clam Shop, they're great. The other place, the Clam Box, is good, but this place . . . ," the fat man put his fingers together and kissed the tips. "So, this kid you're talking about, Sean . . . ,"

"Brancaccio," the other man said.

"He flashin', talking', what?" the fat man said.

"Heard he fenced a load of stones up Hanover Street a few days ago, quality stuff. Made over thirty grand. Told the fence . . . you want to know who?" the other man said.

"He got an office near where the European restaurant used to be but a few doors down, same side of street, third floor, correct?" the fat man said, wiping his mouth. "Incredible clams."

"You got it Bippo. So this kid, Brancaccio, tells Bippo, 'You want more? Can you handle more?' Bippo says, ya sure, but nothing so far," the other man said, opening the Marlboros and tapping one out.

"How'd you find this out?" the fat man said.

"Me and Bippo worked together in the past, the guy's been around a hundred years. He called and asked about this kid and did I know anything more about the stones, seems they were top quality and moved like lightnin', he wanted more. He wanted to know if there were more players involved maybe I could send them his way, he'd send something my way," the other man said.

"So, who else was involved?" the fat man said.

"I'm hearin' things, I'm not sure, but I'm hearin' it was the Curran brothers who made the hit out in Abington. Brancaccio's nothing more than an outside player, a cokehead. The way I figure, Brancaccio came up with the play somehow, got the info on the diamond merchant, gave it to the Currans, and they ran with it. Afterwards, as his end, they threw Brancaccio twenty percent off the top," the other man said.

"Another thing that makes me think it's the Currans. Brancaccio shows up at the door of this dealer I know all jekylled up, flashin' a big wad. He wants a few ounces and talkin' shit while my friend's weighin' the product up. As he's leavin' the house he says to the guy,

'You're thinkin' about gettin' married, see me about the diamond, I'll take care of you.' Now this is out of the blue. There was no mention of marriage, just see me about the diamond, that's what he says," the other man said.

"So, the kid's buying coke talking diamonds. How's that involve the Currans?" the fat man said.

The other man tapped the bridge of his nose with the pack of Marlboros. "Wacko Curran don't like guys doing coke even though his brother's a fiend. Wacko knows coked up guys are sloppy, easily spooked, talk too much. During a score they're liable to grow chemical balls, maybe kill someone who don't need killin', creates all kinds of problems. Wacko don't like problems, you fuck up he'll show you, hard lesson sometimes," the other man said.

"He also don't like his guys gettin' high afterwards either, at least for a while. People like to talk they're high. They don't call the shit 'yak' for nothin'. This kid Brancaccio wouldn't dare ask the Currans for blow; he goes elsewhere and hopes Wacko don't find out. But I did."

The fat man sighed. "You're telling me Wacko Curran, his brother, and this kid Brancaccio pulled this score out in Abington last week and walked away with over a million in diamonds." He squeezed the empty onion and clam boxes, napkins, and salt packs into a large paper bag and opened the door. "I'm gonna dump this, I need some air."

The fat man got out of the car and threw the trash into a large green barrel with MDC written on the side in white. He faced the seawall and raised his arms like he was directing an orchestra to stand. "Wollaston Beach, when can we swim again?" he said. He dropped his arms and shook his head all the way back to the car. He opened the door to the Crown Victoria and got in.

"What you're giving me is stuff for the state police or your buddies in the Boston Police. Why call me?" the fat man said.

"Because you're buddies with that little federal statute, RICO. Seems to me stealin' diamonds, sellin' them, buyin' coke with some of the money, putting the rest of it on the street for shylock to make more cash is a predicate act, what you need for a RICO indictment. That's what I think, but I'm slow about some things," the other man said.

"Could be RICO," the fat man said, stroking his chin. "Could be, but I need more. Something concrete, something when I present it to the prosecutor in the Moakley Federal Courthouse he'll say, 'Ya, this will stick like shit to a chow chow's ass.' We gotta prove this Wacko character pulled off this score, but it's going to be hard; word is they were disguised and the victim isn't talking much. Abington PD thinks he's holding back like he intends to handle it in-house. Maybe he's connected, maybe not. Ain't a guinea on the planet who don't think he's connected somehow or other.

"If you come up with anything more, give me a call," the fat man said, pulling out a foil-wrapped Wash'n Dry® from beneath his seat. He opened it and rubbed his hands with the moist towelette, then threw it over his shoulder. "I hope we can put something together on this so I can keep telling my people in the bureau what a great guy you are. Remember when you gave me that Janowski kid a while back? We walked in on him still had twenty grand traceable to the bank he stole it from under his bed. That was substantial. I need substantial. Stuff that shows my superiors it's worth keeping you and your guys out here cleaning up the streets. You're doing good, do better."

"I'll see what I can do," the other man said, partially rolling down the window and tossing out the unlit smoke. A seagull swooped down from nowhere, plucked it up, and shredded it in his bill, then looked at him directly in the eyes before screaming and flying off.

"This guy Curran's an unguided missile, dangerous. Everyone's served by sendin' him upriver," the other man said. "His brother's just a follower, a cokehead, but guess he'll have to learn to swim too. I'll be in touch." He pulled his ball cap down and slipped on a pair of Ray-Bans. He flipped the collar of his jacket up before glancing over his shoulder and exiting the car. Once outside he looked over the roof, then leaned back in before closing the door.

He said, "Almost forgot. I know DEA's been in Southie keepin' a tab on this jamoke, Mickey Ridge. I've known Mickey since we were kids down the Old Harbor projects. Nice guy, used to work for me, but got sloppy, uses his own shit and talks too much. He lives on Silver Street. What? I say he lives there? More like he stores his coke there, studio apartment, forty-four Silver Street. Tomorrow night after 7:00 if someone real cute was watchin', they'd see maybe six keys of Colombian flake walking up the steps to that number. That's of course if they were interested in watchin'," the other man said.

"After seven someone just might be, Silver Street, thanks," the fat man said.

"Any time," the other man said.

21

DANNY KING STOOD ON THE CORNER of I Street and "Little" Broadway, as East Broadway is also known, and shoved two quarters into the *Boston Herald* machine. He pulled back on the handle; to anyone observing, the machine yanked him forward.

"Motherfucka," he said, stepping back and planting his right size-twelve squarely in the center of the Plexiglas screen just below the headline that read EAST BOSTON CITY COUNCILOR INDICTED ON KICKBACK SCHEME. He staggered back from the impact, then took half a step forward, twisted his hips, and drove his left foot into the screen, cracking it dead center.

He violently rattled the handle. It was at this point Danny plainly heard his two quarters drop ten inches down a steel chute into the yellow collection box at the bottom of the machine. His eyes bugged and his body convulsed like he had just sucked a jolt of 220 electric current through a straw. He raised his right fist over the machine, thought better of it, and coughed up phlegm from the deepest recesses of his throat, then fired the mass, like a paintball, at the screen. It had the desired effect.

As he fumed, a car stopped at the lights behind him and a voice said, "Hey Danny, looking for one of these?" Danny had to shield his eyes from the sun as he turned, though he knew the source of the voice. Marty Fallon always rode low in the seat, peeking over the edge of the door on constant lookout for possible assassins. He waved the *Boston Herald* out the passenger side window as the Impala pulled to the curb.

"These damn machines," Danny said, ignoring the paper. "I'm pissed off anyways, lost three hundred last night on the Bulls, cocksuckers, missed the spread by two points in overtime, now I'm getting beat by this fucking machine."

Marty Fallon waved the rolled up paper like he was conducting the Boston Symphony. "Relax, take the paper," he said and laughed. On the driver's side, Andre Athanas waggled his huge right hand in front of Marty's chest. Danny could only make out Andre's lower jaw and part of his nose.

"Hi, Danny, how are ya?" Andre said.

"Hey, Andre, what's up?" Danny said, taking the newspaper. He rested his forearm on the roof and leaned in.

"What's up? That's a good question, but I wouldn't ask Mickey Ridge you see him. DEA got him last night; kicked in his door and caught him with some weight, he's got big problems," Marty said.

Danny sighed. "Poor bastard, I heard nothin'. Mickey only got out of Allenwood what eighteen months ago after doing a nickel, and now this, put the fork in, he's done."

"Sleep with dogs you get fleas. The kid was dealin' with too many junk balls. I guarantee someone who owed him money dropped the dime. No one to pay off makes life easy for someone. I just hope Mickey holds his water, I heard him and Jackie Curran were runnin' pretty tight," Marty said.

"He'll hold it," Danny said, pushing himself away from the car. He stared over the roof at nothing in particular.

"Hey, Danny boy, I'm not saying he's a rat," Marty said, leaning partially out the window. "If I'm gonna say he's a rat, I'll tell you he's a fucking rat, understand? What I am saying he was usin', like most I know, a little too much of his own product and that my friend can make a mouse out of the strongest man."

Danny leaned on the car again. "Ya, you're right, Marty, no offense. I've seen better guys go down, deliver everything to the cops. The coke takes their manhood, seen it, fact," he said.

Marty picked something off the tip of his nose and flicked it onto the street. "Let's change the subject. You been keepin' up on your payments?" he said, pulling a pack of Marlboros off the dash. He tapped the outside mirror with the box.

Danny's eyes widened and he straightened up. "You know I have, Marty, what's up?" he said.

"You owe me another . . . ?"

"Five grand," Andre said, holding all the fingers of one hand extended.

Danny King took another step back. "Marty, look, you know there's no problem, I —"

To silence him, Marty Fallon pressed an index finger against his lips, then viciously punched the dash. "You fuck, you little fuck, I'll tell . . . me, I'll tell you, understand, when you got a problem, got that?" he said.

Danny's shoulders sagged. Then like someone turned off a faucet Marty stopped. "Hey, kid, relax, you been runnin' the beach lately?" he said. He rubbed the knuckles of his right hand and sunk back into the leather bucket seat. "I haven't seen you runnin', you Andre?" Andre shook his head.

"I've been running different, Marty, ya know nights, days," Danny said.

"Well, running's good for you. It's good to do good things for yourself mind, body, the whole package. Talk about doin' good things, I need a little information, somethin' you might be able to help me with, help you too."

"Whatever you need, if I can help," Danny said.

Marty motioned Danny closer. "Word is Jackie Curran made that diamond score up in Abington recently, nice little pop. Jackie's my friend, but he didn't come to me after. What, I don't treat guys fair, give a fair price? Danny, I want you to talk to him, find out if he's the one, then tell me so I can talk to him. I want to be sure. I don't want to offend him if he had nothin' to do with it."

"I'll talk to him, Marty. Jackie trusts me, we got something in the works too," Danny said.

Marty's face revealed nothing. "Things in the works, huh? You don't mind me asking, what things?"

Danny shook his head. "I can't really talk about it, ya know," he said, looking at Andre.

"Oh, ya, I understand," Marty said. "Ya, Andre, go buy yourself a paper or somethin'."

"I've read the paper, Marty," Andre said.

Marty slapped the top of the dash. "Well, go read the fucking *National Geographic* or the Three Stooges, get the fuck out of the car."

Andre opened the door, leaped out and almost got hit by a minivan. "Hey, fuck you," he screamed as the van sounded its horn.

"Inside," Marty said. Danny came around the front of the car and slid behind the wheel.

"So, can you talk about it now?" Marty said. "I mean, if Jack Curran was involved in another diamond score, as I think he was this one, and you were involved too, then I'd have some hard questions for Jackie boy and you.

"I want you to think about this, you owe me five grand. Can you pay me everything you owe me, vig and all, right now this very minute?"

"Hey, Marty, I —" Danny said.

"Shut up! Shut the fuck up," Marty said. "Or are you going to help me so I can help you, maybe take a little off what you owe me? I want you to find out what Jackie Curran's up to, or do you think this town's wide open like some Wild West freak show? If you do, don't. I run this town; I run everything, I own everything, you forget that for a minute you got problems nightmares don't cover."

Danny hung his head and visibly shook. He spoke into his lap. "I need a cigarette."

"A cigarette, sure, kid," Marty said. He opened the pack and tapped one out. He put it between Danny's lips and lit it. Danny inhaled deeply, then blew the smoke out the window, then stared at his lap again.

"You're right, Marty, I do need help," he said.

22

SMOKEY ROBINSON'S "Tears of a Clown" was just beginning to play on the radio as Kevin Curran drove his red Camaro east up the Broadway hill. As he drew near to the front of South Boston District Court, he tapped the brakes, brought the car to a crawl, and shut the radio off.

Gathered on the sidewalk in front of the courthouse and on its gray, granite steps was the usual collection of lawyers, cops, defendants, and witnesses to get their lies in order. At the sidewalk's edge, next to a mailbox, Bobo Foley leaned against a light pole with a T sign attached overhead that read No Parking Any Time. Bobo, who was six feet tall and stick-figure thin, was garbed in an aquamarine running suit with a pair of maroon Pumas laced to his sockless, bony feet. He tugged at a dark blue Red Sox cap on his head.

"Bobo, hey!" Kevin shouted past his brother's face.

"How 'bout lettin' me get the fucking window down first," Wacko said, hitting the silver button to his right. Kevin signaled Bobo over, then with his right index finger tapped the windshield beneath the rearview mirror.

"Right now, brother, in front of the bowlin' alley, move," Kevin said. The scarecrow glanced up, then away before resettling his gaze on Kevin's face; then Bobo Foley nodded, hunched his shoulders, and headed off in the complete opposite direction.

The Camaro's tires chirped as Kevin threw the car in reverse. He hit the horn. "No, no, you fucking nut, the other way, the bowlin' alley," Kevin said, pointing harder this time. Bobo smiled, flipped his hands in the air, and reversed direction.

"Fucking nipplehead, like he didn't hear you the first time," Wacko said. "What's up with him?"

"He owes us money," Kevin said.

"Tell me you didn't lend him, Kevin, you nuts?" Wacko said.

Kevin grinned. "He owes us. Once removed, but he owes us."

Kevin stopped the Camaro in front of the bowling alley and pointed at Bobo Foley. "Stay there, don't move," he yelled to the nodding figure on the sidewalk.

"No, Jack, I'm not crazy enough to lend to this bum, but someone was, there's always someone crazy enough, just like you were crazy enough to lend to Frankie Popeo."

"How're you comparin' Bobo Foley with Frankie Pop, this guy's a bum. Frankie Pop's a moneymaker," Wacko said.

"Ya, Frankie Pop makes it, he just don't like payin' it back," Kevin said.

"Hey, who the fuck —" Wacko said.

Kevin laughed and bongoed the steering wheel. "Relax, Jack, I'm bustin' your balls. We're gettin' our money back thanks to our friend Bobo here," Kevin said. He waved to Bobo, who ducked.

"Jack, Bobo's a gambler, a keno freak, takes to it like a crow to crack," Kevin said.

"Figures you know him," Wacko said. "How'd he get our money?"

"Funny story. I seen our muscular friend Leppy Mullins outside the L Street Bathhouse a few days ago, he tells me this Bobo character's flush with cash, spendin' it down the Pen Tavern like there's no tomorrow. Naturally I'm curious."

"Get to the point."

"Seems Bobo here was into Frankie Pop for six grand. Now you might say, Why would a guy like Frankie Pop lend so much to a chump like Bobo Foley, who spends most of his free time boosting cigarettes out the back of delivery trucks?" Kevin said.

"You're makin' me anxious," Wacko said.

"Because Bobo's mum, bless her heart, kicked the bucket late last year and left Bobo a huge two-family on Marine Road free and clear, that's why.

"A month or so ago Frankie, who figures he's got the house as collateral, lends Bobo money. Now, Frankie Pop owes us; been scramblin' to get the money since he got out of the hospital. Three days ago he marches this gamblin' degenerate down to Vinny Tessio's joint, River Mortgage Co., and Bobo refinances his house, took out an equity loan too, got him thirty grand at a good rate."

"Bobo gives Frankie the money he owes him, and now Frankie can pay you but he's still scared to death of you, so he asks Bobo to drop two grand off to us, even gives him a double C-note to make the delivery."

"Frankie Pop banged into Leppy Mullins and gave him the lowdown knowin' it would get back to us pretty quick, and I've been keepin' my eyes peeled for this lowlife Bobo ever since. Checked around town but not the Pen Tavern, seems Bobo's been down there every day with his mum's money betting the puppies, playing keno like if he stopped he'd never shit normal again," Kevin said.

"So, keno's a laxative?" Wacko said, his face contorting. "I'll make him shit he don't have our dough." Wacko glared at Bobo Foley. Bobo flinched and took a few steps back.

Kevin pointed his finger at him. "Stay!" Kevin said before getting out of the car.

Bobo kept his head down and his hands in his pockets as Kevin walked up, put his arm around his shoulders, and guided him back up the sidewalk towards the courthouse. Wacko watched in the sideview mirror as Kevin talked and Bobo nodded.

A minute later Kevin returned. "All set," he said, sliding back in behind the wheel. "Noon at the Pen, he'll have the money."

"Good, what's next?" Wacko said.

Kevin looked at him incredulously and laughed. "What, like I got choices now? That's the case, I figure we head up to the stash house on Story Street, check the inventory. I think we'll have to re-up by the end of the week."

"Good idea, but you don't need me, drop me at Paris's, I could use some coffee," Wacko said.

Kevin smirked. "Ya, with red pubic hair in it."

"She ain't a redhead, she's strawberry blond, and watch your fucking mouth, drive," Wacko said.

"Ya, I'll drive, but there's something else. The quality of Marty's coke goes from shit cut with Tums to pure rocket fuel, fucking seesaw. Never know what we're gettin', neither do our customers. Don't make for happy customers," Kevin said.

"They ain't complainin'," Wacko said.

"To our faces."

"Then they ain't complainin'. What about you, you got more I should hear?"

"Ya, I do, come to think about it I —"

Wacko held up his hand. "Buy yourself a notebook, jot everything down, later when I got time I'll read it, pull over."

Kevin stopped the car in the middle of Broadway near K Street, and Wacko got out. "See you in a half hour," he said, attempting to peer past the sun's reflection off the huge front window of Paris's Coffee House.

"She in there?" Kevin said, straining to see inside. "You serious about that notebook thing?"

"Half an hour," Wacko said, closing the door.

▪   ▪   ▪

Wacko Curran opened the door to Paris's Coffee House and paused just inside the doorway as his eyes adjusted to the dimmer light. It always amazed him what Paris, a one-time tailor, had done to a former greasy spoon diner. She had transformed the place, turned it into an upscale coffee shoppe with two gleaming espresso machines imported from Italy, granite countertops, and overstuffed chairs encircling small, strategically placed tables. The air was filled with the scent of baked muffins, croissants, turnovers, and fresh ground coffee from around the world. Elaine Ramsey sat against the wall, at the far end of the counter, beneath a lithograph of Marc Chagall. Wacko sat down beside her. He held out his hand, she grasped it.

"Hello, handsome," Elaine said, removing her glasses. She put her copy of *The Boston Phoenix* down on the counter. As Wacko held her hand, he looked back over his shoulder towards the street.

"Are we under attack?" Elaine said.

Wacko turned and stared into her eyes."Only your beauty on my heart. I thought I might catch you here." He nodded at the paper. "Didn't know they still print that thing. Anything interesting?"

"They do, and you should read more. This paper's loaded with all kinds of interesting things, even the classifieds are great, there are jobs," Elaine said.

"I got a job, chocolate milk," Wacko said to the counter girl. "What about you, still waitin' tables, when you finish school? Seems you've been goin' now what, fifteen years?"

"Fresh, four, and this is my last semester. I'll finish up end of summer," Elaine said.

"And then what?"

"Hopefully find work in a hospital," Elaine said, sipping her coffee.

"See if I can help you out," Wacko said.

"*You* know people in hospitals?"

"No, I send people to hospitals, give you someone to practice on," Wacko said, covering up as Elaine paddled his shoulder.

"Jackie Curran, you're horrible. I'm trying to be serious here," Elaine said.

"I *am* serious," Wacko said.

Elaine rapped his shoulder again. "What about you, Jack? Ever think about going back to school? You had a year under your belt, Boston University. Your mum was so proud you the only one to go." Elaine covered the top of his right hand with her tiny left and gave it a shake. "Come on, Jackie, you've got something, real potential, ability, why don't you go back finish school?"

"I had reasons to drop out, and it's too late to go back, too late for a lot of things," Wacko said.

"Had to drop out, why?" Elaine said.

The waitress put chocolate milk in front of Wacko. He picked it up and held it in front of his face before handing it back. "More chocolate," he said. The waitress looked at him funny. "You want it in Spanish?" She shook her head and hurried away.

"After Steven died, Ma kind of went to hell. He was the oldest, great athlete, good grades, full of promise, all that, but you could see it coming, he was partying all the time, but who would figure on a car crash killin' everyone in the car?" Wacko said.

"By the time Stevie died, Pop had been gone what, two years already, the family was a mess. Kevin got into the coke, then into the gambling, losin' his shirt every day to Morgan Daly down the Quencher, not that I blame Morgan. You know, Elaine, you can see things comin' but when the shit hits the fan you're never ready, for some things how can you be? You've been there with the family heartaches, you know. Bottom line, family comes first. I had to drop out to pull things together," Wacko said.

"I had problems too, Jack, but I got off my butt and dealt with them," Elaine said.

"A good thing you did, it's a pretty one," Wacko said.

Elaine feigned annoyance. "This isn't funny. Get off your butt, do good things with your life, Jack, you can't allow setbacks to keep you down." Elaine squeezed his hand for emphasis. "My troubles might not have been like yours, but I had them and picked myself up, went to school. I'll have a good job soon and a future. The key word is *future*," Elaine said. She paused and sipped her coffee. "I'm sorry, Jack, no more lectures, I just wanted to go on record because I'm your friend."

"You're right, Elaine, I'm listening. You may not believe it, but at times I think about gettin' out but realistically what kind of job could I get that pays a quarter of what I'm makin' now?"

"Everything doesn't have to be about money, Jack, there's more."

"Ya, I heard that before, but the guy sayin' it was on Jay Leno's show, one of them self-help idiots, probably makin' a half million a year sellin' that bullshit," Wacko said.

The waitress put the glass of chocolate milk down in front of him. He sipped it and smiled. "Life should be so easy, throw in a little more chocolate you got perfection. So, what you drinkin' today?"

Elaine picked up her cup then put it down. Wacko examined it. "What kind of forty-dollar Colombian crap is that?"

Elaine pretended to be indignant. "Crap? It's not crap; it's cappuccino with a double shot of espresso. Wakes me up, tastes yummy." She closed her eyes and held the cup up under her nose.

"Yummy? Hope you don't expect me to sit here and listen to that kind of language," Wacko said, looking towards the door. Elaine leaned forward and looked past him towards the large front window and the street.

"That Kevin double-parked out there?" she said. She watched Kevin get out of the Camaro, wildly wave his hands overhead, and tap his watch.

"I got him trained pretty good. Ya know, he can't even see in here, he's just hopin' I'm watchin'," Wacko said.

Elaine giggled, and Wacko leaned over and whispered into her ear. "Gotta go, Scarlett." She smelled like vanilla beans, he lingered, his face in her curls for a moment.

He quickly downed the rest of his chocolate milk, then wiped his mouth with a napkin. "I love the way your hair smells first thing in the morning," he said.

Elaine looked at him incredulously. "And how would you know, Jackie Curran, first thing in the morning?"

"In my dreams, Elaine Ramsey, only in my dreams," Wacko said, pulling some bills from his pocket. He peeled off three twenties and threw them on the counter.

"That's too much," Elaine said.

"What? Forty dollars for your Colombian crap, fifteen cents for my milk, the rest . . . gas money," Wacko said, tickling her under the chin.

"I don't need gas money," Elaine said.

Wacko kissed her on the cheek. "Then buy yourself a few more curls," he said and winked over his shoulder as he headed towards the door.

23

WITH A HERCULEAN EFFORT, Morgan Daly pulled all 315 quivering pounds of himself from the bench of the ancient mahogany booth. Once straight, he twisted his right hip hard and ripped a long, wet fart. Across the room from him, an old man slapped the oaken surface of the bar and wrinkled his nose. Morgan looked offended. "What? I should have been trapped in the booth with that? Fat fucking chance," he said, waddling towards the door. With a shaky finger the old man pointed at the long-necked bottle Morgan had left on the table.

"You gonna finish that?" the old man said.

Morgan Daly stopped just inside the doorway. "Swibby, that beer is three quarters full. It better not be one drop less when I bring my fat ass back to that soft red cushion." The old man looked like he'd swallowed a grape, then spun on the stool and stared at his disappointed face in the mirror. "Michael," Morgan said to the barman. "Give Swibby one on me."

Morgan stepped through the door of the Quencher Tavern into the sunlight and tugged at the seat of his pants. To his right a block up the street, a pencil-thin man in his late twenties wearing a blue tank top, black spandex biker shorts, and a knapsack furiously pedaled a mountain bike the wrong way down I Street. He had almost passed the Quencher before recognizing the enormous figure of Morgan Daly in the doorway. He squeezed the brakes and skidded to a stop. The bike man dismounted and guided the bike between two parked cars in front of the tavern, scraping a pedal on the bumper of one of them.

Morgan reacted like someone had just dragged their nails across a chalkboard. "Hey, you fucking ninny, watch the fucking car," he said, pushing past the bike man and squeezing in between the cars. He scrutinized the gray BMW's bumper and rubbed the chrome with a tissue. "Fucking ninny." The bike man checked his watch, then pulled off his knapsack.

"Sorry, Morgan, no harm done, how you lookin'?" he said, unfastening the straps on his pack.

"Henry, what you pedalin' today, more Gillettes? I got plenty of razor blades. "Used a new one every day, I'd be hairless before they're gone," Morgan said.

Henry pulled a clear plastic bag filled with tiny rectangles from his knapsack. "Come on, Morgan, you can't pass on a deal like this. I got fifty to a bag, fifteen bucks each, c'mon; give 'em away as gifts, everybody fucking shaves," he said.

"Give you twenty-five for two bags," Morgan Daly said.

"Done," the bike man said. "Put it on the Pats tonight, what's the line?"

"I got the Pats three and thirty-nine and a half," Morgan said, tearing open one of the bags. "Hey, these are Mach threes, incredible shaves, expensive, you got more?"

"Ya, give me a quarter A & R the Pats and under," the bike man said. He pulled another bag from his knapsack and tossed it to Morgan.

"Twelve more on the Pats?" Morgan said.

"No, fifteen for my pocket," the bike man said, holding out his hand.

A car horn sounded twice, and Kevin Curran pulled his Camaro alongside the gray BMW. He got out. "Hey, Henry, Morgan, what we got on the Pats tonight?" Kevin said, catching a bag of razor blades.

"Pats three and thirty-nine and a half," Morgan said. "Fucking Henry's beatin' me to death with these razor blades."

"More like you're skinnin' me with my own product," Henry said. "I just took twenty-five A & R the Pats and under, Kev, you should get some."

Kevin high-fived Henry. "Morgan, give me a nickel on the same," he said. "How much I owe you, Henry?"

"Shaves on me," Henry said, throwing on his knapsack. He looked at his watch. "I got more stops to make," he said to no one in particular.

Morgan pulled a small notebook from his back pocket and scratched in it with a stubby yellow pencil. "So, Kev, you want to put a nickel on the same as Henry? If you want you got it, but I gotta tell you, your brother was down here last week sniffin' around askin' if you was bettin'. I told him no like you said, Kev, but it made me uncomfortable, don't want to be caught in the middle."

"Middle's your middle name, you're already there," Kevin said. "Don't worry, Morgan, you're covered. Just take my bets and keep your snout out of my business the way Henry here does."

Henry snapped to attention and saluted. "No problem, sir, Kevin. I see nothin'," Henry said.

Morgan gave Henry a dirty look. "It's Kevin, sir, you fucking lame," Morgan said. He looked at Kevin. "You understand, Kev, I just don't want no trouble."

"Don't worry about trouble, life's too short," Kevin said.

"That's what I'm afraid of, Jack finds out," Morgan said.

Kevin opened the bag of razors and took one out. He examined it from different angles. "Seen Danny King around lately?" he said.

Morgan's neck bulged over his collar as he nodded. "Was here last night around seven, had a beer and a sandwich; seven thirty he left, said he was goin' runnin'. The kid's nutty as a fruitcake that run-nin' thing," Morgan said, patting his ample stomach. "There could be something to it, but by nature, I believe the body to be a sensitive thing. All that jarring on the bones could undermine the spirit."

Kevin frowned. "Hope I hit this game tonight, my spirit's been shit lately," he said. He opened the door to the Camaro and threw the razor blades in. "Thanks again for the blades, Henry; you need some-thin' for the head, let me know."

"Got no problem with that," Henry said, pushing his bike onto the street. "I got more stops to make but, like Arnold Whosenegger, I'll be back . . . first thing tomorrow morning to collect my winnings. Morgan, me and Mr. Curran here are going to undermine your spirit but good."

"Who the fuck wants to look at you first thing in the mornin'?" Morgan said, extending the middle finger of his right hand.

Henry winked. "Have some pity on my poor spirit, Morgan," he said. Morgan flipped him the middle fingers of both hands.

Kevin chortled and climbed into the Camaro."The kid's got a point, Morgan," Kevin said, starting the engine. He turned on the ra-dio, and a classic rock station blared out a song by Men at Work about a land down under and Vegemite sandwiches. "What the fuck's Vegemite?" Kevin said, scratching his chin.

Morgan pulled off his frayed blue scally cap and scratched at the top of his thinning head of red hair. "I think I read somewhere it's a vegetable-like thing they got down in Australia. Like if it had a few more ingredients, minerals or some shit, it would be a full-fledged vegetable, but it don't so it's artificial," he said.

Kevin put both hands on his cheeks and pushed back towards his ears until he looked oriental. "You read that? Jesus, don't make sense. No wonder they're at the bottom of the world makin' sandwiches outta that shit."

A blue Dodge Spirit cruised slowly down I Street, pulled in behind Kevin Curran, and double-parked next to a Chevy SUV. On the same side of the street, opposite the SUV, a second-floor window snapped open and a woman stuck her head out. "Hey, you in the blue car, you gonna be long? You're blockin' me in." she said.

"Long? Sweetheart, how 'bout the rest of my life?" Danny said, twirling his key ring on his index finger as he got out.

Kevin stuck his arm out the window of the Camaro and waved. "Danny boy, your ears must be burnin'," he said.

Danny pulled down on his right earlobe as he approached. "Red hot, Kev, red hot," he said. The two men shook hands.

"Take a ride," Kevin said.

"Where's your better half?" Danny said, looking into the car.

"Just get in the car," Kevin said.

Danny got in. "Jackie called me two days ago; I was there, talked with him, no problem, anything up?" he said.

Kevin smiled and took a left on Seventh Street. He waved out the window to a pretty blond teenager in a soccer uniform standing near the corner. "That's Artie Fano's sister, Meghan. Man, she's somethin' else. I remember her standin' on the corner askin' me for blow pops, now I want her to blow me. Funny, huh?" Kevin said.

At the corner of L and Seventh Streets a group of young men waved, and Kevin nodded back before turning right. As he drove he checked both sides of the street. "Two things. One, how are you at grabbin' cars?" he said.

"No problem," Danny King said.

"We want you to grab them, no one else. We don't want anyone not involved, involved, got it?"

"I can handle it. What else, what's the other thing?"

"We don't need heat from any outside activities you might be currently involved in. We don't want you doin' nothin' for the next few weeks, understand? We don't need something you may be involved in bringin' heat on us. Need dough to tide you over, let me know. Uncle could be on you or the locals. That would put the tail on us. This ain't rocket science, we already got problems," Kevin said.

Danny nodded. "Ya, I know how Jack got strong feelings about stuff like that," he said.

"Jack's real touchy after that shitbag Billy LaGrasse helped send him to Lewisburg, PA for three years," Kevin said. They stopped at the lights in front of the L Street Bathhouse and watched as two older men with gym bags came out the front door.

"You work out today?" Kevin said.

"I'm going to run later, then come down here to the "L" for a steam. I heard about this Billy LaGrasse thing. What happened?"

The light changed and Kevin turned left onto the boulevard. "Billy LaGrasse was movin' and groovin', whackin' them check-cashing joints over the bridge in Revere, Chelsea. Now, for the most part, LaGrasse had his shit together, good with a gun and more than a little common sense, but for some reason, as sometimes city guys do, once he crossed that bridge over the Mystic River he acted like he was in another country, had this force field around him no cop could see through. But he was wrong," Kevin said.

"Now at the same time my brother Jack had this hijacking thing going. He had this guy in Polaroid, over in Cambridge; film's a hot item, easy to get rid of, tippin' him off to loads and truck routes. Jack would be waitin' for them with a master key at the truck stops down Connecticut and Rhode Island way; when they stopped for coffee, bang, he'd nail them.

"One night Jack needed a driver for a run. His regular guy had taken a pinch for somethin' and had to go on the lam. Now Jackie knew LaGrasse from when they were kids growing up down the Old Colony projects. Jack was an up-and-comer then, just gettin' his feet wet. LaGrasse was a few years older, more experienced, a recognized talent. Jack gave him a call, and LaGrasse agreed to step in.

"First thing he asks LaGrasse was You into anything recent I should know about? Any problems, anyone after you for money, anything? LaGrasse answers no to everything. Hey, Jackie's just tryin' to cover his ass, right? Jack puts him to work not knowing the Massachusetts State Police were all over this dude, had a fucking transponder in his car, followed him everywhere. So that night the five of them head off to Rhode Island," Kevin said.

"Five of them?" Danny said.

"Ya, LaGrasse, my brother Jack, and three plainclothes Massachusetts state cops who followed them in an unmarked car to the Rhode Island border, where they were joined by an FBI agent and three Rhode Island state cops. They busted them at the truck stop outside Warwick. That was all she wrote, interstate transportation and hijacking.

"Jack was lucky, he only got five; today they'd smoke him. Thing is, if LaGrasse hadn't been beltin' them check joints, they never would have caught Jack. End of story. You're clean, right?" Kevin said, reaching down his pants. "Here, grab the wheel.

"I got it," Kevin said, producing a small plastic bag. He bit off the knot and grinned. "A little afternoon refreshment, but don't tell Jack," he said, handing the bag to Danny. Danny pressed the bag down gently between his legs and rolled up a dollar bill. He sunk the cylinder into the bag, then tapped it against the inside of the bag. He stuck the bill up his nose, inhaled, and fought the gag.

"Holy shit," Danny said, rubbing one watery eye.

"I'm drivin', load me one," Kevin said, as they followed the road around the edge of the Lagoon. He accepted the bill from Danny and snorted the contents. "You see, you see those two muscleheads coming out of the bathhouse? The big one, the bald guy, Pretzie? The guy's in his sixties and still knockin' other guys out in bars. They say he fought Rocky Marciano to a draw or something back in the fifties; the guy's a fucking animal."

Danny King pressed his finger against the side of his nose and inhaled sharply. He swallowed hard before he spoke again. "Fucking drip and a half," he said. "You're right, Pretzie's a freak."

"We'll be takin' you, maybe next week, out to see the play on the armored truck. We'll contact you by Saturday make sure your voice mail's operating," Kevin said.

"It's working. I'll be home most of the weekend, the girl's coming over," Danny said. He pointed to a large, twin-hulled commuter boat racing across the harbor to his right.

"Heading to Logan most likely," Kevin said.

"Wish I was," Danny said. "Might be soon. I'm thinking of giving Susan a ring."

"Naw, come on," Kevin said.

"Ya, she's a good girl. Keep your eyes open for a diamond, I want somethin' nice," Danny said.

Kevin stuck his finger into the bag between his legs, then into his mouth. He squinted. "Jesus, fucking jet fuel. Diamonds, you want fucking diamonds? Well, I just so happen to have a friend who's movin' some nice two-, two-and-three-quarter-carat stones. Interested?"

Danny reached for the bag. "Mind?" he said.

"Dig in," Kevin said.

"So, what you got you got now?" Danny said, pulling his finger from the bag and putting it into his mouth. He winced. "Jesus, you ain't shittin' . . . I need it soon, Kev, my cousin Billy from the Point may be lookin' too, engagement thing. Maybe I could middle something to him, you know, if there's enough to go around."

"Plenty, we got plenty, me and my friend. I'll bring a couple of stones over Saturday to check out. You got cash?" Kevin said.

"No problem," Danny said.

"The two-and-three-quarter stones retail around twenty-five large, for you, five grand, maybe a little lower, see what my friend says," Kevin said.

He turned the red Camaro right into a space facing the Lagoon just before the Castle Island parking lot. He shut the engine off and wet his index finger. "Don't worry, Danny, when you're ready to ask the missus, we'll take care of you. Now give me the bag, brother, this view's too nice to waste."

24

WHEN MARY ROSE O'CONNELL FLIPPED the covers off her bed, the smell of her own body revolted her. She sat up, swung her feet to the floor, and glanced at her wrist for the time, then remembered how, the night before, she'd traded her Lady Rolex for a half ounce of bad coke. A newer, sick feeling washed over the waves of nausea already nestled in her stomach. As she got up from the bed, her eyes felt sandblasted and the floor unsteady under her feet. Mary Rose struggled to remember some of what she'd done over the past two days, but as soon as an image appeared she tried to erase it.

She remembered sharing her bed with a guy named Twomey she met down the Playwright, who had a ton of hair on his back but none on his head, and her vagina had a tingling itch to it she was certain she hadn't had two days before.

She shuffled down the hallway to the bathroom and sat down heavily on the toilet. Though it hurt to piss and the deepness of the yellow in the water alarmed her, at least there was no blood. She brushed her teeth for the first time in days and spit pink into the basin.

Mary Rose turned on the hot water and stared at the mirror and waited until the steam came up and clung to her face, softening her caked-on three-day-old makeup. She was startled out of her daze when her brother Seamus knocked sharply on the door. "Mary Rose, a guy, some guy named Kevin is in the living room looking for ya."

Mary Rose's stomach convulsed and she choked on the bile in her throat. "Tell him, tell him I'll be there in a sec," she said, looking at her wrist. "Give a girl a few minutes, okay?" The bathroom door opened, and Seamus, standing at doorknob height, peeked around it. Touched by his innocence, she stroked his cheek. "G'wan, go tell him," she said, watching him scurry off.

She dried her face and hurried up the hall to the bedroom. On her way she called down to the living room. "Be there in a minute, Kev."

She closed and locked the bedroom door and removed an orange-and-gold jewelry box from her dresser. She sat on her bed with the box in her lap and opened it. A plastic ballerina spun in front of a tiny mirror to the love theme from *Romeo and Juliet*.

Mary Rose dumped the contents of the box onto the bed, and pieces of costume jewelry clattered to the floor as she pulled the velvet bottom out of the box. She tossed it aside and from the compartment beneath scooped out a small wad of flattened bills. She hurried down the hallway, counting them as she went.

"Hi, Kev, how's tricks?" she said, entering the living room.

Kevin Curran leaned with his right shoulder against the front door. He ignored her and continued to read the back of a CD he held. "Enya, beautiful thing," he said, tossing the CD onto a chair.

Mary Rose wondered if he meant the woman or her music but didn't ask. She held out her hand with the money. "Got some of what I owe you here, Kev. I got lots out on the street. I'm gonna stop cuffing these bums, but my regulars, my bread and butter crew, I gotta cut them some slack, you know."

Kevin glared at her. "Slack, you're talkin' slack? You're the one with the fucking slack," he said.

There was a knock on the door and Seamus came running. "I'll get it," he said. Mary Rose grabbed the back of his shirt as he passed.

"Seamus, get to your room. I'll be in to see you when my friends are gone," she said.

Kevin opened the door, and when Wacko Curran entered the

room and kicked a Barney the Dinosaur doll out of the way, Mary Rose's stomach convulsed for the fourth time that morning. She fought the urge to run, felt foolish, said, "You guys are up early," and instantly regretted it.

Wacko looked at Kevin. "It's one o'clock in the afternoon. Where's our fucking money?" Wacko said.

With her left hand Mary Rose pulled back on the side of her nightdress, like she was going to curtsy, then stepped forward, extending her right hand with the flattened bills. "I got five hundred here, Jack, it's not much but I —"

"You owe us twenty-five hundred cokehead, where's the other two grand?" Wacko said.

Mary Rose balled her fists and pulled both hands to her breasts. "I was tellin' Kevin, Jack, I was tellin' him I got so much out on the cuff. These customers of mine, these fucks are giving me the runaround. Maybe you could —"

"We don't run after cokeheads for nickels, that's your job and our nickels. You better get your dusty butt down to Jones, lady, buy yourself a pair of track shoes, you're gonna need 'em," Wacko said.

Kevin smirked. "You're losin' it, girlie," he said.

"Clean yourself up and get after these bums. You don't owe them a thing, you owe us, remember that," Wacko said.

Mary Rose's eyes filled up. "But it's people like Billy Wallace and Kelly O'Neil, there's seven hundred between them and —"

"I didn't tell you to cuff. You made a real blond move dealin' with those morons. You fucked up, now make good," Wacko said. He stepped through the door into the hallway and turned. "Grow the fuck up and stop being your own best customer."

Mary Rose looked at Kevin. She took a step towards him and lifted her arms. "Kevin, I —"

Kevin backed through the door grinning. He held out his arms, palms facing her. "Whoa, Mary Rose, you smell like ass. Hit the shower girl, that's a good way to start the day," he said. He pulled the door towards him as he backed away, then poked his head back in. "And a good way to end it is to get us our dough." He winked and closed the door.

▪   ▪   ▪

Outside Kevin climbed into the passenger seat of the blue Mercury Marquis. Wacko started the car, looked over his shoulder, and pulled onto Orton Marotta Way. At D Street he took a right.

"Know what I'm thinkin'?" Wacko said. I'm thinkin' our girl's gone bad. Christ, look at her, she's a fucking mess blown everything up her nose."

"Can we write it off?" Kevin said. "You're the one who says you can't get blood out of a rock. We don't want to scare the bitch, have her run to the cops."

Wacko pulled the car sharply to the right, checked the side-view mirror, banged a U-turn, and stopped in front of the D Street Deli. He threw the car in park and shut the engine off. "If we have to, Kevin, we'll cut her some slack, but not just yet. We gotta get more than five hundred bucks from her. I'm not Father fucking Flanagan, but you're right, I don't want to spook her." He nodded in the deli's direction. "Go in the store, see if Walter's there," Wacko said.

Kevin checked his watch. "It's after one, he's there, he's always in his office after one o'clock," he said, getting out of the car and entering the store.

Wacko watched his brother through the glass of the large front window as he talked to a man behind the counter. The man nodded and pointed towards the back of the store. Kevin followed the direction of his finger. The counterman approached the front window, waved to Wacko, then threw his thumb over his shoulder and nodded. Wacko nodded back, then leaned his head against the headrest and closed his eyes.

Behind the Marquis, Mike 'The Winger' Finnerty braked his rickety, three-speed Raleigh bike to a stop, his front tire coming to rest against the Mercury's rear bumper. Wacko watched Mike the Winger in the rearview mirror as he dismounted and approached the driver's side window. Wacko was well aware, as he hit the down button, that Mike Finnerty had the intellect of a ten-year-old trapped in an adult's body. He was also aware of Mike's penchant for buying music CD's, playing them once, then "winging" them into the vast, blue canopy overhead like a demented paperboy as he sprinted, on his ramshackle bike, along Southie's busy thoroughfares.

"What's up, Mike?" Wacko said, over the edge of the glass. Mike the Winger looked over his shoulder towards Old Colony Avenue. He pulled a pack of Bazooka bubble gum from a pocket and offered it to Wacko.

"No thanks, Mike, pulls out my fillings," Wacko said.

Mike the Winger unwrapped the gum and popped it into his mouth.

"Mine too," he said. He chewed with a huge openmouthed grin as he read the funnies. "That Bazooka Joe's a funny guy. Ever notice, Jack, I got a haircut like him?"

"I was just about to comment on it," Wacko said. "So, what's up, Mike?" Mike the Winger stuck his hands in his pockets and looked back towards Old Colony Ave. again.

"You're stopped out here, Jack," he said.

"So?"

"I hate to tell you, but ya gotta pay for parkin' in the city," Mike the Winger said.

"I thought I paid you last week, outside Brigham's, for parkin', even bought you an ice cream cone," Wacko said.

Mike the Winger shifted uneasily. "That's true, Jack, but last week run out, we got new circumstances here," he said. He scraped the bottom of his sneakers on the street like he was trying to rid them of dog shit.

"What I give you last week?" Wacko said.

"You gave me one dollar even on Monday and one dollar even in front of Brigham's Thursday, one dollar even you gave me. Ya know, I'd like to give you a break, Jackie, but taxes don't cover the cost of tires these days," Mike the Winger said.

"So, what I owe ya?" Wacko said, reaching into his pocket.

Mike the Winger stopped scraping and stared at his feet. He pulled an old sock from his left pocket. "Do your windshield?"

"Pass," Wacko said, handing him a five. "There's five there, not one, Mike, we're even for the rest of the week, okay?"

Mike the Winger smiled as he carefully wrapped the dirty sock around the folded five-dollar bill and returned it to his left pocket.

"Now get outta here," Wacko said.

Mike the Winger saluted and shuffled back to his bike and got on. He pulled up to the driver's side window.

"Hey, Jack, this mean it's five dollars even from now on?"

"I want to meet the people who say you're crazy," Wacko said, hitting the up button for the window.

25

WALTER "FEENZO" FEENEY SAT behind his desk and listened to a CD of Johnny Mathis's "Chances Are" bubble from the four Bose speakers he had recently installed in the room. He closed his eyes, intertwined his stubby fingers on top of his bulging stomach, and leaned back into his expensive leather chair until it creaked. The summer before Feenzo had seen Mathis at the South Shore Music Circus, and well, the guy still had it; fag or no fag, he could sing.

Feenzo Feeney owned the D Street Deli. Somewhere behind the wall to his right the compressor for the beer cooler came on. It contained twelve kinds of domestic and imported beer, and that made Feenzo smile because beer trucks arrived twice a week to fill that cooler. The small variety was a veritable gold mine selling beer, wine, and a full array of overpriced canned goods, junk food, and a smattering of deli products primarily to the cash-strapped residents of the huge low-income housing project across the street.

A buzzer on his desk sounded twice, and Feenzo opened his eyes. He had security cameras in the store as well as in the corridor leading to the office located in the back of the building. A movement on the small black-and-white video monitor on the wall to the right of his office door caught his eye, and Feenzo shifted uncomfortably in his seat and looked at his watch. Kevin Curran had just entered the corridor outside his door. Feenzo couldn't pretend he wasn't there, it was after one, almost half past the hour, and like it or not he was opened for business, not store business but the business of being the biggest fence in South Boston.

Ten feet from the office door Kevin stopped, stared directly at the camera, and began to do jumping jacks. Twenty seconds into the exercise he stopped and began to shadowbox. He was midway into his third left jab, uppercut, hook combination when Feenzo hit the release button under his desk for the door. Only when the lock buzzed and the door clicked open did Kevin stop. He bowed for the camera, then ran his fingers through his hair and tucked in his shirt. He pretended to adjust the knot of an invisible tie around his neck before he stepped through the door.

"Hi, Walter," Kevin said with a grin and a wave like he was polishing a large window with a cloth.

"Don't you ever stop?" Feenzo said. He got up and extended his right hand. Kevin reached out to shake, then snapped his hand back, the right thumb extended over his shoulder. Walter's hand remained extended. The game over, Kevin grabbed it and shook it firmly.

"Ever the nut, huh, Kev? Where's your saner half?" Feenzo said, sitting back in the chair.

"Out front in the car, probably being harassed by that lunatic who hangs around your store," Kevin said.

Kevin approached the wall to Feenzo's right. It was covered by a collection of framed, autographed photos of local politicians and sports figures. He ran his finger along the side of one with a cheap, black plastic frame. "Tommy Collins," Kevin said. "Quickest knockout in Boston Garden history, correct?"

Feenzo nodded. "The guy's in his sixties and still in shape. He's tight with my older brother, Danny," Feenzo said. "That night in the Garden, first round, the other guy puts his hands out to touch gloves, and Tommy comes over the top with this vicious right hand. Bing, on the button the other guy goes down, never saw it comin'. Seven seconds into it it's over," Feenzo said.

"You're talkin' kind of like a sucker shot?" Kevin Curran said, staring at the photo.

Feenzo shook his head. "Naw, no such thing in the ring, Kevin. After the ref gives you instructions, there are no rules that say you gotta touch gloves. Anyways, like a lot around here, Tommy was never big on rules."

Kevin hopped away from the wall and threw a brief flurry ending in a left uppercut. "I can appreciate that," he said. "So, you got what we ordered, we all set?"

"Things are fallin' into place. You said you got your own body armor, good stuff with the trauma plates?" Feenzo said.

"We got 'em," Kevin said.

"Gloves? You going with Kevlar gloves and headgear?" Feenzo said.

"Pass," Kevin said, taking two Snickers bars out of his pocket and tossing one to Feenzo. "I don't want it like we're goin' snowmobilin', Walter, we gotta be able to move."

"Hey, Kevin, you should rethink it, they got real light stuff nowadays with plenty of stoppin' power. I can get it. It's expensive, but I can get it. You should put some thought into what you need. You gotta think about what you're doing," Feenzo said.

Kevin cracked a half smile and looked down at the floor for a few seconds before firing his half-eaten candy bar into one of the Bose speakers. Chocolate remnants clung to the black matte cover. He put both hands on the desk and leaned close to Feenzo's face. "You tellin' me, us, my brother and I, that we don't plan our scores like we're some kind of fucking cowboys, you fat bastard? Here, give me my fucking candy," Kevin said, diving across the desk and tearing the half-eaten candy bar from Feenzo's terrified grasp. Kevin pushed away from the desk and fastballed it into the other man's chest.

Feenzo Feeney groaned and covered his face with the backs of his hands. "Kevin, please, hey, relax I —" he said.

"Relax? You fucking beach ball, you tellin' me to relax; who the fuck are you? You sit here every day in your office, everything, everyone comes to you. You take no risks, never taken anything down yourself. Other guys do the hard work, plan the scores, bang them out, and what do you do, you fucking shadow, fucking vampire? You say, ya, I'm the man, I'll take care of you, give you a fifth of the retail of what you stole. Who the fuck are you pay pennies on dollars?" Kevin said.

"I'm a fence, Kevin, that's what I do, always give a fair price," Feenzo whimpered.

"Fair? I'll tell you fair, Walter, fair is me and Jack allowin' you to live, fair is not takin' a pair of needle-nose pliers to those little piggy ears of yours right now and makin' you open the fucking floor safe under your desk."

Feenzo blanched. "I'm always fair with you guys, always get you what you want, did it this time too, didn't I? Think it's easy? Just talkin' to some of the mutts I had to to get the special stuff you need puts me in jeopardy. One of them's a rat, bang, I'm gone ten years, maybe more, but that's my job. My position here is it's worth the risk to help good guys out and maybe make enough for the rent," Feenzo said.

Kevin reached into his back pocket and pulled out a thick envelope folded in half. "Here's the rent for this month, Feenzo, now what you got for me?" he said.

Like an accordion, Feenzo Feeney unfolded in the chair and reached for the envelope. He grasped it daintily between his right index finger and thumb, and pulled it towards him. "Just what you ordered, one H & K ninety-one rifle, four thirty-round clips for it, one hundred and twenty rounds of armor-piercing three-oh-eight ammo, hard stuff to get."

"Can the sales pitch. What else?" Kevin said.

"Four Mossberg riot pumps, four boxes double-o buck, four boxes deer slugs. Two military-issue smoke bombs and, these are as tough to find as eyeglasses on a dog, two fragmentation grenades."

"How much?" Kevin said.

Feenzo Feeney stretched his arms towards the ceiling and shrugged. "Same price me and Jack agreed on. The H & K plus clips, I'm throwin' in the clips, eighteen hundred, a steal. The Mossbergs are brand-new stolen outta Ohio, three hundred a piece, ammo's free. The frag grenades, on this I'm killin' myself, fucking suicide, two hundred each, the smokes are free. You guys always get the best deal, always," Feenzo said.

"My original quote to your brother was three thousand, it was an estimate. You got three here?" Feenzo Feeney held the envelope to his nose and sniffed. "Smells like three," he said, smiling.

"There's twenty-five hundred there," Kevin said.

Feenzo's smile sunk into his jowls like bacon fat into a paper towel.

"I think maybe you owe us some change," Kevin said.

Feenzo groaned and pulled down hard on his right earlobe. "Kevin, I told Jackie three thousand, with the freebies. I figure I got thirty-four hundred worth of equipment here. I'm giving it away, only chargin' *you* twenty-eight. I think maybe . . ."

"I think maybe you didn't listen to what I . . . we just talked about, Walter," Kevin said. He reached into the pocket of his windbreaker and pulled out another Snickers bar.

"Okay, okay, you're right," Feenzo said. His face grew redder. "I'll throw in the frag grenades too; you're killin' me, kid. Me throwin' them in brings us down to twenty-four hundred. I'll tell you something, kid; you oughta sell cars, you'd make a million."

Feenzo opened the manila envelope. "You said there's twenty-five here, Kev?" He reached in and pulled out a one-hundred-dollar bill. He half-stood and offered the bill to Kevin. "Like McDonald's, you get change," Feenzo said. Kevin took the money and shoved it in his pocket.

"At McDonald's we don't tip," Kevin said. "We're takin' the grenades off the twenty-five hundred I gave you, that leaves two thousand your end."

"Jesus, Kevin, the grenades were two hundred a piece, that leaves me with twenty-one hundred, twenty one," Feenzo said, wiping his mouth with a pocket handkerchief.

Kevin held out his hand. "Give me my fucking change. I flunked math before I dropped out of school."

Feenzo leaned back in his chair and briefly stared to his right at the wall of photographs before picking up the remote device off his desk and pointing it at his Aiwa stereo system. Johnny Mathis sang "Misty." "Okay, two thousand, I'm lousy at math too," he said. He handed Kevin four more bills from the envelope.

Kevin tossed him the Snickers bar. "Maybe you should think about a tutor," he said. He opened the door. "We'll give you a call for the pickup."

"Got ya, see you soon," Feenzo said.

Kevin pulled the door closed behind him.

Walter "Feenzo" Feeney tore the top off the Snickers bar with his teeth and spit the wrapper on the floor. He watched the monitor as Kevin walked through the second door. He hit a button on his desk, and the monitor flashed and another scene of Kevin exiting the store appeared.

"Son of a bitch," Feenzo said. He picked up a phone, punched a number and angrily chewed. "Let me speak to Marty Fallon. Marty? How're you doin'? Not so good, I got a problem with a couple of locals. Brothers? Ya, you got it. They certainly are busy little bees. I'd like to see you, tell you just how busy. Mul's? Three o'clock, I'll be there. Thanks, Marty, you're a pal."

26

OUT IN FRONT OF THE D STREET DELI, Kevin Curran gave the roof of the blue Mercury Marquis a tap before opening the door and jumping in. "Home, James," he said slapping the dash.

Wacko glanced at him before turning the ignition key. "How'd it go?" Wacko said. He pulled out and headed east towards the lights on West Broadway.

Kevin laughed out loud. "Did just what you told me, Jack, worked like a fucking charm. I bugged out on cue and poor Walter almost swallowed his tongue," Kevin said.

"Walter's never seen you bug, Kevin, it's good for him, for other people to see it instead of them just thinkin' you're some kind of clown holdin' on to my shirt. People gotta know you got your own shirt," Wacko said. He turned right at the lights.

"Shirt?" Kevin said. "I want a complete fucking wardrobe. Ya know, I almost thought ol' Feenzo wasn't going to bite. He'd never dare say anything, even this much, out of line to you," Kevin said, holding his right thumb and index finger a half inch apart. "So I figured he wouldn't hold back with me either, and he didn't. Soon as he gave me an opening I bulldogged him."

"What he say?" Wacko said.

"He said that we should put more thought into our scores," Kevin said.

Wacko yanked back on the steering wheel. "He said that? That tub of shit tellin' us what to do?"

Kevin slapped the dash again. "Won't be doin' that again, Jack. I jumped so far down his throat his ball-bag wrapped around my Nikes. I felt like I was you, only better lookin'," Kevin said.

"He told me three grand last week. What it cost us?" Wacko said.

"Two grand," Kevin said.

"You're learnin. He get everything we need?" Wacko said.

"Sounds like it. He did mention something about Kevlar gloves and hats, but I don't know about that stuff." Kevin winked at his brother and hooked his thumbs into his shirt. "Hell, I'm just gettin' used to having my own shirt.

"It was classic, Jack. Soon as he got fresh I nailed him with a Snickers bar, hit him square in the chest."

Wacko laughed and high-fived his brother. "Nice touch, beatin' Feenzo with food is like whackin' a vampire in the chops with a neck," Wacko said. "When you tell him we'd make the pickup?"

"I didn't. I said we'd call him, figure we could set up a meet somewhere, maybe in the parkin' lot down the South Shore Plaza. People openin' their trunks all over the place down there, no one will notice a few more," Kevin said. He scratched at his crotch, straightened his legs, and pushed back into the seat. He reached down his pants and pulled out a small plastic bag, and examined it closely. He grasped the knot, shook it, and held it up in the sunlight above the dash.

"Put that fucking thing down," Wacko said, slapping Kevin on the back of the head.

"Hey, what the fuck," Kevin said, rubbing his head with the bag hand.

"Get it out of the window, you moron," Wacko said, pulling over to the right down from Store 24. "You're wavin' it around like it's pancake mix."

Kevin continued to scratch.

"I wasn't waving it, Jack, just checkin' for leaks. My balls are itchy," Kevin said, pulling at his crotch.

"Maybe you got crabs," Wacko said.

Kevin ignored the remark and moved the bag around the palm of his left hand with his finger. "Son-of-a-bitch, it does have a tear, I knew it," he said. He wetted his index finger, touched the bag, then reinserted it into his mouth. "Great stuff, shame to waste it on my balls," Kevin said.

"Ain't the first time it happened," Wacko said.

Kevin opened the tear further and poured out a small pile onto the back of his left hand near the index finger. He dropped his head and pushed his nose into the pile.

"Jesus Christ," Wacko said, looking around.

"You remember, huh? That was a low point in my life, a gutter ball. I never did give you the details, did I?" Kevin said, wiping his nose in the mirror.

"I had a quarter ounce down my budge that night, and I hooked up with Danny O'Leary at Kneeso's old place, On Broadway, what a great joint that was. Remember he booked the Platters, imagine in South Boston the Platters, unbelievable, Jack. No one could figure how Kneeso booked them, but it turned out he didn't, the fuck, not one of them was real. Hell, they were boneheads and all, wore blue tuxes, could dance except one who tore the ass out his pants doin' a split," Kevin said.

"They could sing too or lip-synch; looking back I'm not sure which, but it was a great show. I remember that they were out there, onstage, doing one of their hits, "Only You," everyone's groovin', the whole joint's into it, and then it happened."

"What happened?" Wacko said.

"They're at the part 'You're my dream come true, my one and only —' Crack. This broad's head comes flyin' past me," Kevin said.

"Just her head?" Wacko said.

"Well, no, her body was there too, but I'm all jekylled up, I mean I'm in the fucking corner, and all I see is this head and Danny O'Leary's standin' next to me screamin'. The broad's on the floor, one foot's twitchin', the other's cocked the wrong way, broken," Kevin said.

"Broken how?" Wacko said.

Kevin shrugged. "Beats me, I figure she tried to get fancy when she fell. So she's on the floor, and Danny's standin' there screamin at her, 'Don't want to dance, don't have to dance.' Next thing you know this guy comes up and nails Danny one in the temple, drops him. Now Danny's on the floor next to the broad; except for her leg, they look like they're sleepin'. Then punches start flying like it's free chicken wing night down the Ocean Kai."

"This broad, she had friends, where from?" Wacko said.

"Brockton, there were four guys and this broad, spade lover come to see the Platters like they don't got enough of their own Platters running around down there in Brockton. Next thing you know I'm hit, I'm down, get up, hit a few guys get nailed again. The co come. We all end up in the meat wagon headin' to District Six. Th book us, take our shoelaces and belts, and throw me and Danny the same cell.

"Now my balls are burnin'. The coke bag must have got tor the fight. It feels as though fire ants are doing a line dance on my I drop my drawers, and rocks of coke are fallin' out of my sk

onto the floor. I'm all white down there, 'cept my balls are red. I'm splashin' water out of the fucking toilet onto my balls and wonderin' what the hell they put into this shit to make it burn like that," Kevin said.

"Hot dogs," Wacko said.

"Hot dogs? What the fuck you mean hot dogs?" Kevin said.

"It's the same thing with hot dogs. Everyone loves 'em but if they knew the kind of shit they put in 'em — you know, the eyes, assholes, and tails — no one would eat 'em," Wacko said.

"I guess," Kevin said. "So, there I am, my balls are glowin' like briquettes, and Danny's 'helping' me by picking the rocks up off the floor and eatin' them. I say, 'Hey, you fucking degenerate, you're eating dick coke, that shit's been all over my balls.' He stops for a second, thinks it over, then tells me to stop moving around cause I'm scattering the rocks. The guy's wired. He picks up another rock, looks at my balls, then rubs it on his shirt like he's polishing a ladybug, then pops it in his mouth."

"He sanitized it?" Wacko said.

"More like insane-o-tized it," Kevin said.

"You eat any?" Wacko said.

"Of course I did, I mean the stuff was on my balls. Would have thought twice if it was on Danny's," Kevin said.

"We sat there geeked out for the next three hours waiting for Scribby, the bondsman, to come bail us out, but to tell you the truth Danny was in no hurry. He's sittin' in the corner, grinnin', pickin' leftovers out of my skivvies, the man has no shame. Cop comes by to check on us, and Danny's got the fucking BVD's in his mouth sucking on a spot, his eyes buggin' out like a fucking hoot owl's. The cop's jaw almost hit the floor. I was more than embarrassed."

Wacko tapped Kevin's knee. "Put the leaky bag back in your budge, our man Mark Costa just walked out of Store 24, and he's headed this way." Mark waved.

"He still talkin' that shit about avengin' his brother?" Wacko said, smiling and waving back.

"Heard nothing since that night except that he's been drinkin' a lot. You say anything to Marty about this?" Kevin said.

Wacko shook his head. "Naw, no need to, Mark's a good kid, he was just reactin' to something he had no control over. Think how you'd be, Kevin, that was me," Wacko said.

"They'd be dog meat, Jack, I wouldn't stop. That's why I'm thinkin' maybe Mark won't either, he's capable."

Mark Costa approached from the sidewalk side. Kevin lowered the window. "How're we doin', Mark?"

Mark leaned on the roof, shook Kevin's hand, nodded towards Store 24. "Someone stuck up the place last night," he said. Kevin could smell alcohol on his breath. "They got shit; these days you get nothin' all them stores got drop safes. I hear they got forty-seven dollars and a box of fucking Slim Jims, and people tell me I'm crazy workin' a regular job?"

"I wouldn't say you're crazy," Wacko said.

Mark Costa lowered his head. "My brother used to think I was a sucker, a sap going to work every day. I still go to work every day and Snoopy, well . . ."

"Hey, God bless him," Kevin said. "How's your mum holdin' up? Saw her at O'Brien's Funeral Home that night, and to tell you the truth, I was scared for you, Mark, she took it hard."

"I hate wakes," Mark said. "They're more painful than useful; some people cryin', others standin' around smokin' and jokin'. Weird. I almost skipped it but figured Snoopy would be waiting to give me a ration of shit if I did. Poor Snoop, it was so unnecessary, Jack." He stared into Wacko's eyes like he was trying to detect something, anything.

Wacko spoke first. "Anything I can do, Mark, Snoopy was a good man. He had a few problems but who doesn't?"

Mark looked up and down the street, then squatted his head parallel to Kevin's shoulder. "There is something, Jack, I need a piece."

Wacko leaned closer. "What for, you don't mind me asking?" he said. Kevin pushed back into the seat, and Wacko leaned even closer.

"Got a problem with someone at work, someone who carries got a permit," Mark said.

"You still down South Station?" Wacko said.

Mark stood up and looked up and down the street, then squatted down again. "Still there, will be for the next nine years before I can pull the pin for the pension. This guy, the one at work, makes me nervous, I need protection," Mark said.

"Let's get something straight, Mark, we don't deal in guns." A white Lincoln Continental Town Car went by and honked its horn. Wacko glanced at it and made a disgusted face. "Anyways . . . as I was sayin', we don't deal in guns, but I know someone who might be able to help if you tell him I sent you," Wacko said.

Wacko centered himself behind the wheel. "Kevin, give him Leppy Mullins number, his coke fiend customers are always bringin' him pieces to trade for the yak." Kevin pulled a roll of paper towels from beneath the seat. He tore off a piece, scribbled a number, and handed it to Mark Costa.

"Thanks, Jack, Kev," Mark said, folding the paper and putting it in his wallet.

"Anything I can do for you guys, let me know, okay?" He shook the hands of both men. "I know I don't have to say this, but this is between us, okay. Guns and a federal job don't mix, thanks again," Mark said. He headed back towards Store 24. Kevin put the window up and Wacko started the car. He looked over his shoulder before pulling out into traffic.

"There is something you can do, Mark. When you find your brother's killer do it right the first time," Wacko said.

Kevin gave Mark Costa a wave as they passed. "So, you don't think his problem's at the post office? I've read those postal workers are bugs; they snap, kill people all the time," he said.

"I think Mark's got a special delivery for someone we know and wants to deliver it personally. He's got good reason to take care of that guy and we got good reason to help him, indirectly of course," Wacko said.

His eyes suddenly hardened, and he chopped the steering wheel. "Hey, that Beezo parked in front of the Bayview? The prick can afford to buy clothes but not give us what he owes us? Get me my hammer," Wacko said, pulling over in front of the white Lincoln Town Car parked in front of the Bayview Men's Shop. He threw the car into park, hit the trunk release button, and Kevin jumped out.

"I feel like going shoppin'," Wacko said.

27

KEVIN CURRAN REACHED in the trunk into a dark green gym bag next to the spare tire, pulled out a one-pound ball-peen hammer, and handed it to Wacko. Grasping the hammer, Wacko flipped open his jacket, exposing the satin lining and the heavy canvas loop that was sewn in directly below the left armpit. He dropped the handle through the loop and closed the jacket. It was then he noticed the old woman shuffling up the sidewalk towards him.

She said, "Jackie Curran, doing some shopping?"

Wacko's sphincter muscle tightened, and he squeezed the hammer against his body before he smiled. "Good day to ya, Mrs. Ramsey, a lovely one isn't it?" he said, waving his right hand in the air while pulling down on the hammer's handle with his left.

The old woman squinted at his behavior, half-pointed at the sky and nodded. "Spring's always been my favorite, fall second," she said.

Wacko turned his head, caught Kevin's eye, then playfully wrapped his arm around his brother's neck. He pulled Kevin close and whispered, "Get your ass into the Bayview, tell Beezo he ain't goin' nowhere until we talk." Then he pushed him towards the door of the Bayview Men's Shop.

"And where's your beautiful daughter, Elaine, today?" Wacko said, watching his brother enter the store. As Mrs. Ramsey went on about how this particular stretch of sidewalk always made her sneeze, Wacko searched his memory for a back door to the Bayview but convinced himself there was none.

"She can tell you herself, she's right behind me in Radio Shack buying batteries for her phone. Jackie, did I see you put a hammer in your jacket?" Mrs. Ramsey said, eyeing the coat.

A rush of blood filled Wacko's cheeks, and his neck grew hot. He felt angry, then ridiculous and pulled the jacket tighter to his body. "Actually it's a brace," he said.

Mrs. Ramsey's eyes filled with concern. She touched his arm. "And what did you do to yourself now, dear?"

Wacko stepped back. "Softball, took a fast pitch in the elbow, Sunday. That thing you saw prevents me from bendin' it. It works," he said, stiffly swinging his left arm.

"What ever happened to good old-fashioned slings?" Mrs. Ramsey said.

"Jackie Curran entertaining Momma, you sweet thing?" Elaine Ramsey said, coming up the sidewalk swinging a tiny, black plastic bag in her hand. Her strawberry blond curls bubbled from beneath her black velvet beret.

Wacko looked relieved. "Hey, pal, your mum and I —"

Elaine put her arms out to embrace him, but Wacko retreated a few steps and held out his right hand palm facing toward her. "Whoa, Elaine," he said.

"Elaine, don't hug him, dear, you'll hurt him," Mrs. Ramsey said. Elaine looked surprised and dropped her arms. A gust of wind carried her hair sideways before it rested again on the shoulders of her green suede jacket.

With his right hand Wacko grasped Elaine's left, stiffly bent and kissed it. "Softball," he said.

"I didn't know you played," Elaine said, eyeing him curiously.

"He won't much after this," Mrs. Ramsey said.

Beezo Houlihan poked his head and shoulders through the door of the Bayview Men's Shop. "Hey, Jack, when you get a minute," Beezo said. Kevin bumped him with his shoulder as he walked past him out of the store into the sunlight.

"All right, we'll let you boys talk. Hi Kevin," Elaine said, looping her arm through her mother's. "Momma and I are going to check out some shoes at Bertha Cool's, that new place up Little Broadway." Elaine held her little finger and thumb to her mouth and ear. "I'll call you," she said.

"Good luck, ladies," Wacko said, waving to the departing women. Beezo walked outside. "And your luck's run out, motherfucka," Wacko hissed, opening his jacket. Beezo shoved his arms out like he was pushing open a door and took a step back.

Wacko said, "What's wrong with you, I got to beat you with a fucking instrument to get my money?"

"Look, I seen you guys, didn't avoid ya, I honked, didn't I?" Beezo said.

"Pretty tough to sneak by in a white Conty Town Car," Kevin said.

"Look, you was talkin', not my business to interrupt, a respect thing, Jack, that's all," Beezo said.

"How much you got?" Wacko said.

"Two grand," Beezo said, scratching his cheek with his left hand.

"How much?"

"Three, I meant three," Beezo said, using his right hand on the opposite cheek.

"You owe us another grand," Wacko said.

"I owe Marty too," Beezo said, staring at his shoes.

"Not our problem," Kevin said. "Keep your fat ass away from Suffolk Downs and maybe you'll make the car payments."

Beezo got a look on his face like someone told him his sister slept with lepers. "Hey, I own that car outright," Beezo said.

"Good, then next week we get the pink slip," Wacko said.

"Hey, Jack, give me a break, that car's worth more than a fucking grand," Beezo said. He looked at Kevin, who looked away. "Jesus, all right, you guys, you'll get the grand next week," Beezo said, opening the trunk of his car.

"Eleven hundred," Kevin said. Beezo closed his eyes then pulled a manila envelope out from beneath some old *Boston Heralds*. He turned, and Kevin snapped it out of his hand.

"C'mon, there's four grand there," Beezo whined. "I need something for Marty, he's expectin' somethin' today."

Kevin quickly counted out thirty one hundred dollar bills and handed them to his brother. "Looks like there's another grand here, Jack, want it?" Kevin said.

Wacko folded the wad and stuffed it into his jacket pocket. "Naw, Marty's us, let him take care of Marty too," Wacko said.

Kevin threw the envelope into the trunk, then walked around and opened the driver's side door and scanned the instrument cluster. "Your cruise control work?" he said.

"Everything works. You'll get your dough next week, don't worry," Beezo said angrily.

Kevin singed him with his eyes. "Worried, you think we're worried?

Maybe I should show him worried, huh, Jack?" Kevin said, clenching his fists and stepping towards Beezo.

Beezo held up his hands. "Hey, Kevin, please . . ." Beezo said.

"You seen Kenny Bennet around lately?" Wacko said.

Beezo slowly lowered the trunk, then slammed it the last few inches. "He's my brother, of course I seen him, still lives with Ma."

"You guys got the same disease? You're both behind in your payments, but I got somethin' that will work. Seein' he's your half brother, I'll give you a break; next week you only owe us half his principal, that's two hundred and fifty, got it?" Wacko said.

"Kinda like a fine," Kevin said, wrapping his arm around Beezo's sagging shoulders. "Beezo's in the penalty box."

"So, next week you owe us a total of thirteen fifty, that's by Monday, pal, or find yourself a Hyundai, cause the pink slip for this boat's ours," Wacko said.

Kevin and Wacko climbed back into the blue Marquis. "I almost hope the bum don't show, the cruise control in this thing's been fucking up for months," Wacko said, pulling away from the curb. He looked into the rearview. "That bum's still standin' there with his mouth open imaginin' you behind the wheel of his Conty. You get a hold of Janowski, tell him we're meetin' tonight?"

"Ya, he's meeting us in Quincy, across from the Y, seven-fifteen," Kevin said.

"I feel good about bringin' Mike in," Wacko said. "The kid's solid, hungry, got a lot of both. The other guy I don't know, but I'm gonna find out. Tonight we'll give Mike the score but not the location. A little at a time, don't want to overwhelm him. Tomorrow, if he's around, we'll do the same thing with Danny King. Another thing, I'm going to start lookin' closely at that North End score. I think I figured out a way to determine who's in this for real and who ain't. When we learn that, we might need an alternate plan; if we do, we'll be ready to roll," Wacko said.

"Variety's the spice of life," Kevin said. "Ya know, I forgot to ask Beezo how many miles on the Conty."

"Good chance we'll find out next week," Wacko said.

28

"COME IN OR GET OUT, but close the fucking door," Marty Fallon said.

Andre Athanas stepped into the darkened room and closed the door behind him. "You want I should open the blinds?" he said.

Marty picked up the remote control device off his lap and pointed it at the thirty-six-inch Mitsubishi in front of him. He hit the pause button. "What, you want to ruin this?" he said.

Andre looked at the screen. The image of a girl around thirteen being fucked doggy-style by a heavyset, balding man in his early thirties flickered in the darkness. The man had on a pair of boxing shoes and nothing else.

Andre snorted. "Maggot's earned his nickname," Andre said. "He's makin' these kiddie porn films and still fightin'?"

"Fighting?" Marty said. "In the ring he's a tomato can. His real love is starrin' in his own action flicks. I hear ol' Maggot's makin' some dough selling this shit out on the left coast."

"He payin' you the rent he should on it?" Andre said.

"Naw, don't want a dime from that punk," Marty said. "He's a stool pigeon, has been for twenty years, ever since they chased him out of Jamaica Plain. I shake him for some change on these productions of his and he runs screamin' to the feds, who take me down for kiddie porn. They don't take that rat piece of shit down cause he works for the FBI and the DEA, me they'd hang."

"Don't like him or that stuff," Andre said.

"What, you don't like sweet, young pussy?" Marty said. He hit the play button. "The way I see it, it's okay if you pay for it. I always pay for my pussy."

"Look what I did for Rhonda Allen's family. You remember Lisa, her sister. She was what, thirteen, but an old thirteen, you know, project old, this little cunt wasn't still playin' with Barbie dolls. I pulled them out of the projects, gave her mother that nice two-family house up the point, Columbia Road, for chrissakes, all the trimmin's. Their heads were spinnin' and grateful, let me tell you."

"This kid Maggot, what he give 'em? Dope, booze, then he brings them down Broadway to his little gym, takes 'em in that back room, with the two-way mirror, and rapes them. I swear, somewhere there's a trunk with that guy's name on it," Marty said.

Andre scratched his nose. "Ya, I agree. I didn't want to bother you, boss, but Walter Feeney called, he's down Mul's. Says you're supposed to meet him?"

"Oh, Jesus, I forgot. Poor Walter's havin' problems with a couple of our earners," Marty said.

"Jack and Kevin?" Andre said.

"I gotta talk to him, make sure those two maniacs don't slap him around," Marty said.

Andre pulled an envelope from his back pocket. "And Beezo stopped by," he said, handing the envelope to Marty. "Said he had more but Wacko and Kevin grabbed it off him this mornin'."

Marty hit the off button, then hurled the remote at Andre's face. Like he was waving good-bye with both hands, Andre deflected it into the wall, then reached behind him and opened the door.

"You fuck, you useless fuck, go get Beezo and bring him back. He was supposed to have three grand for me today." Marty tore open the envelope. "A grand? He brings me a lousy, fucking grand?" Marty whipped the cash into the air. "Tell me, Andre, who the fuck are the Currans, they running this town?"

Andre shrugged. "Beezo owes everyone, boss, can't keep cash in his pocket more than five minutes. Those guys, I'm sure Wacko and Kevin just got lucky, got to him first. Ain't sayin' it's right he paid them first, boss, but Wacko's got convincin' ways, ya know, you taught him good," Andre said.

Marty smiled and got up. He came at Andre from around the desk. "Great insight, Andre, you know, some days you make a lot of sense." As quick as a mongoose, Marty lunged and grabbed a fistful of Andre's hair with his left hand. "But today's not one of them." Marty's toes gripped the insides of his shoes as he savagely twisted Andre's head. Simultaneously he twisted his hips and launched a boxer's overhand right, his knuckles crashing into Andre's cheek, splitting him as neatly as if he used a knife.

Andre gasped, his knees buckled, and he crumpled into the doorframe, covering his face with both huge hands. "Oh, God, hey . . ." Andre said.

Marty slide-stepped forward, opened his hands, and slammed both of them into Andre's chest. Andre staggered back and almost fell on his ass.

Marty sighed and straightened up, then ran his fingers through his hair. With the back of his left hand he wiped spittle from his chin, examined it, then wiped it on his pants. He checked his knuckles and smirked. "Andre, you may not understand this, but this was good for both of us . . . Me?" He shook his right fist. "I know I still got it. You? See, scars on a man's face give him character. Every time you lecture me, you get some more character, understand? Now, let me see," Marty said.

Andre nodded and removed the blood-soaked wad of crumpled Kleenex he held to his face with his huge left hand. His right eye teared and his left was swelling shut, the gash below it open almost to the bone.

Marty Fallon smirked again. "Good," he said. "Now clean that shit off the floor. I don't want no one slippin' in your blood; then call Mul's and tell Walter I'm on my way. After you drop me at Mul's, drop yourself at Boston Medical and get some stitches for that. Don't worry about pickin' me up, Walter will drive me home."

29

THE FAT MAN SAT behind the wheel of the black, late-model Crown Victoria peering through the windshield over the seawall into Quincy Bay. His enormous frame shuddered as he tugged at the knot in his tie, the color of a dirty brake light, with a greasy right thumb and forefinger. The knot had a distinct sheen to it. "Clam?" the fat man said, offering the box to the man sitting next to him.

The other man declined but used an index finger to push his sunglasses back from the center then leaned forward to check out the fat man's stomach. "You never made it to the gym, huh? I told my guy

who owns the gym down the waterfront about you; he was waitin',"
the other man said.

The fat man wrinkled his nose. "Let him wait. Gyms are disease
factories. You touch a barbell, bing, you get a cold. Run on a treadmill,
you get the clap. Gyms not for me," the fat man said, chewing an
onion ring. "That kid you told me about, Boocasian? Well, I gave it to
the locals and they ran with it. It went good I hear," the fat man said.

The other man smiled. "Ya, I heard they pinched him too, or
should I say he pinched himself, the stupid prick. The dope left no
prints, nada, inside the jeweler's shop, he wore latex gloves, but the
other area, the construction site he came in from, you wouldn't think
a person had so many fingers. Prints everywhere, even on his can of
diet Coke. Heard he's due to cop a plea next month in Suffolk Supe-
rior, lookin' at a four to six up the Hill. Word is his lawyer wants a
Concord sentence, less time behind the walls but they got you on parole forever, but I think the kid will end up in Walpole, Cedar Junction, whatever the fuck they're callin' it nowadays. It will be his third
B and E conviction, he'll be lucky to get a four to six."

The fat man sighed and chewed with his mouth open. "Whatever.
So . . . ," the fat man wiped his mouth with a napkin. "You didn't
come down here for the clams. What's up?"

"I think I got a line on a few of the boyos who are plannin' to
whack an armored car. Interested?" the other man said.

The fat man whistled and dug deep into his box of clams. "Ya
know, with these things, the nearer you get to the bottom the greasier
it gets. The stuff up top settles down. If there's any such thing as killer
clams, the last inch is where you'll find 'em", he said, popping one in
his mouth.

"So, what you think, interested?" the other man said, pulling a
pack of Marlboros from his right jacket pocket. He rapped the pack
on his knee. "These guys are bad dudes. One of my guys comes to me
tellin' how he's middlin' some heavy weapons to them. He's figurin'
they, knowin' them, are using this stuff for one thing only; it's gotta be
an armored car. Pop 'em at the scene, before the score goes down, and
we're talkin' major headlines, your star will rise with this one, fact."

"We talking full automatics?" the fat man said, crumpling the
clam box and sticking it into a greasy, brown paper bag.

"At least one heavy-caliber machine gun, Mossberg pumps, hand-
guns, body armor, and hand grenades," the other man said.

The fat man whistled again and pulled a paper cup with a lid and straw from the dashboard holder. He sucked on the straw, then pulled it from his mouth. "Well, you know I could say you give me the guy who's actually selling this stuff, he's the target."

"But he's my guy," the other man said.

"No matter, all of us at the Justice Department love machine guns and infernal devices, stuff that makes your balls tingle. We get this bum, down the line if you need it, some judge is going to smile real bright on you," the fat man said.

The other man looked out the window and shook his head. He put the cigarettes back in his pocket. "You don't understand. I'm talkin'a million-dollar score here, maybe more. I got this guy who's part of the crew working for me, trying to figure out where and when."

"You forgot if," the fat man said. He sucked the cup of soda dry and made a face. "You ever notice how diet soda never tastes the same from the tap as the bottle? Beer always tastes better from the tap. What's wrong with this shit?" He tossed the empty cup into the backseat.

"I don't drink diet, it all tastes like shit to me," the other man said. "You want me to find out more, is that it?"

The fat man burped and rubbed his stomach."I have to admit your information is usually good, but sometimes it isn't. I think information is like clams, there are two kinds," the fat man said. "You got clam strips and clams with bellies. Clam strips come from giant sea clams, they shred them, they're all meat. You know what you got when you're eating a clam strip. Now you tell me one of your guys, *your* guys, is moving grenades and machine guns, you know this, and I believe this to be true. That's solid meat, a clam strip.

"I go to the bureau with my report. They put the mechanism in action to pull this piece of shit down. I don't care he's your guy. We send someone to him to set up a buy — machine guns, grenades, whatever. You help with the introduction in such a way that when he goes down, and he will, you'll look as though you've been had too, only it will be his ass will be hitting the slammer in Lewisburg and not yours.

"On the other hand, you're talking about a robbery that may occur, but then again, maybe it won't. That's a clam with a belly, could be delicious, but get a bad one, forget about it. See, we're not dealing with one lone gun dealer anymore; we're dealing with four or five maniacs. That means the good guys have to shift resources, focus an enormous amount of energy and manpower on something that may or may not occur. If it doesn't, I eat a bad clam. If that happens, I want you to remember one thing — food poisoning isn't contagious, but in your case it will be. You won't be sunning yourself out on Castle Island if I'm picking corn husks outta my ass in Omaha," the fat man said.

"Okay, okay, I'll find out more," the other man said, pulling back on the door release handle. "They're taking my guy on a run-through soon. I'll get back to you when they do and I know more." He opened the door.

"I'd like that," the fat man said. "By the way, one of your runners, Eddy Dooley, took a pinch last week out in Tucson, Arizona, with ten thousand OxyContins."

The other man grimaced and closed the door. "And?" he said.

"He's back in town, and seems your name came up — a few times. I don't think he likes confined spaces," the fat man said.

"Can't blame him," the other man said. "Thanks."

30

MIKE JANOWSKI TURNED THE WHEEL of the green Cadillac Coupe DeVille right off of Coddington Street and pulled into the parking lot across the street from the Quincy YMCA. Mike was uneasy; Quincy Police headquarters sat only a quarter mile down the road. He shut off the engine and in the darkness located and pressed a protruding button on the side of his watch with his right hand. Instantly a greenish-white glow illuminated the face of the Timex Expedition as well as the front of the Boston University sweatshirt he wore. It was seven fifteen; he was exactly on time and he wondered where the hell the Currans were, they were never late.

A sudden double rap on the roof made him jump. "Open the door," Wacko Curran said through the glass of the passenger side window. Mike leaned across the seat and pulled up on the release latch.

Wacko opened the door. "What the fuck's wrong with you, let

him in," he said, pointing past Mike's face. Mike Janowski turned his head to see Kevin's face squashed against the driver's side glass. He made squirls on its surface with his tongue.

Mike yowled. "Hey, you fucking nut, my dog, Pooka, licked that window this mornin'," he said.

Kevin backed away from the door spitting. Wacko hit the door release button, and Kevin got into the backseat still laughing. "Son-of-a-bitch, Mike, glass tastes like a dog's ass," he said. "Have to fix that." He raised his hips off the seat and pulled a bag of coke from behind his belt buckle, untwisted the top, and stuck in a straw that he produced from his pocket. He coughed and offered it to Wacko.

"Pass," Wacko said.

"You?" Kevin said, holding the bag over Mike's right shoulder. Mike shook his head.

"I told you this kid was a professional, now put it away," Wacko said. Kevin twisted the bag shut and returned it behind the buckle. "Let's take a ride."

"I didn't even see you guys pull up. Where'd you come from?" Mike said.

"Get us out of this parkin' lot," Wacko said, looking around. "That thing we told you about before, we're talkin' about hittin' an armored car, still interested?" Wacko stared hard at Mike, trying to detect any hint of fear, any weakness.

Mike smiled, turning right out of the lot. "Told you before, I'm down for anything," he said.

Wacko looked at Kevin and nodded. "We want to take you to see the play next week, probably Tuesday morning, you available?"

"Whenever you need me," Mike said. He followed Hancock Street through Quincy Square, quietly eyeing the small shops on either side of the street as he drove.

"Tuesday morning, meet us here in Quincy at the Harbor Express parkin' lot near the Fore River Bridge. Nine o'clock sharp, I don't want you there early hangin' around. There'll be other people, commuters, citizens headin' in town to their cubicles. Once there, park and walk to the rotary. We'll pick you up at the gate. You got it?" Mike nodded. "Good, now bring us back to the Y," Wacko said.

"When we come we might bring along another guy, Danny King, any problem with that?" Wacko said.

"Your show, never heard anything bad about the guy," Mike said.

"And if you did you'd tell us, right?" Wacko said.

Mike grinned. "Bet your ass, my butt's on the line with this thing too, gotta trust my partners," he said.

Wacko patted him on the shoulder and looked at Kevin. "I told you I liked this kid. Naturally, you say nothing to no one about this," Wacko said.

"Don't have to say that," Mike said.

Kevin grabbed Mike's shoulders from behind. "He does have to say that," Kevin said. "We're pals, Mike, but this ain't bullshit, it's business, no room for mistakes, ever. You're in now, know what I mean?" Kevin said.

"No problem with none of it," Mike said.

■   ■   ■

"You wanted a black-and-white?" Kevin said, passing his brother a frappe and a straw through the passenger side window of the big Marquis.

Wacko pulled the paper off the straw and inserted it through the lid of the cup. "Ya, so you're sure you told Danny King we're takin' him Tuesday not Thursday?" Wacko said.

Kevin got into the driver's side holding a cup of chocolate ice cream and a spoon. "Tuesday mornin'," he said. He put a large scoop of ice cream into his mouth, then seconds later said, "Oh shit." He rubbed his forehead with the back of his right hand. "Fucking brain freeze." Kevin put the cup in his lap and rubbed his forehead with both hands. "You said Tuesday, I told him Tuesday, Jesus! My head. What the fuck causes this?"

"Bein' a fucking pig," Wacko said. "What's the deal with you and Dairy Queen? You don't like real ice cream, this shit's like pudding."

"I like pudding, I like Dairy Queen," Kevin said.

Wacko took a sip of his frappe.

"You don't want to hear it, but if there's a problem with Danny King, we're takin' care of it."

"Ya, okay, so what, main thing we're still bringin' him to Weymouth," Kevin said, taking a smaller mouthful of ice cream.

"Ya. But I've been thinkin', Kevin, we might put the Weymouth score on hold," Wacko said.

"How come?" Kevin said.

"The way I see it, scores are like women, smart to have an extra one in reserve, and we got one. Been thinkin' about that North End score, somethin' about it calls me, but we're not tellin' Mr. King about it. Far as he's concerned, Weymouth's the score and that's all he's gonna see," Wacko said.

"And this is how we're gonna handle it. We'll take him there, show him the play, all the details. Then we'll tell him somethin' like we're plannin' to hit it the following week. Tell him we'll pick him up Tuesday morning at nine but we won't, we'll head on up to Weymouth alone. There's a cemetery on a hill across the street from the bank. With a good pair of binoculars, we'll have a clear shot of it. We see the heat, cops crawlin' behind Dumpsters on rooftops, we'll know Danny's bad and we've been had," Wacko said.

"Real poetic, sounds like a plan," Kevin said, digging at the ice cream near the bottom of the cup.

"It is, and this way our friend will be taken care of either way. If on that day Weymouth's cool, then we'll head back to Danny's place, apologize to him for the 'screwup,' and tell him there's been a change of plans, we got another score, a better one. He'll be fine with it. He'll be fine either way I see it," Wacko said.

"The guy don't make me nervous, Jack," Kevin said, licking the spoon. "I know you gotta be sure, but I think you're wastin' your time."

"Maybe, Kevin here, throw this thing out," Wacko said, passing his brother the frappe. Kevin put the cup between his legs. "Look, I'm goin' with my gut on this one, ya know? Tough showin' up game day facin' a SWAT team from the Bank Robbery Task Force," Wacko said.

"Painful too. We'll do it your way, bro'," Kevin said, picking up the frappe.

"Gimme back my frappe," Wacko said, snatching the cup from his brother. He sucked on the straw until it rrrrrrrpppped. He held the empty cup up to the light streaming through the windshield, then without looking, smiled and flipped it sideways off Kevin's head.

"Hey," Kevin said, loading up his spoon with ice cream, bending it, and aiming it at his brother's face.

"You haven't got the balls," Wacko said.

Kevin let it fly.

31

EDDY DOOLEY EXITED Sullivan's restaurant on Castle Island balancing two Kayem hot dogs, with the works, in his right hand. In his left he grasped an extra-large Coke loaded with ice that rattled against the side of the cup and the plastic top. In his teeth was a straw.

Outside the restaurant he banged a left and followed a sidewalk that was bordered on the right side by an ancient green fence festooned along the top with a single row of iron teeth. As Eddy walked a jogger passed a little too close on the left, and Eddy sucked the elbow on that side hard into his ribs. Relish and onions from one of the hot dogs sprinkled the sidewalk, and he was pissed that he had probably overreacted. His stomach grumbled, and he picked up the pace until he came upon a small triangle of trees and picnic tables on the right facing the Lagoon.

He found an empty table in front of an empty boathouse near the water's edge and was determined it remained that way. He plunked his ass down in the middle of one of its wooden benches and popped the top off the Coke, leaned across the table, and poured some on the opposite bench. Confident he'd remain alone, he shielded his eyes from the sun and scanned the Lagoon, watching tiny boats skim across its surface. He picked up a hot dog, bit into it, and smiled as the rush of beef juice, onions, and relish filled his mouth.

As he chewed, Eddy Dooley put both hands on the table, leaned back, and stared at the azure sky through his Maui Jim's. He took a sip of Coke. He had to return on what, the eighteenth, to appear before the federal grand jury in Tucson. He had three weeks, plenty of time to head up north to Manchester, New Hampshire, to gather the money from the three safety deposit boxes he had there. He was glad he was disciplined, unlike the rest of his associates, who spent all their money on cocaine, flashy cars, or women. When he began this ride he swore he'd keep his head on straight, and he had. Now just to tie up some loose ends and collect his money, a considerable sum. When he took that flight out of Logan, courtesy of Uncle Sam, on the seventeenth, he'd wave good-bye to the Lagoon and South Boston forever.

Eddy ate his hot dogs and slurped his Coke and stared out beyond the green, spiked fence that supported a half dozen silent seagulls, to a spot a hundred yards away where a strip of short green grass bled down into a sandy beach, and he reminisced about summer days spent there as a child with his mum and two younger brothers. Days waiting for the tide to come foaming in through the sluice gates, a quarter mile out in the bay, building shipyards in the sand and eating fried baloney sandwiches.

As he ate, others — bicyclists, lovers walking hand in hand — made use of the sidewalk that encircled the island behind him. As Eddy Dooley counted his blessings, a Rollerblader left the cement walkway and rolled onto the grass. As the Rollerblader approached from behind, Eddy broke off a piece of hot dog and threw it to a juvenile gull nearby. The younger bird was instantly swooped on by a screeching adult and shoved aside; the older bird gobbled the morsel.

Pissed off, Eddy waved his hands and shouted with his mouth full, then stood up and broke off a piece of meat and hauled back to throw it at the larger bird. "Hey, you fucking bum, you're outta here," he said.

"You read my mind," said a voice behind him. Eddy turned to face the voice. "You ain't makin' it to Tucson, rat," said the tanned, sunglassed man in the yellow tank top and blue, nylon shorts. The Rollerblader leveled an aluminum-colored automatic to Eddy's face and fired twice. The multilayered right lens of Eddy's Maui Jim's offered no resistance to the punch of the .45 ACP. The first shot exited cleanly above his left ear, nicking the rubberized arm of the glasses. Eddy Dooley died on his feet as the second shot broke the bridge of his nose and cratered the back of his head, spraying three of the gulls behind him near the boathouse with brain matter.

A woman pushing a double baby carriage on the walkway stopped and stared. The gunman turned, drew a bead on her face, and skated awkwardly over the grass towards her. She looked to the left and down as he came up on her, and ran the barrel of his weapon along the base of her skull, flipped her ponytail up, and shoved her head slightly forward. The shooter paused casually, like she had just asked him for the time, then turned, bent low, and leisurely skated back towards Sullivan's. Behind him, the woman made curious squeaking sounds and covered her ears as the seagulls fought for parts of Eddy Dooley's brain.

32

IN BOSTON'S ITALIAN NORTH END, in front of a large window to the right of the doorway to Mike's Pastry on Hanover Street, Gaetano Milano shifted uncomfortably in his cheap metal folding chair. He pressed down with both forearms on the arms of the chair, lifted his ass, and allowed the blood to return to its thinning muscles. Temporarily relieved, he sank back into the seat and picked up and sipped an espresso, the first of two he had every morning, weather permitting, Monday through Friday. He was only slightly annoyed by the brrrrraaapp of the one-hundred-pound jackhammer breaking asphalt less than a block away; hearing diminished by age had it advantages.

At seventy-eight Milano was semiretired from the ranks of the Patriarca crime family that had dominated New England for decades. He had made his bones at twenty-one, the age when most of his peers were thrilled just to be able to purchase alcohol legally. From that point on there was little that Gaetano Milano did that was legal. His slow, steady rise to capo regime was patient, cunning, and above all deadly. Through brilliant manipulation he held that rank for one bloody decade, followed by another of profitable peace, after which he was made consigliere to the family, a title he still held.

To Milano's left behind a window, with MIKE'S PASTRY stenciled on it in white, two men sat at a table. "No one's got cannolis like Mike's," Wacko Curran said, peering out through the glass at the street. He wiped his mouth with a cheap paper napkin, then pointed to the cannoli in front of Kevin. "What's the matter, you ain't gonna eat?"

Kevin removed his sunglasses and rubbed the lenses with a napkin. "I don't know about this thing, Jack. We've been here all of ten minutes and already two state cops have come into this joint for their coffee and Italian donuts." Kevin looked over his shoulder out the window. "I don't like it. A block away you got a police detail, and out front you got an old geeza watchin' everything, the neighborhood lookout, drinkin' coffee out of a midget's cup. Son-of-a-bitch was fillin' the same seat last time we was here."

"He's just an old greaser, you're paranoid and you ain't eatin' your cannoli because you do too much of that shit, especially before you eat. No one can eat on that crap except for Nino, he's the only one, up for days wired like the Flying fucking Wallendas and wolfin' down food like he just smoked a fat one," Wacko said.

Kevin looked down the street. "And what about on the corner of Richmond, there's a Boston cop down there directin' traffic and the bank's ten feet away? I don't like it, Jack, too many cops around here, fucking road construction put us all in jail."

Wacko took another bite of cannoli, wiped his mouth, then stared out the window focusing on nothing. "I'll tell you, Kevin, me, I'll tell you when there's too many cops, understand? My guy down public works says the sewer line project they're workin' on at that intersection is almost done. One more week, maybe two. We watch them, they go, we go, simple. You got a problem with that, you want out let me know, you have that option, only if you pull out it ain't you it's the shit. I'll say it again, you're paranoid; worrying about an old bastard sittin' out there in the sun, you're kiddin', right? The coke's meltin' your common sense, your balls. Now eat your fucking cannoli and relax," Wacko said.

Kevin looked down, shook his head and picked up the cannoli. "How the fuck you eat this thing and not look like you suck dick?" he said, examining the pastry. He put it down and got up. "I'm gettin' a knife and fork."

Mike Janowski walked into Mike's Pastry and nodded at Wacko. He headed to the counter and ordered a cannoli and a coffee half, no sugar. Kevin returned to the table, and Mike joined them.

"Cannoli? You too?" Kevin said. Mike nodded. "We look like faggots."

"What Kevin means to say is that we didn't have you meet us here for the cannolis," Wacko said. "We showed you the Weymouth score Tuesday, you liked it?" Mike nodded. "Good, you liked that you'll love this. We got somethin' better, somethin' the other guy, King, knows nothing about. He'll have to pass an exam to find out; you, being a good student, get to see it first."

Mike sipped his coffee, then put the cup down. "It's your business, Jack, showin' what you want to whoever. Ain't askin' what's up between you and Danny King," he said. He looked through the window at Gaetano Milano, who casually looked him up and down. "The old guy, I know him, seen his mug in the newspapers a few times, he's one of them, a wiseguy."

Kevin glared at Wacko. "Should have known he was more than the neighborhood greeter. Everyone around here seems to know him," Kevin said.

"Then we gotta be cute. This guy didn't get old in his racket bein' dumb," Wacko said. He suddenly became alert and drained the last of his coffee. "Heads up, boys, here comes my honey, right on time," Wacko said, eyeing something up the street the others couldn't see. Seconds later an imposing gray MCI Armored Services truck rumbled past, heading west on Hanover Street. Almost imperceptibly Wacko shook. "You can set your watch by these guys. Never more that three minutes either way. Next stop same side of the street, fifty feet from the intersection with Parmenter, the Shawmut Bank. He'll drive past the bank, then stop, back up at an angle, and get as close as he can to the sidewalk."

Wacko quietly slid out of his chair and stood up. "Mike, you and me are takin' a walk. Kevin, you head back to the car, just sit there and wait, don't bring it around. Mike and me will catch the play," Wacko said.

Kevin got up and tossed his cannoli into the trash. "See ya," he said.

"Ever heard of Piccola Venezia?" Wacko said out loud. "It's only a few doors down the street, Mike, you and Maria gotta check it out before you head back home to Manchester."

The two men left Mike's Pastry, ignoring Gaetano Milano as they turned right. As they walked slowly side by side, Mike smiled and nodded as Wacko pointed out shops and rooftop architectural configurations on either side of the street.

"That's what I mean, some of these buildin's around here date back to the mid-eighteen hundreds and . . . see what I mean, here we go, he's backin' up," Wacko said, lowering his voice. "Now once that truck stops, the guard in back will pop out the side door, on the street side, and walk around to the rear. Once the driver sees everything's cozy, he'll pop the back door from the inside," Wacko said.

"So, this guy, the outside man, doesn't open the back door with a key?" Mike said.

"Uh-uh, the driver's got this release button, usually over the dash above the windshield. The outside man signals everything's cool, then click, the door's opened," Wacko said. He nodded towards the truck. "See, he's signalin' and the door's gonna open. Let's step up near the plate."

The two men crossed Parmenter Street and stopped at the northeast corner of the intersection. In the street a few feet away, two men in hard hats worked an open trench with shovels, while above them, not twenty feet away, another man using a jackhammer made small incisions in the asphalt.

The noise was ear splitting, but the outside MCI guard paid the laborers no mind as he withdrew an aluminum dolly from the back of the truck, followed by two heavy canvas satchels with leather handles, which he lay flat on the dolly. He then, with some difficulty, removed two cardboard boxes from the interior of the truck, and placed them on top of the satchels. Mike looked at Wacko quizzically.

"Change, probably quarters, fifty-pound boxes about three grand each," Wacko said. "We gotta get closer."

Wacko wrapped an arm around Mike's shoulders like the other man had just promised him a free bag of primo reefer. "You like veal? Best veal in the goddamn city over there." He pointed diagonally across the street to Piccola Venezia, a restaurant with huge front windows and a brightly lit interior. They continued to walk down the sidewalk but stopped just past the rear of the truck as if they were crossing to the restaurant. Mike glanced to the right. The guard at the rear of the truck had bent down to readjust the two boxes of change on the dolly, giving Mike a clear shot of the interior.

Bags of money, heavy canvas bags, were stacked on top of one another row upon row parallel to the open rear door waiting to be plucked. Other bags were strewn helter-skelter along the interior sides and under a bench that ran beside the left interior wall of the truck.

The guard closed the rear door, double-secured it with a key, then pushed the dolly to the curb, turned, and pulled it onto the sidewalk. Wacko pretended like he was pointing out features on a building across the street. "There's millions in there, Mike," he said under his breath, using an index finger to push his sunglasses back from the center. "You know, I think you're right, that buildin' is over one hundred years old," he said as the guard pulled the dolly into the bank. Wacko turned Mike by the elbow and headed back up the street.

"Where's all that money come from, Jack, so much in one truck, gotta be thirty, forty bags?" Mike said, glancing over his shoulder towards the truck.

"What we know is this, it makes at least three stops before it gets to this bank," Wacko said. "At nine o'clock sharp they make a pickup at a trust company on Congress Street near the Federal Reserve Bank. They load a ton into it there. From there they make another pickup, a smaller one, at a bank on Atlantic Avenue, then they make a good-sized drop at a bank on Commercial Street near Lewis Wharf. That stop makes me sick, them leavin' our money behind."

"Why then don't we whack them on Congress Street?" Mike Janowski said.

"Because of the traffic, it's much too congested. Commercial Street has less traffic, but there's no good way out of there; Hanover Street's the stop, fact. We're seein' cops around here now, but come game day there shouldn't be any. I know we can do this. I had a friend once, this old-time bank robber who taught me the ropes comin' up. He told me this, 'You can do anything you want, but you gotta do it right.' The guy was smart and I've proved him right a dozen times and I'm gonna do it again," Wacko said.

Mike looked around nervously. "No disrespect intended, Jack, but there's a lot of traffic around here. How do we know we'll have the openin' to take the truck?" Mike said.

"We're blockin' Hanover Street," Wacko said.

Mike's eyes widened. "That takes time. How can we do that with only three guys?"

Wacko put his hand on Mike's shoulder and gently shook him. "We're using the Josephs, the diversion kings," Wacko said.

Mike's eyes widened still further. "The Josephs, you trust them? They're maniacs. That house they live in's a fucking morgue. People go in, come out in fucking pieces," Mike said, slowly shaking his head.

"Talk, all talk. What you seen yourself? I haven't seen shit, known them for years. Strange, ya, so what, who isn't? I'll tell you what I have seen — them in action, pullin' diversions: explosions, fires, car accidents, you name it. You need the cops somewhere else so you can work, you get the Josephs. They may be out there, but they're consistent and solid. They're involved in something it's not all over town the next day like a lot we know," Wacko said.

"What's the plan?" Mike said.

Wacko turned and crossed his arms over his chest and gently pushed Mike.

"They're gonna use a big bread truck, a box job, at the east end of Hanover Street a block or so before Mike's Pastry, and they got a tow truck, one of them ramp jobs, they clipped up in Woburn for the north end of the street. It's wider on that end so they'll pull the thing diagonal across it and throw the ramp down, really fuck things up," Wacko said.

"You'll be drivin' our van, a flower delivery job, perfect, no one questions a flower truck. We'll be parked in front of Mike's Pastry waitin'. Kevin will be in a telephone repair truck double-parked a few feet down from the bank. Again no one should give him a second look. I've had it up here twice in the past month, dry runs, double-parked for almost an hour and no one blinked, cops didn't even bother with it. We'll have walkie-talkies in both vans," Wacko said.

"The armored truck will pass us on Hanover Street. We wait until it stops and backs up, then we'll focus on the rear guard action. When we see the guard rap on the back door and it pops, you'll say 'Sunshine' into your mike and start to move towards the truck but not too fast. 'Sunshine' is Kevin's signal to back up into the truck as we're approaching, but I don't want you hotfootin' it. When we're, say, thirty feet from the back of the truck, you should only be going five, six miles per hour, and I'll exit from the side door of the van on the fly and grab the outside guy. You'll stop the van at an angle so that the side door of the van is parallel to the rear door of the truck, then you'll hop out with the H and K. By this time Kevin will have the van backed up against the front bumper of the truck and will be outside groovin'," Wacko said.

"What about the driver, what's to stop him from turnin' and firin' on you through the inside divider? It's a straight shot through the back door." Mike said.

Wacko smiled and rubbed his hands together. "That's the sweet part," he said. "Kevin ain't comin' to the party empty-handed. When he pops out of the telephone van, he'll be wearin' a sidearm, and he'll also have a hand grenade duct-taped to the front of his wind-breaker."

"Hand grenade?" Mike said incredulously. He stopped walking and stared at Wacko, who stared right back. Both men burst out laughing.

Wacko pulled Mike along by the arm. "Come on, I ain't finished yet. Kevin's gonna monkey over the hood of that truck on his knees up to the windshield, see, then he'll peel the bomb from his chest, slap it on the windshield in front of the guy's face. Kevin orders him out, he's got five seconds before Kevin pulls the pin," Wacko said.

"While all this is goin' on, your job, Mike, is to watch our backs. The rear guard should give it up quick I get the drop on him; he don't, I drop him. You'll be positioned left front of the van near the bumper. If the driver gets out like he should, he'll see your rifle pointed at him. Kevin will put his piece to the guy's head, disarm him, drag him back, and toss him down next to guard number one," Wacko said.

"And if the driver don't come out?" Mike said.

"Kevin pulls the pin and jumps. You get your ass against the side of the truck and wait for it to blow. Once it does you step out and put a ten- or fifteen-round burst through the driver's door. You're using armor-piercing three-oh-eights, go through it like fucking cheese, put 'em in a pattern below the glass you'll get the son-of-a-bitch, fact," Wacko said.

"No problem with it," Mike said.

"On the other hand, the guard comes out he better do it quick. He drags his feet you stitch him, I don't want no hero shooting my brother. Once both guards are at the back of the truck, me and Kevin will start unloadin' into the van, you watch our backs. You gotta remember, this is an Italian neighborhood. Guys like to hang out on the street, be seen, drink their coffee. Anyone sticks their nose in our business you let 'em have it. Nobody's innocent. Any problems with this so far?" Wacko said.

"Anyone sticks their noses in our business I'll give them a new hole to pour their espresso in," Mike said.

"That'll make 'em choke on their cannolis," Wacko said.

"Okay, from start to finish, what kind of time frame we talkin'?" Mike said.

"If that driver comes out like he should, no more than two and a half minutes start to finish. We're grabbin' at least twenty bags."

"And we have to blow him out?"

"That happens, we'll be out of there faster, only one guard to deal with. Plus, the noise should scare most but also draw the curious. How are you with a rifle?" Wacko said.

"As a kid I hunted a lot with my uncle outside Saco, Maine. I'm good enough," Mike said.

"Either way, Mike, we'll be comin' home with a good day's pay, at least two million. If we do use Danny King he'll be out there on back-up with a carbine, but I still ain't sure about him," Wacko said.

"But you will be," Mike Janowski said.

"Ya, I will be," Wacko Curran said.

"Okay, so we're loaded up, how're we getting out of there? There's a hundred little side streets the cops could come at us," Mike said.

"Okay, now we're loaded we back up to Parmenter, head one block down. We turn right onto Salem Street, then take the first left onto Cooper Street. A hundred yards down on the right we'll have an F-three-fifty Ford pickup parked and waitin'.

"Cooper is a narrow street. As we come down it, Kevin will remain in the back with a fifty-pound dry chemical fire extinguisher. Cops come in behind us, he'll unload it; they'll run into a chemical fogbank. Then we'll start shootin'.

"If everything's cool, we'll park the van diagonal across the street, blockin' it off. Kevin jumps out with a knife, flattens two of the tires, now no one's pushin' it out of the way. We load the money into the bed of the pickup. We get into the truck, I'm drivin'. You'll get in next to me; Kevin hops in the back, pulls a tarp over him and the money.

"North Washington Street, the main drag, is only a few hundred yards away, there we take a right. Two blocks up we pull over in front of Sabatino's restaurant, that's the next switch, a Ford Taurus. You'll jump out of the truck into the driver's seat; Kevin jumps into the back, hits the floor. You pull out behind and follow me. Cops won't be lookin' for a lone guy in a Ford pickup driving over the bridge into Charlestown. As soon as you go over the bridge, there's a commuter boat parkin' lot on the left, that's where we'll make the last switch. Kevin grabbed an MBTA shuttle bus last month down in front of Park Street, we throw everything into it. Guaranteed, we get that far we're home free," Wacko said.

"The cops are gonna blame this on the Townies, and those boys ain't gonna like it," Mike said.

"Serves 'em right, they pull the same shit on us," Wacko said. "Billy Kiley's Monument Ave. crew left that stiff in Amrhein's Dumpster last month, a fucking car salesman, for chrissakes. Word is he owed them for coke. I can understand killin' him, but dump him in our town, they couldn't have dumped him in Somerville? Cops don't mind us killin' each other, but kill a fucking citizen, even a cokehead citizen, nothin' but heat. Cops turned the Lower End upside down, crawlin' over each other like roaches, cost Marty Fallon plenty. He still got a hair across his ass about it."

"Speakin' of which, what about Marty Fallon? Around here common knowledge the armored car crews come out of two places, Southie and Charlestown. Just the fact we'll pull this thing off takes the heat off the Townies," Mike said, grinning.

Wacko laughed. "Ya know, you're right, they haven't had much success lately," he said.

"Looks like the heat's on us then, on Marty Fallon too. Marty will take it if the price is right, probably gonna cost us plenty," Mike said.

Wacko patted him on the shoulder. "Let's take care of business first. We'll worry about the details later."

33

KEVIN CURRAN EXITED Osco's on Little Broadway with a huge grin on his face. Above his head in either hand he held a multicolored Massachusetts Lottery scratch ticket. "What you win?" Wacko said, starting up the powder blue Ford Explorer.

"Don't know, haven't scratched 'em yet," Kevin said, climbing into the car. "I'm smilin' because of that store dick in there."

"What's to like about her, she's a fucking mess," Wacko said.

"Like her? Whenever I'm in that store that bitch follows me around like she's a button on my ass. I'm smilin' because one of these days I'm gonna cold-cock her and that makes me happy," Kevin said.

Wacko pulled the car from the lot into the street and headed west.

"She's got a hard on for you, what you expect? Last year she pops you loadin' up your sling with deodorant soap," he said.

"You're tellin' me slings only for broken arms?"

Wacko chopped the steering wheel. "That's just it, Kevin, your arm ain't all that's broken. You're missin' something, a piece, I dunno. You got no shame. You gotta work on it, develop it," Wacko said.

Kevin looked at him incredulously. "I gotta develop shame?"

"Ya, you do. Try to look at it like a tool that helps you make decisions," Wacko said.

"What kind of decisions, Jack, what is this, the Twilight Zone, I'm missin' somethin' here?"

"Listen to me: it ain't shame direct, it's something inside, a little voice that tells you right from wrong. Look, it don't stop you from doin' anything important, but thirty bars of Dial soap, ya, it tells you to pass. You got any clue what I'm talkin' about?" Wacko said before jerking his head in the direction of a bar coming up on the right.

"Hey, ain't that our boy Andre coming out of the Playwright? Bet ya dollars to fucking donuts he just picked up Marty's weekly kiss. I figure, between here and the Cape, that goon makes thirty, forty stops like that for Marty Fallon. Takin' somewhere in between, what do you think, Kev, twenty-five and thirty grand a week? All that dough and Marty still gotta hit us for a piece of everything we make," Wacko said.

Kevin smiled, raised his eyebrows a few times, and waved his right index finger at his brother.

"You're talkin' the diamonds? Well, almost everything," Wacko said, tousling Kevin's hair. "Ya bum, you know what I mean."

With both hands Kevin stroked his hair back into place, then hit the up button for the window and punched the AC button on the dash. "Always been that way, Jack, think it's going to change? How can it, and you and me remain on the street? The bum's expensive, sure, but he gives us a heads-up when there's a problem keeps the heat off. I figure we gotta pay, right?"

"My ass we do. I'm a firm believer in the old saying 'Those who should pay should.' If you can't hang on to your action, you better hang it up or pay the going rate. But that ain't goin' to be us anymore," Wacko said.

They neared the top of the Broadway hill, and Wacko eyed the rearview mirror warily. He pulled the Ford into a space across the street from South Boston District Court and quickly shut the engine off. He checked the side-view mirror. "Here comes Dumbo up the hill behind us. King shit, drivin' the big Audi Marty Fallon gave him. Let's see where king shit's headin', follow his ass for a while," Wacko said.

The silver, late-model Audi approached from an easterly direction, banged a U-turn just before the courthouse, and double-parked in front of the South Boston Bowlarama. The driver's door sprung open, and the Audi vomited the enormous mass of Andre Athanas, chief enforcer for Martin Emmett Fallon, into the middle of busy East Broadway. Andre crossed in front of the car and stopped before the bowling alley's green glass double doors. He knocked twice, then placed both huge hands on his hips, turned, and faced the street.

"Think he made us?" Kevin said.

"Naw, he's never seen this car. That's why I'm a fan of ownin' multiple cars. I'm glad Eddie's got that used car joint down in Rockland; always got good cars on the lot. Pick 'em up cheap, drive 'em a few months, then sell 'em back for something new. Tough for anyone to keep track," Wacko said.

"Even I lose track," Kevin said.

"There you go," Wacko said.

"Whoa, the door's openin', it's Billy Whelan," Kevin said. "What's Andre want with him?"

Wacko said, "Hey, Billy Whelan does a little book on the side, a little shylock too. He's makin', we're talkin' nickels, but the goon's here every Tuesday shakin' him for dimes. Them that should pay . . ."

"They pay, but we won't," Kevin said.

"Don't shit yourself, we've paid our share, more. Maybe not on the nickel-dime stuff like these poor stiffs, but on everything else. An inchworm don't get past Marty Fallon," Wacko said.

"Marty knows better than to shake us too hard," Kevin said. "We'd bite him back."

"But these guys can't or won't. They pay as they should, Kevin. You ain't strong enough to say no, shut your food hole and open your wallet, cause dead's forever."

"Not according to the Hindus," Kevin said. "The Hindus —"

"Fuck the Hindus, hey, Dumbo just took an envelope . . . Hindus," Wacko said, starting the car as Andre climbed back into the Audi. Wacko pulled a pen down off the sun visor. "Here, do something useful. Write down the Playwright, eight o'clock, bowling alley, eight twenty, and today's date. We're gonna start keepin' records on this shit. I want to know exactly where and when he makes his pick-ups, it might come in handy someday."

Kevin scribbled on the back of his hand. "Use a piece of paper, for chrissakes," Wacko said, grabbing a parking ticket off the dash and flipping it sideways.

"What time we pickin' up Danny King?" Kevin said. Both men sunk into their seats as Andre Athanas passed by them in the Audi.

"Ten o'clock, he better be up," Wacko said, banging a U-turn. "Andre's got a few more stops to make on Broadway, then he swings around and starts hitting the joints up the Point. I'll take you back to your car. You head up I Street and wait until he makes his pickup at the Bayview Barber Shop, then goes across the street to the Quencher to see Morgan. Follow him, don't want him to see ya, from there and jot down the exact times he makes his other stops, okay?"

Kevin nodded, his brow darkly furrowed with concern.

Wacko glanced at him. "What, that too tough for you?"

"Ain't that. You're really thinkin' he's bad, Danny King?" Kevin said.

"I don't think Danny's cut out for this," Wacko said. "We're gonna find out if he's bad."

34

WITHIN FIFTY FEET of the northwest corner of a small park near the corner of West Fourth and D Street, Mary Rose O'Connell slammed the creaky driver's side door of her red 1986 Mustang. Only the day before, Gary, at the repair shop on Silver Street, had told her the Mustang's hinges, on both doors, were rotted, gone, and soon a fifty-five-gallon drum of oil wouldn't stop them from squeaking. Soon, he said, the doors would fall off in the street.

Mary Rose walked into the park, kicked the jagged bottom of a broken Heineken bottle out of her way, watching it flip into the air then shatter on impact before spitting and watching the lunga arc through the air before landing at the edge of a dilapidated basketball court. Finished with the preliminaries, she sat down on a bench and, behind her ears, adjusted the arms of the loose-fitting, cheap pair of sunglasses she wore.

What, it was only three or four months ago she was driving a brand-new Camaro. Then what happens? She gets two lousy payments behind and the repo asshole from the bank comes along and snatches it minutes before she's heading out the door on a Friday night. Mary Rose swore that when she pulled herself out of the hole she was in she'd buy something new, used at least with the doors intact, and some new clothes. These days it was tough even keeping the ones she had on her back clean.

She sat on the bench and hung her head and swung her feet in the air and cursed herself for her stupidity. Generosity? She trusted people who took advantage, now everyone owed her and she owed Jackie Curran $2,400. That was chump change to the gangster, but now he was putting on the pressure. At this point he was saying no installments, just get it. Just get it? Talking to her like that? If he wasn't careful, Jackie Curran would get it and he wouldn't like the package it came in. She knew how to use a phone.

Her sister Ellie used to date the cop Kenny O'Donnell down at District Six, and well, the jerk-off still had the hots for her. One phone call to Kenny O'Donnell and big, bad Wacko Curran could kiss the streets good-bye for a long, long time. It was that easy.

She had made him a fortune, and now he was sending messages threatening her? Well, not directly threatening, but it was there, she could feel it, and she was real good at feeling things these days.

Mary Rose took a plastic vial with a rubber cap out of her pocketbook and pulled the cap off with her teeth. She dug the long nail of her right little finger into it and scooped some of the white, crystalline powder within. She held it to one nostril and snorted it up. Ya, she'd take care of Wacko Curran and anyone else who fucked with her. She'd been stand-up, hadn't she? Hadn't she? And now what, $2,400 and her world's caving in? That was dead, it wasn't going to happen.

She pressed her left index finger into the side of her left nostril and inhaled hard. She felt the chill of the drip at the top of her throat, sucked hard again, and swallowed. She looked at the sky and frowned. Who were they, who the fuck was anyone messing with her? She wouldn't let these punks take her down. One phone call, one lousy little phone call and Wacko Curran would be calling her begging. She'd talk to Ellie tonight.

Mary Rose sunk her fingernail into the vial again, held it to her right nostril, and sharply inhaled. She swallowed the drip from the previous blast and got goddamn ready for the next one. Life was more than good. She'd dictate the messages now. She could live with that.

35

WACKO CURRAN PULLED OVER and parked the powder blue Ford Explorer curbside in front of the old Cardinal Cushing School on West Broadway and got out. After waving two cars and a bus along, he crossed the street and entered Mul's restaurant. Kevin sat at a counter on the left, and Wacko sat down next to him on a stool. A short, balding counterman approached. "Benny, coffee," Wacko said to the counterman, then to Kevin, "How long you been here?"

"Not long," Kevin said, folding his copy of the *Boston Herald* in half and pointing at a photo on the front page. "Seems our boy Vinnie Ferrante, our always been good to us North End connection, has decided to run for city council president again, interesting."

"No surprise there, no reason he shouldn't get elected a third term. Forgot to mention it. He called me two weeks ago and told me he was running. Gave him the usual donation, gets the same amount he's elected," Wacko said.

"Nothing like incentive. The photo sucks, makes him look fat," Kevin said, shifting the paper in front of his face, viewing it from different angles as if that would make Vinnie Ferrante thinner.

"So, what else?" Wacko said, sipping his coffee.

"Saw Leppy Mullins this morning on his way to work. Told me a couple of 'Butcher Boy Montillio's wiseguys were snoopin' around the Bayside Club last night askin' questions," Kevin said.

"What they doin' at the Bayside, a little bit out of their territory," Wacko said, nodding at Benny to refill his cup.

"These guys, you know them, Angie Lepore and Peter Oreto, are friends of our friend Jimmy the Bull. They hung around the place for an hour I hear," Kevin said.

"Just because the Bull owns the Bayside doesn't give him license to bring every paisan from the North End, Eastie, and Revere over for tea. Maybe Marty should have a talk with this prick. So, what these guys want, it wasn't social?" Wacko said.

"Naw, well, they pretended social, but they were sniffin', askin' about diamonds from that Abington score," Kevin said.

Wacko put his coffee down and stared at his brother. "And?"

"My guess they got no answers and they were probably happy with that. No one wants to rock the boat, Jack. My guess that guy, that fag jeweler did have some connections and the two gorillas were goin' through the motions for him, they asked around and got nothin', that sort of thing," Kevin said.

"That should be the end of it then. Marty's got a thing going with the Butcher Boy, and he don't want the applecart tweaked. Hell, he never even asked us if we knew anything about it, what that tell ya?" Wacko said.

"I ain't losin' sleep over it, Jack," Kevin said. "So how you make out with our friend Danny King?"

Wacko shrugged. "Dunno, took him out to Weymouth to check that house. He liked it, but can he afford it?" Wacko shrugged again and picked up his coffee cup. He spoke into the cup. "We'll see next Tuesday if this guy got any balls now, won't we?" Wacko sipped and smiled at something in his head. "So, dear brother, what else, anything, nothin'?"

Kevin folded a napkin into a paper airplane. "Stopped at the Quencher this morning to grab the five hundred Morgan Daly owed me. Buffalo kicked the shit out of the Pats last night. What's with that joint? The Quencher used to open every day bright and early at seven. Now they got yuppies in the neighborhood they've gone upscale, don't open until eight thirty."

"You beat Morgan for five hundred but lost two grand to him last week, you're really ahead of the game," Wacko said.

Kevin held up his hands surrender style. "I know, I know, Jack, but these days the guy's too easy, I'm usually ahead of him. It's not like before, really."

"My ass. When Morgan's no longer 'easy', don't come cryin' to me," Wacko said.

"Funny thing about Morgan, he's got the bucks, millions, but he never stops whining," Kevin said.

Wacko scratched his cheek. "They say money ain't everything. The guy lost his prostate last year and now he can't buy a fucking hard-on. Viagra's no good, his ticker's bad; he's got reason to whine," Wacko said.

Kevin grabbed his own crotch and made a face. "Ya, that dick thing's taking its toll on him, plus he's got tenant problems."

Wacko took a bite of Kevin's toast and stared at him. "Ya?"

"You know how he's got those two-family units over on Boston Street?"

"Flophouses, loaded with fleabags, Vietnamese, Section Eight riff-raff, ya, he can have 'em," Wacko said.

"I agree most of them, but some of his tenants are legit workin' stiffs, and one of them, this Irish laborer, he's in Local Two Twenty-three, complained to Morgan about brown stains in the ceiling that kept gettin' bigger," Kevin said.

"Brown stains?"

"From what I hear, Jack, dirty coffee-colored stains that made the apartment smell like the inside of an elephant's ass. So this Irish, the one in Two Twenty-three . . ."

"Get to the fucking point," Wacko said.

"This Irish is sittin' there one night in his livin' room smokin' crack, watchin' the news, sharpening his shovel or whatever the fuck these turkey bastards do, and there's a drip, drip, drip on his head," Kevin said.

"Drip, drip?" Wacko said.

"So he looks up at the ceilin' just in time to catch a fucking mud pie in the face." Kevin starts waving his arms and laughing. "The guy jumps off the couch, wipes his face, and there's a loud crack overhead and right where his Irish ass was four seconds earlier there's now a pile of plaster, chunks of wood, a mound of shitty-smelling earth, and a bunch of tomato plants. He looks up, and there's a three-foot hole in the ceiling and this gook's staring down at him, his mouth wide open, 'awwwww'!" Kevin pulled his eyelids back.

"Jack, you should have seen Morgan telling me this story. Tomatoes? His face is as red as a fucking tomato while I'm laughin' hard enough to shit blood. He nearly pissed himself telling me the story, plus the fact I just beat him for five hundred bucks. No wonder he's got no prostate," Kevin said.

Wacko put his cup down. "You're a fucking bug," he said. He pushed himself away from the counter and stood up. "Keep your cell phone on, I'll call when you start makin' sense."

"Jack, you gotta let me finish, this is classic," Kevin said.

Wacko slid a foot to the right and faked a left hook to Kevin's head. "You *are* finished, Kevin, you're not makin' sense and I ain't gonna sit and watch snot pour out your nose while you do it."

"All right, I'll get to the point. The Irish by now is naturally out of his mind. He stomps upstairs to Bruce Lee's apartment and bangs on the door, no answer but the Irish is persistent. He lays his construction boots to the door, then when the Chink cracks it for a peek, he pushes past him into the livin' room, but it ain't a livin' room no more. It's a fucking farm! They got a foot, foot and a half of dirt coverin' the entire floor and little rows of plants. There are two big watering cans in the corner and a fucking garden hose running from the kitchen sink. They even got those hydrophonic, whatever, lights in the room like the ones Macy used to grow pot out in his barn in Weston. All he's missin' is the pigs, and oh, I forgot, right in the middle of the floor there's this big hole, which is now of course less they gotta water." Kevin burst out laughing and wiped his nose and eyes with a napkin.

"Poor Morgan's fit to be tied. These Chinks mix shit with their dirt, I dunno, makes for bigger holes I guess, and this, this crap is down inside the walls. Morgan's talkin' five grand to fix the place. Plus, he had to put the Irish up in his little apartment over the Quencher while the work was being done. Says the guy's a pig, wants to kill him."

For the first time Wacko smiled. "Poor Morgan, you keep away from him," he said. "Now come outside."

Both men walked out of Mul's into the sunlight. Wacko looked to his left down the street towards the Broadway MBTA station and shook his head. "Remember the night we stole that car on Lansdowne Street, the Audi, and we raced Donnie McAlister all the way home from Kenmore Square?"

"Sure I do. You lost it comin' over the Broadway Bridge, almost killed us," Kevin said.

"I didn't lose it, Kevin, the two-lane road narrows to one by the station, remember, and Donnie got there first, it was a sign," Wacko said.

"A sign?" Kevin said.

"Ya, that we were gonna crash. We were lucky we didn't get banged up too bad, a few cuts, my pant leg completely torn off, but we walked away, strange," Wacko said.

Kevin stared at the station.

"They say a Volvo's good in crashes. We could borrow Marty Hogan's and take another run over the bridge sometime," Wacko said.

Kevin smiled. "Maybe after the score next week," he said.

"Ya, sounds good, business before pleasure," Wacko said. He put his hand on Kevin's shoulder.

"Speakin' about business, when I saw Leppy he told me he needs to re-up, today, same thing with Pauley from the Point," Kevin said.

"Pauley's turned into a good mover; go down fifty dollars on his ounces. I gave him Quincy; he's handlin' all of it for us. We got five bars on line there now, so I threw him a bone. I don't want him over there sneakin' someone else's product in behind our backs," Wacko said.

"That would be bad for him," Kevin said.

"Bad for business too. I ain't interested in puttin' us in a position we have to splash someone to prove a point. I'll catch you later," Wacko said, giving his brother a little shove.

"Where you off to?" Kevin said.

"Headin' over to Charlestown see some guys about a few things maybe a chance to make us some dough," Wacko said.

"Billy Keegan still hijackin' them Polaroid film trucks?" Kevin said.

"Ya, and Marty hasn't been treatin' him the way he should, been shortchangin' him, and Billy don't like it so he gave me a call." Wacko held his right index finger across his lips. "You can't talk about this to no one. You get jekylled up you talk too much," he said.

"Speakin' of which, I could use a blast, I've been pretty good today, Jack, but a man needs a lift now and again," Kevin said.

"Forget about that shit — straight, I need you straight until after the score. I'll call you later."

A marked Boston police cruiser drove past the men heading downtown. The uniformed cop in the driver's seat eyed the brothers warily and nodded. Wacko nodded back, winked at his brother, then stepped off the curb into the street and crossed. He had just turned the key in his door lock when a car horn sounded behind.

"Where you off to, Jackie Curran?" said a female voice. Wacko turned to see Elaine Ramsey smiling at him through the open window of her VW Jetta. A brisk crosswind blew her mantle of red curls in front of her face, briefly covering it. She laughed, it sounded like tiny, silver bells.

Wacko felt himself blush and prayed she hadn't noticed. He opened his door. "Hey, baby, lookin' good," he said over his shoulder.

"You in a hurry got time for a cuppa?" Elaine said.

Wacko nodded in the direction of Mul's. "Just had one with Kevin," he said, getting into his car.

Kevin jumped up and down on the sidewalk and waved his arms. "Hey, Elaine!" he yelled. Elaine giggled and waved back.

Wacko started the engine, and Elaine turned to see the driver's side window going down. "I'll call you soon, maybe tonight, I'll try," Wacko said.

Exaggerated disappointment showed on the redhead's face. She waved a finger at him. "Be sure you do, Jackie Curran, or I'll call your mum and tell her her son's getting a little too uppity to pay attention to the local ladies. She won't like that."

Wacko smiled and hit the up button for the window. "I promise," he shouted over the top of the glass.

36

TWO MEN, one older than the other, walked side by side down the main promenade of the huge, newly renovated South Shore Plaza in Braintree. Perhaps fifteen feet behind they were followed by a lumbering giant of a man who sipped a Frozen Mocha Blast through a straw; the cup almost vanished in his hand.

The two men stopped in front of Long's jewelers and stared into a display window. Three diamond-and-emerald rings were mounted, tantalizingly, on black velvet upright fingers in front of them. The older man spoke first.

"So what you find out about the diamond heist up there in Abington? You sniffed around you, what?"

"I couldn't ask direct, Marty, they're not stupid," the younger man said. "Kevin Curran mentioned somethin' about being able to get me a diamond ring, a nice one; he had access to some stones. Didn't say from where. I know some of the crews that work out of the housin' projects have been bangin' out jewelry scores since early spring. He could be gettin' the stones from them anywhere. These crews are mostly young guys who admire Wacko cause he's like them, done the same stuff comin' up."

"Ya, I can understand that, but it still makes me wonder. I like quality stuff. If Wacko's middlin' for the crews, why didn't he come to me? Why didn't they come to me? They respect Wacko, they don't me?" Marty Fallon said.

The younger man looked uneasy. "Maybe because they don't think they'll get the best price from you," he said.

"You sayin' I'm a cheap prick, Danny boy?"

Danny King blanched and backed directly into the big man behind him, who placed his Mocha Blast cup on Danny's right shoulder.

"Ya know, Andre, I think this punk, this fucking punk is one slap away from a tear, what you think?" Marty said.

Andre rammed the fingers of his left hand down through the back of Danny's belt. He yanked him close enough to fuck him. Andre smiled and looked around. "From all that runnin' you got a skinny neck, Danny. Maybe I should give it a twist," Andre said.

Danny could see his frightened face in the glass. "I didn't mean, ya know, what you're thinkin', Marty. I ain't callin' you cheap. All the times you helped me and I'm callin' you cheap? It's that guys, everyone, want to please you, you're the shit man, the king. Guys want to give you the best break possible, when they can, sometimes at a loss, but they can't always." Andre pulled his hand from Danny King's belt.

"Some days they can't come to you cause they're in debt, you know, whores, coke, gambling, whatever, and they have to get top buck for their goods. Hey, maybe Wacko Curran ain't all that bright, though he wouldn't like to hear that, maybe he pays them more than their product's worth. But I got something you'll like, something good," Danny said, glancing up at Andre.

Marty gave Andre a tap on the shoulder. "Andre, take a walk over to Au Bon Pain and get us a couple Mocha Blasts."

Andre looked at Danny and made a face like he just smelled something nasty. He opened his mouth, but nothing came out before he pivoted and headed in the opposite direction.

Danny King took a deep breath. "Can we walk? I'm nervous. This is my ass, Marty. I'm dead they find out I'm tellin' you this, fact," he said.

"Your ass? I own your ass, talk," Marty said, dragging Danny by the elbow.

"Maybe we shouldn't go far, what about Andre?" Danny said, looking over his shoulder.

"Fuck him, I own him too," Marty said. "Now, what you know?"

Danny took another deep breath. "I know . . . Tuesday morning, ten o'clock, Weymouth they're . . . Wacko, Kevin, and me are supposed to hit an armored car, a Massca, the blue-and-white ones. Supposed to be a good hit, Wacko's talking three, three hundred fifty G's each minimum."

Marty extended his right arm across Danny's chest and stopped him short. On their left was a Foot Locker store. A dozen pairs of sneakers were on display out front on a vertical rack. Marty pointed at them. "Lookee, here, Danny, you see the things they're callin' sneakers nowadays? Except they don't look like sneakers anymore. They look like something some faggot from the circus might wear, and expensive? You need the kind of money you're talkin' about stealin' to afford them."

Marty softly whistled and continued to walk. He put his hand on Danny's shoulder. "So, my guys, my own guys are tellin' you that you'll pull down at least a million dollars from this armored car and the old guy wasn't even invited to the party?" He smiled.

Danny said, "You could make them pay, put the arm on them after. They're crazy but not enough to cross you, Marty. The only thing is you gotta figure out a way you found out, it can't come back to me. Even with you backing me they'd kill me, they'd give you an end, as they should, but dig a hole for me."

Marty smirked.

Andre jogged up behind them, sweating. He held a Frozen Mocha Blast in each hand. Marty took one. "Almost lost you, boss," Andre said. Marty sipped through his straw, then bit down on it hard. He stared straight ahead watching something only he could see.

"I'm going to save you, Danny, you're a good kid. Ya, I'm going to save you, and this is how. You ain't goin' with the Currans Tuesday, you'll be sick, your alarm clock broke, somethin'. You'll stay home nice and comfy and think about the fifteen hundred I just cut from the five grand you owe me. It's like passing Go and not going to jail. You like that, Andre?" Marty said.

"What, Monopoly, boss?" Andre said. With the index finger and thumb of one hand he picked at the front of his shirt, pulling it away from his chest. "It's a great game, boss, for kids I mean, you got the pieces, the dog, wrench, that . . . that shoe. I always took the shoe. Thought it was lucky, I guess."

Marty stared blankly at the giant. "So, you liked the shoe?" he said.

"Ya, boss. The wrench was all right, never took the thimble."

Marty turned his head like he was talking to someone next to him and said, "He liked the shoe." Then he turned back to Andre. "How would you like me to drive mine up your oversized arse?" Marty said.

Danny broke in. "Marty, with all due respect, you want me out of the score I'm out, but what about my end? This is one sweet score, I pull this off I could pay you off. Plus, I'd give you a piece of my end without you even askin', not countin' what you'll take from those other guys."

Marty shook his head. "Naw, do as I say, Danny, I'm tryin' to help you here. Things go right I'll throw you somethin' after. You don't show they'll replace you, these guys always got backup. Besides, these things go bad sometimes. Hittin' an armored car doesn't guarantee you're gettin' away with it." Marty took the other Mocha Blast from Andre and passed it to the younger man. They touched cups together. "Relax, kid, this is the easiest dough you'll ever make."

37

ELAINE RAMSEY PULLED the door to her apartment closed. On her way out she picked a child's glove off the hall floor and hung it on the banister to her left before exiting the outside door. On the sidewalk, Heidi, the neighbors' Labrador mix, greeted her, its tail wagging crazily. Elaine pulled the strap of her pocketbook up over her head. "Hey, wait a minute; didn't I give you a treat this morning?" she said. The Labrador glanced to the right, then up again at her friend, then repeated the process, her eyes shining expectantly. Elaine lowered the bag and frowned. "You're a pretty pooch, you're lucky," she said, opening her bag and removing a ziplock pouch filled with strips of dried beef. She bent down and placed one in the dog's mouth just as a car pulled up on Fifth Street behind her. A car door opened.

"Good morning, Ms. Ramsey," said a voice from the street. Elaine turned to see Jackie Curran standing by the open driver's side door of the blue Marquis, his mouth curled in a grin.

Elaine put her hands on her hips and feigned annoyance. "You said you'd call," she said.

"I did and I have," Wacko said. "Got time for lunch? I'll take you to the L Street Diner — it's cheap, fast, and good."

Heidi nudged Elaine's leg. "No more for you," she said, patting the dog's head.

"We can take the mutt along too, come on," Wacko said.

Elaine sighed. "She's not a mutt, she's a lady, Jackie Curran. Obviously you're not used to dealing with them. You'd think you call, give me some notice, a girl likes notice."

Wacko smiled. "I notice you a lot, Elaine Ramsey, I apologize," he said, bowing and pretending to doff his cap. "Come on, sweetie, the clock's tickin' and we ain't gettin' any younger." Wacko walked around the front of the Mercury Marquis and opened the passenger door. "Come on, I'll make it interesting, I'll make you laugh, I promise." Elaine looked down and shook her head before snapping her pocketbook shut and heading for the car.

Inside the L Street Diner they took the third booth on the right in front of a sunny window overlooking East Fifth Street and the Monsignor Powers elderly housing complex across the street.

"So, how's Mum, the brothers?" Wacko said. A tired looking waitress, a brunette with a large star tattoo on her right bicep, approached. "One regular coffee, one tea with milk, no sugar," he said to the waitress, who nodded and shuffled away.

"Momma's good, thank God, yours still living on Pilsudski Way? You know my auntie Alice, sweet thing, moved in over there last month," Elaine said, nodding towards the Monsignor Powers complex.

"You're lucky," Wacko said. "I heard it's nice over there, it's clean and the food's decent. You're lucky, I can't get my Mum out of the projects. I've offered to move her into a nice place over in Quincy, in my apartment complex. A two-bedroom unit fully furnished, but she'll have nothin' to do with it. I worry about where she is, it's gettin' bad over there with them bringin' the others in. They're breakin' into units, beatin' down old ladies for their pocketbooks, social security checks," Wacko said.

Elaine's shoulders slumped. "It's the way, Jack, some people refuse to move, it's all they know," she said. She nodded at the waitress and took her tea.

"Go wan, order," Wacko said, sipping from his cup.

"Tuna on wheat, tomatoes, pickles on the side," Elaine said.

"It comes with fries," the waitress said.

"I'll pass," Elaine said. Wacko peered at her over his cup. Elaine pinched either side of her waist. "Gotta watch the girlish figure or no one else will," she said. "What about you, eating?"

"Already ate," Wacko said, checking out two construction types who just came in.

Elaine scowled. "You said lunch."

"I did, for you," Wacko said, motioning the waitress away. "Now, tell me some things. How's life treatin' ya?"

Elaine smiled. "Okay, my sister Mary and her husband bought a nice three-family on Swallow Street. Ever think about moving back to Southie? They're looking for good tenants."

"What do you mean, back, I never left. I still got my place on Patterson Way," Wacko said.

"Can't let go of the memories, huh, even the bad ones?" Elaine said.

"I grew up in the projects, it's part of who I am, tough to give it up. Ask the BHA, I still live there, me and Kevin. I pay the rent on time. I don't know, Elaine, you think it's weird?" Wacko said.

"Jack, I heard you got a nice apartment in Quincy. Why not buy a house? Heard you can afford to." Elaine batted her eyelashes at him and sipped her tea.

Wacko smiled. The star tattoo reappeared and put Elaine's sandwich in front of her. Wacko looked up and lifted his cup a few inches off the table. The tattoo returned a moment later with a pot and refilled it.

"A house, too permanent," Wacko said.

"What's wrong with permanence?" Elaine said.

"In my life there is none, don't know if I could handle it. Next thing you know I'd be on the city payroll cashin' a weekly check."

"There's nothing wrong with working an honest job, my father gave us a decent life working water and sewer," Elaine said.

"You still helpin' with your sister's kids?" Wacko said. "How old are they now?"

"The girls are nine and eleven, good kids but she's got her hands full with them. I help out as I can," Elaine said.

"What about your boyfriend, he help out too?"

Elaine looked out the window. "David doesn't get involved much. The girls haven't taken to him. Maybe it's too soon after their Da passed. There's an uneasy peace when David's around, and they can be fresh."

"Fresh? I don't do fresh," Wacko said.

"Not really fresh, but you know kids, they're rude at times. David won't tolerate it. As a result I can't get him to come over," Elaine said.

"Can't blame him," Wacko said.

"David says I spend too much time with them. I'm over there three nights a week and stop by on the weekends."

"They're not your kids."

"I have obligations," Elaine said.

"Ya, to David," Wacko said. He touched Elaine's left hand with his. "Doesn't make for a great relationship. He'll get tired of it."

Elaine pulled away. She picked up her tea with both hands. "It is what it is, Jack," Elaine said.

"You say you're movin' in together, right? You both work. You're saying he'll only see you twice a week for supper?" Wacko said.

"Actually, I work Thursdays until eight thirty. We'll have supper together once during the week," Elaine said.

"And you're at your sister's on weekends too?" Wacko took a sip of coffee and raised his eyebrows. "Some people, like me, are not cut out for relationships, but I don't fake it."

A crimson blush raced across Elaine's cheeks. "Jackie Curran, you and I are not horses of the same color. I love David and our relationship, it's just I have other obligations. I will not turn my back on my sister or those kids," Elaine said.

"Has he asked you to?"

"No, not really, but he's impatient, says I'm rarely with him and when I am I'm tired."

"Ah, family, in the end that's all we really have, isn't that what they say?" Wacko said. He picked up his cup, then put it down. "Eat your sandwich."

Elaine bit off a small piece of crust and quietly chewed. "I'm stuck between a rock and a hard place," she said, wiping her mouth with a napkin. "I love David, it's just between my job and my family he's getting squeezed out. I don't know what to do. I feel like I'm shutting down almost, it's not voluntary, it's just happening."

"That's why I don't get involved with anyone. Don't have the time. Desire? Maybe the desire either. Don't want to be corralled. Sound familiar?" Wacko said.

Elaine took another small bite and stared out the window as she chewed.

"Ya, know, Elaine, I think we're a lot more alike than you think."

The redhead sighed. "I hope Auntie Alice likes it over there, she's comfortable," Elaine said, nodding at the Monsignor Powers apartments. She put down her half-eaten sandwich. "I think I lost my appetite," she said.

"You'll get it back," Wacko said. "I always do."

38

WACKO CURRAN RESTED HIS ELBOWS on top of a pink granite tombstone that read MARY PINCKNEY BELOVED IN OUR HEARTS 1901–1952 and with both hands held a huge pair of Swift binoculars to his eyes. Kevin stood to his left and held, in his right hand, a large bouquet of tulips, baby's breath, and carnations. He propped his left hand above his eyes, palm down, and squinted.

"I can barely make it out, Jack, maybe I need glasses," Kevin said. With his right index finger, Wacko adjusted the focus on the binoculars.

"Naw, that bank's a half mile away, maybe more, and it's hazy. You need these to really bring it in," Wacko said.

Kevin touched his arm. "What you see? Let me take a look, Jack."

"I'm seein' plenty, missin' nothin'. There's a lot of activity around the Union Bank today," Wacko said.

"I'm nervous," Kevin said. "If the heat's down there maybe they got binoculars too and they're watchin' us."

Wacko lowered the glasses and handed them to his brother. Kevin dropped the bouquet and brought the glasses up to his eyes.

"Relax, without rats these guys couldn't catch a cold in a pneumonia ward," Wacko said.

"Boy, these things work, fucking power zoom, wow! You're right, there are a lot of guys around there. What the? See the two on the roof of the pizza joint across the street, construction types it looks like. And that phone guy near the top of the pole to the left of the bank, see him? Just sittin' there lookin'; what's he doing?" Kevin said.

"I counted about eight who look like they don't belong. Like they're tryin', though," Wacko said. "Just wish I could see their faces better. Gimme the glasses." Kevin handed them to his brother. "And pick up them fucking flowers, someone comes along we gotta look like we're payin' our respects, then no one's got nothin' to say," Wacko said.

"Like what are you doin' with those fucking binoculars?" Kevin said, picking up the bouquet.

"Maybe I'm bird-watchin', great birds in cemeteries," Wacko said, readjusting the focus. "Their faces, if I could only make out their mugs, cops, no matter what ya can pick 'em out a mile away."

"But not a half mile?" Kevin said.

Wacko glanced at his brother.

"Watch it or maybe I'll send your skinny ass down there to take pictures," he said. He held the glasses back up to his eyes. "Ya, they're cops, I can smell it. Ho, the pole guy's climbin' down. What gives?" Wacko said, straightening up.

"What's happenin'?" Kevin said.

"And here it comes, Massca Armored." Wacko looked at his watch. "Ten-oh-five, they're five minutes late, unusual." He straightened up and stamped his foot.

"They're parked and just sittin' there, nothing's happening, but the two guys on the roof across from them are leanin' over the edge now watchin'," Wacko said.

"Maybe they're just curious, everyone likes to watch money being moved," Kevin said.

"Hey, the driver's door just opened," Wacko said. "That guy never gets out. Ho, the side door just popped and one, two guys gettin' out. Never had two in the back before. The whole thing reeks." Wacko stepped out from behind the stone and took three long steps forward, the binoculars held tight to his face.

"Let me look, Jack," Kevin said.

"Shit, shit, SHIT! I was right, Kev. Three guys in SWAT get up, just walked out of the bank, fucking cops. They're talkin' to the three guards, fuck, Weymouth police, three marked cruisers pulling in one behind the other. More blue lights coming now from both directions up Washington Street. Can't make out . . . Staties, fucking state police. Fucking Danny boy, our little pal. Those guys on the roof put their tools down, they got rifles in their hands now. I count five, ten, fourteen, there's gotta be twenty cops down there. Would have hacked our heads off. Oh, Danny boy you're gonna burn. We're outta here," Wacko said, pivoting and walking towards the car.

"What about the flowers? Maybe I should save them for Danny?" Kevin said, staring at the bank in the distance. He heard the Marquis's door slam shut and the engine roar to life. Kevin dropped the flowers on the grave of Mary Pinckney and headed towards the car.

■　■　■

On Athens Street, Andre Athanas pulled the blue Chevy Malibu onto the curb near the corner of Dorchester Street and parked. He got out of the car, walked to the corner, and looked up and down Dorchester Street before he cracked a smile and nodded. The Malibu's passenger door sprung open, and Marty Fallon got out, a dark blue baseball cap with the red-and-blue Modern Continental Construction logo on it snug on his head.

As he headed up the sidewalk, Marty removed his reflective Vuarnets and rubbed the lenses with a tissue he took from his pocket. "I just can't figure it out, Andre. We picked up nothing on either scanner, Weymouth or state police, maybe they're using a special frequency? If we only had a scanner for the feds, but nothing on the other two means nothin' happened, right? What's with that? You think Danny told 'em?"

Andre stuck his right index finger into his ear and wiggled it hard. "Dunno, boss. Maybe Wacko got spooked, you think? Maybe he went to pick up Danny this morning and when Danny was a no-show he got spooked."

"Danny told me they had backup, someone else in the wings just in case. Jack Curran doesn't get spooked; he's cold and fucking capable. Somethin' happened, somethin'," Marty said.

"Cops? Maybe there was an extra car or two in the bank parking lot when they got there. That would spook me, might throw him off. Maybe it was just bad vibes, boss," Andre said.

"Vibes? What the fuck you talkin', vibes?"

"Vibes, you know, it's kind of hard to describe, boss, but when I was out there workin', if something didn't feel right, I mean it had to feel good. If it didn't we'd pass, no questions asked. Had a rule if someone wanted to pass on game day it was kind of like a right," Andre said.

"Cocaine paranoia," Marty said.

"I don't do coke," Andre said.

"Kevin does."

"Wacko don't, and he's the boss," Andre said.

"Vibes, huh? You can put your vibes in Kevin's crack pipe and smoke it; I think there's more to this. My gut tells me something's goin' on, but what?"

"Your gut? That's vibes, boss, no disrespect intended," Andre said, stepping away.

Marty rammed his Vuarnets back with his middle finger; his teeth flashed as he grinned. "What I tell you about lecturing me?" he said, stepping towards the giant. He hurled the balled-up tissue in Andre's face.

Andre bent over, picked it up, and stuffed it in his pocket. "We . . . we still gonna visit Danny?" he said.

"You talk too fucking much," Marty said, turning and heading down the sidewalk. Andre caught up with him. "Put your hat on, you moron, and keep your head down. I gotta tell you everything?"

Side by side the pair continued down Dorchester Street then stopped in front of number 18. Andre checked the house. "This is it, boss, Danny King's joint," he said.

Marty looked up and down the street, then both men climbed the three steps and entered the foyer. Over one of two buzzers on the left the name King was written on a piece of torn paper in runny, black ink. Marty watched the street through the window of the outside door. "Go ahead," he said.

Andre pressed the buzzer. As they waited a huge Boston Sand and Gravel cement truck, its barrel spinning slowly, rumbled down Dorchester Street, and the building vibrated.

A shrill entry buzzer sounded, and Andre twisted the doorknob and flicked the cheap wooden door aside. In the hallway to the right was a stairway, cluttered with boxes, old clothes, and a single black Rollerblade, leading to the second floor. On the left, fifteen feet down, a dead bolt snapped and a door warily opened a crack. "Ya, who is it?" Danny said.

"Danny, it's us," Andre said. Like a frightened turtle, Danny King stuck his head outside, then as quickly pulled it back. Andre grabbed the doorknob and jammed the door with his foot. Danny grunted and threw his shoulder against the door. "Danny, what the fuck? Open up we gotta talk," Andre said over his shoulder.

"Marty, please, fucking Jesus, please, I don't . . ." Danny King said.

Marty slid to Andre's left and reached through the narrow opening, placing his right hand on top of Andre's while simultaneously placing his foot on top of the giant's. With Marty in place, Andre pulled both his foot and his hand back, put his palms on the door, and rammed it with his shoulder. The center panel cracked and the door swung back on its hinges, knocking Danny to the floor. Like a toad, Marty leaped inside with Andre following, pulling the door closed behind him.

"Ho, Danny, not very hospitable," Marty said breathing hard and straightening his jacket.

Danny warily watched both men from the floor. "I'm sorry, I didn't mean to panic, it's just I didn't expect . . ."

Marty Fallon waggled an index finger, and a smile spread across his face like fungus on a rain forest floor. "Expect? You little fuck. Expect what?" he said. He took a pair of latex gloves from a pocket and pulled them on while Andre did the same. Danny got up. Andre shoved him into the wall as he passed by to search the rest of the apartment.

"Marty, I don't understand, what gives, did it go down?" Danny said.

Andre came back down the hall and shrugged. "Nothing, empty," Andre said.

"Naw, Danny, it didn't go down. Go down, hmmm. See, we got these scanners, and at ten o'clock this morning there was no activity on them, nothin'. You'd think there would have been maniacs tipping an armored truck in Weymouth for two million, but naw, nothin'," Marty said, following Danny, who now backed up the hallway.

"What can I say, Marty, ya know, they told me, showed me, I told you. Told you everything I knew; you guys maybe want coffee? Wacko Curran told me ten o'clock this morning, and he was here when he said he'd be, at least the doorbell rang at eight fifteen, but like you said I didn't answer. I must have overslept," Danny said, smiling weakly.

Marty removed his Vuarnets. "Get into the bedroom," he said.

"I like this place," Andre said looking around then turned and savagely punched Danny in the face then grabbed and tossed him like a doll left through a doorway. Danny stumbled over his running shoes and fell onto his back on the bed.

"Marty, I don't know what happened, I swear," Danny said, wiping blood from his nose with the back of his hand. He stared at it horrified and said, "They came lookin' for me, the doorbell rang, then there was a noise in the alley outside, someone lookin' in the fucking window. They went to Weymouth to do it, Marty, I know they did, I saw the play."

Andre kneeled on the edge of the bed. Marty nodded, and Andre planted his right foot on the floor, then grabbed Danny by the seat of the pants and the hair and flipped him face-first onto the mattress. Danny's scream was cut short by Andre's fist, driven pile-driver style, into the middle of his back, knocking the air from his lungs.

"No screamin'," Andre said, pinning Danny's shoulders.

Marty said, "Danny, you offered me coffee a minute ago but I declined, too much caffeine. They say too much caffeine can make you high, you know that, Danny?" Marty Fallon pulled a two-inch, blue-black, Smith and Wesson Chief's Special from his back pocket. "I think you lied to me, Danny, or gave me lousy information. Either way it cost me plenty," he said. He came around the back of Andre and stopped. "Ya, coffee makes you high. No, I don't want any coffee, Danny. If I want to get high, I kill people, and right about now . . . I feel like gettin' high."

Quicker than a shark turns, Marty grabbed a pillow and covered Danny's head. Danny felt pressure at the base of his skull, saw darkness, then stars multiplying, twirling, growing larger before mutating into the shape of a giant arctic snowy owl unfolding its wings overhead.

39

HIS MIND RACED at a hundred while Wacko Curran gunned the Marquis along at seventy down Route 3 to Boston. Precisely at the 93 merge he rammed his palm into the center of the steering column. The horn blared. "Move it, move it, you piece of shit, accelerate," he screamed at the green Chevy van in front of him. He looked at Kevin. "You see that? The way that piece of shit drifted into my lane; no signal, didn't even turn his empty, fucking head? Son-of-a-bitch," Wacko said.

Kevin checked the side-view mirror.

"Cool down, Jack, we're all set, just cool down, stay in the right lane, we want Quincy," he said.

Wacko took the Furnace Brook Parkway exit and stopped at the lights at the bottom of the ramp. He slapped the steering wheel again. "Ya know, the more I think about it, we would've been dead, fucking dead, any survivors doing thirty years at Lewisburg," Wacko said, shaking his head. The light changed, and Wacko's breathing was labored as he followed the meandering parkway towards Wollaston Beach.

"I know the way it looks, Jack," Kevin said, trying to calm his brother.

"Looks, what you mean 'looks?'" Wacko said.

"You think Danny lost his balls then went to the cops, but why?" Kevin said.

"Fucked if I know, but we're gonna find out," Wacko said.

"We going to his house?" Kevin said.

"First thing we're doin' is heading out to Squantum, Marina Bay, use a pay phone to call Janowski, tell him to sit tight," Wacko said.

"Mike's gonna want to bang him he finds out," Kevin said. "Him and Danny had a falling out years ago over Ralphie Iianella's sister. Crazy shit, neither one dates her now, but the feelin's run deep, go figure."

"I don't want Janowski involved in this, we'll handle it ourselves," Wacko said.

At the lights at Dunkin' Donuts, Wacko turned right, then took a left a quarter mile up at the huge white sign that read MARINA BAY. They passed a condominium complex on the right that looked like a French palace. Kevin pressed his forehead against the door glass. He said, "I could live out here real easy."

"Everything goes good on Thursday, buy yourself a fucking penthouse," Wacko said. He glanced at his brother and grabbed at the back of his neck. "But you won't. Why? Cause we don't flash, we never flash," Wacko said. Kevin frowned.

At the end of the road Wacko turned right and pulled over in front of a bank of pay phones. He got out, threw some change into one.

While Wacko talked, Kevin turned on the radio. Michael Jackson sang "Beat It." "Beat this," Kevin said, staring out the windshield at another condominium development a hundred yards down the road near the waterfront.

Wacko got back in. "Mike's sittin' tight," he said.

"You tell him what we saw?" Kevin said.

"No, I'll tell him everything when I see him," Wacko said, pulling out into the roadway.

"Those condos near the water, I could live there too. What good's the money we can't spend it?" Kevin said.

"You need a doctor, right, you're sick?" Wacko said.

"I'm not sick," Kevin muttered.

"Good. You hungry? Need a roof overhead, a car? What you need, Kevin, tell me?"

Kevin sunk in the seat and put his feet up on the glove box.

Wacko said, "You . . . we have everything we need and more. You want. This, that, whatever, that's fine, Kevin, and that's what money's for, but remember this, everything in life is timing. Now's the time, brother, the time for takin'. Thursday we're takin' a bundle, and why's that? Because the timin's right. The feds are going to relax after that fiasco today out in Weymouth, afraid to make a move, and that's why we're goin' to," Wacko said.

"So, we make the move, you're sayin' we wait until we're gray haired to spend the money? What happens we don't get old, Jack, what happens then? What happens I don't want to wait? There's lots out here who make it fast and spend it the same way. They drive nice cars, buy clothes off the rack on Newbury Street, broads all over 'em. Hell, even Beezo got a nice condo down Farragut Road and he don't have money," Kevin said.

They crossed the Neponset Bridge and headed down Morrissey Boulevard.

"Here's the deal, Kevin. We do well Thursday, you take your end of it and do what you want. I ain't your keeper. But if you do that, you're on your own. When this score goes down there'll be major heat, you spend like a drunken sailor, you'll throw logs, big logs on the fire. Me, I'll be lyin' low hopin' to stay out of jail. That's my thing, Kevin, stayin' out of jail; you been there, be your thing too," Wacko said.

Kevin sighed, put his feet on the floor, and sat up. "Okay, Jack, we'll do it your way," he said.

Wacko gave Kevin's ear a tug. "Good, now you're talkin'."

At the rotary in South Boston near the state police barracks, Wacko depressed the accelerator and followed the seawall that stretched like a thick, gray rope along Day Boulevard. At L Street he turned left and, obeying the speed limit, headed toward Danny King's.

40

AT THE CORNER OF D STREET and Old Colony Boulevard, Marty Fallon instructed Andre Athanas to pull the Malibu into the Merit gas station. "Fill it, I'll make the call," Marty said, getting out of the car.

He walked to a phone stand at the back of the lot and picked up the receiver. After casually looking over either shoulder and seeing no one around, he removed a cup-shaped device from his pocket and fitted the rubber end over the mouthpiece of the phone. He flicked a switch on the device, and a small, red light on it glowed. Marty dropped a quarter and a dime into the pay phone and punched a number. He leaned against the stand and casually checked the nails of his right hand.

"Ya, District Six? You need to send someone down to eighteen Dorchester Street. Someone's dead recently," he said. He pushed down on the clicker with his right index and middle finger, terminating the call. He removed the device from the mouthpiece and returned it to his pocket. He checked the area around him again, then removed two alcohol wipes in foil packages from a pocket in his shirt, then with his back to the street, carefully wiped the phone and clicker. He stuffed the wipes in his pocket and returned to the car. Andre had just finished squeegeeing the windshield as he approached.

"Good job, Andre, glass is fucking beautiful. Why don't you check the oil," Marty said, reaching into the car and pulling on the hood release. He hit the trunk release button, walked around back, and took a roll of paper towels from it. He tore off a couple of sheets and handed them to Andre, who had just located the dipstick. Both men hovered over the engine.

"The way I see it, Andre, when Wacko Curran sees he's been had by his little partner, Danny King, he's gonna want to do him. Wacko's not one to wait. My guess he's on his way from Braintree to Danny's house as we check our fucking oil."

"You think he'll go straight to Danny's, boss?"

"We're gonna find out, Andre. I just put a bug up the BPD's arse. They say a bee can't sting twice, but maybe we'll prove 'em wrong. With a little luck when the Currans arrive at Danny King's place they're gonna get stung, and it's gonna be one hell of an allergic reaction."

▪   ▪   ▪

Wacko Curran turned onto East Third Street and followed it until the post office came up on the right. He cut the wheel left and parallel-parked across the road from the three mailboxes out front. Both brothers exited the Marquis simultaneously, then walked down the middle of the street towards Emerson Auto Service. Near the garage entrance the men casually turned right and, careful to keep their heads down, continued down Emerson Street.

At Dorchester Street they turned right and stopped in front of number 20. Once inside the foyer, Wacko turned back towards the street and checked either end through the dirty, lace-curtained door glass. "Hit it again. Where the fuck is he?" Wacko said, as Kevin hit the buzzer again.

Wacko stepped in front of the solid wooden door and anxiously scraped the soles of his feet on the mat as Kevin kept his eye on the street. Wacko pressed the buzzer again. Kevin suddenly pulled away from the window. "Whoa, we got something comin' up the street, Jack," he said, nodding in the direction of the Broadway merge. "Heat comin' behind a cement truck." Wacko peeked out the window.

Two huge Boston Sand and Gravel trucks rumbled slowly towards them down Dorchester Street. The floor of the building vibrated from their enormous combined weight. The second truck briefly shifted to the left, revealing directly behind it the alternating high beams and flashing blue lights of a Boston Police cruiser.

With a fistful of doorknob Wacko cursed softly, put his shoulder to the wood and rammed. There was a barely discernible splintering noise; the door held fast.

"Somethin's bad here," Wacko said. He looked through the curtains up the street again. A white Saab had just turned left off East Third Street midway into Dorchester Street and stopped. Unable to pass around the front of the first cement truck in the narrow street, it sat there in a stand-off. "Saved by an idiot. Come on, we're outta here," Wacko said, pulling Kevin by the arm down the steps as the air was sliced by three sharp blasts of the cement truck's air horn and the Saab's backup lights flared.

On the sidewalk Wacko shifted his attention to the other end of the street. A police car turning off West First Street, its blue lights flashing, entered his line of vision and was heading their way. "Be cool, we're headin' back to East Second," Wacko said. He stopped and squatted like he was tying his shoe, then got up and headed in the opposite direction.

Kevin followed Wacko's lead, his eyes glued to the sidewalk. "Maybe it's nothin', Jack, cops escortin' trucks through the neighborhood because of the kids, ya know?" he said, his lips barely moving.

"You idiot, cops escort from the front, what's wrong with you? Maybe it's nothin', but my gut's twitchin'. We'll circle the block, come back," Wacko said.

They turned the corner at East Second Street and picked up the pace. Seconds later they were moving along at a slow jog towards the post office. "We're gettin' the car," Wacko said.

"But you said —"

"Fuck what I said, I don't like this. We're outta here," Wacko said.

As they got close to the blue Marquis, a white Lincoln Town Car pulled up. The passenger window went down, and Beezo Houlihan, hands on the steering wheel, leaned halfway across the seat, wearing a huge grin on his face.

"Jack, Kevin, how're you doin', something cookin' around the corner, three cruisers over there. Looks like they're gonna pull an entry on a house. Doesn't Danny King live on Dorchester Street?" he said.

"Wouldn't know," Wacko said. He nodded towards the post office. "Just paid a few bills. Fucking credit card companies, miss a payment. You think I'm bad, try stiffin' Visa."

Beezo nodded. "Tell me about it, my credit's shot . . . on the cards I mean. Got something goin' on at Foxwoods this weekend, Jack, thinkin' I'd borrow fifteen hundred, two grand. You all right with that?" Beezo said.

Wacko opened the door to the Marquis. "We're square on that other thing; ya, Kevin will take care of you. You just take care of that car," Wacko said, winking.

"She's my baby," Beezo said. "I'll see you Friday, Kev. Remember now, don't head that way, they got Dorchester blocked off."

"Thanks for the tip," Wacko said, getting into the car. Kevin started to do the same, then stopped and yelled over the roof of the Marquis. "Remember Beezo, the only accessory that Conty's missin's me," Kevin said. Beezo gave Kevin the finger and drove away.

41

MARTY FALLON LEANED BACK into his brown leather, heavily padded chair, his elbows up and his fingers intertwined behind his head. His eyes were closed, and he was thinking.

There was heat in South Boston today. They had found that King kid dead in his house down the Lower End shot execution style, and the new captain at District Six, Declan Connerty, an up-and-coming maniac with a penchant for detailed investigation, was turning the town upside down. The old captain, Freddy Blasidell, would have handled it differently, Freddy believed in low key. Don't muck up the waters too much; you can't see the bottom, especially when you're trying to find the fish that ate a bottom-feeder like Danny King. Connerty was different, like a fucking hurricane, he didn't care what was disturbed or who.

This guy didn't use the proper channels. He just kept ripping at things until a bug popped out of the wood, and then he'd squeeze it. Marty was good at supplying bugs, getting just the right information to the right guy. But with someone tearing around, how you going to get one in, give the cops something to work with so they'd leave legitimate guys like Marty Fallon alone? This was part of doing business in the city, he knew it, but knowing something and accepting it were horses of different colors.

There was a knock at the door, and Andre Athanas stuck his head in the office. "Boss, the Currans are downstairs in the bar, they want to talk. You busy, got a headache or somethin'? Maybe I should tell them come back later?"

Marty rocked forward in the chair and flicked the switch on the small halogen lamp on his desk, the base of which was a pirate ship, sails unfurled, with eight tiny cannons jutting from either side.

"Tell 'em . . . tell 'em to come in," he said, pushing the ship slightly forward.

"Kevin too?"

Marty repositioned the lamp. "Ya, Kevin too, tell 'em." He leaned back in the chair and returned to his former position.

There was a knock on the partially opened door, and Wacko Curran entered the room, followed closely behind by his brother. "How're we doin', boys, what can I do for you?" Marty said.

Wacko approached the desk while Kevin closed the door and stood in front of it, "We got problems," Wacko said.

Marty Fallon's eyes narrowed. "What do you mean *we*?" he said, unlocking his hands and rocking forward.

Wacko put both hands on the desk, purposely crowding Marty's space. "I haven't done a fucking thing lately that anyone would want to question me about, but still I hear the cops are lookin' for me, why?"

Marty shook his head and shrugged. "You must be talkin' about that kid, King. I hear he had problems, you don't far as I know," he said. "Danny King got himself killed or he killed himself, either way seems I'm the one with the problem, not you. That bum died owing me five grand, what he owe you?"

Wacko pushed away from the desk and walked around to the window. He separated the blinds, glanced out, and let them snap back into place. He tapped the back of Marty's chair. "Mind I open this?" Wacko said. Marty nodded. Wacko twisted the Levolor bar counterclockwise, and sunlight chased shadows into the corners.

"Danny King didn't owe me a thing, never did business with him. Knew him to say hi to, what's up, but I got word from someone, a cop, that other cops and the feds are sniffin' around and my name's comin' up. Seems the feds were down the Quencher first thing this morning askin' Morgan Daly questions about me, what's with that?" Wacko said.

Marty pointed at Kevin. "You. Get away from the door. Andre

comes in, he'll launch you like a fucking rocket," he said. He shut off
the halogen lamp.

"Listen, Jack, we're — they're talkin' Danny King being murdered. Murder or suicide, Jack, why would the feds be askin' questions about you? If anything, why wouldn't it be the locals?"

Wacko stared out the window and said, "My man tells me it's the
feds, actually it's a bank task force, combined state and federal. Maybe
they were investigatin' Danny for banks. Hell, everyone knew he was
into banks," Wacko said.

"What he was into was too much coke, maybe that's what killed
him," Marty said.

"I hear he was capped," Wacko said.

Marty Fallon's face contorted like he'd sat on a porcupine. "Shot,
overdosed, hung from the fucking rafters, who the fuck cares? I say
worry about yourself. You got an alibi where you were when he died,
right, volunteer for a paraffin test whatever, on this you're covered,
but there are other things," Marty said.

Wacko screwed the Levolor rod half a turn clockwise, and the
room dimmed. "I'm listenin'," he said.

Marty pulled a pack of Marlboros from his pocket. Kevin clapped
once, pointed, and laughed. "I thought you quit," he said.

"I thought you quit gamblin', sit down," Marty said. Kevin sat
down in a chair by the door and looked at the floor. Marty turned in
his chair and stared at Wacko.

"Jack, I was going to reach out to you, a little bird told me you
got problems. One of your earners, a broad, can't never trust a broad,
is a rat. Seems she's talkin' to some cop down at Six whose brother's
DEA. I hear she's supposed to meet with him the day after tomorrow
down the federal courthouse."

Wacko released the Levolor rod; it slapped loudly on the blind. "I
only got one broad movin' product for me, you sure about this? How
sure?" he said.

Marty got up from his chair and slowly walked around his desk
to a small white refrigerator against the wall beneath an autographed
photo of Bobby Orr. "I'm sure about two things," he said. "One is
that I like you, Jack, always have. Two, I hate rats. Coke, water, Diet
Pepsi?" Marty said, opening the refrigerator door. He took out a six-
teen ounce Poland Spring, cracked the top, and offered it to Wacko.

Wacko waved it away. Marty sipped. "Actually, I'm sure of three things; I know what to do with rats. Do you, Jack?"

"I'll look into it," Wacko said.

"I would I was you, I'd do more than look into it. A slow leak in one of your tires, your girlfriend gettin' a little on the side, maybe your dog scratches its balls too much, these thing you look into. This —" Marty put the Poland Spring in the center of his desk and sat down behind it — "this you do something about, something to discourage any son-of-a-bitch from opening their mouth wide enough to put your ass in the slammer for ten years."

Kevin shifted uneasily in his seat, then got up. "I'm hungry, going out to the car, the other half of my sandwich," Kevin said, beginning to stand.

"Sit the fuck down," Marty said, gripping the Poland Spring tight enough that water bubbled slightly from the neck. "I'll tell you when we're done, chew on your fucking fingernails you're hungry."

Kevin looked at his brother, who closed his eyes and almost imperceptibly nodded. Kevin sat down.

"So, we all set on this, Jack? She's your man, do something about it. Better you, me she'd be suspicious I came sniffin' around. Arrange a meet, somethin'. Talk to her," Marty said.

"I'll handle this, Marty. She's lucky her brother's still up the Hill. He caught wind of this she'd be in intensive care, fact," Wacko said.

"Talk to her, Jackie. I don't want intensive care," Marty said.

42

"THERE'S SOMETHING ABOUT BURGER KING that puts McDonald's to shame," the fat man said. He unwrapped the bacon double cheeseburger, ketchup only, and bit into it. "Hmmm, ya know, you rarely get something cold, since they cook it to order hot, right out the bull's ass, you say ketchup only." He took another bite, then reached into the bag and pulled out a huge order of fries. "Fries?" he said.

The man sitting next to him declined. "Already ate," he said.

The fat man took another bite and smiled. "So here we are, sitting in Wollaston, not the beach, mind you, I got reasons not the beach, but Wollaston still the same. You guys from South Boston thinking Wollaston, this Burger King on Adams Street is in another country, am I correct? It's easy to get locked into your own weird little world. Sure you don't want some fries? And painful is you become locked out of your own little world for whatever reason, and that can happen. Me, I'm comfortable anywhere, Wollaston, Weymouth, hell, even South Boston I'd be okay in."

The other man shifted uneasily in his seat. "Do we have to go through all this? I can explain what happened," he said.

The fat man put the half-eaten cheeseburger on the dash and wiped his mouth with a paper napkin. "Go through this, like we're talking it's going to happen, that what you're saying? Let me tell you something, my friend, this has already happened. Tuesday morning I ate that bad fucking clam and my supervisor corn-holed me from here to fucking Provincetown. Friday there's an in-house meeting at the Moakley Building regarding this situation, my involvement in it, and your reliability as an informant. They want to cut you loose, Marty, and you know when that happens the clock's ticking until they convene a grand jury and throw a net over you and yours. That happens, my friend, no one from uncle's coming aboard to say how great Marty Fallon has been to the office in the past. I can see the write-up now in the *Globe* Metro section: 'Feds Clean House of Career Mob Rat,'" the fat man said.

Marty Fallon smiled. "Roy, I've been good in the past, haven't I? Made you look like a champ how many times? In anyone's book that counts for somethin'."

"You want to know what happened Tuesday? I'll give you a news flash. I don't fucking know either, but I'll tell you one thing, I'm gonna. But you gotta realize that these things take time. It's not like I'm takin' a book from the library for my information. My guy, the information he gave me was good. You think I'd give you shit info knowin' what was on the line?"

The fat man dabbed at his chin with the napkin. "And this reliable source, your guy, he the same bum they found down the Lower End with the two extra holes in his ear?"

Marty grimaced and lowered his head. "Ya, you're right, Danny

King, the poor bastard. The way I figure, these guys, for whatever reason, paranoid, cocaine paranoid probably, they're whacked out half the time, figured King was weak, rotten, whatever. My guess, trustin' no one, they put it to him, a little torture he talked; they whacked him," he said.

"But what could he tell them. He knew nothing about us," the fat man said.

"You're right, but he must have told them I was snoopin' around lookin' for an end from their score. My guess these guys have forgotten where they came from, who taught them what and what's owed. They forgot this, and these bums killed this poor kid for remindin' them, for doin' the right thing," Marty said.

The fat man nodded solemnly and sipped through his straw. "Ya know, I like Wendy's too, I tell you that? The food's always hot, not as hot as my ass this point in my career, but hot," he said, staring at his passenger.

"Marty, you should eat more. I eat when I'm nervous, you're not nervous? I'm surprised. I also eat when I'm pissed, helps me relax. Right now I'm pissed and nervous, that's why this is my second number-four king-sized combo today; can't beat it for five bucks and change." The fat man threw a fistful of fries into his mouth like he was eating peanuts.

"Did you know on Tuesday we had a complete tactical unit up there in Weymouth, plus a seven-man team from the Mass State Police, good boys. The locals had another twelve for backup. All that firepower for nothing, and the boys were itching to get it on, geez. Massca Armored's laughing at us, like we're ham-and-eggers. My supervisor eyeballing me like I'm useless as gum on your foot. Ya, I'm mad, and mad makes me hungry, can't stay away from places like this, a goddamn vicious cycle."

The fat man patted his belly, then grabbed a fold with both hands and violently shook it. He sighed. "My boss tells me they got Burger Kings in Montana; he gave me the address of one in Missoula. It didn't relax me. Nothing does these days, but I was thinking you could relax me, Marty, change my mood, help me lose some weight."

The fat man crushed his bag into a tight little ball and fired it into the windshield. Marty ducked, and it ended up in the backseat. "When I'm finished I always throw my trash away. I'd hate to throw you away, Marty. Can you tell me anything?" the fat man said.

Marty pulled a pack of Marlboros from a pocket inside his jacket. He tugged the cellophane off with his teeth and spit it on the floor of the car. He pulled one out. "You mind?" he said. He quickly put the butt in his mouth, then removed it the same way.

"Roll down the window," the fat man said, pushing in the cigarette lighter with a chunky index finger.

"I wasn't there in Danny King's apartment, I can't tell you I was, but I'm sure, surer than shit, those guys, Wacko and his pals, killed that kid." The cigarette lighter popped, and Marty snatched it out. He held the cigarette in his lap as he pressed the glowing lighter to one end.

"You're supposed to suck on it," the fat man said.

Marty glanced out the window, coughed, then shoved the cigarette between his lips. He touched the lighter to the end and sucked hard. His head was spinning. What the hell was happening? If they cut him loose, his game, all of it, was over. He pondered how much money he could gather before he was forced to run for his life. He was already losing a fortune. His loan-shark customers were making themselves scarce, the heat was on, there was blood in the water; at the very least the parasites knew they had a grace period.

Most of his income came from drugs. He had plenty of pot in the warehouse down off of D Street, enough to last until things cooled down, but cocaine was another matter. Fifteen kilos was a three-week supply. He had eight left but was afraid to go to the stash house, afraid of transponders in his car, bugs in his phones, fear was costing him plenty. He was hurting in other areas too.

His bookmakers were operating out of closets, their offices shut down by Boston police infuriated by the fact the feds were crawling all over their backyard.

In another area Marty was losing four to five grand a week from guys who specialized in hot credit cards. Marty gave them weekly marching orders for whatever was in demand: winter coats, TV's, laptops, etcetera. It was clean, no heat; his men hit stores across state lines, in malls in Manchester, Hartford, and Providence. He paid twenty-five percent of the retail for goods, then charged his dozens of eager customers seventy-five percent, but crossing state lines with criminal intent was a federal crime, and now that the feds were everywhere the store was closed.

"I think I got somethin', maybe," Marty said.

The fat man rolled his eyes. "What you got, their equipment in the trunk? Their machine guns, and hand grenades, for chrissakes. We done it my way, I'm out of my mind listening to you, we'd have guys with buying and selling bombs and guns. Great headlines, the public would have eaten it up. I'm a hero; you've got a bigger license to do whatever you want.

Now we got guys running around out there with this stuff planning God knows what and my appetite's growing in leaps and bounds. Now I'll ask you one more time, can you give me anything that's not gonna make me hungry?" the fat man said.

"They're gonna kill a girl," Marty said softly. "One of their earners got her knickers up in a knot owin' them, and she's talkin' to the BPD. A meet with the DEA's been set."

The fat man leaned back into the headrest and closed his eyes like he was trying to sleep. After a moment he opened his mouth like he was going to say something, then closed it like he changed his mind. Seconds later he opened it again. "How do you know this?"

"The Currans, in a face-to-face, told me."

"Not interested," the fat man said, opening his eyes. "It's a local beef murder. I need something that the federal statutes go on and on about, something with hair on it."

"Maybe they'll use a machine gun on her," Marty said.

"You really think they'll do her?" the fat man said, picking a loose fry off the seat between his legs. He examined it, rotating it between his thumb and index finger, like it was a two-carat diamond on the end of a stickpin before dropping it to the floor.

"I think," Marty said. "Get them on this, who knows where it might lead. Kevin's a cokehead, and I've never known one to hold his water."

The fat man tore open a Wash'n Dri, wiped his mouth and hands with the moist towelette, then rolled down the window and tossed it out. "Maybe I'm not as hungry as I was before," he said.

43

WACKO CURRAN STOOD at the pinnacle of Dorchester Heights and had to shield his eyes from the glare of the sun reflecting off the ninety-foot white marble tower in front of him. A mile away Boston Harbor sparkled in the early morning sun. More than two hundred years ago, in this very place, American patriots fired cannon, hauled from Fort Ticonderoga in New York, onto British frigates anchored in the harbor.

Wacko often came here as a child. It was the highest place in South Boston. Wacko figured the air was probably cleaner, and the place was usually empty — he liked to be alone. On hot summer days he'd come and sit in the shade at the base of this monument, imagining how it must have been during those revolutionary times, the cannons booming, the men shouting, loading, reloading, and the desperation of those in the harbor, the fearful eye they cast to the very spot on which he stood. Today he wasn't alone.

Wacko sat down on a bench next to Kevin and closed his eyes and enjoyed the warmth of the early morning sun. Kevin casually surveyed the area, seeing no one, then slyly glanced at his brother before he bent and retrieved something from his sock. He removed the rubber cap of the small plastic vial and tapped out a pile of pale yellow powder on top of his left hand. He snorted it up through a straw and gagged.

Wacko's eyes snapped open like someone unloaded a gun next to his ear. "What the fuck's wrong with you? You got no respect, this is a national park. Besides, we got the score comin' up. What I tell you about waitin' until after?" Wacko said.

"It *is* after," Kevin said, shaking his head. "After that clusterfuck up in Weymouth Tuesday and the shit with Danny King, I figure this is as after as it's gonna get." He pressed his left index finger alongside his nose and inhaled hard. "Wow, this shit's wild. Step on it three times, Jackie boy, we still got an excellent product." He jumped up off the bench and threw a couple of uppercuts in the air, then jabbed and danced to the right.

"You still plannin' to move on the North End thing next week?" Kevin said, his arms moving faster and faster.

"Ya, I'm plannin'," Wacko said.

"I think you're nuts, becomin' a real nutcappa, Jack, I dunno," Kevin said.

"I decide what we're gonna do," Wacko said.

Kevin threw a right lead, left uppercut, hook combination. Wacko closed his eyes.

"But what about Danny King? Before we make a move shouldn't we know more than just the fact he set us up, like why, and who the fuck whacked him? And that O'Connell bitch, what we gonna do about her, huh? All this and still we're movin' ahead next week?" Kevin continued to air-box, crouching and throwing a right to the body, followed by a left hook to the body and a hook to the head. He danced around and was breaking a sweat.

"Who am I, the Wizard of fucking Oz, got all the answers?" Wacko said. "I need time to figure this out."

Kevin stopped moving and dropped his arms to his sides. "Time? Sorry, Jack, all out of it. Like I said, for me this is after, cause I'm nervous and I don't know which end's up. It's like I got all this hair in my eyes and I'm only catching glimpses of things. I'm missin' the picture. Hey, can you help me with this, what is the fucking picture?" Kevin said.

"You want to see a picture, go buy a ticket at the Bughouse," Wacko said.

"The Bughouse? Won't work, Jack, they're closin' it down. The Broadway Theatre the only one in Southie, and they're makin' condominiums out of it, can you believe it?" Kevin sat down on the bench, pulled off his T-shirt, and wiped his face and body with it. "Maybe it's right they close the Bughouse, too dark in there anyways, made me paranoid, and my feet stuck to the floor." Kevin poured another mound of coke onto his hand.

"Ain't darkness makin' you paranoid," Wacko said. He slapped the vial out of his brother's hand. "It's that shit. I ain't tellin' you again."

Kevin leaped after the vial, and Wacko was on him like a puma. With his right hand he grabbed a fistful of Kevin's hair, yanked him to his feet, and twisted him towards him, using his left foot to sweep both of Kevin's from beneath him, slamming his brother solidly to the sidewalk on his back. Wacko felt the impact in his soles and took a diagonal step, raised his right foot, and stomped the coke vial flat.

Wacko was breathing heavily as he sat back down on the bench. He wiped his mouth with the back of his hand before he spoke. "After means after, need better instructions let me know," he said.

Mike Janowski had just bounced up the last of the three steps leading from Thomas Park as Wacko was stomping the vial. As he approached, he comically eyeballed Kevin. "You guys havin' fun?" he said.

Wacko shrugged and stretched. "How're you doin', Mike? Kevin here's just missin' the Bughouse is all," Wacko said. Kevin groaned and rolled onto his side.

Mike clapped his hands and pointed at Wacko. "Ya, ya, I heard that, they're closin' the end of the month, right? The new cinemas, like the one in Randolph, killed it, killin' all the small theaters." He squatted down next to Kevin. "You been to Randolph, Kev? They got stadium seating?"

He winked at Wacko. "I got your message on the recorder for the meet. So what's up, boss, we on, off, what?"

"Technical difficulties, should have them ironed out by next week, though; plan on next week, Mike," Wacko said.

Kevin was on his back now, shielding his eyes from the sun with both hands. Mike extended his right hand and pulled him up. Kevin touched his lip, examined his fingers, spit, and slapped at the seat of his pants.

"Heard about Danny King, figured that might crimp the operation. What the fuck happened?" Mike said.

"Heard everything from his bug of a girlfriend, caught him with something strange, so he owed the Townies for a bundle of pot," Wacko said.

Mike paced in front of the bench. He said, "When I heard about it, I went, like hey, what the fuck."

"Not to worry, he ain't part of our technical difficulties. Just fine-tuning a few things. We don't roll, ever, unless we're one hundred percent," Wacko said.

"That's your rep, and I like that. Need any help with your 'difficulties' let me know, anything, in for a penny, in for a pound," Mike said. "Another thing, Jack . . ." Mike stopped in front of Wacko and stared into his eyes. "The feds are up Marty Fallon's ass, what about yours? You're gettin' any heat over Danny King or anything else, I'd appreciate a heads-up. Word on the street is we're together now, the heat's on I gotta know," he said.

"No more than usual," Wacko said. "But you're right, Marty's takin' a hit. I don't know what's up with that, but I hear anything you'll hear it next, okay?"

Mike grinned and brushed a lock of blond hair away from his forehead. "I trust you, Jack. You need me, call," he said.

Wacko stood up and looked over his brother's head to a spot somewhere in the harbor. "Just be ready. When you hear from me next, we'll be movin', and nothin's gonna stop us."

44

PORKY LINEHAN WAS BROUGHT UP as a middle-class kid from the Point, but he had no problem acting lower-class. Here it was eight o'clock on a Friday night, and he was pointing the nose of his father's black Lincoln Navigator, surfing the asphalt of West Broadway, heading towards the D Street housing projects in search of the magic marching powder.

As he neared the traffic lights at D Street, Porky turned down the voice of the guy on the AM talk radio station who loudly complained about the lack of quality viewing after nine o'clock. "Fuck it, do some lines after nine," Porky said, marveling at his poetic flair.

He turned left at the lights, passed the Condon School on the right, then the D Street Deli on the left, with its usual collection of gangsters hanging around out front, a fixture there, who coldly eyeballed him as he passed.

Psychos, Porky thought, the whole damn area is filled with psychos, welfare cheats, and a general assortment of daylight duckers. Porky wondered how anyone could live down here as he took the next right at the lights at West Seventh and followed that road a short distance before pulling over and parking.

A half a block down on the same side of the street, Mary Rose O'Connell peeked through the faded orange acrylic curtains of her apartment and watched as, three stories below, two young men in their early twenties exited her red brick building and descended the steps to the walkway. Suddenly one of them turned and stared up directly at her. Mary Rose released the curtain and took one step back, her right hand covering her mouth as if she had seen a ghost.

"Come on, Mary Rose, we seen ya, what gives? We got money, what gives, you crazy bitch," said a muffled voice on the other side of the glass. Mary remained frozen until she heard the sound of two car doors slam, a peel of rubber, and an engine overaccelerating away.

How had these coke fiends found her? She'd been out of business for two weeks and still they had searched. But why shouldn't they? Everyone said she always had the best product, though it hadn't done her much good. She was deeply in debt and in trouble at home, accused of smoking crack in front of her younger brother. Her mother threw her skinny ass out. It was all a mistake. She was in her bedroom getting high, minding her own business, when that little rat Seamus stuck his head in the door. Now she was sleeping on the pullout of her girlfriend Megan Sullivan's apartment down the D. Megan shared the joint with her boyfriend, Stick, who worked for housing and dealt pot on the side. There was no love lost between Stick and Mary Rose. Stick told Megan that coke dealers brought nothing but heat.

Porky had just exited the driver's door of the Navigator as two young men in an old Ford wagon came roaring past. Fucking idiots, Porky thought, as he hit the car alarm device on his father's key chain on, then off, then on again, listening to the chirps. In this neighborhood it paid to be certain it worked before he headed to 64 West Seventh Street and climbed the stairs to Megan's apartment.

Mary Rose couldn't believe her black luck as she sat on the couch, picked up the remote, and hit the switch for the twenty-seven-inch Toshiba in front of her. As she glumly stared at the tube, watching a rerun of *Hollywood Squares* and pondering how the fuck Whoopi Goldberg always rated the center square, there came an insistent knock at the door. "Who is it?" Mary Rose said.

"Porky Linehan."

"Fuck off."

"Mary Rose, please, I know you're in there, Clemmy Richards told me you're here. Now, we gotta talk," Porky said.

Mary Rose ripped open the door. "What? And who told Clemmy Richards I was here?"

"Mary Rose, I haven't got a lot of time," Porky said, looking over his shoulder and stepping through the door into the living room. Mary Rose didn't try to stop him and was grateful Megan's pot-dealing boyfriend worked nights.

Porky pulled out a roll of bills and waved it in her face. "Look, Mary Rose, I know you're on again, off again dealin' these days, but I got a grand here, I need six eightballs, good stuff, you got it? Can you get it?"

Mary Rose twirled the ends of her hair as she stared at the money in Porky's fist. "Why you botherin' me? I'm out of business because of stiffs like you stiffin' me. I owe people, got enough headaches. Get outta here," she said, grabbing the doorknob.

Porky grinned and waved the roll in Mary Rose's face. "What don't you get here, Mary? This is money, baby. Ol' Porky's willing to set you up, put you back in business. I got four guys waiting on me-you, and here's the money, one thousand dollars. You got the connections, make it happen. You always get the best. I'm sick of buying crap. I bought a couple of crappy eightballs from Billy Bertucci two weeks ago."

"He sells shit," Mary Rose said.

"Goddamn right, cuts his blow with fucking aspirin. The only time it's good is you're drinkin' all night, have a fucking hangover. Now, take the money and make everyone happy." Porky pressed his palms together like he was praying for a field goal in overtime. "Please!" he said.

Mary Rose plunked her ass down on the couch. She felt a tingle in the pit of her stomach. Hell, with the G-note she could probably pick up just about an ounce, whack it with another half ounce, and still have a decent product, a product miles ahead of the shit out there whacked with CVS aspirin. She'd take care of Porky, sell the rest, and still have enough to get high, not too high, just enough to get a good drip going, or she could even pocket the profit. It wouldn't be much, but it might put her back in the game.

Porky held out the money again, and Mary Rose got up. "All right, you prick, for you I'll try. She counted the money then picked up the phone and fingered a number. "Ya, Mark, Mary Rose." She looked at Porky nodded, and winked. "Ya, I know, I hear you, but this . . . Mark, Mark?" She slammed down the phone. "Son-of-a — cocksucker!"

She snatched the phone up again and stabbed another number. "Andy, Mary Rose. Not bad, honey, better soon I hope." She winked again. "So, how we doin' tonight, good? Good. Ya, I'd like to see her, your girlfriend's a beautiful lady, classy, ya. I should talk to her. I got about a thousand things to say. Ya, old friends are like that. Oh, you're jealous, huh? I can be over there in about twenty minutes or so. You gonna bring her out to see me, or should I come in and surprise her? Okay, sounds good, see ya soon."

She hung up the phone and smiled at Porky Linehan. "Tell me I'm good. Naw, don't bother, I know it." She waggled a finger at him and pirouetted. "I'd let you kiss me, Porky, but you Point kids get around a real woman it does something unnatural to ya's. I'd have to call the cops," Mary Rose said. She coquettishly pivoted, glanced over her left shoulder, and batted her eyelashes. "A girl's gotta freshen up, give me five minutes."

"You got a car, need a lift?" Porky said, heading for the door.

"I'm all set," said a voice from the bathroom. "Wait in your car. I'm only going to Braintree, back in an hour."

In the hallway outside the apartment, Porky pulled out his cell phone and dialed a number. "Leo, Porky, we're all set, give me an hour, I'll hang here." He snapped the phone shut, descended the stairs, and exited the building.

Out on the sidewalk he put his hands over his head, spun once, then mamboed towards his car, though the folds of his stomach revolted against the demands of his feet. He pointed the key ring at the car; the alarm chirped, the lights blinked on and off, and Porky got in.

Inside he turned the ignition key to accessory and the radio sparked to life. K.C. and the Sunshine Band sang "Shake Your Booty," and Porky did, increasing the volume and pounding the steering wheel like a conga drum.

K.C. was halfway through the second chorus when the front door to 64 West Seventh Street opened and Mary Rose stepped outside, illuminated by a single overhead light. Porky could see her clearly at the top of the steps and watched as she cautiously paused, almost like she was sniffing the air, before she descended the four steps to the courtyard.

Porky was just about to flash his headlamps and lower the passenger window, blasting the music into the neighborhood, when on the sidewalk side next to his car, two hooded figures passed so close they were almost in the gutter. One behind the other, Indian style, they hugged the car ahead and the next one too, drawing ever closer to Mary Rose. As he watched, Porky's scrotum twisted into a tight little ball. He turned the ignition off and involuntarily sunk, as far as his belly would allow, into the padded, brown seats of the Navigator.

Now on the sidewalk next to her car, Mary Rose fumbled through her pocketbook for her keys. She never saw it when the larger of the two figures stepped out into the middle of the sidewalk and marched deliberately towards her, with his right hand pointed at her head.

There was a muffled pop, like a party balloon exploding, and Mary Rose fell down straight, almost as if a shallow hole had opened in the sidewalk. The other figure stood fifteen feet away, a gun held waist high in either hand as the shooter closed on the fallen figure, raised his left hand chin high, palm facing out, and fired the remainder of the five-shot Smith & Wesson .38 Airweight Centennial into her head. Porky's stomach spasmed, and the stench of shit quickly overpowered the smell of the Lincoln's fine Corinthian leather.

Shoulder to shoulder, both gunmen turned and, with no urgency in their gait, headed back up the street toward Porky's car. As the gunmen drew near, Porky struggled to control the urge to bolt. His lips barely moved. "Jesus, help me, Jesus, I am invisible, fucking invis —" Both men stopped next to the Navigator, and the smaller of the two bent until his face, covered by a Scream mask, was only inches from the glass. With a simple wrist motion he tapped the passenger window with the barrel of one of the two .45 ACP's he held and slowly shook his head. Porky shook his head back, then closed his eyes and sobbed. When he opened them, seconds later, they were gone.

45

IN BOSTON'S NORTH END, Gaetano Milano was aggravated as he sat at the small faux marble table in front of Mike's Pastry on Hanover Street. Seconds earlier he had twisted his left wrist a half turn to check the time on his diamond-encrusted Rolex Presidential, and a corner of his starched, white Armani cuff had come in contact with the surface of the steaming double espresso in front of him. Disgusted, he muttered something in a Sicilian dialect and looked around as though someone might offer to help him or at least sympathize before he picked up a napkin, pressed the corner against his tongue, and dabbed at the light brown stain on his cuff.

Less than half a block west from where he sat, Steve Sweeney, a fourteen-year veteran driver for MCI Armored Transit, sat behind the wheel of his truck. While he idled at the red light at the intersection of Parmenter and Richmond Streets, he considered the fate of his younger brother Albert, recently diagnosed with prostate cancer. The kid was five years younger, and Sweeney wondered what twist of fate had delivered up the insidious disease to his younger brother and not to him. "God help him," he said out loud as the light turned green and he slowly accelerated towards the Shawmut Bank a short distance up on the right.

"Ya, got a car blocking your spot, an Explorer," Billy Phillips, the guard in back said through the gunport of the steel and bullet-resistant-glass divider that separated the driver's compartment from the rest of the truck. Phillips had been Sweeney's partner for the past six years, a long time in a field where the pay sucked, the hours were long, and the work was sometimes dangerous.

"I could double-park, Bill. Up to you, it's a quick one," Sweeney said.

"Up to me, pal, I'd let you, but if the company's tailing us or the bank reports a nonregulation drop, then both our asses are grass. Let's wait a minute; the dip's probably in the bank, should be out in a minute. Pull up ahead," Phillips said.

With both hands on the wheel, Sweeney drove slowly past the green Ford Explorer and said, "Asshole," under his breath before coming to a stop ten feet in front of it and double-parking next to a red Eldorado. Fifteen feet ahead of him a telephone truck, its yellow roof lights flashing, quietly idled in the cool morning air.

Farther up Hanover Street, Gaetano Milano had cleaned his cuff as best as he could, then twisted the platinum pinkie ring on his left hand with its huge, flawless blue-white diamond in a way that reflected the morning sun on the stone just so then settled back in his chair and sipped his espresso. He picked up his copy of *The Boston Globe* and glanced briefly at the headlines before his attention was drawn to something peculiar happening farther up the street.

Less than a block east from where he sat, in front of Cristano's Pizzeria, a thirty-foot Sunbeam bread truck heading west down Hanover Street had suddenly stopped, veered to the left, then stopped again and backed up, diagonally, blocking the street. In front of the Sunbeam truck, two vehicles, a black late-model Mustang and a sky blue van with commercial lettering on the side, were also stopped and idling in the middle of the street.

Milano put down his paper and shifted his chair, resting both forearms on the table as he stared intently up the street. He watched a man he assumed to be the driver of the truck get out, sprint to the Mustang, and climb in back. The Mustang and the van slowly passed his table, then stopped at the lights at Parmenter and Richmond.

For a few seconds the Mustang paused for the red light, then with a chirp of tire rubber, took a left through the light and disappeared down Richmond. The van didn't follow but continued to idle at the lights. When the lights turned green, it remained there unmoving. Milano's instincts were aroused; something was happening, but what? He casually pushed his espresso towards the outer edge of the table. There was the scent of bad in the air, and if he had to move fast he didn't want more coffee on his shirt.

Milano watched, transfixed, as sixty feet ahead of the van on the right, a heavyset woman in her mid-twenties exited the Shawmut Bank. She paused for a moment outside the door counting her money, then climbed into a green Ford Explorer and pulled away from the curb. After she passed, the armored truck's backup lights flicked on and the heavily armored vehicle rolled briefly in reverse before stopping in the vacant space at an angle to the curb.

Milano's attention was drawn away from the sky blue van and returned to the bread truck, where now a small crowd had gathered. A few men were attempting, with little luck, to push it out of the way.

Meanwhile, in front of the Shawmut Bank, Phillips, after looking out the back window and checking the side mirror, hopped out the side door and casually walked around back. He rapped twice on the door with the knuckles of his right hand.

Sweeney heard the familiar signal and absently reached overhead to the right of the visor to hit the toggle switch that released the rear door lock. Phillips pulled on the latch, and the heavy steel door swung open.

Like a cat watching a bird, Milano subtly shifted his weight in the chair as the sky blue van inched towards the armored truck, then suddenly accelerated. As Sweeney sat and contemplated the extent of his cancer-ravaged brother's health insurance coverage, he heard a commotion at the rear of the truck. He had just enough time to see in the side-view mirror a masked man with a rifle running towards his partner, who was kneeling, arms up, in the street. Then his attention was forced to the front as the armored car was violently jolted by the impact of a telephone truck.

Kevin Curran leaped from the van and scurried, like a winged monkey, over the hood of the armored car. He skidded up to the windshield on his knees, peeled the duct tape X from his chest, and slapped the bomb onto the glass. Sweeney reacted by squashing the brake pedal to the floor and pushing himself, arms locked at the elbows, straight back into the seat. Kevin screamed through the glass, "Get the fuck out, get out or you're dead." Sweeney found himself counting the flecks of the gunman's bubbled spittle on the windshield before the ski-masked figure grabbed one of the wipers for stability and put the other hand on the grenade's pin.

"All right, I'm out, out," Sweeney yelled. He raised one hand to the ceiling, cocked his body crazily to the right, and opened the door with the other. Outside, an unseen hand yanked the door open.

"Out, out, get out," screamed someone to his left. Sweeney had the faint sensation of something grabbing his jacket, and suddenly he was flying through the air. He landed hard on the pavement, cracking ribs, the wind knocked from his lungs. A rifle barrel pushed into his cheek while unseen hands yanked his sidearm and pat-frisked his legs.

"This is fucking beautiful," the rifleman standing over him said.

Mike Janowski stood in the street covering the prone figures of the guards as Wacko threw money bags from the truck to Kevin, who tossed them sideways into the van. "Forty seconds," Mike said, checking the huge military-style watch he wore on his left wrist.

"It's a beautiful thing," Kevin said.

Mike nodded and turned his head as a slight movement from the Atlas Bank diagonally across the street caught his attention. An ancient guard had stepped outside the bank's double-glass front doors. His eyes were wide and unblinking as he drew his weapon and backed up the sidewalk towards Richmond Street.

"Heads up," Mike yelled, before he twisted and fired two thundering rounds from the big H and K in the guard's direction. The guard staggered under the rounds, losing his hat as bullets smashed through the windshield of an empty Audi parked behind him, leaving gaping sunflowerlike holes in the edge of the roof. Boom, boom. The next two rounds hit the granite facade of the Atlas Bank, right above the A, spraying bits of rock like buckshot into the guard's face. The old man flipped his weapon crazily into the air and raked his eyes with his hands before he staggered and fell.

Farther up the street, on the same side, three young men holding small coffee cups, attracted by the sound of gunfire, cautiously poked their heads outside a café and noticed the stricken guard. Boldly, one of them strode towards him, motioning the others to follow. Mike saw them coming and calmly shouldered the H and K 91, unloading a three-round burst inches above the heads of the café gawkers. As they dove to the sidewalk and rolled, Mike cackled and howled like a wolf.

Seconds before the telephone truck rammed the front of the armored car, Milano had realized what was happening, and his years of criminal experience paid off. Categorized as a "career violent offender" by law enforcement, he was a suspect in a half dozen murders and had been investigated for ordering the deaths of at least eleven others. He'd been subpoenaed before several grand juries and never once opened his mouth. He never blinked or ran and that wouldn't change today. He had simply sat and watched.

He was glad he'd made no sudden movements after seeing how quickly the rifleman reacted to the security guard from the bank, but now the time had come to move. Almost imperceptibly he pushed away from the table and was edging towards the door of Mike's Pastry when the curious assholes across the street left the safety of the café to help the stricken guard. Milano squinted when he first heard the booming report of the H and K rifle and witnessed the effect of the first two rounds as they drilled their way like evil moles through the café's huge plate-glass window. He never heard the third shot or saw it pass through the phone stand in front of the café, angling off the frame, crossing the street, then deflecting off the end of a rusted steel H-beam, used in the past for hoisting, above the door of Mike's Pastry.

Milano heard himself gasp as something hit him hard in the chest, directly above the right nipple. Jerked from his feet and thrown sideways, he fell on the table, which flipped onto its side. On the sidewalk he rolled onto his back, his head resting on the leg of a chair, and was amazed to see a hole in his shirt and red blood bubbling from it. As feeling drained from Milano's hands, he fumbled for a paper napkin that lay twisted on the concrete next to him. He dabbed weakly at the blood on his shirt, then dropped the napkin, cursed his bad luck in Sicilian, and died.

Down the street, Wacko jumped from the back of the armored car. "Let's go, we're outta here," he yelled to Mike. Kevin slammed the side door of the van shut and jumped into the passenger seat as Mike leaped through the open back doors. He left them that way as Wacko threw the van in reverse, backed up, then headed west down Parmenter Street.

The van hadn't traveled fifty feet when Mike slapped the inside wall. "Ho, stop, we got company!" he ordered. From a crouch he kicked open one of the partially closed doors and sprang from the still moving van into the street. On the opposite side of Hanover Street a marked Boston Police cruiser, its blue lights flashing, was approaching in a direct line up Richmond.

With no hesitation Mike shouldered his weapon and headed directly for it. Kevin followed close behind, making little 360-degree turns in the street, the barrel of his Mossberg pump rising and falling as he covered the buildings on either side. At Hanover Street the cruiser jerked to a halt.

From inside the cruiser, both cops visually checked the wounded security guard, who was now sitting up against the Atlas Bank building holding a bloody handkerchief over his eyes. Mike was a hundred feet away and closing when suddenly the cop on the passenger side pointed at him and removed his hat, revealing a square-jawed, boyish face and a close-cropped marine-style haircut. The driver's left hand gripped the steering wheel; his right wrapped around the cruiser's microphone into which he screamed frantically.

"Take 'em out, boy," Kevin yelled, then flinched from the first report of the big H and K. Boom, boom, boom, boom. Mike stalked the cops, taking smaller steps now but still moving towards them. Boom, boom, boom, boom. The chrome molding at the top of the front glass flipped thirty feet into the air as a half dozen holes cratered the cruiser's windshield.

Both cops crouched under the dash. Mike lowered the barrel and stopped thirty feet from the car. Boom, boom, boom, boom, boom, boom. A rapid series of shots and the headlamps exploded. A section of grille cut free and whipping sideways, ricocheting off the door of a Volkswagen Passat parked nearby. Mike lowered the weapon to his hip and continued to fire. Armor-piercing .308s churned their way through the engine compartment, mangling pistons and crushing the intake manifold, while other rounds shattered the dash, radio, and computer before exiting the trunk. The hood release shot away, another round severed the right hinge, causing the hood panel to spring crazily upwards and to the left.

Miraculously both cops, though wounded superficially from flying debris, were still alive but had to move or die; both cruiser doors opened at once. The driver bailed first, hit the street and barrel-rolled beneath a silver Toyota Land Cruiser covered with tiny cubes of glass.

Satisfied, Mike ceased fire. He swung the barrel like a pendulum as he retreated towards the van. Suddenly the marine haircut popped up from behind the open passenger door of the police cruiser. He swung both arms up, leveled his Glock through the shattered window, and fired a six-round burst.

Zit, zit, zit. Three rounds passed dangerously close to the left of Mike's head. He dropped to one knee, becoming a smaller target, and fired a ten-round burst, emptying the clip, through the right fender and door of the cruiser. He ejected and reversed the empty clip, and slapped home a fresh thirty-round magazine. He pulled back on the receiver and chambered a round. Looking down the iron sights, he waited. He heard sirens in the distance.

"Come on, he's finished," Kevin yelled, running up alongside him. He pointed at the young cop, who had now regained his feet. Blood flowed freely from a deep gash that ran the length of his skull from the corner of his left eye. He stared incredulously at his right arm, which was missing from the elbow down. He glanced up once more at the retreating robbers, then staggered to the right and fell sideways into the doorway of 153 Richmond Street.

As the van raced down Salem Street, then turned left onto Cooper, Kevin grabbed the dry-powder fire extinguisher, pointed the hose towards the back doors, and said, "Want me to dust the street?"

"Put it down," Wacko said over his shoulder. "It's clear, don't draw attention. Get ready, I'm stoppin'." Mike slung the H and K over his shoulder as Wacko pulled the van to a stop diagonally across the narrow street, lined on either side by closely parked cars. Ahead of the van on the right was a forest green F 350 pickup truck. "Hit it," Wacko said.

He removed the ignition key and pushed himself between the two seats into the back. Kevin exited the side door, shotgun at the ready. Mike jumped out the back, holding a heavy money bag in either hand. Kevin watched both ends of the street as Wacko threw bag after bag to Mike, who tossed them into the bed of the pickup.

"Tires," Wacko said, jumping from the van. He climbed into the cab of the F 350 and started it. Now Mike covered the street as Kevin pulled a double-edged knife from a sheath on his ankle and quickly stabbed the van's two left tires. Task complete, he hopped into the bed of the pickup and pulled a nylon tarp, rolled beneath the rear window, over him and the money bags like a blanket. Mike climbed into the truck and stared through the windshield. "Looks good," he said.

Wacko pulled from the curb and forced himself to drive slowly. Less than a block away on North Washington Street, two cruisers streaked past, lights flashing, sirens wailing. Mike glanced at Wacko, bit his lower lip, and adjusted the butt of the assault weapon just below his armpit.

At the corner of North Washington Street, Wacko paused and took in both ends of the street. A few blocks to his left a half dozen police cruisers, a cacophony of sound and lights, converged on the area from various points downtown. Wacko turned right and flicked on the radio, his eyes glued to the rearview mirror. As he drove, he lightly tapped the steering wheel to the 5th Dimension song "Aquarius."

"We got this, boys," Wacko said. "Age of A-quar-i-us. . . . Mike, when we stop take the rifle; here we go." Wacko flicked on the right turn signal and pulled over in front of Sabatino's restaurant next to a black Ford Taurus. "Get out, stay right behind me. Remember, we get stopped we all get out." Wacko reached behind and rapped twice on the glass. In a flash Kevin popped from beneath the tarp and jumped from the back of the truck. He covered the money, then climbed into the rear of the Taurus and lay on the floor.

"Less than four minutes to the next switch, see ya in Charlestown," Wacko said. Mike got into the Taurus and fired it up. Using his left index finger, he made tiny circles in the air, then pointed towards the Charlestown Bridge. With a chirp of rubber Wacko pulled away, the Taurus tight to his ass.

46

MARTY FALLON PAID THE COUNTERMAN $5.25 for two slices of Sicilian pizza and two medium Cokes. He took the bag and walked out of the store back to his car.

"Anything yet?" he said through the Chevy Malibu's open window to the giant sitting behind the wheel.

Andre Athanas shook his head. "I'm lookin', boss. Only seen one Ford Crown Vic near the bank. It was red, you said blue, right?" Marty passed Andre the bag with the slice and Coke in it and took a general view of the parking lot over the roof of the car. "You see anything?" Andre said, his mouth full of pizza.

"Ya, I do, there he is," Marty said, pointing with his pizza. He grabbed his Coke off the roof, took a sip, then passed the cup to Andre. "Stay put."

A few hundred yards away, opposite the drive-through window of the Rockland Trust Bank, a late-model blue Crown Victoria had pulled into a space between a Chevy Tahoe and a small foreign job. Marty took one last bite of pizza, then tossed it on the ground before making a wide loop in his approach to the Crown Victoria. When he got alongside, the driver of the Crown Vic was looking in the opposite direction. Marty banged his fist on the passenger door glass, and the other man jumped. The electric door locks popped, and Marty got in.

"Sneaky prick, huh? You got pizza on your face," the fat man said, pulling a Kleenex out of a box on the floor below the radio. He handed it to Marty, who ignored it and wiped his mouth with the back of his hand.

"You got egg on yours," Marty said.

The fat man snickered, shook his head, then crumpled the Kleenex and stuffed it into the right pocket of his sport coat. "Ya know, somehow I have to admire a guy who can still crack wise when his life is going down the shitter." He tipped his huge head to the left. "What gives? You never brought the goon before?"

"Since that thing up the North End, I got a feelin' there might be problems with the guineas, so now Andre's like American Express, I don't leave home without him," Marty said.

The fat man bit his lower lip. "So, what you been hearing?"

"So far not much," Marty said.

"You think maybe the same guys who stood us up out in Weymouth pulled this North End horror show? Rolaids?" The fat man offered a cylindrical package to Marty, who declined. The fat man peeled back the wrapper and popped two into his mouth. He crushed them with his teeth as he spoke.

"The heat's on . . . Marty . . . really on. That rookie cop . . . on the job . . . all of nine months, nine fucking months, and now his arm's gone missing along with his career, bad, real bad, and you're sitting here telling me you know nothing? What you think I'm from, Mars, some fucking Venusian, you know nothing? I'm hungry, Marty, give me something here. Your guys, Townies, who, Marty?" The fat man grabbed the steering wheel with two beefy hands and tugged it towards him. "Who the fuck did this?"

Marty's hand shook as he reached into the pocket of his windbreaker and pulled out a pack of Marlboros. "I'm workin' on it," he said, opening and closing the top of the pack with his thumb.

"Ya? Well let me tell you something, my former ace. While you're 'workin' on it' my bosses are going to start tossing this town upside down. Remember back when you were in the joint and someone fucked up, got caught with dope, stabbed someone, whatever, and the heat came down on everyone in the block? Remember the Inner

Perimeter Security team, the IPS, how they'd roll in and toss every cell, tear your world to fucking shreds? Well, it's about to happen out here, Marty. Your world's coming apart the same way, you don't get me something to hang my fucking hat on," the fat man said.

Marty stared out the passenger window. "Fuck you and your threats; don't you see there's more involved here? Does the name Gaetano Milano ring a bell?" he said.

"Fuck Gaetano Milano," the fat man said.

"There you go, just like that, fuck him, ya. But the wiseguys are lookin' just as hard for the guys who killed one of their own, accident or no, and how many places do you think they'll look, how many places would you?" Marty said. He stuck the cigarette in his mouth and sparked the turquoise Bic in his hand.

"Please open the fucking window," the fat man said.

"They find who did this, and they will, someone's goin' *out* a fucking window, fact," Marty said, blowing the smoke towards a one-inch crack at the top of the glass. "Later today I got a meet with Angelo Scarpa over in his joint at the Prudential Center, talk about things, clear the air."

Like it carried an electric shock, the fat man pulled his hands from the wheel. He said, "Small world, I talk to Angelo too."

Marty stared at him.

"He was a Top Echelon Informant before you," the fat man said.

Marty slowly pulled the drooping cigarette from his mouth and attempted to flick the ash out the window, but a gust blew it back onto his jacket. He snorted softly and flicked at the ash with the little finger of his left hand. He shook his head. "Sometimes bein' number one ain't so good, eh? He know about me?"

"You want him to?"

Marty lowered the window, pitched the cigarette, and smirked. "Ya know, I'm feelin' pressure here from you, from them. Makes me wonder I find out somethin', who do I come to? If it's someone I knew done this, them Italians might clip me." He snapped his fingers. "Or if I'm lucky it will only cause a war, bad for business for us, them, hmmm. I hear they pulled a few million out of that truck, true?"

The fat man sighed. "Actually, between us more. Why?"

"It's business. In the end that's all the Outfit's about: business, money. To smooth things over the guineas will want a piece of that North End pie, half, three quarters of a million," Marty said.

"Smooth things? Should be like fucking glass that much money," the fat man said.

"Ya, that's what's good about those guys, they're up-front with how they can be bought, unlike guys like you," Marty said.

"You can't buy me."

"Who you shittin'? I buy you every day. The currency's information. You know, I'm tired of you threatenin' me, real tired. You need knowledge things comin' down, already gone down, I'm there, have been for years. It was me made you a star. You doubt it, cut me loose," Marty said.

The fat man held up his hands. "Okay, okay, relax, I'm not going to argue. Maybe some of what you say is true, but it don't change things. The heat's on, and nothing short of a fire hose is going to cool it down."

Marty shook his head. He opened the door, put one foot on the ground, then stopped. He turned and looked at the fat man. "By the way, in that score, what kind of equipment they use?"

"Why?"

"Could mean something."

"I'll find out," the fat man said.

Marty got out of the Ford, then leaned back in. "I'll find out too, we got a primary interest here."

"And that's?" the fat man said.

"Ourselves," Marty Fallon said, closing the door.

47

IF NOTHING ELSE Walter "Feenzo" Feeney had always considered himself to be a fair man, especially when it came to lending money and then, of course, collecting that money from some of the bums he lent it to. Feenzo wasn't violent, was not into the leg breaker routine; besides, if you were good there was rarely the need for violence. It was all in the choices you made, who you lent the money to. It didn't take rocket science to know if eight out of ten customers paid up what they owed, you were ahead of the game.

But like most there was a downside to the business. Sometimes guys got into trouble, lost their jobs, got busted or hooked on drugs or gambling, and the money Feenzo lent them went down the toilet; you couldn't get blood out of a stone. And occasionally somebody mushed him, simply declared they weren't going to pay, and that was bad for business and had to be straightened out. But if something had to be straightened, Feenzo had an ace. It paid to have a thousand-pound gorilla like Marty Fallon in your corner. Everyone knew Marty was a murder waiting to happen, and if he told someone to pay back the money, Feenzo's main concern was paper cuts as it flew past his face.

As Walter Feeney sat at his desk counting receipts, he glanced up at the video monitor mounted above the door. Two men, dressed like carpenters, stood in the hallway outside the door and stared up at the camera. One of them waved and smiled. Feenzo threw the receipts in a drawer and buzzed them in.

"Hey, Boots, what ya hear?" he said to the taller of the two. He stood up and shook both men's hands.

Boots looked at his companion. "Tell him about it, Jerry," Boots said.

Jerry licked his lips and used a finger to tug at the collar of his shirt. "Walter, they hit the Pen Tavern about twenty minutes ago. I seen them go in, it wasn't pretty. Figured you knew, did you?" He pulled a small roll of bills from the right side pocket of his Carhartt vest and counted out five twenty-dollar bills. "Got a C-note here. Pay you the rest next week, okay?"

Feenzo ignored the money as he slowly rose from his chair.

"You talkin' raid, a fucking raid, what they do?" he said.

Boots laid two hundred-dollar bills on the desk. "There's two for me, Walter, it was nasty. I came along after they were into it, me and Jerry watched from across the street. Looked like feds to me. Must have been twenty. There was a whole lot of screamin' and yellin' comin' from inside, sounded like dogs killing each other. They took 'em out in a conga line, old man Cagney was horizontal wearin' the cuff links, he didn't go easy. Sorry to bring you bad news, Walter," Boots said, pushing the bills to the middle of the desk.

Feenzo snatched up the phone, hit some numbers, listened, made a face, then dropped the receiver on the desk. His eyes bugged as he put both hands on the edge of the desk, and he seemed to sway ever so slightly. "Ya, it's okay guys, thanks," he said. He picked up the money and stuck it in his pocket.

Boots and Jerry looked at one another, then at the man behind the desk. "Okay Walter, we know you've got a lot going on, but please don't forget we paid," Boots said, backing out the door. He pulled it towards him a few inches and stopped. "Feenzo, it ain't safe, maybe you should get outta here, get some air, know what I mean?"

Walter Feeney stared at the phone. "Don't worry guys, thanks, I'll mark it down, close the door," he said. He picked up the phone again, lifted it halfway to his ear, then made a face like something stunk, slammed the receiver down, snapped it up again. As he pecked in the number, sweat gathered in tiny beads on his forehead and upper lip.

"Frankie, it's me. He in? Listen, I don't give a shit he ain't answerin' his buzzer, don't mean dick. Get off the fucking bar and check." Feenzo mopped at his forehead and swiped his mouth with a handkerchief. "Ya, hello, Frankie, ya, I know about the Pen. Marty comes in have him give me a call on my cell. Tell him I called his and got the fucking voice mail. No, you daft, of course I didn't leave a message. I'm leaving the office now." He hung up the phone, then pushed a white button set in a rectangular silver plate on his desk next to a framed photograph of a girl around seven.

"Ya, boss, what's up?" said a voice from a speaker on the edge of his desk.

"Vinny, I'm going out the back door. The Pen just got hit, we might have visitors too. We do, let them in, I don't want no broke doors."

"Gotcha, Walter," said the voice.

In the right front corner of the room, Feenzo stepped between a large, black fireproof filing cabinet and a bottled watercooler. He reached up with both hands and firmly pressed on the wood-paneled wall near the ceiling. Something clicked, and the panel swung noiselessly away on hidden hinges, exposing a gray, rectangular wall safe with a stainless steel knob.

After a few quick spins he grabbed the handle and opened the door. He reached in and, with both hands, grabbed a pair of leather-bound ledgers the size of phone books and stuck them under his left armpit. Then he reached with his right hand and pulled out a roll of cash five inches thick, secured by a thick, red elastic band.

Feenzo closed the door, careful not to lock it, and pressed the wooden panel shut. If they found the safe, at least they wouldn't have to drill it.

He left the office door unlocked, turned right, and followed a short corridor leading to the back of the store, lined on the left with empty cases of Budweiser and Miller Lite. At the end of the corridor he used a peephole in a gray steel door before taking his key ring out and selecting a triangular-shaped key that he stuck with some difficulty into the lock.

The door swung outwards on its hinges, and Feenzo stepped outside, gazed up at the blue sky through the black runners of the fire escape landing twelve feet above him. He walked past a blue, padlocked Dumpster on his right and pointed his key ring at an emerald green Cadillac Eldorado on his left. Just beyond the car was an alleyway leading to the street. The car alarm chirped, and the doors unlocked.

Feenzo got in, locked the doors, and checked the rearview before starting the engine. He put the Eldorado in reverse and backed away from the two rows of empty steel beer kegs piled against the wall in front of the car. But something was wrong. Puzzled, he stopped. He got out of the car and walked around back. Feenzo angrily slapped his thigh as he stared at the right rear tire which was as flat as Vinnie Pazienza's nose.

"Motherfucka," Feenzo said, pulling out his handkerchief and wiping his mouth and the back of his neck.

He opened the trunk, pulled out his cell phone, and angrily poked it. "Ya, hello, ya fucking mook, I'm still here, out back, got a fucking flat. Send the stock boy out to change it," he said before he flipped the phone shut and returned it to his pocket. "Son-of-a-bitch," he said as he bent into the trunk and moved things away from the spare tire compartment. Slightly winded from the effort he tugged at his Callaway golf bag and clubs, stood them upright, and admired them.

He had just wiped his forehead with a balled-up wad of Kleenex when a voice behind him said, "No golf today." Mike Janowski had miscalculated the big man's speed as he turned to face him. The first shot from the .22 Beretta caught Walter Feeney a few inches below his right cheek. His molars shattered, Feenzo groaned and defensively threw his arms in front of his face as he partially fell into the trunk. With the ease of a ballroom dancer, Mike slid to the right and fired two more .22 CCI Stingers in quick succession over the wounded man's ear. Feenzo's feet remained on the ground as his upper torso folded into the trunk.

Mike glanced up the alleyway, then bent down and, with a grunt, flipped the body into the trunk onto its back, stuck the gun under Feenzo's chin, and fired once more. He closed the trunk and headed up the alley.

He had walked less than a hundred feet east up D Street when a white Toyota Camry pulled alongside. Mike got in and took off his dark blue Red Sox cap and sunglasses. The driver said nothing.

At the West Broadway lights, they stopped at the red. Near the corner Kevin Curran leaned against a building reading a *Boston Herald*. Mike put his window down as Kevin approached and leaned with both arms on the door, his left arm over his right. "How're ya doin'?" Kevin said.

"Doin' good," Mike said, slipping the .22 Beretta up the vinyl door panel into Kevin's open right hand.

Kevin slipped the gun into the Herald. "See ya," he said and walked away.

The light turned green and the Camry turned left, heading for the Broadway Bridge. Wacko said, "We'll dump this hotbox in the South End near the Cathedral projects. Let the Mau Maus steal it again. Kevin will dump the piece, then pick us up in front of the Cathedral on Washington Street. How'd it go? Any chance Feenzo will be testifyin' against us about gun sales in the future?"

"Doubt it, and I really fucked up his golf game," Mike Janowski said.

48

AS MORGAN DALY WALKED OUT the door of the Quencher Tavern into the South Boston sunlight, he spoke over his shoulder to someone inside the place. "Ya, Rooney, maybe when elephants fly; pay me what you owe me for your last bet, you fucking deadbeat, then maybe I'll hear ya, right now I'm deaf" (which he pronounced "deef").

On the sidewalk Morgan looked to his left towards the water, yawned and stretched, and checked his Baume & Mercier for the time. He brought the crystal up to his mouth, hawed it, and then polished it with the inside of his left cuff. Satisfied, the heavy work of the day done, he put both hands in his pockets and scratched his balls with his right and rocked on his heels until the blue Chevy Malibu stopped in front of him. The driver, who filled the entire side window, motioned him over.

"Hey, Andre, what ya hear?" Morgan said.

"Boss wants to see ya," Andre said through a small space between the glass and upper doorframe.

"What?" Morgan said.

"Get in the car," Andre said.

Morgan pulled his hands from his pockets and rubbed them together like he was wiping off peanut salt. "Uh, can't. I'm waiting on someone made a good hit last night, supposed to meet and pay him any minute now," he said.

"You'll be back in time," Andre said, getting out of the car. "I ain't askin', Morgan, get in the car."

Morgan's face dropped like his cheeks had suddenly filled with BB's. He gingerly put his hands in his pockets like he had an egg in each he was afraid might break.

He walked around the front of the Malibu, pulled his hands from his pockets, and checked his watch again. "We ain't gonna be long, huh, Andre?"

"Get in the fucking car," Andre said. Morgan got in.

"So, how's things with you? Still workin' out?" he said as they stopped at the lights opposite the Gate of Heaven church. Andre picked his nose and flicked the snot through the small opening at the top of the glass.

"Hit the L now and then, but the joint's gettin' dirty. Ain't like the old days when the old guys took care of it." Andre turned onto East Broadway, then the first right off it down Emerson Street.

"Things get old they get worse," Morgan Daly said.

"Some things get worse fast," Andre said, pulling over and stopping in front of the Dudley Tavern. He got out, quickly walked around the front of the car, and waited for Morgan to get out.

Andre noticed Morgan looking across the street at the fire station. "Fucking sirens drive me crazy, you? Boss don't mind, go figure," Andre said. He put a huge mitt on the back of Morgan's neck, and both men entered the bar.

Inside, Andre nodded at the bartender, who unblinkingly watched them pass before subtly reaching beneath the lip of the bar. The electric buzz of a remote lock releasing preceded Andre's hand on the brass knob of the mahogany door, next to an ancient oak-wood and glass phone booth at the back of the room.

"I got him, boss," Andre said as they climbed the twelve steps to the second floor. The door across the hall at the top of the second-floor landing was open.

Marty Fallon was behind his desk watching the news when they came in. Morgan glanced over his shoulder at the screen. "CNN?" he said.

Marty kept his eyes on the screen. With his left hand he indicated a chair in front of his desk. "Sit," he said.

Morgan sat down uncomfortably in the chair. "Me, I can take the news or leave it, too depressin' most the time," he said.

Marty took his eyes from the screen and turned them on the man sitting in front of him. The eyes seemed to smolder. "Most the time the news pisses me off," he said. He raised his hands to shoulder height and made little circles in the air with his index fingers. "And there's enough round here that pisses me off already."

Morgan shifted uneasily and lifted one cheek off the seat like he wanted to fart. "I can appreciate that, Marty. The cops have been hittin' us, your bookies, pretty hard. They got Cagney at the Pen, Bobby Kiley at the Coachman, Stooey down Street Lights. Not to mention, least what I heard, all your other books in J.P., Dorchester, Quincy. You must have just about had it. Why they botherin' you?" Morgan patted the vest pocket of his shirt and frowned. "Gum, thought I had gum. Ya know, I'm lucky, they haven't bothered me, but not to worry, even if they do I've moved my books, they ain't findin' nothin'."

Andre crossed the room and stopped directly behind Morgan Daly's seat. Marty continued to stare.

Morgan looked over his shoulder at Andre's dick, then back at Marty. "Whoa, Jesus, ya know, I almost forgot about Walter, sorry about Walter, a shame. I hear a robbery?"

Marty hit the mute button on the remote control. "The only one gettin' robbed here's me. I want you to tell me somethin', Morgan.

Anyone of your customers, anyone bettin' large these days that never used to?"

Morgan glanced over his shoulder, put his hands on his knees, and slowly began to rise out of the chair. He said, "No disrespect intended, Marty, but who's bettin' what's kinda my business, ain't it?"

Marty savagely slammed his fist on the desk. "Who — who the fuck is this guy, Andre?" he said, hoisting himself out of the chair. Andre moved even closer. "I gotta tell you, Morgan? Everything you do in your miserable fucking life is my business. Now sit the fuck down."

Like he was hit behind the knees with a sock full of sand, Morgan plopped into the chair. "Sorry, Marty, I didn't mean . . . it's just that with all the heat, business has been off. No one's bettin' large that doesn't usually except . . ." He looked over his shoulder at Andre's dick again. "Kevin Curran. He usually bets between three hundred and a grand a game, mostly on basketball, football, sometimes baseball, and . . ."

"Get to the point."

"The point's this, he calls me last Friday, bets thirty-three hundred on the Celts to win three grand over the Knicks. The Celts were a nine-point favorite. The Knicks got the money, he was bullshit." Morgan shrugged.

"Last night he comes down the bar around six and drops another thirty-three hundred on L.A to win against the Suns. You follow the game, good game, L.A. got the money. I got sixty-three hundred to hand him when I get back to the Quencher," Morgan said, pulling his pager off his belt and checking it. "I'm surprised he ain't paged me yet for the dough."

Marty stroked his chin with his left hand. "Interesting," he said. "That's a lot of dough to be throwing around for a guy usually bettin' a helluva lot less. Funny too this same kid dropped twenty-five hundred last week down the Coachman to Bobby Kiley on a fucking Bruins game."

Morgan hesitantly eased himself out of the seat like he expected the cushion to suck his butt back down. "The kid's lousy, Marty. Usually can't hit the side of a barn, but he always pays," Morgan said.

Marty's chair creaked as he leaned back into it and put his feet up on the desk. "Strange, Kevin throwin' his money around bettin' large and Wacko Curran's not been down to see you? You know how he badgers guys who take his asshole brother's bets," Marty said.

"Tell ya the truth, Marty, I'm hopin' I don't see him until I win my money back, cause I will, ya know," Morgan Daly said.

"Maybe not," Marty said. "Maybe the kid will discover the error of his ways." Morgan looked at him weird.

Marty removed his feet from the desk and got up. He came around and put his hand on Morgan's shoulder dismissively. "Okay, Morgan, that's all for now. Tomorrow's Thursday. Andre will stop by as usual to pick up my envelope."

Morgan nodded and moved towards the door. "You got it, boss, end of the week, with your dough I'm never late, even though it's been a tough month up to now."

"Now's just a speed bump, it'll get better," Marty said, patting Morgan's back. "It's all because of that North End thing plus with poor Walter Feeney getting — robbed don't help none." He pointed at the door. "Go outside, wait in Andre's car; he'll give you a lift back."

Morgan left the room, and Marty listened for the sound of footsteps descending stairs before he turned up the volume on the TV.

"When you drive him back, Andre, make sure Morgan understands how important it is his books aren't found. Don't need no feds hammerin' down my door."

Marty walked over to the window, separated the blind with two fingers, and watched as two floors below Morgan pulled up on the door latch of the blue Malibu and staggered back a step; embarrassed, he looked around. "You locked the car?" Marty said.

"Ya, boss," Andre said, looking out the window.

Marty grinned and turned away from the glass. "You're learning, Andre. See, life's a learnin' experience, and I try to learn one new thing each day. Today I learned Kevin Curran's spendin' large. That plus the fact his brother's not threatenin' anyone over it tells me Wacko Curran's got bigger fish to fry. Know what kind of fish that is, Andre?"

Andre clenched his jaw and nodded.

"Ya, me too," Marty said. He patted Andre's back. "Now go give Morgan his ride, he's got bills to pay."

49

AT EMERSON CLEANERS on Fourth Street near M, Elaine Ramsey paid for her clothes with money from a small brown leather purse, then carried them folded over one arm to her car. She opened the Jetta's trunk, unfolded the clothes, and laid them flat on the floor of the compartment. As she smoothed the plastic covering with her palms, she was vaguely aware of a car passing slowly on the left. The dark blue Mercury Marquis rolled to a stop, then backed up and the passenger window went down.

"Cute butt, honey, kinda looks like cupcakes," Wacko Curran said with a huge grin on his face. Elaine straightened up; with her right hand she flipped the hair from the nape of her neck. "Hey, Jack, how are you doing? I'm heading out the island to roller-skate," she said, closing the trunk. "Want to come?"

"My skating days are over, Elaine, sorry," Wacko said.

"Don't know about that. From what I've seen, Mr. Curran, you've been skating your whole life," Elaine said. The redhead batted her eyelashes and grinned.

Wacko turned his ignition key off and rested his right elbow on the nearby headrest. "Been thinkin' about going on vacation," he said.

Elaine comically arched an eyebrow.

"Why the look, ya, a vacation, like I don't deserve one?" Wacko said.

Elaine folded her arms on her chest. "Jackie, people who work for a living take vacations. People who don't simply do what they generally do in a warmer climate."

"And that's?"

"Nothing," she said, waving her finger at him.

"You tellin' me I don't work? My work . . . my work's more demandin', more time consumin', more . . ."

"Illegal, Jack, the word you're searching for is *illegal,* and you, my friend, are heading up the wrong road. And as someone who cares, I refuse to watch you go down it, good-bye," Elaine said, turning away from the car and climbing into her own.

Wacko pulled alongside her door. "Hey relax, Lainey-bear, calm down. Geez, you redheads got a temper."

Elaine pushed her palms against the steering wheel and pretended to be angry.

"You know, I've been thinkin', Elaine, maybe you're bored, need a break. You could come with me on vacation, you know, strictly as friends. You'd get your own room, do whatever you want, we could hang out," Wacko said.

Elaine tried to restrain herself from smiling and stared at him. "Hang out?" she said.

"Ya, you know, go out to eat, see the sights, hang glide, I always wanted to hang glide," Wacko said.

"You want to hang out and hang glide?" Elaine said.

Wacko looked down and shook his head. "Ya know, Ramsey, you're a wise guy, but I like that about you. But really, I'm serious about this vacation thing. You could skate down there just as easily," Wacko said.

"Jackie, down there, what are you talking about, where are you going?"

"Anywhere, someplace nice, Australia?" Wacko said.

"Australia? It's winter there," Elaine said.

"Then how about China? You like Chinese food, or the islands?" Wacko said. Elaine covered her ears.

"I'm going out to Castle Island, my island, it helps me think," Elaine said.

"Then think about it while you're skatin'. You got my number, right?" Wacko frantically searched his glove box for a pen.

"Jackie, don't bother. Whenever you give me a number, within a week it's no good. You call me, same number all these years," Elaine said.

"Gotcha," Wacko said, keeping his foot on the brake but putting the car in drive. "Call you in a few days. If you can think of someplace nice to go, write it down. Makes no difference to me long as they take American money. They take it in China, you think?"

"Taiwan or Red?" Elaine said.

Wacko scowled.

"There's two Chinas, Jack."

"Fine, then we'll see 'em both, fly to one, do day trips to the other," Wacko said.

Elaine blinked twice and stared straight ahead. "Call me," she said, putting the car in gear.

50

GENNARO SCARPA SUCKED UP a big, fat line of pink Peruvian bubble gum cocaine through a sterling silver straw and went "Ahhh!" With the little finger of his right hand he dug at a collection of residue in the corner of one nostril and stuck it in his mouth, then stepped to the right in front of a small porcelain sink, turned on the tap, and washed his nose and upper lip, inhaling some of the liquid. For the third time in four minutes he checked the bathroom door to make sure it was still locked, then with his right index finger, pressed up the few remaining flakes of cocaine on top of the toilet tank and rubbed the residue on his gums. "Fucking A," he said to himself as he gave his zipper one last tug and flushed the toilet. He opened the door and walked into the room.

In the center of the small third-floor room, Sonny Falcione sat at an oversized card table with five other men. He gave Scarpa an icy stare. "Drinkin' a lot of water," he said. Scarpa sat down on a couch against the wall and stared at a rectangle of sunlight on the floor from the only window in the room.

Falcione shook his head "As I was sayin' . . ." He glared at Scarpa. "Somebody killed one of us, an accident? Maybe, but I'll be fucked —" he slammed his fist on the table — "fucked if I give anyone credit being smart enough to come into our backyard, kill one of us, steal two million fucking dollars, and get away clean."

Every head at the table nodded in grumbling agreement.

"Now I gotta ask you, was it them Irish bastards that did this? It's a fact they'd like to kill every one of us."

"And I'd like to kill every scallycap-wearing son-of-a-bitch on the planet, dig 'em up, and kill 'em the fuck again," Teddy Limone said, almost poking a hole through the table with a beefy index finger.

Joe "The Animal" Lombardo sat at the head of the table facing the door. He quietly listened as one after the other his men said their piece before he held up his right hand and the table fell silent. He slowly, almost painfully removed his glasses and laid them down, gently, as if the frames were made of nitroglycerin. He placed his palms together, intertwined his fingers, closed his eyes, and lowered his head as if he were readying himself to pray. The four men around him grew anxious. When J.L. took off his glasses, it was like cocking a pistol, bad things were sure to happen. J.L began.

"Most men got real problems they pray, but God forgive me, I gave up the church long ago," he said. He closed his eyes, and the men at the table shifted almost imperceptibly towards him as though he were a magnet and they sharp-edged bits of steel.

Lombardo opened his eyes. "For some time it troubled me to think I had no religion. I figured this was my lot until one day it came to me, like a fucking spear, an electric bolt of white-hot energy from somewhere, I don't know. I did have a god; my religion, my god is Mafia." He paused again for emphasis while the other men softly patted the table.

"This thing of ours has been attacked on two fronts. Gaetano Milano, my dear friend and consigliere, an accidental death by working men perhaps, but aside from his loss, and it's huge, the police, since one of theirs was also shot, are pressuring everyone for information. We are unable to operate our many businesses, collect our money in the fashion we are accustomed, and the cost to us in less than two weeks is close to a quarter million dollars," Lombardo said. There were a few audible gasps.

With the side of his Bally shoe, Scarpa flicked at a dead moth on the floor. Like most of his kind, he couldn't get high enough. The package of Peruvian coke was burning a hole in his pocket, and here this old guy was rattling on like someone from a B gangster flick. Scarpa had had enough. He pulled himself slowly off the couch as though his ass was attached to the cushion by long, stringy bands of rubber. He was about to straighten his knees, which were aimed at the bathroom door, when Lombardo pointed.

"You! Sit the fuck down. What you got in there, a date?" the old man snarled. He put both hands on the table and pressed himself halfway up. "You, kid, are good for one thing and one thing only, and if Salvatore here hadn't spoken for you, your ass wouldn't be within ten miles of this room. Now sit the fuck down and stay there." The old man's eyes burned through Gennaro Scarpa and pinned him to the couch like a beetle to a Styrofoam board.

Though the veins in his neck visibly pulsed, the old man responded to the outstretched hands at the table imploring him to sit. He tugged at his shirt collar and began again. "We got problems. This ain't rocket science what's happenin' to us. Someone comes into our town to do business, no warnin', but some things can be understood the circumstances. But the end result is one of us is dead and it's like we got jet fuel up our ass there's so much heat.

"Who knows why this happened, but I'll tell you one thing — someone's gonna pay. They, whoever *they* are — Irish, Polish, Italian, orangutan, or goddamn Chink — is gonna pay. So, what we got so far?" Lombardo said.

Biaggio Vitale, a heavyset, balding man, twisted two diamond rings on the soft outermost fingers of his left hand as he spoke. His eyes were hard. "Joe, the rest of ya's, I got my network out there, every bookmaker, loan shark, collector whatever, lookin' for unusual activity, heavy gamblin', heavy borrowin' from people we know or don't know, don't matter. They see anything weird they'll reach out for me."

Sal "The Monster" Cristallo frowned and leaned back in his chair. Salvatore was middle-aged, squat, dark, and muscular. The nickname came from the Arizona Gila monster, a lizard so fierce that once its jaws were locked on a victim, it was said release required removing its head.

"Tell me, Biaggio, why would guys with two million plus need a shark? Don't make much sense," Cristallo said. "I say we got any idea who did this we grab, shake, and kill 'em — bing, bang, boom, end of story."

"And if they're the wrong guys?" Vitale said.

Sal shrugged. "Things happen. You perfect, Biaggio?" Cristallo said.

Joe Lombardo held up his hand. He said, "To answer your question, Salvatore, why would these men need to go to a shy? These guys are smart, hell, they stole two million fucking dollars, but smart guys don't throw money around: it attracts cops, makes people jealous. But a smart man might go to a shylock, borrow a little, then maybe a little more. He pays it back, then turns around and borrows more, a lot more. Then, a little bit down the road, when he does start to flash — a new car, trip to Paradise Island, fur coat for the old lady — the talk is he's dealin' dope or havin' a good run at the track. Other guys see him figure he's into the loan sharks and thank God it's not them. It's human nature, they wait for the bum to fall on his face, 'cept these guys don't fall."

Cristallo waggled a finger at Lombardo. "Ya, Joe makes sense. Everyone knows when a guy's big into the shylocks, no one thinks about when he starts to show a little here and there. Maybe we should just start grabbin' guys who took out big loans after Gaetano bought it," he said.

J.L. put his glasses back on and stared at the Monster, then suddenly yanked them off and threw them across the table. "Whatsa matter with you, you nuts?" he said. "Lendin' *is* our business. Why don't we set fire to our pants, burn the fucking buildin' down while we're at it? We ain't grabbin' anyone until we know, know! Nothing's bringin' Gaetano back, but he ain't gonna die in vain, naw. An accident? Okay, we'll *fine* the bastards, like they do when there's an oil spill in the Arctic, six hundred thousand dollars it's gonna cost 'em. If they don't wanna pay then we let the "Monster" here loose with his man Scarpa." Lombardo glared at the young man on the couch. "That is, if he can stay out of the fucking bathroom long enough."

51

THE BLUE MERCURY MARQUIS'S driver's side window framed the irregularities of the Atlantic coast as Wacko Curran sped south on Route 93 and passed the huge, multicolored Keyspan gas tank on the left before taking the Neponset exit. At the bottom of the ramp, after passing a small strip mall on the right, he turned right onto the Neponset Bridge and crossed the murky, slow-moving river sixty feet below before bearing left at the split and taking the first right after it.

Boston Harbor stretched out to his left as Wacko followed a desolate stretch of road that eventually led to a rotary. He followed it halfway around, went straight, then turned right at Victory Road. A short distance down he pulled into a small, L-shaped parking lot opposite the Marina Point Apartments. He parked the Marquis between a neon green Dodge and a silver, late-model Porsche with a vanity plate and got out.

Wacko crossed the street bordering the front of the gray, multiform building that rose fifteen stories and entered through double glass doors. On a stainless steel control panel to his right he pressed a black, rectangular button next to the number 46. As he awaited a response, he turned and faced the outside door and cursed softly as a white Chevy van with blacked out windows cruised slowly by.

"Ya?" said a voice that sounded like someone talking through the bottom of a popcorn box. Wacko turned and pressed a button alongside the speaker that had TALK embossed in the metal next to it. "It's me, open the door," he said.

"Jack?"

Wacko didn't reply but angrily tugged on the inner door handle until the buzzer released the lock.

He quickly descended three steps to the lobby, crossed to the elevator in front of him, and hit the up button. As he waited he glanced over his shoulder, focusing on a framed oil painting of water lilies on the wall to the left of the stairs. Below it was a chair with a sky blue cushion and bright mahogany railings. Wacko approached the painting and prodded the frame. It didn't move. Both picture frame and chair were discreetly but firmly affixed to their respective positions by screws. Wacko chuckled softly to himself as the elevator door slid open behind him.

On the fourth floor he stepped out and took a left. The door to number 46 was slightly ajar; hip-hop music emanated from inside. Without knocking Wacko walked in past a small kitchen on the left into the living room, where a gum-snapping, twenty-something bleached blond with a Who-the-fuck-are-you? look on her face sat on a brown leather couch.

"You. Get the fuck out!" Wacko said without breaking stride.

At the end of a hallway off the living room, Kevin stepped out of the bathroom, the exhaust fan humming noisily behind him. In one hand he held a glass pipe; a long cylindrical lighter with a trigger was in the other. He looked up at his brother as he put the pipe stem in his mouth and sparked the lighter. Kevin held the hissing blue flame to the bowl and sucked hard on the stem.

"We gotta talk," Wacko said, glancing at the walls on either side, then down at the floor.

"And nice to see you again," Kevin said, his mouth streaming smoke.

"Who's the broad?"

"Hired help."

"Get rid of her," Wacko said.

Kevin cupped his left hand, dumped the contents of the pipe into it, and shoved the flakes around with his finger. He pouted, then turned over his hand, the ashes falling like lethal bits of chemical confetti to the floor. "You do it, Jack, she thinks I'm nice," he said, reentering the bathroom.

Wacko almost ran into the living room. "Hey, you understand American? Get up, get the fuck out," Wacko said. Before the woman could react he grabbed one of her wrists, yanked her off the couch, dragged her to the door, and flung her into the hallway. Seconds later a handbag ricocheted off the startled hooker's hip and the door slammed shut.

"Good job, Jack," Kevin said, walking into the kitchen. He came out with a beer in either hand. "Sayin' good-bye's always been tough for me." He grinned and tossed a Bud Light to his brother. "Ice cold," he said, cracking his.

Wacko put his beer down on a glass coffee table, sat on the couch, and collapsed back into it. "We're being watched, you know that? Christ, the cops, feds, some kind of heat cruised past as I waited for you to buzz me in. What I tell you about partyin', Kevin?"

Kevin grinned and shrugged and took a sip of beer. "Why you gotta be a buzzkill, Jack? You said I could after the score, this" — he raised his beer — "is after. I ain't no priest. One or two ladies in the house ain't a party, Jack," Kevin said, falling backwards, his legs splayed in front, into a black leather La-Z-Boy recliner. "Me, I don't see no party. What I do see are nosy fucking neighbors. Maybe I'll cut someone's nose off, stop that," Kevin said. He chugged the remainder of his beer, crumpled the can with both hands, and tossed it behind him. "These snotty pricks round here see a Ne-gro in the hall come all unglued."

"What are you talkin' about?" Wacko said, putting his hands on his knees and sitting up.

"Manny tells me how they check him out like he's got feathers sprouting from his butt when he makes his drops," Kevin said.

Wacko threw his hands in the air and dropped his chin to his chest. "Dominicans? You got fucking Dominicans movin' dope here?" he said.

Kevin pressed down with his legs on the chair's support and sat up. "Jack, you told me stay out of Southie, don't be buyin' product over there. Where you want me to go, Home Depot?"

Wacko closed his eyes tight and rubbed his temples hard like he was trying to squeeze some obscene image through the top of his head. "Kevin, right about now anyone else I'd have my hacksaw out and they'd be in separate Dumpsters," he said. Wacko grabbed his beer and cracked the top. He licked the spray off his thumb and index finger, gulped down half the contents, and belched. He put the beer down and got up. "That does it, we're outta here."

Kevin walked into the kitchen and reappeared in the living room with another beer in his hand. "Ya, where we goin'?" he said.

"We're goin' down south a few months."

"South? You're talkin' Florida, right? Pass, too hot," Kevin said. He opened his beer and sucked on it hard.

Wacko got up, walked over to a sliding glass door that led to a small balcony overlooking Boston Harbor. He pressed his palms overhead against the glass. "You don't get it, Kev. This is heat, and you're so high you can't see it's burnin' you up as we speak. Dominicans? Fucking Dominicans? How many times I tell ya, we deal with our own kind? They bust this shithead Manny, down the line they'll squeeze him. Fed says, 'Hey, Manny, your ass is headin' to Lewisburg, Lompoc ten to twenty. What you got to trade?' Manny says, 'Hey man, I ain't a bad guy, but I can give you one. I'm sellin' the yak to this crazy Irish bastard over in Quincy, Kevin Curran. Maybe you know him?' Now the fed's foaming, lickin' his lips, thinkin' fuck the Dominican we'll take down this Southie hood, real badass, bigger headlines. You're buyin' ounces, no matter there for your head, Kevin, ounces is distribution. You'll do ten just for that, and while you're doin' it they continue to investigate you for God knows what. Maybe hit you with superseding indictments for other shit like money launderin' and nail you with another twenty. Seen it done to others," Wacko said.

Kevin turned from his brother and headed towards the bathroom. "If you're tryin' to make me nervous, Jack, it's workin'," he said.

"Good, you should be nervous," Wacko said, turning from the window.

Kevin came out of the bathroom carrying his pipe. He dropped something into the bowl, then pulled the lighter from his back pocket. "Cops know so much, why ain't they doin' anything?" he said.

Wacko picked up his beer and drained it. He had a wry smile on his face when he put it down. "You that far gone? You can't stay away from that shit?"

"This is the end of it, Jack, gettin' rid of the evidence, ya know?" Kevin pulled the trigger of the lighter, held the flame to the bowl, and inhaled.

"That better be the fucking end, like they can't smell that shit out in the hall. I'll tell ya, Kevin, I'm sick of it. Maybe I should just leave your sorry ass here. Hasn't anything I said sunk in?"

Kevin nodded, then his eyes suddenly bulged and he dropped the lighter and pipe to the floor. He clutched at his chest with both hands, clawed the area around his heart, slid down the wall to the floor on his side, and lay there.

Wacko rested his fists on his hips and stared at his brother. "I should be so lucky," he said.

Kevin rolled onto his back and exhaled a pencil-thin stream of white smoke. He got up on one elbow. "Okay, I'll ask you again, cops know so much why ain't they doin' anything?"

"Listen, you psycho, knowin' and provin' are two different animals. At this point they can't prove shit but can still make our lives miserable. We gotta get outta here. I'm thinkin' Florida's no good, everyone round here on the lam heads to Miami, Fort Lauderdale, and Disney World."

Kevin sat up and wrapped his arms around his knees. "Remember Jimmy Caldwell, Jack? Remember years ago he's passin' funny money all over the south and the story goes he's in Disney World leavin' the ticket booth for the Tiki Room or one of them stupid rides and somethin' grabs his arm, remember? Turns out it was Pluto, Goofy, one of them fucks tryin' to snap a headlock on him along with a bunch of rabbits, clowns, and fucking elves tacklin' him and pinchin' his ass. Almost tore his clothes off," Kevin said.

"Ya, I remember. We ain't hittin' Disney World either, goin' further than Florida," Wacko said.

"Like where? It get hotter the farther we go?" Kevin said.

"Naw, it gets hotter the longer we stay. Maybe China," Wacko said.

"China's south?" Kevin said.

"South of somewhere. Marty's feelin' the heat from our score, Kevin. I heard the cops found Feenzo's books in his car, records of payoffs to Marty. Marty's got problems. He's lost a fortune since the score. He ain't certain it's us, but you know Marty, he don't have to be sure. He got the hounds out sniffin', and something's gotta break. I don't want to be here when it does," Wacko said.

"What about Janowski?" Kevin said.

"Janowski's smart, he's long gone, down New York with his girl relaxin'. Spoke to him last night, told him continue to," Wacko said.

"New York's south. `Maybe we could head down there?" Kevin said.

"Somethin' tells me we'll be needin' someplace closer to China," Wacko said.

52

JOE LOMBARDO PULLED his red Lincoln Town Car in front of the three-story red brick building at 40 Salem Street in Boston's North End and double-parked. After he got out he purposely left the door unlocked, slipped between two parked cars onto the sidewalk. The door in front of him, faced with riveted steel plate, swung open, and a heavyset, square-shouldered middle-aged man stepped through it, extending his right hand palm up. "What ya say, boss, they're expectin' ya," the man said, catching Lombardo's keys.

Lombardo patted the other man's shoulder and said, "Who's up there, Frankie?"

"Just Biaggio and Sonny Falcione; Vinnie Sculli left fifteen, twenty minutes ago. They were all up there talkin' for a while, then Vinnie left. Now it's just you guys," Frankie said.

"Thanks, Frankie, good job," Lombardo said as he headed up the stairs.

He entered a third-floor room just as Biaggio Vitale was coming out of the bathroom pulling up his fly. "Hey, boss," Vitale said.

Sonny Falcione laid his deck of cards down on the table and stood up. "You missed Vinnie, Joe, he had some news," Falcione said.

Lombardo shook Falcione's hand but ignored Vitale's, waving his index finger and pointing to Vitalie's crotch.

Vitale grinned. "Hey, Joe, I wash after always, you know that," he said.

"How would he know that?" Falcione said, looking suspiciously at Lombardo, who waggled his hands over his head. "Enough," he said. Vitale shook his fist at Falcione and chuckled.

Lombardo walked over to an espresso machine on a table beneath a framed, tourist-type poster of Palermo. "All right you two, what we got?" he said.

"Vinnie, Joe, he's got the escorts, three, four offices and expandin'," Vitale said.

"I know all that, what he say?" Lombardo said.

"He told me he's got a girl, works out of the Harbor Towers, high priced, pretty," Vitale said. The smell of strong, fresh-brewed coffee filled the room. "She's kinda special, see. Vinnie's puttin' the salami to her on the side, and she's talkin' to him last night, you know bullshit, pillow talk, tellin' him about how some guy roughed her up, tossed her out of a place, one of her stops. Vinnie don't like it."

J.L. filled a tiny cup and smelled the coffee before he sipped. "What she say, tell me exact," he said.

"Seems she's been seein' the same guy the past few weeks, a big spender, cokehead. The guy gets whacked and talks a lot, the coke. Take a guess who," Vitale said.

Joe Lombardo blew lightly across the top of the cup. "C'mon, don't jerk me around," he said, bringing the cup back up to his lips.

"Wacko Curran's brother," Vitale said.

J.L. frowned and lowered the cup."Them are Marty Fallon's boys," he said. The other two men nodded. "You tellin' me she's been seein' this guy . . ."

"Kevin."

"She's been seein' this Kevin regular, how regular? She's expensive we're talkin' four, five hundred dollars a night, correct?" J.L. said.

Vitale nodded again. "He rents her by the day, Joe. All day, all night. He's smokin' the shit, her too; has her parade around naked, play with herself. He gets so high he can't even fuck her. She's been to his joint in Quincy two days once, three days the next time, then two more days after that. He must have given her ten, twelve grand."

"That's a lot of dough. What's he into?" J.L. said, putting his cup down on the table and pulling out a chair.

"Same shit as his brother, a little bit of everything: shylock, dope, stickups, both are hitters, dangerous. Remember a while back Sal Montillio called me from Revere complainin' how he's got a jeweler friend out in Abington who recently took a big hit? Wanted to know if we could put some feelers out and we did?" Vitale said.

"Ya, I remember, get to the point," J.L. said.

"Well, Joe, we sniffed around, got word, nothing direct, no one would say anything direct — that it was these two, the Currans, who banged out this guy. We checked it out best we could but . . ." Falcione shrugged.

The cheap metal folding chair creaked as Lombardo leaned back into it and sipped his espresso. "Bit of a jump, Sal, whacking some jeweler in the boondocks and taking down an armored car in our backyard," he said.

"I agree, boss, but . . . You tell him, Biaggio," Falcione said.

Biaggio Vitale sat down at the table. "That's just it, Joe, this kid, Kevin Curran, told the broad that he had more money than God, that if she married him he'd need one of them prenuptial agreements them fucking movie stars get."

"Sounds like a fucking bug," Joe Lombardo said, pushing himself to his feet.

"There's more," Vitale said. "This broad, while the kid's smoking crack in the bathroom, I guess it stinks so the fan's going and —"

"Get to the fucking point."

"Well, this broad, Vinnie's girl, strolls into the bedroom looking for his stash, ya know, something for the head for later. She looks under the bed and spots these shoe boxes. But they ain't filled with shoes, Joe, it's all cake. She figures an easy quarter million, three hundred thousand just under that bed."

Joe Lombardo turned the chair towards him and slowly lowered himself into it. Vitale drummed his fingers on the table. "Joe, maybe they just got lucky, nailed some coke dealer," he said.

Lombardo shook his head and with the back of his hand flicked the air in front of his chest like he was shooing away a fly. "Naw, Marty Fallon, that fucking bum. He's up to his eyeballs in this; I knew it from the start." He balled his fist and hammered the table over and over. "I knew it! I knew it!" He leaped to his feet and grabbed the underside of the table like he intended to flip it. Vitale almost fell over backwards in his haste to get out of the way. Lombardo released his grip, grabbed his espresso cup, and fired it into the wall, then ripped off his glasses and spun them onto the table. "Get the Monster and that fucking crackhead he runs with, tell them they got work." He ran his fingers through his thinning hair.

Falcione looked at Vitale and gushed like he'd been holding his breath before speaking. "All due respect, Joe, what about the money? The 'fine' you called it, you said you were going to fine 'em, right?"

Joe Lombardo pulled a paper towel and tore it off a roll attached to the wall. He folded it neatly in half, then into quarters. He picked up his glasses and polished the lenses as he spoke. "Marty Fallon's a weasel, a weasel with fangs, and he ain't afraid to use 'em. You want I should draw you a diagram?" he said.

"Boys, we got one shot at this prick. We miss we got a fucking war, and that happens we'll lose more than that son-of-a-bitch could give us. There's always enough for a squirrel but never enough for a pig, capesh? I live by that. Clip him. After this pig is dead, we'll take over his rackets, make up our end then. The Currans won't say shit, they know the rules, their boss is in the wrong."

"You think the Currans will lay down that easy, Joe?" Vitale said.

J.L. put on his glasses. "What I'm hearin' there's no love between them and Fallon. Besides, we kill one, have to kill the other and their friends, gets very complicated. It's true, maybe they had something to do with this Hanover Street deal. If that's the case they can keep the fucking money, which should keep 'em in line."

Falcione pulled opened a narrow closet door in the corner of the room and removed a broom and dustpan. He swept the pieces of the broken cup into a pile. "I hear the Currans are smart, Joe, they'll catch on fast," he said.

Joe Lombardo made a fist, put an index finger to his temple and cocked his thumb. "They get it fast or they will," Joe Lombardo said, dropping the thumb.

53

TRAFFIC WAS LIGHT on Route 93 south in Quincy when Marty Fallon took the Furnace Brook Parkway exit and cut across the city to Route 3A, on the way to the coastal town of Hull. It might have been quicker had he remained on 93 then taken Route 3 to Rockland, cut through Hingham, but he needed time to think, and it was hard to think when he was angry.

It was Thursday, Thursday was collection day. He should have been with his man Andre Athanas, making stops in South Boston, Quincy, the rest of his towns, collecting his due from the assortment of bookmakers, loan sharks, and drug dealers who operated by his grace alone. Today Andre would handle the chores himself, and the pickings would be meager. Ever since that job in the North End turned up the heat in the city to such a degree, the very air Marty breathed seemed filled with cinders.

There had been an endless scream coming from his wallet since the cops raided three of his largest gaming operations and shut them down tighter than the skin on Joan River's face. But at least they didn't discriminate. They also slammed the mahjong parlors in Chinatown and the Italians in East Boston, the North End, and Revere. Even the black and Puerto Rican gangs of the South End and Roxbury were feeling the heat. The headlock was on and would remain, choking the lifeblood from everyone, until they broke the case in which two million was grabbed and a Boston cop lost his arm.

If that wasn't enough, Marty Fallon had gotten the word that Joe Lombardo was rattling sabers over the loss of his man Gaetano Milano. J.L. was looking hard for whoever did this, and if it was the Currans, if it was, then the heat would be squarely on Martin Emmett Fallon, and he hadn't made a dime.

The headaches came in waves. A few days earlier one of his earners, a coke dealer named Buttso Connaughty, got popped. The cops hit his stash house on Cottage Street and walked away with eight kilos of coke. Marty's coke.

Marty hated Buttso's I'm-smarter-than-you attitude and his habit of constantly filling his face with food, but Buttso was an earner. Now Buttso was a headache looking at fifteen years. These days the average dope dealer couldn't hold his mud for six months, never mind a decade or more. Would Buttso hold his water? Marty didn't think so. Marty planned to bail him out, talk to him, see what he told the cops, then dig a hole and be done with Buttso Connaughty, but that was down the line. His immediate concern was another fat slob, his FBI handle just dying to meet him.

At the southernmost end of Nantasket Beach in Hull, Marty Fallon pulled the blue Malibu into the nearly empty parking lot of the defunct nightclub Blackie's on the Rocks. He parked between two faded white lines, got out, walked a short distance to where a black Crown Victoria sat idling, and got in.

Without a word the driver put the car into reverse, backed up ten feet, threw it into drive, and turned right as they exited the parking lot. A half mile up the road, just before the public bathhouse, he pulled into a space in front of the seawall next to a stairway leading down to the beach and shut the engine off. For a few nerve-wracking seconds the driver stared hard at the dash, as if memorizing the reading on the odometer, before he turned and looked at his passenger.

"I'll tell you honest, Marty, it's not me wants to cut you loose, it's them. I don't know I can help," the fat man said, pulling a cylindrical package from his shirt pocket. He bit through the top, removed the piece from his mouth, tore the paper off the white tablet, then popped it onto his tongue. He offered one to the other man. "Rolaids?" Marty stared out the passenger window and said nothing. "No? I'm surprised."

Marty turned and looked at the driver. "After all I done for you that's it, fucking sayonara?" he said.

"Done? That's just it, Marty, the SAC thinks you're done, put the fork in, he told me," the fat man said. He crushed the Rolaids with his teeth. Marty dropped his chin to his chest, closed his eyes, then snapped them open and looked out the side window.

"Hey, c'mon, Marty, the guy's nervous some of the things he, shall we say we, looked the other way on. You being Top Echelon, you got a lot more play than the average informant; could cause trouble, a lot, down the road it gets out. At this point you're more of a hazard than a help, understand? Hey, I gotta fart, let's take a walk," the fat man said, pulling up on the door latch.

He opened the driver's door and swung his chunky left leg out. He hesitated for a second, took another breath, then pushed on the steering wheel and forced the rest of his body, like toothpaste from a tube, out of the black Crown Vic. Before he straightened, he farted loudly, with a sound like a wet sheet tearing.

A gust off the ocean blew the rancid cloud into Marty's face. He clawed the air, ripped open the door, and leaped out. "Fucking Jesus," he said.

"Sorry," the fat man said.

Marty walked up to the seawall, still fanning the air in front of his face. He stared out at the vast expanse of rolling, green Atlantic like he was looking for something. He pointed diagonally to his left. "That Boston Light over there?"

"Don't know, your city," the fat man said.

Marty turned and looked at him. "Well, I'll tell you something else you may not know. Ever hear the name Joe Barboza? He was the first guy ever in the Witness Protection Program. Back there in the mid-sixties, while he was waitin' to testify in the Teddy Deegan murder case, over in Chelsea, they stashed him out there on Boston Light or some other godforsaken island."

"Ya, I think I heard about that," the fat man said.

Marty smirked. "That lyin' piece of shit put four innocent men — Peter Limone, Joe Salvati, Henry Tameleo, Louie Greco — away for life, and your guys, your fucking bureau, knew and let him, and you say I'm a hazard?"

The fat man turned away from the ocean and rested the considerable bulk of his ass on the seawall. "That was a long time ago," he said.

"Not for those guys. If the state hadn't overturned the death penalty they'd all be dead, and that's what the bureau hoped for. Tameleo and Greco died in prison; the other two did thirty years before they flipped the case."

The fat man looked at his feet and shook his head. "They were wiseguys every one, comes with the territory."

"Wiseguys? Who says? You want to find out what else 'comes with the territory'? Who you think might be interested in the story of a guy who had a license for the past fifteen years to do whatever he wanted when? The *Globe,* the *Herald,* fucking *Newsweek?*" Marty said.

"You threatening me?" the fat man said.

"You're threatenin' me. Comes with the territory, right?" Marty said.

The fat man sighed. He attempted unsuccessfully to cross his legs, gave up, and simply repositioned his ass. He nodded across the street towards a row of ancient one- and two-story wood-and-concrete structures.

"That restaurant over there, Joseph's, been there? Used to have the best seafood around when I was a kid, steamers, scallops, couldn't beat them with a fucking stick. Used to go there with my mother and younger brothers after riding the amusements all day out back in Paragon Park. Remember Paragon Park, Marty, the Jungle Ride, the roller coaster made of wood, the goddamn Roter, the way it spun you stuck to the wall and the floor dropped out from beneath?" The fat man grinned, shook his head again, and extended both huge arms towards the sky, then slowly lowered them.

"This place, this whole place was beautiful, and what happened? Decent people stopped coming, riffraff poured in, the place got seedy, antiquated. They shut it down and put up condos no one wanted for the longest time. Now who can afford them? Go figure." The fat man stood up and stretched, then rubbed his belly vigorously like he was hoping some kind of genie might spring from it.

"That's life, Marty, what's good never stays that way, what's bad, well, you don't mind waiting, it sometimes comes around." The fat man licked the tip of his right index finger and dabbed at a spot of something three buttons down from the base of his enormous neck. "Time's a-passin', Marty, things are bad, and I don't have time to wait. Any suggestions?"

"Ya, take me back to my car," Marty said.

The fat man got into the Crown Victoria and turned the engine over. The other man got in next to him.

"Of course things could change instantly you come up with some-thing to hang my hat on," the fat man said.

"Like what?"

"Like who the fuck stole two million and blew a young cop's arm off."

"I'm workin' on that, gettin' close. What, I don't move fast enough? You never complained before. You and yours seem to forget what I've done for them over the years, but I haven't, get my drift, I haven't," Marty said.

"What's that supposed to mean?" the fat man said, looking at his passenger.

"I got tapes," Marty said.

The fat man's look turned into a glare.

"That's right, every time we shared so much as a cuppa Salada tea I got tapes."

The fat man winced like he had just swallowed something sharp. "And anything not on 'em is locked tight up here," Marty said, tapping his temple.

The fat man pulled out the Rolaids. "You're in a talkative mood, tell me more," he said, pushing two into his mouth.

"All the little shit, like me lendin' you five grand here, five grand there, not to mention that eleven grand debt of yours I took over because of your problem at Suffolk Downs. You forget you had problems, Roy, and I always had the solutions?" Marty said.

"You forgot about Christmas too, huh? How every year those fucking holidays cost me ten, twelve grand your lousy FBI office alone. Them bums you work with walkin' outta Rotary Liquors, my store, with cases of my booze. Funny thing those security cameras in the parking lot outside. Well, genius, they're not for security — well, not in the regular sense." Marty laughed out loud and pointed. "All of ya's are movie stars. I got ten years of you guys walkin' out the door of my store grinning like mako sharks, fingers buried in free cases of my booze. I got enough for a feature-length film."

Marty Fallon gave the fat man's shoulder a squeeze and a pat. "Roy, you throw me to the dogs, I'll make sure they're gnawing on your leg before I go under."

"I don't respond to threats," the fat man said.

"You don't but I do? Hey, c'mon, I want things like they were before, you?" For almost a minute the fat man stared over the steering wheel and said nothing. Marty pulled on the door release. "I'm walkin'," he said.

"Tide's coming in," the fat man said, nodding over the seawall. "Ever notice how it buries everything when it does? Tide goes out, things look the same, but get down close everything's different."

"What's your point?"

"No point, Marty, tide's coming in. Just an observation," the fat man said.

"Take me to my car, unless of course you got more observations. I got work to do," Marty said.

The fat man pulled the black Ford into the parking lot of Blackie's and stopped twenty feet away from the other man's car. Marty got out.

With both hands gripping the steering wheel, the fat man leaned to the right. "Hey, Marty, that shit about the tapes, you serious?" he said.

Marty patted the right pocket of his blue, nylon windbreaker. "You like clams?" he said, slamming the door.

The fat man pulled himself straight and watched the other man drive off. He reached down, removed an envelope from between his seats and pulled a letter from it. "Too bad you're so bad, Marty," the fat man said, opening the letter. It read:

Federal Bureau of Investigation
Boston, Massachusetts
June 5, 1998

From: Special Agent in Charge: Earl C. Duntoff
To: Special Agent Roy Sheffield

Please be advised that recent intelligence sources have informed us that the New England branch of LCN has designated the Fallon group of South Boston as the party or parties responsible for the recent holdup of the Shawmut Bank on Hanover Street with the resultant death of one of their members. Sources indicate a contract has been issued on group leader Martin Emmett Fallon. As TOP ECHELON INFORMANT handler in charge of said Martin Emmett Fallon, you have permission to advise target of LCN intention if by doing so it will not jeopardize the confidentiality and security of other currently active TOP ECHELON INFORMANT operatives in the Boston area.

Sincerely,
Special Agent Earl C. Duntoff

The fat man refolded the letter, tore it in half, then quarters then eighths. He placed the pieces back inside the envelope, took a pen out of his vest pocket, and printed 'Shred' across the face of it before returning it between the seats.

"Ya, I like clams . . . helluva lot tastier than dirt," he said, putting the car in gear.

54

LEPPY MULLINS STEPPED OUT the front door of the L Street Bathhouse onto the sidewalk bordering Day Boulevard and snorted the rancid scent of sweat and old gym from his nose. He wiped below it with his right wrist, then pulled a pair of sunglasses from his gym bag. He looked at the sun, squinted, and slid the glasses on before he stopped at the crosswalk directly opposite the front door and purposefully hammered the pedestrian light button.

As Lep reveled in the warmth of the sun, the light changed from green to red-yellow and a car horn sounded to his left. Three cars down, a familiar head protruded from the passenger side of a shiny, red VW Passat. A flat-topped, smiling Mike Janowski motioned him over. "Leppy, need a lift, come on," he said.

Leppy grinned, waved back. The light changed to green as he walked to the Passat, and a guy in a BMW behind it leaned on the horn. Leppy glared at the driver as he opened the back door of the Passat and tossed his gym bag in.

"Hey, maggot, you in a fuckin' rush?" Leppy screamed. The guy in the BMW pulled his hands from the wheel and shrank into the seat. "Fuckin' yuppies," Leppy muttered, crawling into the back of the Passat.

The two men shook hands, and Mike stroked the driver's hair. "You know my girl, Jenna?" Jenna flashed a smile, Leppy nodded. Jenna headed up L Street.

"I'm headin' to my house. Nice car," Leppy said, squeezing the leather seats.

"Jenna's," Mike said. "Picked it up last week down New York."

"Long ride to buy a car," Leppy said.

"She's got an uncle in Poughkeepsie, small dealership, gave her a deal," Mike said, stroking Jenna's hair again.

"How's everything else?" Leppy said.

"No complaints, your end?"

"Been good, Mike, a few headaches. The cops are pressurin' everyone on account of that North End thing. It's affecting everyone, but things are startin' to relax," Leppy said.

"Things usually do. Jenna, left at the lights," Mike said. Jenna turned left at the lights onto East Broadway. "Ah shit, I should've gone straight, would have been quicker," Mike said, punching his knee.

"Naw, you did just fine, but pull over a sec, will ya?" Leppy said, leaning between the front seats, eagerly staring to his right through the windshield. Jenna pulled over sharply in front of the Boston Beer Garden. Leppy was out of the car before it stopped.

"Stay right where you are, Foley," Leppy said, jogging towards a man and woman who were standing talking in front of the bar. A short, muscular man in his twenties with close-cropped, bleached blond hair wearing a black nylon workout outfit turned from the conversation he was having with the older heavyset woman in jeans and a hooded sweatshirt. "Mike, this will only take a minute," Leppy shouted over his shoulder.

With a demonic grin Leppy extended his right hand as if to shake, then nimbly, as he got within range, leaped and landed a crisp lead left hook on the other man's chin. Like someone had lassoed and pulled Bobby Foley's feet from the front, he instantly went horizontal and bounced off the sidewalk.

Mike tooted the horn and yelled out the side window. "Great shot, Lep, haven't lost ya touch." Horrified, the woman backed against the bar's large front window, then slid sideways and sprinted inside. Bobby groggily picked himself up off the sidewalk and rubbed his jaw. He looked over at Mike, cringed, and waved his hands out in front.

"Leppy, hey, please, Lep, I'm sorry I screwed up," Bobby said. Leppy screamed something unintelligible and pointed to his left hand. "Hey, I'm sorry about your hand too, okay?" Bobby whined.

"Tonight, you piece of shit, be here with my money, understand?" Leppy said, half-turning away. He shook his fist. "No excuses."

Leppy climbed back into the Passat. "Sorry, folks, a straggler. Gotta deal with 'em as you find 'em, ya know?"

"No problem," Mike said. "Nice touch. You twisted into it good, fucking airborne when you hit him, tough shot."

"All in the feet, Mikey boy. Perfect balance is important when it comes to collectin' from deadbeats," Leppy said.

At K Street, Jenna took a right, then a left on East Third. She pulled the car over in front of the IA restaurant across the street from Leppy Mullins' house. "Food here any good?" Jenna said, indicating the IA.

Leppy shrugged. "Live there, I don't cook," he said. He tapped Mike on the shoulder. "Talk to you a minute?"

Both men got out of the car and diagonally crossed to a yellow house on the corner of Emmet Street. Leppy grimaced as he looked at the gutters. "Gotta get up there and clean 'em, birds makin' a nest in the corner," he said.

"So what's up?" Mike said, coming up behind him and putting a hand on his shoulder.

Leppy turned. "Wanted to let you know, Mike, would have before now but haven't seen you much lately. Course I had somethin' like that," Leppy said, nodding towards Jenna, "I wouldn't be around much either."

"Thanks. So what ya got?" Mike said.

"You know that kid Mark Costa, Snoopy's brother? Well, a few weeks back Wacko, I mean Jack Curran sends him down to see me about a piece."

Mike shook his head, stepped back, and waved his hands. "Maybe you should talk to Jack about this. I know nothin' about it, don't want to," he said.

Leppy continued like he hadn't heard him. "Thought it strange, Mike, him bein' a citizen and all. But he told me, the guy told me that Jack Curran had okayed the sale. I ain't questioning Jack, ya know? Just thought it strange."

Mike scratched his head and looked down towards L Street. "What kind of piece was he lookin' for?" he said.

"I had three, two Smiths and a Glock. He checks them all out real close, then, like a light goes on, he grabs the Glock. It's a nice piece, gave him a deal, three hundred bucks. Could have got four, he would have paid four, but for Jack, ya know?" Leppy said.

"Three hundred's more than fair," Mike said. "He said Jack sent him, right?"

"Wouldn't have done it he hadn't, Mike. Right after, the same day, I beeped Jackie, no answer. Never got back to me. I figure there was a problem I'd know."

"I'd figure too, but I'll check on it. Say why he wanted it? Mark's a fucking citizen far as I know," Mike said.

"Said somethin' about protection, how he works nights for the post office, drives around Roxbury, Mattapan. I hear that, I'm thinkin' maybe he should have gone for a machine gun," Leppy said. "Mike, could you do me a favor? You see the boss, tell him I'm low, need to re-up early next week? I used to use Buttso Connaughty as a backup but he got popped. I still got customers to take care of," Leppy said.

"I'll tell him, Lep, relax. Jack told that fat prick Connaughty to move his stash at least twenty times," Mike said, then shrugged. "Didn't listen." He grabbed Leppy playfully by the back of the neck. "People get lazy, don't you, and don't mention that gun thing to no one."

"Hope I ain't bein' a problem," Leppy said.

"Naw, you ain't no problem. Jackie likes you, Lep." Mike winked. "You were a problem, you'd be ridin' the trunk, not the backseat."

55

DOWNTOWN, ON THE PERIMETER of the old Combat Zone, Kevin Curran and Elbow Moriarty stood on the corner of Tremont and Stuart Streets and waited to cross the heavy line of traffic. Kevin glanced at Elbow. "Fix your tie . . . good. How I look?" he said, using his right hand to adjust the knot in his tie.

"Better than perfect," Elbow said. The light changed, and the two men crossed, heading south up Tremont Street. They quickly passed a parking lot and a small bar on the right before traveling another fifty yards and pushing their way through the revolving door of the Tremont Hotel.

"You gotta relax, remember you belong here, act it. By the looks of ya, I was a dick I'd pinch you for suspicion of bein' suspicious," Kevin said, guiding Elbow through the hotel lobby.

Kevin wore dark-framed, clear glasses and carried in his left hand a black leather valise with an attached shoulder strap. Both men were similarly dressed: black Dockers trousers, crisp, white shirts, blue ties. Both wore blue cotton barracuda-style jackets. They looked amazingly identical, like messengers from one of the large investment firms in the Financial District on their way to service some out-of-town client. No one in the busy lobby gave them a second look.

They walked past the front desk, turned left, then took the first right into a dead-end corridor with a bank of brass-doored elevators on either side.

"People are starin'," Elbow said, glancing back over his shoulder towards the lobby.

Kevin pushed the up button. "It's that shit, I told you not to do any before. Get a fucking grip," Kevin said.

The elevator doors opened. Both men got in and turned as the door began to close. Suddenly, a business type in a suit jumped in between them. Elbow gasped and viciously fingered the door open button. He jumped out without looking back, Kevin hot on his tail. Kevin grabbed a fistful of Elbow's jacket and jerked him to a halt. "What the fuck you doin'?" he hissed. He looked over his shoulder, then into Elbow's frightened eyes.

"Kevin, that guy, I think he was a cop. They got 'em in hotels, right. Could've been a Boston dick. I've seen —"

"Shut up, you seen. You got spooked is all by some stone citizen, you bug, fucking nutcappa, relax." Kevin smiled and nodded at a middle-aged, professional woman pulling a small wheeled American Tourister past.

"She a cop, Elbow? Relax." Kevin guided Elbow back to the elevator.

On the way up Elbow checked his reflection in the mirrored walls. He tilted his head sideways and fidgeted with his tie. "Looks real," Elbow said.

"Good thing we found these clip-ons since neither of us knows how to tie the real ones you boosted out of Macy's," Kevin said.

At the twenty-second floor they got out, turned right. "You sure of the room?" Kevin said.

"Dead on," Elbow said. "My guy's been workin' this thing six months. This card crew uses four of five different rooms, always the same ones, though, something to do with lucky numbers."

"Their number won't be lucky today," Kevin said.

As they walked down the hall, Kevin threw the shoulder strap over his head and settled the bag on his hip. He reached into it and pulled out a Charter Arms two-inch .38 revolver he handed to Elbow. His hand disappeared back inside and came out holding a two-inch Smith & Wesson .357, which he stuck in his pocket.

"Your man's always on the door, right, always?" Kevin said.

Gun by his side, Elbow reversed himself and traveled backwards a few steps. "Ya, always, and he knows what to do, don't worry," Elbow said, turning around again.

"All clear?" Kevin said.

"Lookin' fine," Elbow said.

"Feelin' better?"

"Ya, just had to get out of that fucking lobby, think the Valium's kicking in," Elbow said.

The men slowed in front of room 1154, hugged the wall, then stopped in front of room 1156. Kevin put all his weight on his left knee, leaning close to the door, listening. Behind it he heard the murmur of voices, music, and the clink of glasses. Kevin looked over his shoulder at Elbow, whose mouth was a grim line, and nodded.

Kevin whispered, "You wondered why we can't wear masks? They gotta see us, see?"

Kevin stood directly in front of the peephole, smiled. He rapped on the door with the barrel of the gun. Footsteps approached.

"Who's there?" said a voice.

"Room service," Kevin said, tightening his left-handed grip on the valise.

"One of you guys order up?" the voice inside said. The dead bolt barked, the door opened slowly.

Kevin held the .357 shoulder height as he reared back and booted the door as hard as he could. The doorman caught it square in the forehead and flew backwards, landing unconscious on the floor.

"Jesus," Elbow said, as Kevin leaped over the doorman and rushed down a short hallway that opened into a spacious room.

Five startled men holding cards were seated at a table in the center of the room. Piles of cash, like miniature cityscapes, lay before each of them. "Everyone, hands in the air, manos arriba!" Kevin yelled. All hands went into the air, but no one dropped his cards.

The dealer leapt up. "Hey, motherfucker, you can't —"

Kevin marched to the table's edge and pointed the gun at the dealer's head. "Sit the fuck down," he said. The dealer dropped into his seat. "The rest of ya's keep 'em in the air where I can see 'em."

In a corner, next to a door leading into a bedroom, a lanky blond man in a white, open-collared shirt and black pants stood behind a makeshift bar. He held his hands in the air. "Anyone in there?" Kevin said. The bartender looked over his shoulder, shook his head. "Over here on the floor, hands behind your head," Kevin said, indicating a spot near the table.

Elbow giggled as he shoved the bloody-faced doorman into the room. "He just woke up," Elbow said, pushing him down on the floor.

"Take his piece?" Kevin asked. Elbow waved a 9mm Walther PPK in his left hand, then stuck it in his budge.

One of the card players, an ultrafat man whose face grew redder by the second, snarled at the dealer. "Artie, you said, you said this fucking game was protected."

Kevin turned the gun on him. "Hey, beach ball, shut your yap," he said. He tossed the valise to Elbow. "This guy's comin' around, I want all of ya's to throw your money and your cell phones into the bag. Make it neat now, it's all gotta fit."

As Elbow came around, the card players scooped their money and a few phones off the table and pushed them down into the bag. The dealer got up and, with both hands, gathered the pot towards him. He hastily arranged the bills before stuffing them into the bag.

Elbow handed the bag to Kevin, who threw the strap over his head.

"You got your money, get the hell out," the dealer said.

"We ain't finished," Kevin said, shoving the dealer's head with the gun. "The bank, where is it?" The dealer pulled his head away. Kevin cocked the gun and stuck it in the dealer's ear. "Gonna go bang."

"Tell him, Artie," Ultrafat squeaked.

"The bed, under the fucking bed," the dealer said. Kevin nodded at Elbow, who crossed the room and dropped to his knees next to the bed opposite the makeshift bar.

He put his gun hand on the mattress, reached beneath the bed with the other, and pulled out a medium-size green nylon bag. He switched the gun to his left hand and pulled back on the zipper with his right. He looked down and smiled. "We're outta here," Elbow said.

"You're in over your heads," the dealer said.

"That so? Worry about yours," Kevin said, swatting the dealer hard with the gun on the back of the head. The dealer pitched forward onto the table. "Any other comments before we go? Last chance," Kevin said, backing towards the door. Gym bag in hand, Elbow tore the hotel phone from the wall and headed towards the door.

Like he was hosing a lawn, Kevin waved his gun back and forth over the men. "Listen up, you've just met number one and number two. Number three's out in the hall with a cell phone scanner. Any you guys weren't exactly honest, have a phone, use it, we'll know. Stick your head out the door the next fifteen minutes you'll be lookin' for a new one. Have a nice day," Kevin said.

Out in the hall, Kevin jammed the .357 down his budge. Elbow handed him the gym bag and bolted towards the elevator. Kevin was surprised by the heaviness of the bag. Elbow hit the elevator button, jogged back down the hall, and both men headed for the stairs.

"Tell me again, Kev, why we takin' the stairs?" Elbow said.

"To avoid a shoot-out. You want to be out here waitin' on an elevator one of them cardsharps grows some balls, has a piece we missed? You hit the up button for the elevator, right? We'll take the stairway two flights down, run to the elevator, hit the down button; elevator should only be two floors above us. We're on our way down nice and safe," Kevin said.

"What happens they're in the elevator?" Elbow said.

"Won't happen. It does, they won't expect us there. They're in there, they get it," Kevin said.

On the twentieth floor, both men got into the elevator. "By the way, how's your pal the doorman?" Kevin said.

"I think you broke his nose, forehead's cut too," Elbow said. "He thinks you overdid it."

"He'll change his tune when he gets his twenty percent," Kevin said. "Another thing, we're changin' plans; we're gettin' out at the mezzanine, takin' the back stairway to the parkin' garage. I got a Camry waitin' for us."

Elbow laughed out loud. "You said we were taking a cab outta here," he said.

Kevin pinched Elbow's cheek. "Naw, cabs cost money," he said.

56

WACKO CURRAN STEPPED OUT of the air-conditioned comfort of the Farragut House restaurant on P Street and wiped ketchup off his chin with a huge paper napkin. Then, like he was making a snowball with both hands, he compacted the paper and tossed it to his right before walking down three steps to the sidewalk. He spit out a tiny piece of gristle as he checked his watch, then something to his left up the street caught his eye. Wacko focused on the doorway of the Cozy Corner Store, half a block away on the corner of Seventh and P Streets.

Ralphie Fantasia had just exited the place and was staring hard at the Leaping Millions scratch ticket he held in his tight little fist inches from his acne-scarred face. He furiously scratched away with a nickel, then squinted, squealed, and spun around. Wacko watched mesmerized as Ralphie hugged the ticket to his chest, then brought it to his lips and loudly smacked it. Next, Ralphie held the scratch ticket like a dance partner and tapped, Fred Astaire like, down the steps, touching the sidewalk with his toe. He said, "Five hundred bucks," before he hopped two steps up and gave a little kick.

On the opposite corner across the street, three teenage girls leaned against a mailbox and watched Ralphie's antics in open mouthed amazement. Ralphie noticed his audience, twiddled his fingers at the girls. They scowled and turned away. "Yep, five hundred buck-eri-nos," Ralphie repeated, loud enough for the girls to hear.

As he crossed the street heading towards the Farragut House, he took his eyes off the ticket for a second, looked up and spotted Wacko. As if he had fully extended on a bungee cord, he suddenly stopped and shot backwards towards the store. Wacko pointed at Ralphie and pulled his index finger slowly towards him, then stepped out from the restaurant shade into the sunlight.

For a second Ralphie had a vision of Wacko exploding into flames, but nothing happened, he just kept coming. "Don't even think about running," Wacko said.

Ralphie's head jerked unnaturally to the side, and he tugged at his fly with his right hand like maybe something was showing. "Hey, Jackie," he said.

"What you got there, a winner?" Wacko said. He grabbed the ticket, but Ralphie held fast with his thumb and index finger. "Ralph, those fingers better open faster than a hooker's legs, or I'm going to break 'em," Wacko said in a sing-song voice.

Ralphie released the ticket and folded into himself. "Jack, please, I don't owe much. I took care of Lep, we're square for the last time, only I still owe him a little on what I owe him now."

"What? When you talk you should have subtitles on your chest," Wacko said. He examined the ticket, then flipped it against Ralphie's chest. "I don't want your ticket, and your beef with Leppy's yours. You seen my brother?"

"Kevin?" Ralphie said.

"No, my other brother — Kevin."

Ralphie ran his fingers thought his greasy hair and thought it over. He shoved the ticket into his pocket. "Kevin, ya, right, Kevin. Ya know, Jack, I was sittin' on a bench M Street Park; he drove by me with a new set of wheels. I froze, couldn't move," Ralphie said.

"Scared? You owe him too?" Wacko said.

"No, the car it was beau-ti-ful, kinda touched me, you know? I waved back, thought he might pull over," Ralphie said, waving both hands overhead.

"That how you waved?" Wacko said.

Ralphie grinned. "Naw, I'm wavin' at him now behind you, Jack, look."

Wacko turned in time to see his brother exiting the driver's door of a jet-black Cadillac Eldorado parked directly in front of the Farragut House. Kevin grinned and waved back at Ralphie Fantasia.

"Jack, we cool, I can go?" Ralphie said.

Wacko turned away from Ralphie, flipped his hand over his shoulder as he headed towards his brother.

Kevin did a little jig that ended with a bow in the middle of the street. "Hey, bro' what happenin' dog," Kevin said.

Wacko grabbed both of Kevin's shoulders and stared hard into his eyes. "Where you been — *dog*? We were supposed to meet here an hour ago remember?"

A light inside Kevin's eyes seemed to dance a two-step, and Wacko fought the impulse to smile.

"Nice to see you too," Kevin said.

"You're late, asshole. C'mon, get in the car, we're goin' for a ride," Wacko said.

Both men got into the Caddy. "I thought we were eatin' — on you," Kevin said, starting the car.

"Where'd you get this boat? What I tell you about flashin'?" Wacko said.

"Relax, Jack, it's only for the weekend, it's a rental. I had Beaver O'Connell put it on his card, paid him cash for it plus a little incentive." Kevin clipped the horn twice, then pulled from the curb. Two of the teenage corner girls shyly waved.

"See that, see it? They love it, Jack. I should be drivin' this carumba wagon all the time. Hell, why can't I get credit, huh? I got money," Kevin said.

"You can't get a card, you got no credit history," Wacko said.

"How am I supposed to get history I can't get a card?"

"You gotta work, you don't work," Wacko said.

"What you mean? I work harder than most," Kevin said.

"Ya, sometimes too hard: we got problems," Wacko said wryly.

Kevin gunned the accelerator across Farragut Road, turned left at the statue, and followed the Lagoon on the right. "Problems?" he said, turning on the radio. "Check out these speakers." Wacko turned the radio off. "What's with the eyes?" Kevin said.

"Seen Elbow lately?"

Kevin whistled softly.

"You won't anymore, pull over," Wacko said.

Kevin pulled into a parking space, beneath a maple tree, facing the Lagoon. "What do you mean, not anymore?"

Wacko stared out across the water. "What's the matter, Kevin, you don't got enough? You're sittin' on almost three quarters of a million bucks and you gotta rob one of Marty Fallon's games?"

Kevin clicked on the radio. "This is a beautiful stereo, the sound —"

Wacko ripped the knob to the left, silencing it. Kevin smirked.

"A joke, this is a fucking joke? You — we! — got problems. They're after you, you gotta get out of town. You're late for lunch today, and I'm thinkin' you're already dead," Wacko said.

"Fuck! Fuck! Fuck!" Kevin pounded the steering wheel, pulled it violently to the left. He jumped out of the car. Wacko shut the engine off and watched Kevin pace in front of a bench. He flailed his arms, ranted until foam flecked around his mouth.

Wacko got out of the car, and Kevin turned. "How'd they find out?"

"The doorman, you greedy prick, his end you cut him short, he gave up Elbow," Wacko said.

"Short? That piece of shit got twenty percent of a hundred seventy grand."

Wacko looked at his brother oddly. "One hundred seventy? Marty says he's out over two hundred G's. The bank alone was a hundred and twenty, and the players claimed you clipped them for a hundred thousand more," Wacko said.

"A hundred grand . . . from the table? We got fifty-six thousand. Fucking lyin' scum," Kevin said, hammering his fist into his palm. "Fucking thieves." Kevin looked at Wacko. "You gotta believe me, Jack, you do, don't you?"

Wacko nodded. "But Marty won't."

"Jack, I wasn't cuttin' you out, your end's in a big plastic makeup pouch in my closet next to my porno tapes. I just didn't know how to give it to you without you goin' off on me," Kevin said.

"Why, Kev? You're sittin' on a ton of cake, why?"

Kevin sat down on the bench, and met Wacko's eyes as he sat down next to him. "Hey, man, it's stealin', stealin', Jack. Like you always said, Can't steal it, it ain't worth havin', right, right? Elbow's dead?" Kevin said. He covered his face with his hands.

"They snatched him comin' out of the Black Rose wasted, took him to the bloody den," Wacko said.

"They're still using that cellar on Fourth Street?"

Wacko nodded. "Busy place. Tore off two of his fingers. He was drunk, heard he held up good until they went for his teeth; he gave you up. You gotta get out of here. I got a room booked for you at the Plaza in New York. First, go to the stash house, it's safe, grab a hundred G's for me and some for yourself, pack a ditty bag: underwear, shave kit, toothbrush, all the little shit you'll need right off, and meet me in an hour. I'm figurin' this thing out best I can. I'll meet with Marty, give him the money, buy some time. We got nowhere to go now. Gotta put plan B into action," Wacko said.

"Plan B, what was plan A?" Kevin said.

"You fucking up," Wacko said. He shoved his brother and stood up.

Kevin got up and stood next to his brother. His gaze seemed to carry far beyond the locks, centered on the access road, a quarter mile out from where he stood. "The Lagoon never changes, notice that, Jack? Remember we were kids and Ma, to get us out from underfoot, would send us down here for sailin' lessons? Freebies for the project rats. I never learned to sail, you? Hell, I could barely swim, but we had fun, didn't we? You know what I'm thinkin', Jack? I'm thinkin' wouldn't it be cool if the ocean had a memory. Your brain's made out of water, right? Could happen. And all the good times and all the laughs we shared down here were recorded somewhere, somehow, huh. What ya think?" Kevin said.

Kevin picked up a stone and side-tossed it into the lagoon. It skipped once, then disappeared beneath the shimmering surface. He shook his head. "No good skippin' stones round here anymore, they've all been thrown."

"*We* ain't gonna be tossed away," Wacko said. "I've talked with Mikey Janowski, he's down with us, naturally. He's lined up Denny Condon's Old Colony boys, shooters every one, and they're with us too. Marty goes down, everyone else will fall in line, fact," Wacko said.

Kevin slammed his fist into his hand. "I don't want to run, Jack. I can handle myself," he said.

"Ain't the point, you gotta go. With you around I'm more vulnerable. I want you outta here. Marty might try to clip me, that's what I'd do; so I'm gonna arrange a meet in a public place. I'll tell him you're fucked up, coked, you're in a rehab trying to pull it together, when you get back you'll talk to him, smooth things. I'll give him the one hundred G's right then and there," Wacko said.

"Fuck givin' him anything," Kevin said. "I say we drop him same way as Mary Rose."

"That's what he'll expect us to do and he'll be ready. I'll pretend, not too much, just enough, that I'm nervous, you know, fucked up over this, tryin' to make things right. The money will draw him out, it's the only thing that will," Wacko said.

"Once we meet, I'll tell him I need a few more days to come up with the other one hundred and twenty grand. That greedy prick won't think anything's up and he'll meet me. First chance I get I'll pop him and his goon. I'll put a hole the size of the Ted Williams Tunnel in both of 'em," Wacko said.

"A man with a plan," Kevin said. "Ya, we got a plan, we got a plan." He danced across the sidewalk, then pretended to swim. "Look, Jack, I'm great on land but shit in the water, go figure." Kevin did the backstroke for a moment, then stopped and pulled a small plastic bag from his pocket. He bit off the knot and poured the contents in a half-assed line on top of his left hand. Half-dropped to the sidewalk as he snorted it up.

"Hey!"

"Relax, Jack, it's cool, that's the last of it, I swear," Kevin said. He licked his hand and pinched his nostrils together. "Ooo-wee that bites."

"That shit, you gotta stop, Kevin," Wacko said.

"I will — someday," Kevin said. "Manana. Banana. Cabana. Tomora." He burst out laughing.

"You fucking bug, drop me at my car," Wacko said. Kevin threw his arm around his brother's shoulder and guided him towards the Eldorado.

Wacko put Kevin in a headlock. "Don't call Ma, understand? I'll tell her you went down the Cape for a few days. It's eleven-thirty. We'll meet back at Kelly's Landing in an hour. Can you handle that?"

Kevin pulled away from his brother. "I can handle any-*thang*," he said, doing the backstroke.

57

IN DARKNESS Marty Fallon sat in his office and tapped the middle finger of his left hand on his desk without any sense of rhythm. He thought big thoughts about what he considered very small people, the furrow in his brow grew deeper. There was a knock on the door, and a laser line of light split the wall in front of him. Like something from Fantasmic Features, the enormous skull of Andre Athanas protruded from the center. "They're here, boss. You want more light?" Andre said.

"I got a choice? Open the fucking shades. Where are they?" Marty said, sitting up in his chair.

"Downstairs, end of the bar. I recognize one of 'em, Biaggio Vitale. There's some young guy with him too, powerful build, up-and-coming muscle, I guess," Andre said, twisting the Lucite rod of the Levolors.

"Hope he didn't get the bull on you," Marty said.

Andre's eyes narrowed. "No one on this fucking planet gets the bull on me," he said.

Marty stopped tapping. "No one?" Marty said.

Andre looked like he swallowed a centipede. "Hey, you're the boss, I'm talking regular planet types, not you," he said morosely.

The man sitting behind the desk scratched his cheek. "You know, Andre, just shut the fuck up, go down and get them."

Marty was standing in front of his refrigerator as Biaggio Vitale walked into the room, followed closely by a twenty-something, heavy-set man with a receding hairline who wore a brightly colored Hawaiian-style shirt outside his pants. Andre came in behind him and closed the door. Marty nodded at Vitale and offered him a small, chilled bottle of Orangina but ignored the muscle.

Vitale faced his palm towards Marty and shook both it and his head. "Orangina? No thanks, where'd you find that? One time the only place would be in the Italian neighborhoods," he said.

"Some of the supermarkets carry it now," Marty said, unscrewing the cap and taking a sip.

He walked over to his desk and sat down. "So tell me, how's Joe? When you see him, let him know there are a few things I'd like to discuss he gets some time."

"Anything I can help you with?" Vitale said. Without it being offered, he pulled a chair from the wall and sat down facing the desk.

"Naw, just a couple ideas I'd like to run by him. Could be moneymakers. We both know how Joe loves a buck."

Vitale leaned towards him. "Speakin' of which, we hear you lost a chunk of your own dough at the Tremont Hotel recently. One of the card players is my wife's cousin. I want to thank you personally for makin' it good with him and the others," Vitale said.

Marty put the bottle down and wiped his mouth. "Surprised it happened, a couple of cowboys, out-of-towners we think. We got some idea who, want to be sure, don't want to grab the wrong guys," he said.

"God forbid," Vitale said. "If there's anything we can do, let us know. We, none of us can allow anyone to get away with that kind of shit. Makes us look weak, we gotta swat 'em. Remember, Marty, you're us, any assistance you need, reach out and we're there."

"So that's what the visit's about?" Marty Fallon said.

"That's why we're here. Joe wanted us to make a special trip to let you know how much we appreciate what you did. Friends take care of friends," Vitale said.

"To friends," Marty said, raising the Orangina bottle and draining the contents. A cell phone rang, and all four men reached for their pockets.

"Mine," Marty said, pulling his from the pocket of a jacket hanging on the back of the chair. He flipped the phone open. "Ya?" Marty smiled at Biaggio Vitale and rolled his eyes. "Ya, Ma, I'll tell him. I'll take care of it, I promise. Milk don't go bad in a day, Ma. Me too, ya, I'll call you later." Marty closed the phone. "My mother. One more errand for my friend over here." He nodded at Andre. "Could you guys please excuse us?"

"Sure, we're outta here anyways," Vitale said. The enforcer stood up with him and discreetly adjusted something at the small of his back beneath his shirt.

"Nice shirt," Marty said. "Like Hawaii Five-O, no offense."

Vitale nodded in the muscle's direction and smiled. "A young guy's thing, I guess, a little too tropical for me," he said.

Both men left the room, and Andre closed the door behind them.

"See the look on Five-O's face?" Marty said.

"Serves him right, looks like a faggot that shirt," Andre said. "So, Mum needs milk?"

Marty got up and walked to the window, separated two of the blind louvres and looked down. He watched as Vitale and Five-O crossed Emerson Street and entered Joseph's bakery. "Guineas must be getting their pizza fix," he said. He turned to Andre. "Got your piece?"

"In the car behind the radio, always there," Andre said.

"Good, get in your car and head down to Marine Road," Marty said.

Andre looked surprised. "Spider Keenan's place? Boss, he can't be out already. He paid us cash for a pound two nights ago. What, he smokin' the shit?"

"You're right, he's not, he called to tell me Kevin Curran's on his way over to pick up some coke. Said he needed the package for a trip. That punk steals from me and thinks he's takin' a vacation, huh? I want you to meet him, Andre, give him a grand send-off. Be careful, park a few blocks away, down on M Street near Sixth. When you get there, Spider will leave you two alone. Don't waste any time. Leave the body in the house and get out.

"When it's done, return to your apartment, pick up what you'll need for your own trip. You do like I told ya, keep a ready bag in the closet?" Marty said.

Andre nodded. "Ya, boss, just like you told me, I got socks, underwear, deodorant, one shirt, one pair of pants, a razor —"

Marty Fallon cut him off. "Okay, good, that's why they call it a ready bag, you're ready to roll on a moment's notice. Now, when you leave your apartment, I want you to drive to the North Quincy T Station. Leave your car in the lot, keys above the visor, I'll send someone later to get it. Take the Red Line to South Station."

"How long am I goin' and where?" Andre said.

"You're goin' to Maine, a week, maybe more," Marty said.

Andre made a face like someone had just asked him to spell Ticonderoga.

"Buy whatever else you need when you get there," Marty said, pulling a roll from his pocket and handing it to the giant.

"Maine, boss?"

"The Cliff House in Ogunquit, nice place. From South Station you take the Amtrak to Portsmouth, New Hampshire. Rent a car there and drive to Ogunquit. I'll pick you up in a week. Don't call me, and stay off your cell phone unless this number comes up on it. You got all this?" Marty said.

Andre blinked twice and nodded. "What are you going to do with the body?" he said.

"I want to know when Kevin Curran's dead," Marty said. "When you get to North Quincy, call me from the T station lot. Say something — 'boyos,' say 'boyos,' and hang up. I hear that, I'll send Digger Feeks and his man over to get rid of it. Try not to make a mess."

▪   ▪   ▪

Biaggio Vitale ordered four slices of Sicilian pizza and two Cokes and paid the overweight teenage girl behind the counter. While the pizza heated in the oven, he walked over next to a potato chip rack and took out his cell phone. He hit a preprogrammed number. "Ya, how you doin'? I'm doin' fine, just fine," he said. He nodded over at Five-O, who was taking the tray with the pizza and Cokes off the counter. "Ya, he's up there as we speak, spoke to him myself. His man's with him, but he's sendin' him on an errand. I'm eatin' pizza and waitin' for the big guy to leave. I'll call you when. Ya, it's good pizza. Go ahead, send them. I'll leave when they get here."

Vitale closed the phone and returned it to his pocket. He sat at a window seat facing the intersection of Fourth and K. He took a bite of pizza and winked at Five-O. "Cavalry's on the way," he said.

58

KEVIN CURRAN STOPPED the Cadillac Eldorado in front of 30 Story Street and checked both the rear and side-view mirrors before he got out of the car and hurried into the gray, vinyl-sided, three-story building. He climbed one flight, then followed a hallway to the rear of the building, where he entered through a red door into a studio apartment. After stepping over a partially deflated air bed, he kicked a pair of Nike sneakers out of the way and opened the door to the only closet in the room.

He reached up to the solitary shelf and removed two stacks of porno tapes and a small, red plastic toolbox with a silver latch and put everything on the floor. He bent down and removed an eighteen-inch, black-and-white television set from the top of a black plastic milk crate in the corner the closet, pulled the crate out, and stepped up on it. Kevin ran the fingertips of his right hand above the shelf, along the upper juncture of the back wall, and located a thin white wire, which he pulled towards him. The fourteen- by twenty-six-inch panel popped from the wall, and Kevin dangled it by the wire briefly in the air before dropping it to the floor.

The compartment behind the panel contained twelve five-inch blocks of currency, each secured by clear plastic shrink wrap. He removed five bundles, tossed them on the bed, and softly said "One hundred," then removed an extra one and threw it with the others. Kevin replaced the panel and everything else on the shelf, then kicked the milk crate into the closet corner, put the TV on it, and closed the door.

In the opposite corner of the room, an empty black leather valise with a shoulder strap slouched against the side of a small, four-drawer mahogany bureau. Kevin opened the top drawer, grabbed a silver .25 Bauer automatic in a shiny brown leather clip-on holster from it, and stuck it in his pocket. He removed socks, underwear, a T-shirt, and a pair of black nylon drawstring shorts from the second drawer. He opened the valise and threw everything in, then went into the tiny bathroom and scooped a bottle of Old Spice cologne off the back of the toilet and a razor and can of shaving cream from beneath the sink and tossed them into the bag.

Next to the bed, partially hidden beneath a coverless pillow, was a blue cordless phone. Kevin picked it up and dialed. While the number rang, he walked to a corner window, moved the shade aside with two fingers, and looked out. "Ya, Spider, I'm headin' out of town for a week, how things look? Good. Me? Dry, but I've decided to break the monotony, I need some assistance. Put somethin' together for me, I'll be over in fifteen minutes." Kevin shut the phone off and lobbed it onto the bed.

He pulled a green plastic garbage bag from a box next to the door and shook it out. He gathered the money off the bed into the bag, then picked up the valise and threw the strap over his shoulder. He left the room without looking back.

Once outside, Kevin looked up and down the street. With the exception of one old lady watering her lawn at the South Boston High School end of Story Street, there was little activity.

Kevin hit the trunk release button on the key chain he pulled from his pocket, and the rear deck of the Eldorado sprung open. He tossed the valise and garbage bag inside and closed it. He slid in behind the wheel, hit the door locks, and pulled out the Bauer. He stuck the empty holster under the seat, chambered a round, flicked the safety on with his thumb, and stuck the gun between his legs.

Aware of how easily he could be ambushed, he drove the wrong way up the one-way street, waiting patiently at the end until the last of three slow-moving cars coming up G Street passed before he turned left, then took the first right onto Thomas Park. When a van approached from behind, he pulled over, allowed it to pass, then continued on, taking a right onto Telegraph Street, then another at the bottom of the steep hill leading from Dorchester Heights.

Kevin followed the road across South Boston, up the Broadway hill. At the top of the hill, Ralphie Fantasia sat on a bench in M Street Park, smoking a joint and watching the traffic go by. He took a hit, pulled the spleef from his mouth, and waved as Kevin passed. Kevin hit the horn twice. At the end of Broadway, Kevin turned right onto Farragut Road, then right again just before Kelly's Landing.

He followed that road another eighth of a mile, bearing right onto Marine Road, and stopped in front of number 129. Kevin cupped the gun in his right hand and flicked the safety off as he got out of the car. He felt confident and ready as he climbed the four brick steps to the front door and hit the buzzer.

The heavy six-panel door swung open. "How're you doin', Kev?" Spider Keenan said, offering Kevin his hand.

Kevin ignored the hand. "Who's with you?" Kevin said, looking over Spider's shoulder down the hallway that led to the kitchen.

Spider looked over his shoulder. "Nobody but Phoebe — my parakeet. She's a real talker, like most broads."

Kevin walked past him and peered left into the living room.

Spider closed the door. "Gina's not here either. She took off for a week with her sister and her kids, Disney World. I even paid for her sister; you know Helen used to be married to that fucking loser Arkie, the cook down Amrhein's. When Helen was a kid, what a fucking bombshell, go figure why she married that nipplehead." Spider spotted the gun in Kevin's hand. Alarmed he said, "What's with the piece?"

"Shut the fuck up," Kevin said. He grabbed the doorknob to a closet on his left, ripped open the door, then closed it. "Come here," Kevin said. Before Spider could move, Kevin grabbed his arm and yanked him ahead of him. "Move."

"C'mon, Kev, what gives, the gat, you're scarin' me," Spider said, as Kevin halted him in front of a doorway to the right. "My bedroom," Spider said, looking back. "I told you no one was here."

Kevin peeked around the doorframe of the bedroom, then prodded Spider towards the kitchen. A sound came from it, and Kevin grabbed the back of Spider's shirt with his left hand.

"The kitchen, I heard somethin'," he hissed. He pressed the Bauer into the back of Spider's neck.

"Kevin, please, it's the fucking bird, my parakeet, Phoebe, she moves around, please. You going to rip me off?"

Kevin shoved Spider hard into the kitchen, then came in low behind him, sweeping the gun from left to right. Phoebe chirped crazily. Kevin spun and looked down the hallway, then turned and pointed. "Where's that go?" he said, indicating a door with a white lace curtain in the kitchen corner next to the refrigerator. Spider stepped towards the door. "Whoa," Kevin said, pointing the gun at Spider's head.

Spider flinched and put his hands in front of his face. "Hey, man, it goes out to the driveway and yard. C'mon, I keep trash in the hall. Wanna see?" Spider said. Kevin lowered the gun. Spider pulled a paper towel from a roll on the wall and wiped his forehead. "Jesus, Kevin, how long I known you? Christ, relax, okay, have a seat." He pointed at the table. "I whipped up something nice for ya. It's in the bedroom, can I get it?"

"Sorry, Spider, ya, go ahead. These are crazy times, maybe I'm nuts. Remember I told you when I called I needed assistance," Kevin said.

Spider left the room but returned seconds later carrying a legal-size manila envelope folded in half secured by a thick rubber band. He removed the elastic. "I got your 'assistance' right here, this shit is the shit, man, rocket fuel, pure nitro." Spider pulled out a plastic ziplock bag from the envelope, unrolled it, and held it, up to the light. He made a disgusted face. "Fuck, it figures, I grabbed the wrong package. Got a half ounce for this college faggot over on P Street, put aside an ounce for you. I grabbed College Boy's package by mistake." Spider shrugged. "Hey, what the fuck, College Boy won't miss a taste, right?" He opened up the bag, took out a two-gram rock, and dropped it onto the table. "Got a card?"

"Credit card? I don't rate," Kevin said. He pulled out his wallet and removed his license. "Amazed I got this." He laid the card on top of the rock and pressed down with the heel of his right hand. He rubbed his hands together like he was warming them over a fire, then pulled out a chair and sat down.

Spider threw a straw on the table. "Chop it good," he said, edging towards the kitchen door. "You want I should grab the ounce in the trunk, I'm in the driveway."

"Ya, go ahead," Kevin said, focusing on the task in front of him. He wet the tip of his index finger, touched the pile, and put it in his mouth. "Oooo-wee," Kevin said. He compressed the crystals with the flat side of the card and dragged it to the right before using one corner of the card to make a ten-inch line. He chopped the line left to right, stopping every few seconds to put some of the increasingly fine powder in his mouth.

Kevin heard Spider leave through the back door and go down a few outside steps to the driveway. He heard a car door open. Hadn't Spider said the stuff was in the trunk? Kevin eyed the .25 but continued to chop. He smiled as the tip of his tongue grew numb.

The straw rested against the trigger guard of the Bauer, and Kevin reached for it. He heard Spider's footsteps on the stairs, and the kitchen door opened. "Nice product, Spider, here goes," Kevin said, sinking the straw into one end of the long line of coke. He inhaled hard, gasped, and raised his head. His eyes began to water. "Jesus," Kevin said.

Suddenly at the base of his neck on the right, Kevin felt the warmth and weight of an enormous hand. He turned his head in time to see Andre's right fist shoot in front of his immense chest, carrying with it a looping white blur that closed around Kevin's neck.

With a bull-like grunt, Andre pulled the wooden ends of the knotted nylon rope in opposite directions. He yanked the seated man backwards, and Kevin immediately shit himself and kicked the table into the air. The table crashed onto its side in front of the sink as Kevin fought to turn his body, but Andre held him close to his chest, utilizing every muscle fiber in his shoulders, arms, and back.

Kevin's face was like a mime's as he tore at Andre's sleeves, then went for the rope around his neck. He tore the nails from his right hand as his fingers struggled to get beneath the knots that were turning his windpipe to mush. Kevin fought desperately as Andre attempted to flush the life force from his body and raked at his antagonist's cheeks with the remnants of his nails.

Andre silently dragged him backwards across the floor heading towards the door but slipped on something wet and the momentum temporarily shifted. Using his legs, Kevin drove the larger man back into the bird stand. The cage crashed to the floor and was followed closely by the giant, who momentarily relinquished his grip on the rope.

Kevin felt the release of pressure and could see the knotted rope fall away to his chest but was amazed he could still barely breathe. He willed his hands to grab the rope, but his arms were filled with sand. Who would fill his arms with sand?

For a brief moment the deadened muscles in his legs surged and he twisted to the right, but Andre immediately realigned himself onto his side, parallel to his victim. The rope snapped tight again, the knots burrowing like rabid badgers into Kevin's neck.

Now Kevin's legs were filled with sand and his tongue protruded. As his right ear touched his shoulder, there was a cracking sound from his neck. He was tired beyond words, the screeching bird circled madly overhead, and Kevin discovered that letting go was easier than he ever imagined.

59

SEVENTEEN-YEAR-OLD MOLLY KILROY took the ten-dollar bill Wacko Curran offered her over the counter and watched him pick up the frappe she had just poured into the tall paper cup. He pushed a straw through the plastic lid, brought it to his lips, and sipped. Wacko pulled the straw from his mouth, made a face, and looked down at the cup like he was at the edge of a pool searching for a quarter at the bottom before he sipped again. He looked at the girl. "Keep the change, but tell me how come? How come they sell black cherry ice cream now, not red maraschino?" Wacko said.

The pretty blond in the white halter top and pink terry-cloth cutoff shorts looked up at him through her foot-long eyelashes, turned and faced the register, and shifted the soft curve of her butt to the left. "Couldn't tell ya," she said over her shoulder as she rang the money in.

"Since I was a kid Frosty Village always had red cherry ice cream. What, you don't believe me? I gotta get my kid brother down here as a witness?" Wacko said. As he sucked on the frappe, he stared at the muscular ridges that formed the backs of her legs just below her ass.

She turned and faced him and looked bored. "Hey, my first summer at Frosty's, thanks for the tip," she said, dropping the money into a clear quart jar marked "Tips" on the counter.

"Not your fault, but I'll tell you somethin', kid, this being your first summer, Frosty's got tradition, red cherry ice cream's tradition," Wacko said. "This shit" — he took another sip — "must be a yuppie thing, huh?" The little blond shrugged. "Actually, it ain't all that bad," he said, then walked outside.

Wacko sipped the frappe on the busy corner of I Street and Marine Road and watched traffic stream off Day Boulevard from the lights up I Street as they headed into the heart of South Boston. He walked up I Street towards his car and checked his watch. He picked up the pace, took another sip, and made a mental note to take out the irritating change in his pocket when he got back to the car. Just as his cheeks were contracting from another chunk of cherry in the straw, his cell phone rang. He shifted the frappe and snatched the phone off his hip. "Ya?"

"Ya, hi, Jack, how're ya doin'?"

"Not bad," Wacko said, recognizing the voice of Mike Janowski.

"You'd never guess who I'm with, Denny Condon, he says hi," Mike said.

"So, what's up?" Wacko said, stopping outside the blue Marquis. He put the frappe on the roof and stuck the key in the door.

"We've been out and about, grabbed a car early this morning up in Brookline Village. We stashed it back in Southie. As we speak, I'm drivin' a nice Lexus we grabbed up in Newton Center a half hour ago. I figure good chance we're gonna have trouble with Marty Fallon over Kevin, we might be needin' cars, Jack."

Wacko switched the phone to the other ear. "I agree, hold on," he said, opening the door to the Marquis. He took the frappe off the roof, reached inside, put it on the dashboard, then closed the door. He wiped his fingers on his pants, walked farther up I Street, then leaned against a tree. "Go ahead."

Mike continued. "And then a funny thing happened. We were drivin' up Old Colony —"

"Where are you now?" Wacko said.

"I'm gettin' there, listen. We were drivin' up Old Colony, and who do we see all by his lonesome gassin' up in the Merit station? Andre Athanas. I'm sittin' here as we speak watchin' him," Mike said.

"Alone?" Wacko said.

"Ya, he's alone, thought it strange, like him and his boss don't know what's up? Like we're gonna let them whack Kevin over a card game and do nothin' about it," Mike said.

"They don't think anyone will fuck with them," Wacko said.

"I hope they continue to think no one will fuck with them," Mike said.

"He still there gassin'?" Wacko said, heading for his car.

"He's payin' his tab. Want me to follow him, see where he's goin'?"

"Ya, do that. I have to meet Kevin in about ten minutes at the Landing. Call me back," Wacko said, closing the phone. He climbed into the Mercury, put the car in gear, and took the first right off I Street heading towards Kelly's Landing.

▪   ▪   ▪

At Kelly's Landing, Wacko pulled into a parking space adjacent to an empty space that used to house a fried food restaurant and killed the engine. He got out of the car and walked to the green steel railing that sprouted like something living from a seawall constructed of huge, rough-hewn granite blocks.

He scanned the area for signs of his brother or the black Eldorado, but there was nothing, and something in the pit of his stomach seemed to flop over onto its back. He became angry. No matter how hard he tried to pound discipline into Kevin's stubborn head, the kid resisted. Kevin never listened, everything was a joke, and Wacko swore the next time he saw him he'd put it to him hard, really get in his face about his attitude towards business and life.

His cell phone rang. He picked it off his hip. "Ya, where the fuck are you?" Wacko said.

"Hi, Jack, you must be expectin' someone," said the voice on the other end.

"Who the fuck is this?" Wacko said.

"Digger — Digger Feeks," the voice said. The sound of Digger's voice made Wacko's skin crawl like maggots had suddenly sprung to life beneath it. In the riptide of personalities that made up the South Boston underworld, there were few like Digger Feeks. His unique cold-blooded skills were highly valued by men like Marty Fallon; he was a man who cleaned up after their bloody messes. If the boyos left a body behind, a call to Digger would guarantee it would never be found. Digger was also one of Marty's gofers, incapable of committing any crime that required guts but with a vicious streak as deep as a canyon and a total lack of morals. He was also a gambling degenerate and one of Wacko's loan-shark customers.

"Just got a phone call from Marty Fallon, said he had some housecleanin' for me, gave me an address," Digger said.

Wacko checked his watch; there was still no sign of his brother. The thing in his stomach flipped back onto its feet and began to claw its way towards his heart. "Housecleanin', huh?" he said, trying to remain calm.

"Ya, things have been slow, but I got a feelin' they'll be pickin' up."

"Listen, Digger, what do you want? I'm expectin' a call. You wanna make a payment on the twenty-two hundred you owe me, and I strongly suggest you do, see Mike Janowski. Have a nice day," Wacko said.

"Hey, hey, Jack, hold on. You want to talk to me," Digger said. "Word is you're on the outs with Marty Fallon over the matter of a card game. When he told me he had housecleanin', I figured it might be you. Hadda check."

"You thinkin' maybe you didn't owe me anymore, I might be dead? My rising blood pressure proves I'm alive, you prick. You want to stay that way, see Mike Janowski," Wacko said, moving the phone from his ear, but the shrill voice called him back.

"Look, Jack, you there?"

"I'm here."

"I ain't into causin' problems, just coverin' my ass, don't want to be lookin' for no dead guy to pay. But since you're alive, I figure maybe we can make a deal. You tear up my debt, and I'll give you the address Marty gave me," Digger said.

"Why should I give a rat's ass who you're diggin' a hole for?" Wacko said.

"Because it could have been you," Digger said.

Wacko checked the boulevard again for signs of his brother, saw none, and tried to breathe deeply but couldn't. He willed his legs towards the Marquis.

"Who you diggin' for, Feeks? You know more than you're lettin' on," Wacko said.

There was silence on the other end of the phone.

"I got an address for you, Jack."

"Tell me, Digger, how much you into Marty Fallon for?"

"Over five grand."

"And if Marty were gone, that's two debts cleared up, correct?" Wacko said.

"I got an address for you, Jack. I'm tryin' to do the right thing here. You interested or not?" Digger said. Wacko's watch said twelve twenty-five.

"Ya, give it to me."

"Number one twenty-nine Marine Road," Digger Feeks said and hung up.

60

WACKO CURRAN WALKED OUT the back door of number 129 Marine Road and stopped on the landing. As if pressed into an icy wind, he visibly shook and almost dropped the driver's license in his right hand. He wavered slightly, tightened his grip, and slowly descended the four steps to the driveway, where he paused, placing one hand on the trunk lid of a derelict Buick to brace himself, then gazed back up the stairs before continuing, in a determined way, up the driveway to the street.

He walked with his head down and his hands clenched into fists by his sides and rounded the corner on M Street, where he continued on to the rear of the blue Marquis half a block away. He opened the trunk, laid the license gently in the center, and from the corner grabbed a red hand towel, which he shook out and slung over his shoulder.

Next, he picked up a gallon jug of antifreeze, pulled the false bottom, and removed a small paper bag from inside. He threw the bag and towel onto the front passenger seat as he got in. He headed down Day Boulevard and called Mike Janowski, steered with his knees as he opened the paper bag.

"Ya," Mike said.

"Where is he, you still behind him?" Wacko said, as he used one hand to pull a .357 Smith & Wesson revolver from it. The gun was still wrapped in a plastic freezer bag.

"Ya, he's made a few stops, acting kinda weird, spooked, lookin' over his shoulder every time he gets out of the car, but we're on him. I'm thinkin' what's with the stops but it's Thursday, pickup day for those guys. I figure maybe he's grabbin' the boss's envelopes, probably headin' to Quincy to do the same thing. Didn't you tell me, Jack, that you guys made a list of their stops? If you got it, check it I can get there ahead of him if you want."

Wacko shook the freezer bag off the gun. "Forget that, just stay with him; that Condon kid still with you?" Wacko said, opening the chamber, checking the rounds, then snapping it shut with a flick of the wrist.

"Ya, the kid's here. Why, Jack? You okay, you don't sound —"

"Fuck how I sound. Drop him off the next set of lights. Get rid of him. Give him cab fare back to Southie and my thanks," Wacko said.

"You just want me to drop him off in the middle —"

"Just fucking do it and keep the line open, don't disconnect. I'll hook up with you shortly. I just want you and me there, get my drift?" Wacko said.

"Ya, I'm thinkin' I do," Mike said. Moments later, as Wacko held the cell phone to his ear, he heard Mike say good-bye to his passenger and the car door slam.

"Where are you now?" Wacko said.

"Stopped at the first set of lights after the Neponset bridge across from the Chink restaurant. I'm five, six cars behind him," Mike Jansowksi said.

"I just passed the Stop and Shop on Morrissey Boulevard. I'll be pullin' behind you in a few minutes. Stay on him," Wacko said.

▪ ▪ ▪

In North Quincy, Andre Athanas sat in his Lincoln Continental at the traffic lights on Hancock Street, part of a small line of cars waiting to get into the MBTA lot. Once inside the parking area he found, as usual, it was jammed with the vehicles of early morning South Shore commuters heading into Boston. Andre was aggravated as he searched for a space. He finally spotted one in the middle of a row to the right of the station entrance, sped towards it, only to be beaten by a woman in a dark green Saab who accelerated faster from the opposite direction. "You fucking cow," Andre said through the glass at the unblinking woman behind the wheel. "Fucking cow," he said again before resuming his search.

On the other side of the lot near a tall security fence, a red Chevy Tahoe backed out of a space, and Andre raced over, sat idling with his left turn signal on as the Tahoe pulled out. After backing in, he carefully surveyed the lot before he shut off the engine, removed the ignition key, and slipped it over the visor. He checked his watch; it was twelve fifty-two. He pulled his cell phone from the dashboard mount and hit the trunk release button. The rear deck sprung open, and Andre got out.

At the back of the car, he opened the phone and poked a number. He casually made a three-hundred-and-sixty-degree turn as he held the phone to his ear. Satisfied he was safe, he reached into the trunk and removed the ready bag. He straightened, dropped the bag to the pavement, idly looked over his shoulder, nodded, and said 'boyos' into the phone, then snapped it shut and slipped it into his pocket.

As Andre bent to pick up his bag, he wondered briefly how long the trip to Portsmouth would take before his thoughts were interrupted by the sound of a car horn blowing twice. He peeked around the edge of the trunk. A black Lexus sat idling in front of his car. Led Zeppelin music that Andre recognized as "The Immigrant Song" loudly blasted from the quickly sinking driver's side window. The driver was in his late twenties, and wore sunglasses and a baseball cap turned backwards. For an instant Andre thought he recognized him, then dismissed the notion, thinking how all those morons looked the same. The driver said something indiscernible.

"What?" Andre snapped. The driver mouthed the word *sorry* and turned down the radio.

"Excuse me, are you coming or going? Helluva time finding a space," the driver said.

Andre scowled. "I just got here, I'm stayin'," he said, coming around the bumper and stopping just before his side-view mirror.

"I just thought —"

"I don't care what you thought, I told you I'm stayin'," Andre said, waving the man off and turning away. The music blared again.

Andre slapped the upright trunk lid as he turned the back corner of the car but saw the gun too late. Wacko was crouched, almost on his knees, behind the left side of the Lincoln bumper, his .357 revolver pointed at a steep angle directly at Andre's head.

He fired once, and the top of the other man's head geysered brain matter and bone. Almost simultaneously Wacko lunged, grabbed the front of Andre's shirt, and savagely yanked the collapsing giant sideways into the trunk. The big man folded half in, half out of the compartment, his right foot on the pavement, the other leg over it. Wacko grabbed what remained of his victim's hair, twisted the head to the side, and drove the butt of the gun, in a vicious crushing arc, again and again into Andre's temple. Satisfied he was dead, Wacko felt his chest heave as he rammed the slippery gun down his budge, foot-swept the other man's leg off the ground, tugged the body into the trunk, and closed it.

Wacko picked up Andre's ready bag, then looking neither left nor right, walked to the passenger side of the Lexus and got in. As Mike pulled away, Wacko grabbed the red hand towel off the floor and wiped away the flecks of blood and brain matter clinging to his hands, face, and the front of his shirt.

"He killed Kevin. Turn off the music," Wacko said. Mike's eyes widened as he stared at Wacko.

"Eyes on the fucking road, slow down," Wacko said, checking the side-view mirror.

"We switchin' back to your car?" Mike said.

"We can't switch back to my car since we didn't have time to wipe this one down. We'll take our chances in this," Wacko said. Mike pulled out onto Hancock Street, turned left, and headed for the bridge. Wacko checked the side-view mirror again, then looked over his shoulder out the back window. "Everything's cool now, just go nice and easy." He gingerly rubbed the side of his right hand. "I think I broke my little finger on that piece of shit," he said.

"I take it Andre's dead?" Mike said as they passed over the Neponset Bridge.

"Like that piece of shit said, he's stayin'," Wacko said through lips that barely moved. "Take Morrissey Boulevard back to Southie and head to the D Street garage; we'll leave the Lexus there and grab one of the other cars. I ain't wastin' time. We're going after Marty Fallon today, right now. We gotta get him before he finds out about his goon. Today's collection day, he'll be makin' the rounds himself. Kevin had the right idea. I'll go down the list, pick a stop, set up, and wait for him to arrive. I'll kill him with my bare hands," Wacko said. "I'll . . ." He throttled the air in front of his face until the veins in his neck bulged and his knuckles were white.

Mike looked at him nervously. "Can understand how you'd want to, Jack, but I'm thinkin' we can't get fancy, we just gotta clip him, get the hell out. It's daytime, a lot of eyes."

Wacko dropped his hands and stared straight ahead, then patted Mike on the shoulder. "You're right, and I'm gonna shoot him through one of his," Wacko said. "We'll grab the gray Jeep Cherokee in the garage and go straight to the Dudley Tavern, see if he's in. He is, might do him there," Wacko said, pulling the .357 from his budge. He lay the gun flat on his left palm and rubbed it with the other hand like he wished a genie might appear.

Mike glanced at the gun. "Gotta get rid of that piece first," he said.

Wacko picked the red towel off the floor and used the clean side to wipe down the gun. "We're going over the Malibu Bridge, I'll toss it into the channel," he said. "You got another piece with you?"

"I got," Mike said, reaching under the seat. He pulled out a paper bag and handed it to Wacko. "It's a five-shot forty-four Smith. My backup piece. If you want we could swing by my house, grab a couple of automatics."

Wacko pulled the gun from the bag, opened and closed the chamber. "This will do. Now slow down, we're comin' up on the bridge. How's the traffic behind us?"

"All clear, do it," Mike said.

Wacko flipped the gun sideways through the window over the railing into the channel. "We'll approach the Dudley down Emerson Street; he won't be able to see us. If we spot his car out front, we'll stop halfway down, park. When the son-of-a-bitch leaves, we follow him," Wacko said.

He pulled out a small notebook from his back pocket and tapped it softly on his knee. "Unless Marty made pickups this morning, he'll cover the Point area first. My guess, he'll make one, maybe two stops up on Broadway, then head down K Street to Miller's Market for the little envelope they pay him to insure their windows remain intact. Then it's over to the Quencher to see Morgan Daly for a big, fat envelope that he pays to insure his face remains intact while he runs his book."

"You got their routine down," Mike said.

Wacko waved the notebook at him. "It's all here, Mike. Every Thursday for the past few weeks me and Kevin followed Marty and his boy. The routine never varied. His routine. Marty Fallon got real comfortable, and it's gonna be the death of him," Wacko said. "We could hit him at the Quencher, but I don't want to bring no heat on Morgan. Morgan's an earner, and now he's gonna earn for us."

Mike said, "Think Miller's Market's better, Jack. It's on an intersection, more ways outta there. We could park on Seventh, watch him go in; hit him when he comes out. We'll pick up two cars at the garage, have a switch parked down the beach just in case. Should be out of there quick."

The veins in Wacko's neck throbbed as he nodded. "Marty's going to be out of there even quicker after I put a rocket in his pocket," he said.

61

AT TEN MINUTES TO TWELVE, Sal "The Monster" Cristallo and Gennaro Scarpa parked the black, four-door Pontiac Grand Am in the back lot of Stop and Shop supermarket facing Fourth Street. Scarpa shut the engine off but left the radio on and bounced his head to the beat of a song by Eminem about losing yourself in a woman. He swilled down the last of his large Dunkin' Donuts coffee, half-crumpled the cup, opened the door, and tossed it out.

The Monster turned and with both hands grabbed him by the front of his overalls and pulled him into the armrest. "What the fuck's wrong with you? What I tell you about throwin' shit from the car?" The Monster scowled at the radio. "And turn that shit off." Scarpa wrenched himself away.

"You bitch when I throw cups in the back, I got nowhere to throw 'em and I don't give a flyin' fuck you don't like rap, it's a comin' thing," Scarpa said.

"Ya, you want to be a goin' thing, keep playin' that shit, and while we're at it, why you gotta drink so much coffee? Who the fuck are you, Juan Valdez?" the Monster said.

"Who?"

The Monster sighed. "Ya know, I'm gettin' tired of schoolin' you, but cause I like you a little, I'll tell you one more time, you — don't — throw — shit out of a hotbox, ever, and this is a hotbox, remember? Cop comes and sees you litterin' — you followin' me so far, if I'm movin' too fast here tell me, I'll use fucking flash cards. Now this piece of shit catches your bad behavior, comes over, complains about you litterin', asks for your license, registration, the fucking gun permit you don't have, and the next thing ya know you're killin' this guy over a paper cup or going to jail. Capeesh? I hope so. C'mon, take a walk, I need some air," the Monster said, opening the door.

Both men who got out of the car were dressed the same: dirty, worn Carhartt overalls and work boots. Each man pulled on an equally dirty baseball cap before they crossed the street diagonally towards Joseph's Bakery.

Once inside Scarpa walked directly past Biaggio Vitale and Five-O to an empty table that offered a full view of the intersection. At the counter the Monster ordered two coffees, paid the girl, and turned with the cups just as Biaggio Vitale and Five-O passed in front of him, without acknowledgment, and left the store.

The Monster put the coffee on the table and sat opposite Scarpa facing the Dudley Tavern. He took off his hat, wiped his brow, then pulled it back on. "There they go, Juan, now it's just you and me, drink your coffee," the Monster said.

Scarpa picked up the cup and blew across the top. "Those guys sure Fallon's still up there? What are they, psychics?" he said into the cup before taking a sip.

The Monster raised his eyebrows and nodded, then rested his forearms on the table and leaned closer. "Biaggio says the guy's there, he's there. When he made his bones, kid, you were dancin' with Muppets in feety pajamas."

Scarpa glared. "Never liked the fucking Muppets," he said.

The Monster feigned surprise."Not even the broad, the pig?" he said before suddenly stiffening. "Be cool, don't turn around, I think our man just came out."

Marty Fallon stood in the sunlight directly in front of the doorway to the Dudley Tavern. He put a cigarette in his mouth, struck a match, and lit it, then flung the match to the sidewalk before he walked into the street and opened the door to the blue Chevy Malibu double-parked out front and got in. The Monster cooly put his cup down, nodded at Scarpa, then both men casually got up and walked outside.

"I'll watch him, you get the car," the Monster said. As he sat in the Malibu with the engine idling, Marty checked a folded computer printout, a list of names and addresses with dollar amounts next to them. Scarpa stopped the Grand Am in front of Joseph's Bakery, and the Monster got in.

"What's he doin'?" Scarpa said.

"You want I should ask him? He looks like he's readin' somethin'," the Monster said.

The Malibu began to move, and Scarpa tightened his grip on the wheel. "He's movin', get ready," the Monster said, resting both hands on the dash and leaning towards the glovebox.

Marty turned left, heading the wrong way up K Street towards East Broadway. Scarpa threw the Grand Am into gear and pulled into the intersection but was forced to hit the brakes as a gray Jeep Cherokee with two occupants shot down Emerson Street in front of him, turning, with a hint of tire rubber, left onto K less than a block behind Marty Fallon. The Mafiosi looked at each other. "What the —? Scarpa said.

"Don't ask me," the Monster said. "Get on 'em for chrissakes; you're losin' the other guy."

Scarpa accelerated up K Street in time to see the ass end of the Cherokee turning right onto East Broadway. "Think they're cops?" he said.

"Could be, but remember round here, Fallon's used to bein' tailed, usually cops, but he knows when it's the cops," The Monster said.

At the East Broadway merge, Scarpa was forced to stop as an MBTA bus approached on the left.

"C'mon, move it, don't let that thing get between us," the Monster said.

"Go slow, hurry up. What the fuck? Let me drive, will ya?" Scarpa screamed, looking to his right past the Monster's chest. "I see Fallon's car. It's double-parked in front of the Stop and Shop and he's gettin' out," Scarpa said, rounding the corner and pulling over a short ways down.

Like a pointer dog the Monster locked on to the figure of Marty Fallon as he crossed the busy street.

"Here we go. He's headin' into the Boston Beer Garden, gotta be for a pickup,"

Scarpa turned on the radio, then punched the seat cushion. "Whoa, shit, there it is. That gray Cherokee's doubled-parked three cars up. Them guys are watchin' him too."

"Relax, they, whoever *they* are, ain't watchin' us, and what I tell you about the radio, you —"

"Look, the Cherokee's movin'," Scarpa said, pointing. The hitters watched as the Jeep pulled out into traffic and passed the Malibu just as Marty Fallon exited the Boston Beer Garden, holding a small brown paper bag in one hand. The Cherokee turned right onto L Street and was gone.

Scarpa and "The Monster" turned slowly, met each other's eyes. "Don't ask me," the Monster said. "My guess nothin' to do with him."

Marty Fallon opened the Malibu's trunk, tossed the bag inside, and got back into the car. Suddenly the Malibu lurched to the left, cutting across the line of traffic heading east, forcing oncoming cars to jam on their brakes. "Think he made us?" Scarpa said.

"For chrissakes don't look at him," the Monster said, snapping his head to the right as the Malibu roared past. Scarpa eyed the rearview mirror and watched as the Malibu turned, without slowing, down K Street. The Monster checked the side-view mirror. "Relax, he didn't make us, those quick U-turns are probably part of his regular routine to lose a tail if he's got one."

"Well, he's got one tail now he ain't losin'," Scarpa said, banging a U-turn and accelerating until he was only a block behind the Malibu.

As they passed the Dudley Tavern, the Monster handed Scarpa a pair of sunglasses with a black elastic restraining band attached to the arms.

"The strap's for the back of your head, keeps 'em from fallin' off, put 'em on," the Monster said. He pulled his glasses on and held the steering wheel in his left hand as Scarpa did the same.

"This guy better have more stops," Scarpa said.

"There's more. The giant usually does the collectin' for him, but Marty Fallon don't mind gettin' his hands dirty. We gotta bang this thing out quick or he'll make us, the guy's sharp."

"If we only knew his route," Scarpa said.

"Then we'd be waitin'. I don't like this cowboy shit any more than you, but Joe says he goes today, he goes today," the Monster said.

Scarpa punched the dash. "Why the big fucking rush? How come it's gotta be today?" he said, slowing for an intersection.

The Monster cast his eyes on Scarpa like he was viewing something already dead. "Because Joe says. You don't want to, he could say today for you too," the Monster said.

Marty drove through the intersection of K and Seventh Streets, pulled to the right, and stopped directly across from a small market. The Monster tapped Scarpa's arm. "Pull over, must be one of his pickups."

The men watched as Marty got out, crossed the street, and climbed the steps to Miller's Market. Scarpa rested his chin on the steering wheel like somehow that would bring him closer to his prey. "There's a space up there on the left, two cars back from the intersection," he said. "I'm takin' it." He pulled up and backed the car in. Now both driver and passenger checked their side mirrors. "Sidewalk's clear, how 'bout you?" Scarpa said.

"Street's empty," the Monster said. Scarpa shifted nervously in his seat, refusing to take his eyes off the doorway to Miller's Market.

"Uh-oh, something's up, but it don't fucking matter, we're takin' him here," the Monster said in a singsong voice. Scarpa looked at his partner, who faintly moved his head in the direction left of the doorway to Miller's Market.

Scarpa subtly shifted just his eyes. From out the corner he saw the gray Jeep Cherokee parked three cars back from the intersection next to the building. The two men sat in it. Scarpa pretended to adjust the radio. "If they're cops, what we gonna do?" he said.

"Don't think they're cops, probably Fallon's muscle shadowin' him instead of the giant. Don't matter. Those two get in the way, they're goin' too," the Monster said. He opened the door and got out, then opened the back door and slid across the seat behind the driver. "Give it to me," he said.

Scarpa leaned slightly to the left and pulled from under the seat a small green plastic bag. "Here's your lunch," he said, handing the package over his shoulder. The Monster opened the bag, pulled out a blue, four-inch six-shot Charter Arms .38 revolver. He opened the chamber, checked the rounds. As the Monster snapped it shut, Scarpa took from his own bag a Browning sixteen-shot 9 mm.

"Gotta love a revolver, never jams. You ready?" the Monster said.

"When I'm packin' this bazooka, I'm always ready," Scarpa said. He looked at the Jeep with disdain. "Only one of them looked this way once, don't think they made us," he said.

The Monster held the revolver tightly in his right hand while resting his other hand on the door latch. "I don't care if they jump out, finger-fuck each other, when Fallon comes out we're takin' him. You watch the Jeep, either of them puts a foot on the street, start blastin'. They stay put, stay put. Unless you gotta, wait until I hit the intersection before you move. If we get out the same time, it might spook Fallon," the Monster said.

"If someone stops in a car?" Scarpa said, looking over his shoulder.

"Point that cannon at their head, move 'em but don't say a word. You don't want some asshole down the line sayin', 'I'll never forget the sound of that voice'."

Scarpa tugged on the brim of his hat. "That's him in the doorway, Sal, holdin' a paper bag and an envelope. Seems like he's givin' the store owner some shit."

"I got him," the Monster said, cracking the door. "Once you're outside the car, you stay out until you see him drop."

Marty Fallon said something loud and unintelligible to the store owner and shook the envelope at him. The owner cringed and held up his hands like "What do you want from me?"

Marty was still talking to the man over his shoulder as he headed down the stairs, then stopped on the middle one. The Monster got out of the Grand Am, took a step, and froze. On the same side of the street, half a block past the store, a man wearing a gray jumpsuit and a white Patriots football cap, the brim pulled down to his sunglasses, advanced.

"Jesus, a fucking citizen," the Monster said, getting back in and quietly closing the door. Marty continued to chastise the store owner from the step. The Monster retrieved the plastic bag from the floor. "I don't fucking believe —"

Scarpa said, "Here we go! One of the Jeep guys is gettin' out holdin' a piece cute by his side."

The Monster glanced up momentarily, then continued to re-bag the gun. "Must be muscle, sees his boss yellin', plus he's probably keepin' an eye on the citizen," he said, then stopped wrapping the gun and slowly raised his eyes. "But he can't *see* the citizen."

"He ain't no citizen," Scarpa said.

The report of a powerful handgun made the Monster's stomach convulse. He ducked, then raised his head just high enough to see Gennaro Scarpa lying across the seat peering over the dash on the passenger side. Both men watched in amazement as dollar bills floated in the air around Marty Fallon's head. A shredded bag containing more bills lay at his feet. The man from the Jeep had frozen midstep and was now backing away, aiming his gun with both hands at the corner.

Marty Fallon hopped down onto the sidewalk and turned to face his attacker. The Patriots man, both arms extended in front, was twenty feet away now and closing. At ten feet he stopped, and Marty raised his arms in a defensive posture across his face. "You fucking punk," he snarled.

The gunman fired once, then twice more in quick succession. Marty twisted slightly as the first shot shattered his right elbow and clipped the top of his shoulder. The second slug passed cleanly between his forearms, leaving a bloody furrow on the left side of his neck. The third round entered the apex of the sternum and exited his back, neatly severing his spinal cord. Marty dropped to the sidewalk like a sack of wet rags, his head coming to rest on the bottom step of Miller's Market. For the first time in his life, Marty Fallon had nothing to say, then lost his chance to as the gunman stood over him and fired twice more. The first round shattered a section of the cement step to the left of his head, the second passed through his forehead, churned through his brain, carrying with it, in a stream, the final image of the flash at the end of Mark Costa's arm.

In the black Grand Am up the street, the driver turned, grinned at the man in the seat behind him. "Lousy shot, and the muscle ain't muscle," Scarpa said.

"Get us out of here," the Monster said, sinking down in the backseat.

"Makes me want to do a line."

"You fucking maniac, get us the hell outta here, take a left," the Monster said.

Scarpa pulled out and turned left onto Seventh Street. Neither man looked at the occupants of the Cherokee as they passed. Scarpa stared at the rearview mirror like he was viewing a tiny movie screen. In the glass, framed by cheap black plastic, played a scene of people running towards the fallen figure on the sidewalk. The Jeep Cherokee had pulled out and, leaving a trail of tire smoke, the backup lights glowed a full moon white as it raced in reverse up Seventh Street a hundred yards behind the Grand Am.

Scarpa cackled and said, "Those guys in the Jeep are followin' us — in reverse."

The Monster looked out the back window and snorted. "Think you can lose 'em?" he said.

Scarpa centered his sunglasses and turned on the radio. "Ya, if I can pick the station." Scarpa said.

EPILOGUE

WACKO CURRAN HAD ARRIVED in Playa del Carmen, on Mexico's "Mayan Riviera," four days earlier and spent the entire first afternoon at the bar of the Via Maya Hotel. He barely remembered having dinner alone in his room that night before returning to the same barstool afterwards, remaining there until closing. He spent the second day in his room overlooking the harbor, recovering from the alcohol and cursing himself for his weakness, for what he perceived as an inability to cope with the events of the recent past. By the second night, though, he was back in control, the way he knew Kevin would have wanted, and he swore to lay off the booze or anything else that might bring him down in the future.

As he sat on the beach bright and early the morning of the fourth day, a familiar waiter from the hotel carrying a tray of fruit approached from behind and squatted in the sand next to him. Wacko sat up in his lounge chair and watched as a sliver of sun danced along the serrated blade deftly manipulated by the Oriental waiter as he completed his task of slicing up an assortment of mangoes, papayas, and pineapple. He arranged the pieces in a delicate pattern on a silver tray shaped like an oyster shell, then placed it on a small plastic table next to Wacko's lounge chair. "Nice-a day, Mr. Bennett sir, you enjoy fruit with your sun?" the waiter said.

"Ya, I always like fruit with my sun," Wacko said, taking a bite of mango. He nodded. "Very good," he said. Pleased, the waiter smiled.

"Remember now, sir, you want anything, anything at all, you ask cabana boy for me, Jim-san, he your waiter, sir, Jim-san." The waiter handed Wacko a bone-colored linen napkin.

Wacko wiped his mouth. "You a China man, Chinese?" he said.

Jim-san pressed his palms together under his chin and tilted his head slightly to the side. "You ask . . . why? I no Chinese, Jim-san Okinawan," Jim-san said.

"And this Okinawa's nowhere near China, huh?" Wacko said, chewing a piece of pineapple.

Jim-san dropped his hands by his sides, glanced back over his shoulder towards the hotel. "China across sea from Okinawa, but Jim-san don't understand why —"

Wacko waved his hand to cut him off. "Ain't no big deal, Jim, it's only because I was thinkin' about headin' down China-way before comin' here. It's further south, see, and that was the plan, head south. So what's an Oky-man doin' in Mexico? Ain't south from your home-town, I bet," Wacko said.

Jim-san looked over his shoulder again at the hotel.

"Relax, Jimmy, your bosses won't spike your ass for talkin' with a hotel guest. So, what's up? Chinamen here rare as honest cops," Wacko said.

"No Chinese, Okinawan," Jim-san said insistently.

"My book, cuppa soup from the same pot," Wacko said.

Jim-san's brow wrinkled as he contemplated the observation. Then he half bowed, remained in that position when he spoke. "Entire life Jim-san sailor. Work huge ship, freighter, *Kyoto Maru*, haul pig iron ship. Captain bad man. My cousin, Yoki, small, work ship too. Yoki do good job but captain no like. Captain beat Yoki," Jim-san said, shrugged. "Next morning Jim-san beat captain. Jim-san put in brig, ship officer say once in port Jim-san go to land jail. We reach Mexi-can port, Yoki free Jim-san. Captain bad man, maybe Jim-san too," Jim-san said.

Wacko picked up the tray and offered the waiter a piece of fruit. "Take a piece, you ain't bad," he said.

Jim-san looked towards the hotel like he was fearful someone might be watching and declined with a subtle wave of the hands. "I can't, Mr. Bennett sir, there are rules," he said.

"G'wan, take a piece," Wacko said, holding up the tray and wig-gling it.

Jim-san took a slice of mango and held it cupped in his hand by his side. He pretended to cough and slipped it into his mouth, then al-most spit it out when both men laughed. He wiped his eyes as he chewed.

"Such a beautiful place, Jim-san, a shame I got no one to share it with," Wacko said.

The waiter's eyes twinkled. "Ah, yes, I agree, too beautiful not to share with another person, a female person?" Jim-san made a fist with his right hand near his belt, then covered it with his left and stared hard into Wacko's eyes.

Wacko shifted uneasily then sat up in the chair. "Hey, knock that shit off. I like girls, get it, girls. And if I want one I'll get my own," he said.

Jim-san's eyes bugged, and he covered his open mouth with his hand. "Do not mean to offend, Mr. Bennett, sir, I only ask because businessmen here sometimes —"

Wacko held up his hand. "Jimmy, I don't give a rat's ass what businessmen do, I know what I do, and now what you can do is get me a phone."

Jim-san recovered his smile. "Pleased to, Mr. Bennett, sir," he said.

Wacko reached into the pocket of his blue bathing trunks and pulled out a small, damp roll of bills. He peeled off a twenty. "Here's twenty bucks. I was swimmin', it got a little wet, but it'll still spend good down here," Wacko said.

Jim-san stepped back and waved his hands at Wacko. "No, Mr. Bennett, sir, house rules, gratuities always end of visit, last day only."

"Come here," Wacko said. He grabbed Jim-san by the sleeve and gently pressed the bill into the waiter's hand. "Any day could be the last day, remember that," he said.

The waiter looked confused. "But the rules?"

"G'wan, take it. I don't mix with rules, and maybe you don't either," Wacko said.

Jim-san bowed and examined the bill in front of his face, pulling either end of it taut. "Thank you, Mr. Bennett, sir," he said. He folded the bill, then like he was tucking in his shirt, discreetly slid it into his pocket.

"What about home, you must miss it?" Wacko said.

Jim-san closed his eyes like he was about to sneeze. "I do, but some things can't be changed. In the West you have a saying about cards, Mr. Bennett, and how a man must play the dealt ones."

The waiter inhaled deeply, paused, and exhaled as his gaze took in both ends of the beach. He smiled, then held up his arms like "Look at me." "I work in paradise, Mr. Bennett. I have had worse cards in these hands. I'll get your phone," Jim-san said, trotting off towards the hotel.

Wacko grabbed some fruit off the tray and stood up. He gazed towards the eastern end of the beach, where a half mile away, copper-colored sandstone cliffs rose from the water's edge hundreds of feet in the air. Wacko had to shield his eyes from the tropical sun. He squatted and retrieved a pair of Ray-Bans from his blanket, put them on, and now could see tiny figures diving from outcrops of rock near the base of the cliffs into an aquamarine sea.

As he walked, Wacko barely noticed the young girls who passed singly and in pairs in colorful string bikinis, who gave him more than a passing glance, or the Windsurfers cavorting in the roll and spray of the ocean a few hundred yards offshore.

The sand burned his feet, and he traveled to the water's edge and followed the foam line slowly towards the cliffs. It was then they appeared, as they had for weeks, images he could not strike from his mind. Marine Road, visions of his brother lying on the floor, his crooked neck, and the aftermath at Miller's Market.

It was a miracle they weren't spotted at the scene. Jackie Curran, the master planner, the guy who left nothing to chance, jumping out of a stolen car with a gun to kill in broad daylight. Out of his mind, he couldn't grasp it was July, that people were out, windows open. If it hadn't been for the quick thinking of Mike Janowski, he might have been identified.

Mike had backed out of the space as the first timid customers edged out the door of the store and headed for the intersection, only to slam on the brakes when a Corvette traveling down K Street did exactly what Mike thought it would do — stopped dead in the center and blocked the way. If Mike had remained there, even a moment longer, they may have been identified. Instead, he raced in reverse up Seventh Street as the Corvette driver stuck his head out the window and screamed something about an ambulance to the curious, who like ants to blood, gathered to examine the oozing form on the step of Miller's Market.

Wacko's thirst for revenge remained unquenched, had left him sleepless and angry for days since he wanted to pull the trigger. Nonetheless, he could not fault the other man and decided, should the need ever arise, there would always be an opening in his organization for Mark Costa.

The horror didn't end at Miller's Market. Wacko had to ensure his brother's body would be found in such a way that neither he nor anyone with him could be incriminated in his death. Spider Keenan claimed no knowledge of Kevin's fate. He was out of beer, he said, when Kevin came, went out for some, returned to find him dead.

The same night Spider helped Wacko and Mike carry the body, Wacko made plans to carry Spider's body later. They lay Kevin on a bench facing the Lagoon; he appeared to be sleeping. A call to the authorities assured he'd be quickly found. When questioned by police, Wacko Curran had nothing to say.

With pressure building in the weeks following Marty Fallon's death, Wacko had little choice but to move decisively to prevent Fallon's empire from fracturing into unmendable pieces. The Boston branch of La Cosa Nostra searched diligently for a breech in the wall of the town Fallon had ruled for twenty years. There was searing heat from the cops. Wacko thought it curiously strange that following the gangster's execution the fires of law enforcement were stoked to such a degree — almost as if one of their own had been killed.

With Mike and a handpicked crew, Wacko quickly laid the groundwork for the new regime. Protection rackets didn't skip a beat. Fallon loyalists were either absorbed or eliminated. Area loan sharks and bookmakers who attempted to hoard their money were sharply warned, anything owed to Marty Fallon was still owed and must be paid. But it was easier said than done. Volunteers would not be knocking on Wacko's door begging him to take their money. Once invisible, Wacko had to break with the routine that had served him so well. To make his presence felt, he was forced to move from the shadows into the light, since no man paid tribute to a ghost. For the first time in years he was vulnerable.

■　　■　　■

Behind him, someone called his name. Wacko turned to see Jim-san jogging towards him holding a phone. Every other day he had placed a call, at a predetermined time, to pay phones in Braintree and Weymouth, to Mike Janowski. Things seemed to be running smoothly, but the last time they talked Mike had mentioned something about a possible alliance with the wiseguys along the same lines the North End Italians had with Marty Fallon. Alliance? Wacko's mind raced.

Who had Mike been talking to?

Wacko knew Mike was capable, had left everything in his hands, but now he was having second thoughts, maybe he had given the kid too much. Who was this guy that he'd brought under his wing to be talking to anyone about alliances? What was Mike Janowski thinking?

Jim-san stopped alongside and offered the phone to Wacko. "I wait for the phone, Mr. Bennett, sir, over there?" he said, pointing to a small outcrop of smooth boulders fifty feet away.

"Fine, Jimmy, should only be a few minutes," Wacko said, deciding not to call Mike today. Maybe that little prick should think about what I'm doing, Wacko thought.

He sat down at the water's edge and dialed another number. As he awaited the connection, he could faintly hear the roar of a powerboat a mile offshore pulling a parasailer seven hundred feet in the air. "Hey, Elaine," Wacko said.

"Jack? I've been worried, where are you?" Elaine said.

"You know me, always disappearin', reappearin', same old shit," Wacko said.

Elaine was briefly silent. "Nothing's the same, Jack. What are you talking about? Nothing's the same. I thought something happened to you, something terrible."

"Nothin' happened to me. What's happenin' there?" Wacko said, trying hard to steady his voice.

"Talk, there's a lot of talk about Marty Fallon and that animal who worked for him, people are glad they're dead. Police are promising to find the killers, but no one really cares. Papers say what's going on is a gang thing — Italian-Irish, but I'm not sure they know. There's been more killings, one of Marty Fallon's loan sharks was shot in the doorway of the Mexican restaurant on Dorchester Street two weeks ago, but you probably already know that, Jack, don't you?" Elaine said.

"What they sayin' about me?" Wacko said.

"In the papers they're saying you're Marty Fallon's successor and how the federal authorities are now targeting you. Around Southie it's another story. You know how people talk, you're already the new monster. I hear these things and I want to cover my ears and close my eyes. I can't defend you anymore," Elaine said.

"And you have such beautiful eyes," Wacko said.

"I'm not kidding, it's not a joke. People are afraid, Jack. People are being murdered, and your name keeps coming up," Elaine said.

"Elaine —"

"Jackie, please," Elaine said. He thought he heard her sob, and something twisted inside him.

"I went to Florida, Key West," Wacko said.

"You're in Key West?"

"No, two weeks ago that was my first stop. People told me I couldn't go any further south, so I went. Stayed awhile, it was nice, you'd like it there, laid-back, but I needed more, hell, maybe less. I headed further south."

"Are you going to tell me where you are?"

"If you'll come to visit I will. Ah, hell, I'll tell you anyways. I'm in Mexico somewhere," Wacko said.

"I've got a job, Jack. I just can't leave and fly off to Mexico," Elaine said.

"You told me before you have vacation time, use it. In one hour I'll have a ticket in your name waiting at the American Airlines desk at Logan. Come on, Elaine, it's the same arrangement, your own room, do whatever you want, we can hang out. Hey, I'll buy you some shoes . . . and a sombrero. What d'ya say, pal, c'mon, I need you," Wacko said.

"Jackie, you're right, I do have vacation time, but me coming down there's not going to change things," Elaine said. "Aren't you tired of all the shit in your life? Christ, what's important to you? Your brother's dead, your mother's a wreck, you could change but you won't, and I just can't 'hang out' and watch you destroy yourself, I'm sorry," Elaine said.

"I need a friend, Elaine. Give me a chance, we'll talk, just give me a chance. All I'm askin' is you think about it and call me tomorrow, manana they call it around here," Wacko said. He gave her the number of the hotel.

"Elaine?"

"Yes, Jackie."

"The plane ticket's first class, it's gonna be a real comfortable flight."

"First class?" Elaine sighed. "Okay, Jack, we'll see, maybe. I'll call you in the morning."

"I'll be waiting," Wacko said and swung the phone by his side.

He gazed out across the Mexican Gulf for a moment and watched a young man and a woman cross wakes on their Jet Skis every hundred feet or so before he shut the phone off and tossed it to the approaching Jim-san. The waiter smiled as he caught it and scrutinized Wacko's face. "Jim-san may be bold, Mr. Bennett, but your face say female person?"

"You heard me over there?" Wacko said.

Jim-san shook his head. "I hear nothing but see clearly what is said here," he said, circling his face with his index finger. "Face betray thoughts of beautiful woman, the kind that make fruit taste even better," Jim-san said. The waiter's eyes twinkled as he backed away, then turned and jogged back towards the hotel.

As Wacko watched the receding figure, he was aware of the intensity of the sun on the back of his neck and shoulders. He cupped his hands, squatted, and scooped Gulf water, rubbing it into the hottest spots, cooling them temporarily, and thought about Elaine Ramsey and the similar effect she had on his life. Did he really want to go back into the fire? He closed his eyes and wondered if Elaine would come and subconsciously pressed the fingers of both hands into his abdomen as an uneasiness settled in his stomach.

All of his life Wacko Curran had convinced himself that a large part of what he did was for family, but now that his mother had finally agreed to move and Kevin was gone, he had no excuse. There was no question of money; he had more than he needed. His time away from South Boston had cleared his head, and he knew, like a drug addict who remained clean for a time, there'd be no guarantee he'd survive if he returned to the life.

He walked into the water of the Mexican Gulf until it lapped just below his knees, then stopped and listened to the voices of couples happily chatting as they passed behind him on the beach. It was the first time in his life that he had strangers at his back and he was not afraid. Wacko was aware of the subtle tug of the outgoing tide on his legs. He liked the way he felt and wondered if he could live like this.